Theodore Sturgeon was born in New York City in 1918. His career as a science fiction writer began—after a large succession of varied jobs—in 1939 with the publication of *Ether Breather*. In the three years following he produced more than 25 stories using the pseudonyms E. Waldo Hunter and E. Hunter Waldo. He then went on to write a number of highly praised works including *The Dreaming Jewels*, *The Cosmic Rape*, *Venus Plus X* and *More than Human* which won the 1954 International Fantasy Award.

Other Theodore Sturgeon novels available from Carroll & Graf:

The Dreaming Jewels
Venus Plus X

THE GOLDEN HELIX

THEODORE STURGEON

Carroll & Graf Publishers, Inc.
New York

The stories in this book first appeared in various publications as follows:

"The Golden Helix" was first published in *Thrilling Wonder Stories*, 1954, © 1954 by Standard Magazines, and reprinted by permission of the Fawcett Books Group, The Consumer Publishing Division of CBS, Inc.

"The Man Who Lost the Sea" and "And Now the News . . ." in *The Magazine of Fantasy and Science Fiction*, © 1956, 1959 (respectively) by The Mercury Press, Inc.

"The Clinic" in *Star Science Fiction Stories No. 2*, edited by Frederik Pohl, © 1953 by Ballantine Books.

". . . and my fear is great . . ." in *Beyond Fantasy Fiction* and "The Skills of Xanadu" in *Galaxy*, reprinted with permission of *Galaxy* magazine (UPD Publishing Corporation). Copyright © 1953, 1956 (respectively) by UPD Publishing Corporation under International, Universal, and Pan-American copyright conventions.

"The Dark Room" in *Fantastic*. Copyright 1953 by Ziff-Davis Publishing Co.

"The Ultimate Egoist" and "Yesterday was Monday" in *Unknown*, Copyright 1941 by Street & Smith Publications, Inc. in the U.S.A. and Great Britain; reprinted from *Astounding Science Fiction*.

"I Say . . . Ernest . . ." In *The Los Angeles Weekly News*. Copyright 1973 by Theodore Sturgeon.

To my oldest and most faithful friend,
EMANUEL MARCUS STAUB,
whose love Is precious metal
and
whose precious metal is love

Contents

Introduction

Shaping this collection has been a roller-coaster experience for me, and I wish I could share the total experience with you. But to do that you would have had to live inside my skin for all those years in all those places, undergoing a good deal of joy but a fairly heavy load of stress, of poverty, of loneliness, of self-denial and self-abnegation. You'd have had to experience the same sense of failure and unworthiness and certain peaks of joy so great they created guilt.

Some of these stories were written quite recently, two of them forty years ago by a kid I look back on with a little recognition and a lot of amazement. When I think of him I want to jump into a time machine and go back and yell, "Kid, look out! Watch yourself! You're going to do dumb things, you know that?"

These stories were written in furnished rooms, in homes I have had, and in other people's houses; in cellars, on tropical beaches, in a dune house with snow outside coming horizontally for days with such ferocity that it never lay on the ground. They have been penciled into notebooks and rapped out on typewriters, sent out first-draft and unread, or hoarded and polished. Funny ones have been written with pressure and terror all around, strictly laugh-clown-laugh. Frightening ones have been written in peaks of joy. (The horridest horror story I ever wrote—not for this book—was done on my honeymoon. Catharsis works that way too.)

I've tried here and there in the rubrics—the notes before each story—to share some of this with you. And I'm proud that I can do this. I have learned that the greatest payment a writer can receive for his work isn't money or banquets or standing ovations or trophies and medals and plaques. It's the knowledge that one can reach people all over the world; people one has never seen, might never meet; people who write and say, in one way or another, in one language or another: "It isn't so much that you understand your characters' problem. You understand *mine*." I shall launch into acknowledgments in a moment, but I would like to head the list with The Reader—the reader who has so encouraged me all these years, who has, at the very worst of times, let me know that I have reached out and touched, and that my touching is a good thing. For that, with all my heart: thank you.

This book would not be in your hands without the generosity and assistance of editor and friend Don Bensen; of editor Jim Frenkel with his compliments and his whip; of the very best agent in this or any other world, Kirby McCauley; of Stanley Apfelbaum, who gave me a roof when I needed it; of Kyle Hennefeld who lent me a typewriter at a moment when I needed it possibly even more than a roof; of the proofreaders, typesetters, printers, salesmen, and distributors whose names are never given to a writer, and of my Lady Jayne.

Theodore Sturgeon
Queens, New York, 1979

The Golden Helix

Far more remarkable, to me, than any other aspect of the intricate plot of this story is the fact that it was written in 1953, a good span of years before the double spiral of the DNA molecule was discovered, with its astonishing role in evolutionary structures. This makes the story a sort of quasi-mystical precognition—something I was not and could not be aware of when I wrote it. This is by no means the only time this has happened. Well after the fact, readers have unearthed in my work devices, events, or phenomena that I couldn't possibly have known of at the time I wrote them: Velcro, illuminated watch-dials, certain break-throughs in cancer research, automobile smog devices, and a good many other things. The average gap between these appearances in my typewriter and the emergence of them in the real world seems to be about fifteen years. I claim no special superiority for this, and admit to a good deal of humility. There are times when I feel like no more than a length of pipe, through which Something pours these things into my manuscripts.

1

Tod awoke first, probably because he was so curious, so deeply alive; perhaps because he was (or had been) seventeen. He fought back, but the manipulators would not be denied. They bent and flexed his arms and legs, squeezed his chest, patted and rasped and abraded him. His joints creaked, his sluggish blood clung sleepily to the walls of his veins, reluctant to move after so long.

He gasped and shouted as needles of cold played over his body, gasped again and screamed when his skin sensitized and the tingling intensified to a scald. Then he fainted, and probably slept, for he easily re-awoke when someone else started screaming.

He felt weak and ravenous, but extraordinarily well rested. His first conscious realization was that the manipulators had withdrawn from his body, as had the needles from the back of his neck. He put a shaky hand back there and felt the traces of spot-tape, already half-fused with his healing flesh.

He listened comfortably to this new screaming, satisfied that it was not his own. He let his eyes open, and a great wonder came over him when he saw that the lid of his Coffin stood open.

He clawed upward, sat a moment to fight a vicious swirl of vertigo, vanquished it, and hung his chin on the edge of the Coffin.

The screaming came from April's Coffin. It was open too. Since the two massive boxes touched and their hinges were on opposite sides, he could look down at her. The manipulators were at work on the girl's body, working with competent violence. She seemed to be caught up in some frightful nightmare, lying on her back, dreaming of riding a runaway bicycle with an off-center pedal sprocket and epicyclic hubs. And all the while her arms seemed to be flailing at a cloud of dream-hornets round her tossing head.

The needle-cluster rode with her head, fanning out behind the nape like the mechanical extrapolation of an Elizabethan collar.

Tod crawled to the end of his Coffin, stood up shakily, and grasped the horizontal bar set at chest level. He got an arm over it and snugged it close under his armpit. Half-suspended, he could then manage one of his feet over the edge, then the other, to the top step. He lowered himself until he sat on it, outside the Coffin at last, and slumped back to rest. When his furious lungs and battering heart calmed themselves, he went down the four steps one at a time, like an infant, on his buttocks.

April's screams stopped.

Tod sat on the bottom step, jackknifed by fatigue, his feet on the metal floor, his knees in the hollows between his pectorals and his shoulders. Before him, on a low pedestal, was a cube with a round switch-disc on it. When he could, he inched a hand forward and let it fall on the disc. There was an explosive tinkle and the front panel of the cube disappeared, drifting slowly away as a fine glittering dust. He lifted his heavy hand and reached inside. He got one capsule, two, carried them to his lips. He rested, then took a beaker from the cube. It was three-quarters full of purple crystals. He bumped it on the steel floor. The beaker's cover powdered and fell in, and the crystals were suddenly a liquid, effervescing violently. When it subsided, he drank it down. He belched explosively, and then his head cleared, his personal horizons expanded to include the other Coffins, the compartment walls, the ship itself and its mission.

Out there somewhere—somewhere close, now— was Sirius and its captive planet, Terra Prime. Earth's first major colony, Prime would one day flourish as Earth never had, for it would be a planned and tailored planet. Eight and a half light-years from Earth, Prime's population was composed chiefly of Earth immigrants, living in pressure domes and slaving to alter the atmosphere of the planet to Earth normal. Periodically there must be an infusion of Earth blood to keep the strain as close as possible on both planets, for unless a faster-than-light drive could be developed, there could be no frequent interchange between the worlds. What took light eight years took humans half a lifetime. The solution was the Coffins—the marvelous machine in which a man could slip into a sleep which was more than sleep while still on Earth, and awake years later in space, near his destination, subjectively only a month or so older. Without the Coffins there could be only divergence, possibly mutation. Humanity wanted to populate the stars—but with humanity.

Tod and his five shipmates were hand-picked. They had superiorities—mechanical, mathematical, and artistic aptitudes. But they were not all completely superior. One does not populate a colony with leaders alone and expect it to live. They, like the rest of their cargo (machine designs, microfilms of music and art, technical and medical writings, novels and entertainment) were neither advanced nor extraordinary. Except for Teague, they were the tested median, the competent; they were basic blood for a mass, rather than an elite.

Tod glanced around the blank walls and into the corner where a thin line delineated the sealed door. He ached to fling it open and skid across the corridor, punch the control which would slide away the armor which masked the port, and soak himself in his first glimpse of outer space. He had heard so much about it, but he had never seen it—they had all been deep in their timeless sleep before the ship had blasted off.

But he sighed and went instead to the Coffins.

Alma's was still closed, but there was sound and motion, in varying degrees, from all the others.

He glanced first into April's Coffin. She seemed to be asleep now. The needle-cluster and manipulators had withdrawn. Her skin glowed; it was alive and as unlike its former monochrome waxiness as it could be. He smiled briefly and went to look at Teague.

Teague, too, was in real slumber. The fierce vertical line between his brows was shallow now, and the hard, deft hands lax and uncharacteristically purposeless. Tod had never seen him before without a focus for those narrow, blazing green eyes, without decisive spring and balance in his pose. It was good, somehow, to feel that for all his responsibilities, Teague could be as helpless as anyone.

Tod smiled as he passed Alma's closed Coffin. He always smiled at Alma when he saw her, when he heard her voice, when she crossed his thoughts. It was possible to be very brave around Alma, for gentleness and comfort were so ready that it was almost not necessary to call upon them. One could bear anything, knowing she was there.

Tod crossed the chamber and looked at the last pair. Carl was a furious blur of motion, his needle-cluster swinging free, his manipulators in the final phase. He grunted instead of screaming, a series of implosive, startled gasps. His eyes were open but only the whites showed.

Moira was quite relaxed, turned on her side, poured out on the floor of the Coffin like a long golden cat. She seemed in a contented abandonment of untroubled sleep.

He heard a new sound and went back to April. She was sitting up, cross-legged, her head bowed apparently in deep concentration. Tod understood; he knew that sense of achievement and the dedication of an entire psyche to the proposition that these weak and trembling arms which hold one up shall *not* bend.

He reached in and gently lifted the soft white hair away from her face. She raised the albino's fathomless ruby eyes to him and whimpered.

"Come on," he said quietly. "We're here." When she did not move, he balanced on his stomach on the edge of the Coffin and put one hand between her shoulder-blades. "Come on."

She pitched forward but he caught her so that she stayed kneeling. He drew her up and forward and put her hands on the bar. "Hold tight, Ape," he said. She did, while he lifted her thin body out of the Coffin and stood her on the top step. "Let go now. Lean on me."

Mechanically she obeyed, and he brought her down until she sat, as he had, on the bottom step. He punched the switch at her feet and put the capsules in her mouth while she looked up at him numbly, as if hypnotized. He got her beaker, thumped it, held it until its foaming subsided, and then put an arm around her shoulders while she drank. She closed her eyes and slumped against him, breathing deeply at first, and later, for a moment that frightened him, not at all. Then she sighed. "Tod. . . ."

"I'm here, Ape."

She straightened up, turned and looked at him. She seemed to be trying to smile, but she shivered instead. "I'm cold."

He rose, keeping one hand on her shoulder until he was sure she could sit up unassisted, and then brought her a cloak from the clips outside the Coffin. He helped her with it, knelt and put on her slippers for her. She sat quite still, hugging the garment tight to her. At last she looked around and back; up, around, and back again. "We're—there!" she breathed.

"We're *here*," he corrected.

"Yes, here. Here. How long do you suppose we . . . "

"We won't know exactly until we can take some readings. Twenty-five, twenty-seven years—maybe more."

She said, "I could be old, old—" She touched her face, brought her fingertips down to the sides of her neck. "I could be forty, even!"

He laughed at her, and then a movement caught the corner of his eye. "Carl!"

Carl was sitting sidewise on the edge of his Coffin,

his feet still inside. Weak or no, bemused as could be expected, Carl should have grinned at Tod, should have made some healthy, swaggering gesture. Instead he sat still, staring about him in utter puzzlement. Tod went to him. "Carl! Carl, we're here!"

Carl looked at him dully. Tod was unaccountably disturbed. Carl always shouted, always bounced; Carl had always seemed to be just a bit larger inside than he was outside, ready to burst through, always thinking faster, laughing more quickly than anyone else.

He allowed Tod to help him down the steps, and sat heavily while Tod got his capsules and beaker for him. Waiting for the liquid to subside, he looked around numbly. Then drank, and almost toppled. April and Tod held him up. When he straightened again, it was abruptly. "Hey!" he roared. "We're here!" He looked up at them. "April! Tod-o! Well what do you know— how are you, kids?"

"Carl?" The voice was the voice of a flute, if a flute could whisper. They looked up. There was a small golden surf of hair tumbled on and over the edge of Moira's Coffin.

Weakly, eagerly, they clambered up to Moira and helped her out. Carl breathed such a sigh of relief that Tod and April stopped to smile at him, at each other.

Carl shrugged out of his weakness as if it were an uncomfortable garment and went to be close to Moira, to care about Moira and nothing else.

A deep labored voice called, "Who's up?"

"Teague! It's Teague . . . all of us, Teague," called Tod. "Carl and Moira and April and me. All except Alma."

Slowly Teague's great head rose out of the Coffin. He looked around with the controlled motion of a radar sweep. When his head stopped its one turning, the motion seemed relayed to his body, which began to move steadily upward. The four who watched him knew intimately what this cost him in sheer will-power, yet no one made any effort to help. Unasked, one did not help Teague.

One leg over, the second. He ignored the bar and stepped down to seat himself on the bottom step as if it were a throne. His hands moved very slowly but without faltering as he helped himself to the capsules, then the beaker. He permitted himself a moment of stillness, eyes closed, nostrils pinched; then life coursed strongly into him. It was as if his muscles visibly filled out a little. He seemed heavier and taller, and when he opened his eyes, they were the deeply vital, commanding light-sources which had drawn them, linked them, led them all during their training.

He looked toward the door in the corner. "Has anyone—"

"We were waiting for you," said Tod. "Shall we . . . can we go look now? I want to see the stars."

"We'll see to Alma first." Teague rose, ignoring the lip of his Coffin and the handhold it offered. He went to Alma's. With his height, he was the only one among them who could see through the top plate without mounting the steps.

Then, without turning, he said, "Wait."

The others, half across the room from him, stopped. Teague turned to them. There was no expression on his face at all. He stood quite motionless for perhaps ten seconds, and then quietly released a breath. He mounted the steps of Alma's Coffin, reached, and the side nearest his own machine sank silently into the floor. He stepped down, and spent a long moment bent over the body inside. From where they stood, tense and frightened, the others could not see inside. They made no effort to move closer.

"Tod," said Teague, "get the kit. Surgery *Lambda.* Moira, I'll need you."

The shock of it went to Tod's bones, regenerated, struck him again; yet so conditioned was he to Teague's commands that he was on his feet and moving before Teague had stopped speaking. He went to the after bulkhead and swung open a panel, pressed a stud. There was a metallic whisper, and the heavy case slid out at his feet. He lugged it over to Teague, and helped him rack it on the side of the Coffin. Teague immediately plunged his hands through the membrane at one end of the kit, nodding to Moira to do likewise at the other. Tod stepped back, studiously avoiding a glance in at Alma, and returned to April. She put both her hands tight around his left biceps and leaned close. "Lambda. . . ." she whispered. "That's . . . parturition, isn't it?"

He shook his head. "Parturition is Surgery Kappa," he said painfully. He swallowed. "Lambda's Caesarian."

Her crimson eyes widened. "Caesarian? Alma? She'd never need a Caesarian!"

He turned to look at her, but he could not see, his eyes stung so. "Not while she lived, she wouldn't," he whispered. He felt the small white hands tighten painfully on his arm. Across the room, Carl sat quietly. Tod squashed the water out of his eyes with the heel of his hand. Carl began pounding knuckles, very slowly, against his own temple.

Teague and Moira were busy for a long time.

II

Tod pulled in his legs and lowered his head until the kneecaps pressed cruelly against his eyebrow ridges. He hugged his shins, ground his back into the wall-panels, and in this red-spangled blackness he let himself live back and back to Alma and joy, Alma and comfort, Alma and courage.

He had sat once, just this way, twisted by misery and anger, blind and helpless, in a dark corner of an equipment shed at the spaceport. The rumor had circulated that April would not come after all, because albinism and the Sirius Rock would not mix. It turned out to be untrue, but that did not matter at the time. He had punched her, punched *Alma!* because in all the world he had been given nothing else to strike out at, and she had found him and had sat down to be with him. She had not even touched her face, where the blood ran; she simply waited until at last he flung himself on her lap and wept like an infant. And no one but he and Alma ever knew of it. . . .

He remembered Alma with the spaceport children, rolling and tumbling on the lawn with them, and in the pool; and he remembered Alma, her face still, looking up at the stars with her soft and gentle eyes, and in those eyes he had seen a challenge as implacable and pervasive as space itself. The tumbling on the lawn, the towering dignity—these co-existed in Alma without friction. He remembered things she had said to him; for each of the things he could recall the kind of light, the way he stood, the very smell of the air at the time. "Never be afraid, Tod. Just think of the worst possible thing that might happen. What you're afraid of will probably not be *that* bad—and anything else just has to be better." And she said once, "Don't confuse logic and truth, however good the logic. You can stick one end of logic in solid ground and throw the other end clear out of the cosmos without breaking it. Truth's a little less flexible." And, "Of *course* you need to be loved, Tod! Don't be ashamed of that, or try to change it. It's not a thing you have to worry about, ever. You are loved. April loves you. And I love you. Maybe I love you even more than April, because she loves everything you are, but I love everything you were and ever will be."

And some of the memories were deeper and more important even than these, but were memories of small things—the meeting of eyes, the touch of a hand, the sound of laughter or a snatch of song, distantly.

Tod descended from memory into a blackness that was only loss and despair, and then a numbness, fol-

lowed by a reluctant awareness. He became conscious
of what, in itself, seemed the merest of trifles: that
there was a significance in his pose there against the
bulkhead. Unmoving, he considered it. It was comfortable, to be so turned in upon oneself, and so protected,
unaware . . . and Alma would have hated to see him
this way.

He threw up his head, and self-consciously straightened from his foetal posture. *That's over now,* he told
himself furiously, and then, dazed, wondered what he
had meant.

He turned to look at April. She was huddled miserably against him, her face and body lax, stopped, disinterested. He thumped his elbow into her ribs,
hard enough to make her remember she had ribs.
She looked up into his eyes and said, "How? How
could . . ."

Tod understood. Of the three couples standard for
each ship of the Sirian project, one traditionally
would beget children on the planet; one, earlier, as
soon as possible after awakening; and one still earlier,
for conception would take place within the Coffin.
But—not *before* awakening, and surely not long
enough before to permit of gestation. It was an impossibility; the vital processes were so retarded within the
Coffin that, effectively, there would be no stirring
of life at all. So—"How?" April pleaded. "How
could. . . ."

Tod gazed upon his own misery, then April's, and
wondered what it must be that Teague was going
through.

Teague, without looking up, said, "Tod."

Tod patted April's shoulder, rose and went to
Teague. He did not look into the Coffin. Teague, still
working steadily, tilted his head to one side to point.
"I need a little more room here."

Tod lifted the transparent cube Teague had indicated and looked at the squirming pink bundle inside.

He almost smiled. It was a nice baby. He took one step
away and Teague said, "Take 'em all, Tod."

He stacked them and carried them to where April
sat. Carl rose and came over, and knelt. The boxes
hummed—a vibration which could be felt, not
heard—as nutrient-bearing air circulated inside and
back to the power-packs. "A nice normal deliv— I
mean, a nice normal batch o' brats," Carl said. "Four
girls, one boy. Just right."

Tod looked up at him. "There's one more, I think."

There was—another girl. Moira brought it over in
the sixth box. "Sweet," April breathed, watching them.
"They're sweet."

Moira said, wearily, "That's all."

Tod looked up at her.

"Alma. . . ?"

Moira waved laxly toward the neat stack of incubators. "That's all," she whispered tiredly, and went to
Carl.

That's all there is of Alma, Tod thought bitterly.
He glanced across at Teague. The tall figure raised a
steady hand, wiped his face with his upper arm. His
raised hand touched the high end of the Coffin, and
for an instant held a grip. Teague's face lay against his
arm, pillowed, hidden and still. Then he completed
the wiping motion and began stripping the sterile
plastic skin from his hands. Tod's heart went out to
him, but he bit the insides of his cheeks and kept silent. *A strange tradition,* thought Tod, *that makes it
impolite to grieve. . . .*

Teague dropped the shreds of plastic into the disposal slot and turned to face them. He looked at each
in turn, and each in turn found some measure of control. He turned then, and pulled a lever, and the side
of Alma's Coffin slid silently up.

Good-by. . . .

Tod put his back against the bulkhead and slid
down beside April. He put an arm over her shoulders.

Carl and Moira sat close, holding hands. Moira's eyes were shadowed but very much awake. Carl bore an expression almost of sullenness. Tod glanced, then glared at the boxes. Three of the babies were crying, though of course they could not be heard through the plastic incubators. Tod was suddenly conscious of Teague's eyes upon him. He flushed, and then let his anger drain to the capacious inner reservoir which must hold it and all his grief as well.

When he had their attention, Teague sat cross-legged before them and placed a small object on the floor.

Tod looked at the object. At first glance it seemed to be a metal spring about as long as his thumb, mounted vertically on a black base. Then he realized that it was an art object of some kind, made of a golden substance which shimmered and all but flowed. It was an interlocked double spiral; the turns went round and up, round and down, round and up again, the texture of the gold clearly indicating, in a strange and alive way, which symbolized a rising and falling flux. Shaped as if it had been wound on a cylinder and the cylinder removed, the thing was formed of a continuous wire or rod which had no beginning and no end, but which turned and rose and turned and descended again in an exquisite continuity. . . . Its base was formless, an almost-smoke just as the gold showed an almost-flux; and it was as lightless as ylem.

Teague said, "This was in Alma's Coffin. It was not there when we left Earth."

"It must have been," said Carl flatly.

Teague silently shook his head. April opened her lips, closed them again. Teague said, "Yes, April?"

April shook her head. "Nothing, Teague. Really nothing." But because Teague kept looking at her, waiting, she said, "I was going to say . . . it's beautiful." She hung her head.

Teague's lips twitched. Tod could sense the sympathy there. He stroked April's silver hair. She responded, moving her shoulder slightly under his hand. "What is it, Teague?"

When Teague would not answer, Moira asked, "Did it . . . had it anything to do with Alma?"

Teague picked it up thoughtfully. Tod could see the yellow loom it cast against his throat and cheek, the golden points it built in his eyes. "Something did." He paused. "You know she was supposed to conceive on awakening. But to give birth—"

Carl cracked a closed hand against his forehead. "She must have been awake for anyway two hundred and eighty days!"

"Maybe she made it," said Moira.

Tod watched Teague's hand half-close on the object as if it might be precious now. Moira's was a welcome thought, and the welcome could be read on Teague's face. Watching it, Tod saw the complicated spoor of a series of efforts—a gathering of emotions, a determination; the closing of certain doors, the opening of others.

Teague rose. "We have a ship to inspect, sights to take, calculations . . . we've got to tune in Terra Prime, send them a message if we can. Tod, check the corridor air."

"The stars—we'll see the stars!" Tod whispered to April, the heady thought all but eclipsing everything else. He bounded to the corner where the door controls waited. He punched the test button, and a spot of green appeared over the door, indicating that with their awakening, the evacuated chambers, the living and control compartments, had been flooded with air and warmed. "Air okay."

"Go on then."

They crowded around Tod as he grasped the lever and pushed. *I won't wait for orders*, Tod thought. *I'll slide right across the corridor and open the guard plate and there it'll be—space, and the stars!*

The door opened.

There was no corridor, no bulkhead, no armored port-hole, no—

No *ship!*

There was a night out there, dank, warm. It was wet. In it were hooked, fleshy leaves and a tangle of roots; a thing with legs which hopped up on the sill and shimmered its wings for them; a thing like a flying hammer which crashed in and smote the shimmering one and was gone with it, leaving a stain on the deck-plates. There was a sky aglow with a ghastly green. There was a thrashing and a scream out there, a pressure of growth, and a wrongness.

Blood ran down Tod's chin. His teeth met through his lower lip. He turned and looked past three sets of terrified eyes to Teague, who said, "Shut it!"

Tod snatched at the control. It broke off in his hand. . . .

How long does a thought, a long thought, take?

Tod stood with the fractured metal in his hand and thought:

We were told that above all things we must adapt. We were told that perhaps there would be a thin atmosphere by now, on Terra Prime, but that in all likelihood we must live a new kind of life in pressure-domes. We were warned that what we might find would be flash-mutation, where the people could be more or less than human. We were warned, even, that there might be no life on Prime at all. But look at me now—look at all of us. We weren't meant to adapt to this! And we can't . . .

Somebody shouted while somebody shrieked, each sound a word, each destroying the other. Something thick as a thumb, long as a hand, with a voice like a distant airhorn, hurtled through the door and circled the room. Teague snatched a folded cloak from the clothingrack and, poising just a moment, batted it out of the air. It skittered, squirming, across the metal door. He threw the cloak on it to capture it. "Get that door closed."

Carl snatched the broken control lever out of Tod's hand and tried to fit it back into the switch mounting. It crumbled as if it were dried bread. Tod stepped outside, hooked his hands on the edge of the door, and pulled. It would not budge. A lizard as long as his arm scuttled out of the twisted grass and stopped to stare at him. He shouted at it, and with forelegs much too long for such a creature, it pressed itself upward until its body was forty-five degrees from the horizontal, it flicked the end of its long tail upward, and something flew over its head toward Tod, buzzing angrily. Tod turned to see what it was, and as he did the lizard struck from one side and April from the other.

April succeeded and the lizard failed, for its fangs clashed and it fell forward, but April's shoulder had taken Tod on the chest and, off balance as he was, he went flat on his back. The cold, dry, pulsing tail swatted his hand. He gripped it convulsively, held on tight. Part of the tail broke off and buzzed, flipping about on the ground like a click-beetle. But the rest held. Tod scuttled backward to pull the lizard straight as it began to turn on him, got his knees under him, then his feet. He swung the lizard twice around his head and smashed it against the inside of the open door. The part of the tail he was holding then broke off, and the scaly thing thumped inside and slid, causing Moira to leap so wildly to get out of its way that she nearly knocked the stocky Carl off his feet.

Teague swept away the lid of the Surgery *Lambda* kit, inverted it, kicked the clutter of instruments and medicaments aside and clapped the inverted box over the twitching, scaly body.

"April!" Tod shouted. He ran around in a blind semicircle, saw her struggling to her feet in the grass, snatched her up and bounded inside with her. "Carl!" he gasped, Get the door. . . ."

But Carl was already moving forward with a needle

torch. With two deft motions he sliced out a section of
the power-arm which was holding the door open. He
swung the door to, yelling, "Parametal!"

Tod, gasping, ran to the lockers and brought a
length of the synthetic. Carl took the wide ribbon and
with a snap of the wrists broke it in two. Each half he
bent (for it was very flexible when moved slowly)
into a U. He placed one against the door and held out
his hand without looking. Tod dropped the hammer
into it. Carl tapped the parametal gently and it adhered to the door. He turned his face away and struck
it sharply. There was a blue-white flash and the U was
rigid and firmly welded to the door. He did the same
thing with the other U, welding it to the nearby wall
plates. Into the two gudgeons thus formed, Moira
dropped a luxalloy bar, and the door was secured.

"Shall I sterilize the floor?" Moira asked.

"No," said Teague shortly.

"But—bacteria . . . spores . . ."

"Forget it," said Teague.

April was crying. Tod held her close, but made no
effort to stop her. Something in him, deeper than
panic, more essential than wonderment, understood
that she could use this circumstance to spend her tears
for Alma, and that these tears must be shed now or
swell and burst her heart. *So cry*, he pled silently, *cry
for both of us, all of us.*

With the end of action, belated shock spread visibly
over Carl's face. "The ship's gone," he said stupidly.
"We're on a planet." He looked at his hands, turned
abruptly to the door, stared at it and began to shiver.
Moira went to him and stood quietly, not touching
him—just being near, in case she should be needed.
April grew gradually silent. Carl said, "I—" and then
shook his head.

Click. Shh. Clack, click. Methodically Teague was
stacking the scattered contents of the medical kit. Tod
patted April's shoulder and went to help. Moira

glanced at them, peered closely into Carl's face, then
left him and came to lend a hand. April joined them,
and at last Carl. They swept up, and racked and
stored the clutter, and when Teague lowered a table,
they helped get the dead lizard on it and pegged out
for dissection. Moira cautiously disentangled the huge
insect from the folds of the cloak and clapped a box
over it, slid the lid underneath to bring the feebly
squirming thing to Teague. He studied it for a long
moment, then set it down and peered at the lizard.
With forceps he opened the jaws and bent close. He
grunted. "April. . . ."

She came to look. Teague touched the fangs with
the tip of a scalpel. "Look there."

"Grooves," she said. "Like a snake."

Teague reversed the scalpel and with the handle he
gingerly pressed upward, at the root of one of the
fangs. A cloudy yellow liquid beaded, ran down the
groove. He dropped the scalpel and slipped a watch-
glass under the tooth to catch the droplet. "Analyze
that later," he murmured. "But I'd say you saved Tod
from something pretty nasty."

"I didn't even think," said April. "I didn't . . . I
never knew there was any animal life on Prime. I wonder what they call this monster."

"The honors are yours, April. You name it."

"They'll have a classification for it already!"

"Who?"

Everyone started to talk, and abruptly stopped. In
the awkward silence Carl's sudden laugh boomed. It
was a wondrous sound in the frightened chamber.
There was comprehension in it, and challenge, and
above all. Carl himself,—boisterous and impulsive,
quick, sure. The laugh was triggered by the gush of
talk and its sudden cessation, a small thing in itself.
But its substance was understanding, and with that an
emotional surge, and with that, the choice of the one
emotional expression Carl would always choose.

"Tell them, Carl," Teague said.

Carl's teeth flashed. He waved a thick arm at the door. "That isn't Sirius Prime. Nor Earth. Go ahead, April—name your pet."

April, staring at the lizard, said, *"Crotalidus,* then, because it has a rattle and fangs like a diamondback." Then she paled and turned to Carl, as the full weight of his statement came on her. "Not—*not Prime?"*

Quietly, Teague said, "Nothing like these ever grew on Earth. And Prime is a cold planet. It could never have a climate like that," he nodded toward the door, "no matter how much time has passed."

"But what . . . where . . ." It was Moira.

"We'll find out when we can. But the instruments aren't here—they were in the ship."

"But if it's a new . . . another planet, why didn't you let me sterilize? What about airborne spores? Suppose it had been methane out there or—"

"We've obviously been conditioned to anything in the atmosphere. As to its composition—well, it isn't poisonous, or we wouldn't be standing here talking about it. Wait!" He held up a hand and quelled the babble of questions before it could fully start. "Wondering is a luxury like worrying. We can't afford either. We'll get our answers when we get more evidence."

"What shall we do?" asked April faintly.

"Eat," said Teague. "Sleep." They waited. Teague said, "Then we go outside."

III

There were stars like daisies in a field, like dust in a sunbeam, and like flying, flaming mountains; near ones, far ones, stars of every color and every degree of brilliance. And there were bands of light which must be stars too distant to see. And something was stealing the stars, not taking them away, but swallowing them up, coming closer and closer, eating as it came. And at last there was only one left. Its name was Alma, and it was gone, and there was nothing left but an absorbent blackness and an aching loss.

In this blackness Tod's eyes snapped open, and he gasped, frightened and lost.

"You awake, Tod?" April's small hand touched his face. He took it and drew it to his lips, drinking comfort from it.

From the blackness came Carl's resonant whisper, "We're awake. Teague? . . ."

The lights flashed on, dim first, brightening swiftly, but not so fast as to dazzle unsuspecting eyes. Tod sat up and saw Teague at the table. On it was the lizard, dissected and laid out as neatly as an exploded view in a machine manual. Over the table, on a gooseneck, was a floodlamp with its lens masked by an infrared filter. Teague turned away from the table, pushing up his "black-light" goggles, and nodded to Tod. There were shadows under his eyes, but otherwise he seemed the same as ever. Tod wondered how many lonely hours he had worked while the two couples slept, doing that meticulous work under the irritating glow so that they would be undisturbed.

Tod went to him. "Has my playmate been talking much?" He pointed at the remains of the lizard.

"Yes and no," said Teague. "Oxygen-breather, all right, and a true lizard. He had a secret weapon—that tail-segment he flips over his head toward his victims. It has primitive ganglia like an Earth salamander's, so that the tail-segment trembles and squirms, sounding the rattles, after he throws it. He also has a skeleton that—but all this doesn't matter. Most important is that he's the analog of our early Permian life, which means (unless he's an evolutionary dead-end like a cockroach) that this planet is a billion years old at the least. And the little fellow here—" he touched the flying thing—"bears this out. It's not an insect, you know. It's an arachnid."

"With *wings?*"

Teague lifted the slender, scorpion-like pincers of the creature and let them fall. "Flat chitinous wings are no more remarkable a leg adaptation than those things. Anyway, in spite of the ingenuity of his engineering, internally he's pretty primitive. All of which lets us hypothesize that we'll find fairly close analogs of what we're used to on Earth."

"Teague," Tod interrupted, his voice lowered, his eyes narrowed to contain the worry that threatened to spill over, "Teague, what's happened?"

"The temperature and humidity here seem to be exactly the same as that outside," Teague went on, in precisely the same tone as before. "This would indicate either a warm planet, or a warm season on a temperate planet. In either case it is obvious that—"

"But, *Teague*—"

"—that a good deal of theorizing is possible with very little evidence, and we need not occupy ourselves with anything else but that evidence."

"Oh," said Tod. He backed off a step. "Oh," he said again, "sorry, Teague." He joined the others at the food dispensers, feeling like a cuffed puppy. *But he's right,* he thought. *As Alma said . . . of the many things which might have happened, only one actually has. Let's wait then, and worry about that one thing when we can name it.*

There was a pressure on his arm. He looked up from his thoughts and into April's searching eyes. He knew that she had heard, and he was unreasonably angry at her. "Damn it, he's so cold-blooded," he blurted defensively, but in a whisper.

April said, "He has to stay with things he can understand, every minute." She glanced swiftly at the closed Coffin. "Wouldn't you?"

There was a sharp pain and a bitterness in Tod's throat as he thought about it. He dropped his eyes and mumbled, "No, I wouldn't. I don't think I could." There was a difference in his eyes as he glanced back at Teague. *But it's so easy, after all, for strong people to be strong,* he thought.

"Teague, what'll we wear?" Carl called.

"Skinflex."

"Oh, no!" cried Moira. "It's so clingy and hot!"

Carl laughed at her. He swept up the lizard's head and opened its jaws. "Smile at the lady. She wouldn't put any tough old skinflex in the way of your pretty teeth!"

"Put it down," said Teague sharply, though there was a flicker of amusement in his eyes. "It's still loaded with God-knows-what alkaloid. Moira, he's right. Skinflex just doesn't puncture."

Moira looked respectfully at the yellow fangs and went obediently to storage, where she pulled out the suits.

"We'll keep close together, back to back," said Teague as they helped each other into the suits. "All the weapons are . . . were . . . in the forward storage compartment, so we'll improvise. Tod, you and the girls each take a globe of anesthene. It's the fastest anesthetic we have and it ought to take care of anything that breathes oxygen. I'll take scalpels. Carl—"

"The hammer," Carl grinned. His voice was fairly thrumming with excitement.

"We won't attempt to fasten the door from outside. I don't mean to go farther than ten meters out, this first time. Just—you, Carl—lift off the bar as we go out, get the door shut as quickly as possible, and prop it there. Whatever happens, do not attack anything out there unless you are attacked first, or unless I say so."

Hollow-eyed, steady, Teague moved to the door with the others close around him. Carl shifted the hammer to his left hand, lifted the bar and stood back a little, holding it like a javelin. Teague, holding a glittering lancet lightly in each hand, pushed the door open with his foot. They boiled through, stepped aside for Carl as he butted the rod deep into the soil and against the closed door. "All set."

They moved as a unit for perhaps three meters, and stopped.

It was daytime now, but such a day as none of them had dreamed of. The light was green, very nearly a lime-green, and the shadows were purple. The sky was more lavender than blue. The air was warm and wet.

They stood at the top of a low hill. Before them a tangle of jungle tumbled up at them. So vital, so completely alive, it seemed to move by its own power of growth. Stirring, murmuring, it was too big, too much, too wide and deep and intertwined to assimilate at a glance; the thought, *this is a jungle,* was a pitiable understatement.

To the left, savannah-like grassland rolled gently down to the choked margins of a river—calm faced, muddy and secretive. It too seemed astir with inner growings. To the right, more jungle. Behind them, the bland and comforting wall of their compartment.

Above—

It may have been April who saw it first; in any case, Tod always associated the vision with April's scream.

They moved as she screamed, five humans jerked back then like five dolls on a single string, pressed together and to the compartment wall by an overwhelming claustrophobia. They were ants under a descending heel, flies on an anvil . . . together their backs struck the wall and they cowered there, looking up.

And it was not descending. It was only—big. It was just that it was there, over them.

April said, later, that it was like a cloud. Carl would argue that it was cylindrical, with flared ends and a narrow waist. Teague never attempted to describe it, because he disliked inaccuracies, and Moira was too awed to try. To Tod, the object had no shape. It was a luminous opacity between him and the sky, solid, massive as mountains. There was only one thing they agreed on, and that was that it was a ship.

And out of the ship came the golden ones.

They appeared under the ship as speckles of light, and grew in size as they descended, so that the five humans must withstand a second shock: they had known the ship was huge, but had not known until now how very high above them it hung.

Down they came, dozens, hundreds. They filled the sky over the jungle and around the five, moving to make a spherical quadrant from the horizontal to the zenith, a full hundred and eighty degrees from side to side—a radiant floating shell with its concave surface toward, around, above them. They blocked out the sky and the jungle-tops, cut off most of the strange green light, replacing it with their own—for each glowed coolly.

Each individual was distinct and separate. Later, they would argue about the form and shape of the vessel, but the exact shape of these golden things was never even mentioned. Nor did they ever agree on a name for them. To Carl they were an army, to April, angels. Moira called them (secretly) "the seraphim," and to Tod they were masters. Teague never named them.

For measureless time they hung there, with the humans gaping up at them. There was no flutter of wings, no hum of machinery to indicate how they stayed aloft, and if each individual had a device to keep him afloat, it was of a kind the humans could not recognize. They were beautiful, awesome, uncountable.

And nobody was afraid.

Tod looked from side to side, from top to bottom of this incredible formation, and became aware that it did not touch the ground. Its lower edge was exactly horizontal, at his eye level. Since the hill fell away on all sides, he could see under this lower edge, here the jungle, there down across the savannah to the river. In a new amazement he saw eyes, and protruding heads.

In the tall grass at the jungle margin was a scurry

and cease, scurry and cease, as newtlike animals scrambled not quite into the open and froze, watching. Up in the lower branches of the fleshy, hook-leaved trees, the heavy scaly heads of leaf-eaters showed, and here and there was the armed head of a lizard with catlike tearing tusks.

Leather-winged fliers flapped clumsily to rest in the branches, hung for a moment for all the world like broken umbrellas, then achieved balance and folded their pinions. Something slid through the air, almost caught a branch, missed it and tumbled end-over-end to the ground, resolving itself into a broad-headed scaly thing with wide membranes between fore and hind legs. And Tod saw his acquaintance of the night before, with its serrated tail and needle fangs.

And though there must have been eater and eaten here, hunter and hunted, they all watched silently, turned like living compass-needles to the airborne mystery surrounding the humans. They crowded together like a nightmare parody of the Lion and the Lamb, making a constellation, a galaxy of bright and wondering eyes; their distance from each other being, in its way, cosmic.

Tod turned his face into the strange light, and saw one of the golden beings separate from the mass and drift down and forward and stop. Had this living shell been a segment of curving mirror, this one creature would have been at its focal point. For a moment there was complete stillness, a silent waiting. Then the creature made a deep . . . *gesture*. Behind it, all the others did the same.

If ten thousand people stand ten thousand meters away, and if, all at once, they kneel, it is hardly possible to see just what it is they have done; yet the aspect of their mass undergoes a definite change. So it was with the radiant shell—it changed, all of it, without moving. There was no mistaking the nature of the change, though its meaning was beyond knowing. It was an obeisance. It was an expression of profound respect, first to the humans themselves, next, and hugely, to something the humans represented. It was unquestionably an act of worship.

And what, thought Tod, *could we symbolize to these shining ones?* He was a scarab beetle or an Egyptian cat, a Hindu cow or a Teuton tree, told suddenly that it was sacred.

All the while there flooded down the thing which Carl had tried so ineptly to express: *"We're sorry. But it will be all right. You will be glad. You can be glad now."*

At last there was a change in the mighty formation. The center rose and the wings came in, the left one rising and curling to tighten the curve, the right one bending inward without rising. In a moment the formation was a column, a hollow cylinder. It began to rotate slowly, divided into a series of close-set horizontal rings. Alternate rings slowed and stopped and began a counter-rotation, and with a sudden shift, became two interlocked spirals. Still the over-all formation was a hollow cylinder, but now it was composed of an upward and a downward helix.

The individuals spun and swirled down and down, up and up, and kept this motion within the cylinder, and the cylinder quite discrete, as it began to rise. Up and up it lifted, brilliantly, silently, the living original of that which they had found by Alma's body . . . up and up, filling the eye and the mind with its complex and controlled ascent, its perfect continuity; for here was a thing with no beginning and no end, all flux and balance where each rising was matched by a fall and each turn by its counterpart.

High, and higher, and at last it was a glowing spot against the hovering shadow of the ship, which swallowed it up. The ship left then, not moving, but fading away like the streamers of an aurora, but faster. In three heartbeats it was there, perhaps it was there, it was gone.

Tod closed his eyes, seeing that dynamic double helix. The tip of his mind was upon it; he trembled on the edge of revelation. He *knew* what that form symbolized. He knew it contained the simple answer to his life and their lives, to this planet and its life and the lives which were brought to it. If a cross is more than an instrument of torture, more than the memento of an event; if the *crux ansata*, the Yin-and-Yang, David's star and all such crystallizations were but symbols of great systems of philosophy, then this dynamic intertwined spiral, this free-flowing, rigidly choreographed symbol was . . . was—

Something grunted, something screamed, and the wondrous answer turned and rose spiraling away from him to be gone in three heartbeats. Yet in that moment he knew it was there for him when he had the time, the phasing, the bringing-together of whatever elements were needed. He could not use it yet but he had it. He had it.

Another scream, an immense thrashing all about. The spell was broken and the armistice over. There were chargings and fleeings, cries of death-agony and roaring challenges in and over the jungle, through the grasses to the suddenly boiling river. Life goes on, and death with it, but there must be more death than life when too much life is thrown together.

IV

It may be that their five human lives were saved, in that turbulent reawakening, only by their alienness, for the life around them was cheek-and-jowl with its familiar enemy, its familiar quarry, its familiar food, and there need be no experimenting with the five soft containers of new rich juices standing awestruck with their backs to their intrusive shelter.

Then slowly they met one another's eyes. They

cared enough for each other so that there was a gladness of sharing. They cared enough for themselves so that there was also a sheepishness, a troubled self-analysis: *What did I do while I was out of my mind?*

They drew together before the door and watched the chase and slaughter around them as it subsided toward its usual balance of hunting and killing, eating and dying. Their hands began to remember the weapons they held, their minds began to reach for reality.

"They were angels," April said, so softly that no one but Tod heard her. Tod watched her lips tremble and part, and knew that she was about to speak the thing he had almost grasped, but then Teague spoke again, and Tod could see the comprehension fade from her and be gone. "Look! Look there!" said Teague, and moved down the wall to the corner.

What had been an inner compartment of their ship was now an isolated cube, and from its back corner, out of sight until now, stretched another long wall. At regular intervals were doors, each fastened by a simple outside latch of parametal.

Teague stepped to the first door, the others crowding close. Teague listened intently, then stepped back and threw the door open.

Inside was a windowless room, blazing with light. Around the sides, machines were set. Tod instantly recognized their air-cracker, the water-purifiers, the protein-converter and one of the auxiliary power-plants. In the center was a generator coupled to a light-metal fusion motor. The output buses were neatly insulated, coupled through fuseboxes and resistance controls to a "Christmas tree" multiple outlet. Cables ran through the wall to the Coffin compartment and to the line of unexplored rooms to their left.

"They've left us power, at any rate," said Teague. "Let's look down the line."

Fish, Tod snarled silently. *Dead man! After what you've just seen you should be on your knees with the weight of it, you should put out your eyes to remem-*

ber better. But all you can do is take inventory of your nuts and bolts.

Tod looked at the others, at their strained faces and their continual upward glances, as if the bright memory had magnetism for them. He could see the dream fading under Teague's untimely urgency. *You couldn't let us live with it quietly, even for a moment.* Then another inward voice explained to him, *But you see, they killed Alma.*

Resentfully he followed Teague.

Their ship had been dismantled, strung out along the hilltop like a row of shacks. They were interconnected, wired up, re-stacked, ready and reeking with efficiency—the lab, the library, six chambers full of mixed cargo, then—then the noise Teague made was as near to a shout of glee as Tod had ever heard from the man. The door he had just opened showed their instruments inside, all the reference tapes and tools and manuals. There was even a dome in the roof, and the refractor was mounted and waiting.

"April?" Tod looked, looked again. She was gone. "April!"

She emerged from the library, three doors back. "Teague!"

Teague pulled himself away from the array of instruments and went to her. "Teague," she said, "every one of the reels has been read."

"How do you know?"

"None of them are rewound."

Teague looked up and down the row of doors. "That doesn't sound like the way they—" The unfinished sentence was enough. Whoever had built this from their ship's substance worked according to function and with a fine efficiency.

Teague entered the library and picked a tape-reel from its rack. He inserted the free end of film into a slot and pressed a button. The reel spun and the film disappeared inside the cabinet.

Teague looked up and back. Every single reel was

inside out on the clips. "They could have rewound them," said Teague, irritated.

"Maybe they wanted us to know that they'd read them," said Moira.

"Maybe they did," Teague murmured. He picked up a reel, looked at it, picked up another and another. "Music. A play. And here's our personal stuff—behavior film, training records, everything."

Carl said, "Whoever read through all this knows a lot about us."

Teague frowned. "Just us?"

"Who else?"

"Earth," said Teague. "All of it."

"You mean we were captured and analyzed so that whoever they are could get a line on Earth? You think they're going to attack Earth?"

" 'You mean . . . You think . . .' " Teague mimicked coldly. "I mean nothing and I think nothing! Tod, would you be good enough to explain to this impulsive young man what you learned from me earlier? That we need concern ourselves only with evidence?"

Tod shuffled his feet, wishing not to be made an example for anyone, especially Carl, to follow. Carl flushed and tried to smile. Moira took his hand secretly and squeezed it. Tod heard a slight exhalation beside him and looked quickly at April. She was angry. There were times when he wished she would not be angry.

She pointed. "Would you call *that* evidence, Teague?"

They followed her gesture. One of the tape-readers stood open. On its reelshelf stood the counterpart of the strange object they had seen twice before—once, in miniature, found in Alma's Coffin; once again, huge in the sky. This was another of the miniatures.

Teague stared at it, then put out his hand. As his fingers touched it, the pilot-jewel on the tape-reader flashed on, and a soft, clear voice filled the room.

Tod's eyes stung. He had thought he would never

hear that voice again. As he listened, he held to the life-line of April's presence, and felt his lifeline tremble.

Alma's voice said:

"*They made some adjustments yesterday with the needle-clusters in my Coffin, so I think they will put me back into it . . . Teague, oh, Teague, I'm going to die!*

"*They brought me the recorder just now. I don't know whether it's for their records or for you. If it's for you, then I must tell you . . . how can I tell you?*

"*I've watched them all this time . . . how long? Months . . . I don't know. I conceived when I awoke, and the babies are coming very soon now; it's been long enough for that; and yet—how can I tell you?*

"*They boarded us, I don't know how, I don't know why, nor where . . . outside, space is strange, wrong. It's all misty, without stars, crawling with blurs and patches of light.*

"*They understand me; I'm sure of that—what I say, what I think. I can't understand them at all. They radiate feelings—sorrow, curiosity, confidence, respect. When I began to realize I would die, they gave me a kind of regret. When I broke and cried and said I wanted to be with you, Teague, they reassured me, they said I would. I'm sure that's what they said. But how could that be?*

"*They are completely dedicated in what they are doing. Their work is a religion to them, and we are part of it. They . . . value us, Teague. They didn't just find us. They chose us. It's as if we were the best part of something even they consider great.*

"*The best . . . ! Among them I feel like an ameba. They're beautiful, Teague. Important. Very sure of what they are doing. It's that certainty that makes me believe what I have to believe; I am going to die, and you will live, and you and I will be together. How can that be? How can that be?*

"*Yet it is true, so believe it with me, Teague. But—find out how!*

"Teague, every day they have put a machine on me, radiating. It has to do with the babies. It isn't done to harm them. I'm sure of that. I'm their mother and I'm sure of it. They won't die.

"I will. I can feel their sorrow.

"And I will be with you, and they are joyous about that. . . .

"Teague—find out how!"

Tod closed his eyes so that he would not look at Teague, and wished with all his heart that Teague had been alone to hear that ghostly voice. As to what it had said, the words stood as a frame for a picture he could not see, showing him only where it was, not what it meant. Alma's voice had been tremulous and unsure, but he knew it well enough to know that joy and certitude had lived with her as she spoke. There was wonderment, but no fear.

Knowing that it might be her only message to them, should she not have told them more—facts, figures, measurements?

Then an old, old tale flashed into his mind, an early thing from the ancient Amerenglish, by Hynlen (Henlyne, was it? no matter) about a man who tried to convey to humanity a description of the super-beings who had captured him, with only his body as a tablet and his nails as a stylus. Perhaps he was mad by the time he finished, but his message was clear at least to him: *"Creation took eight days."* How would he, Tod, describe an association with the ones he had seen in the sky outside, if he had been with them for nearly three hundred days?

April tugged gently at his arm. He turned toward her, still avoiding the sight of Teague. April inclined her shining white head to the door. Moira and Carl already stood outside. They joined them, and waited wordlessly until Teague came out.

When he did, he was grateful, and he need not say so. He came out, a great calm in his face and voice, passed them and let them follow him to his methodical examination of the other compartments, to finish his inventory.

Food stores, cable and conduit, metal and parametal rod and sheet stock, tools and tool-making matrices and dies. A hangar, in which lay their lifeboat, fully equipped.

But there was no long-range communication device, and no parts for one.

And there was no heavy space-drive mechanism, nor tools to make one, nor fuel if they should make the tools.

Back in the instrument room, Carl grunted. "Somebody means for us to stick around."

"The boat—"

Teague said, "I don't think they'd have left us the boat if Earth was in range."

"We'll build a beacon," Tod said suddenly. "We'll get a rescue ship out to us."

"Out where?" asked Teague drily.

They followed his gaze. Bland and silent, merciless, the decay chronometer stared back at them. Built around a standard radioactive, it had two dials—one which measured the amount of energy radiated by the material, and one which measured the loss mass. When they checked, the reading was correct. They checked, and the reading was 64.

"Sixty-four years," said Teague. "Assuming we averaged as much as one-half light speed, which isn't likely, we must be thirty light-years away from Earth. Thirty years to get a light-beam there, sixty or more to get a ship back, plus time to make the beacon and time for Earth to understand the signal and prepare a ship. . . ." He shook his head.

"Plus the fact," Tod said in a strained voice, "that there is no habitable planet in a thirty-year radius from Sol. Except Prime."

Shocked, they gaped silently at this well-known fact. A thousand years of scrupulous search with the best instruments could not have missed a planet like this at such a distance.

"Then the chronometer's wrong!"

"I'm afraid not," said Teague. "It's sixty-four years since we left Earth, and that's that."

"And this planet doesn't exist," said Carl with a sour smile, "and I suppose that is also that."

"Yes, Teague," said Tod. "One of those two facts can't exist with the other."

"They can because they do," said Teague. "There's a missing factor. Can a man breathe under water, Tod?"

"If he has a diving-helmet."

Teague spread his hands. "It took sixty-four years to get to this planet *if*. We have to find the figurative diving-helmet." He paused. "The evidence in favor of the planet's existence is fairly impressive," he said wryly. "Let's check the other fact."

"How?"

"The observatory."

They ran to it. The sky glowed its shimmering green, but through it the stars had begun to twinkle. Carl got to the telescope first, put a big hand on the swing-controls, and said, "Where first?" He tugged at the instrument. "Hey!" He tugged again.

"Don't!" said Teague sharply. Carl let go and backed away. Teague switched on the lights and examined the instrument. "It's already connected to the compensators," he said. "Hmp! Our hosts are most helpful." He looked at the setting of the small motors which moved the instrument to cancel diurnal rotation effects. "Twenty-eight hours, thirteen minutes plus. Well, if that's correct for this planet, it's proof that this isn't Earth or Prime—if we needed proof." He touched the controls lightly. "Carl, what's the matter here?"

Carl bent to look. There were dabs of dull silver on the threads of the adjusting screws. He touched them. "Parametal," he said. "Unflashed, but it has adhered enough to jam the threads. Take a couple days to get it off without jarring it. Look here—they've done the same thing with the objective screws!"

"We look at what they want us to see, and like it," said Tod.

"Maybe it's something we want to see," said April gently.

Only half-teasing, Tod said, "Whose side are you on, anyway?"

Teague put his eye to the instrument. His hands, by habit, strayed to the focusing adjustment, but found it locked the same way as the others. "Is there a Galactic Atlas?"

"Not in the rack," said Moira a moment later.

"Here," said April from the chart table. Awed, she added, "Open."

Tensely they waited while Teague took his observation and referred to the atlas and to the catalog they found lying under it. When at last he lifted his face from the calculations, it bore the strangest expression Tod had ever seen there.

"Our diving-helmet," he said at last, very slowly, too evenly, "—that is, the factor which rationalizes our two mutually exclusive facts—is simply that our captors have a faster-than-light drive."

"But according to theory—"

"According to our telescope," Teague interrupted, "through which I have just seen Sol, and these references so thoughtfully laid out for us . . ." Shockingly, his voice broke. He took two deep breaths, and said, "Sol is two-hundred and seventeen light-years away. That sun which set a few minutes ago is Beta Librae." He studied their shocked faces, one by one. "I don't know what we shall eventually call this place," he said with difficulty, "but we had better get used to calling it home."

They called the planet Viridis ("the greenest name I can think of," Moira said) because none among them had ever seen such a green. It was more than the green of growing, for the sunlight was green-tinged and at night the whole sky glowed green, a green as bright as the brightest silver of Earth's moon, as water molecules, cracked by the star's intense ultraviolet, celebrated their nocturnal reunion.

They called the moons Wynken, Blynken and Nod, and the sun they called—the sun.

They worked like slaves, and then like scientists, which is a change of occupation but not a change of pace. They built a palisade of a cypress-like, straight-grained wood, each piece needle-pointed, double-laced with parametal wire. It had a barred gate and peepholes with periscopes and permanent swivel-mounts for the needle-guns they were able to fabricate from tube-stock and spare solenoids. They roofed the enclosure with parametal mesh which, at one point, could be rolled back to launch the lifeboat.

They buried Alma.

They tested and analyzed, classified, processed, researched everything in the compound and within easy reach of it—soil, vegetation, fauna. They developed an insect-repellent solution to coat the palisade and an insecticide with an automatic spray to keep the compound clear of the creatures, for they were numerous, large, and occasionally downright dangerous, like the "flying caterpillar" which kept its pseudopods in its winged form and enthusiastically broke them off in the flesh of whatever attacked them, leaving an angry rash and suppurating sores. They discovered three kinds of edible seed and another which yielded a fine hydrocarbonic oil much like soy, and a flower whose calyces, when dried and then soaked and broiled, tasted precisely like crab-meat.

For a time they were two separate teams, virtually isolated from each other. Moira and Teague collected minerals and put them through the mass spectroscope and the radioanalyzers, and it fell to April to classify the life-forms, with Carl and Tod competing mightily to bring in new ones. Or at least photographs of new ones. Two-ton *Parametrodon,* familiarly known as Dopey—a massive herbivore with just enough intelligence to move its jaws—was hardly the kind of thing to be carried home under one's arm, and *Felodon,* the scaly carnivore with the catlike tusks, though barely as long as a man, was about as friendly as a half-starved wolverine.

Tetrapodys (Tod called it 'Umbrellabird') turned out to be a rewarding catch. They stumbled across a vine which bore foul-smelling pods; these the clumsy amphibious bats found irresistible. Carl synthesized the evil stuff and improved upon it, and they smeared it on tree-boles by the river. *Tetrapodys* came there by the hundreds and laid eggs apparently in sheer frustration. These eggs were camouflaged by a frilly green membrane, for all the world like the ground-buds of the giant water-fern. The green shoots tasted like shallots and were fine for salad when raw and excellent as onion soup when stewed. The half-hatched *Tetrapodys* yielded ligaments which when dried made excellent self-baited fish-hooks. The wing-muscles of the adult tasted like veal cutlet with fish-sauce, and the inner, or main shell of the eggs afforded them an amazing shoe-sole—light, tough, and flexible, which, for some unknown reason, *Felodon* would not track.

Pteronauchis, or "flapping frog," was the gliding newt they had seen on that first day. Largely nocturnal, it was phototropic; a man with a strong light could fill a bushel with the things in minutes. Each specimen yielded twice as many, twice as large, and twice as good frog-legs as a Terran frog.

There were no mammals.

There were flowers in profusion—white (a sticky green in that light), purple, brown, blue, and, of course, the ubiquitous green. No red—as a matter of fact, there was virtually no red anywhere on the planet. April's eyes became a feast for them all. It is impossible to describe the yearning one can feel for an absent color. And so it was that a legend began with them. Twice Tod had seen a bright red growth. The first time he thought it was a mushroom, the second it seemed more of a lichen. The first time it was surrounded by a sea of crusher ants on the move—a fearsome carpet which even *Parametrodon* respected. The second time he had seen it from twenty meters away and had just turned toward it when not one, but three *Felodons* came hurtling through the undergrowth at him.

He came back later, both times, and found nothing. And once Carl swore he saw a brilliant red plant move slowly into a rock crevice as he approached. The thing became their *edelweiss*—very nearly their Grail.

Rough diamonds lay in the streambeds and emeralds glinted in the night-glow, and for the Terran-oriented mind there was incalculable treasure to be scratched up just below the steaming humus: iridium, ruthenium, metallic neptunium 237. There was an unaccountable (at first) shift toward the heavier metals. The ruthenium-rhodium-palladium group was as plentiful on Viridis as the iron-nickel-cobalt series on Earth; cadmium was actually more plentiful here than its relative, zinc. Technetium was present, though rare, on the crust, while Earth's had long since decayed.

Vulcanism was common on Viridis, as could be expected in the presence of so many radioactives. From the lifeboat they had seen bald-spots where there were particularly high concentrations of "hot" material. In some of these there was life.

At the price of a bout of radiation sickness, Carl went into one such area briefly for specimens. What he found was extraordinary—a tree which was warm to the touch, which used minerals and water at a profligate pace, and which, when transplanted outside an environment which destroyed cells almost as fast as they developed, went cancerous, grew enormously, and killed itself with its own terrible viability. In the same lethal areas lived a primitive worm which constantly discarded segments to keep pace with its rapid growth, and which also grew visibly and died of living too fast when taken outside.

The inclination of the planet's axis was less than 2°, so that there were virtually no seasons, and very little variation in temperature from one latitude to another. There were two continents and an equatorial sea, no mountains, no plains, and few large lakes. Most of the planet was gently rolling hill-country and meandering rivers, clothed in thick jungle or grass. The spot where they had awakened was as good as any other, so there they stayed, wandering less and less as they amassed information. Nowhere was there an artifact of any kind, nor any slightest trace of previous habitation. Unless, of course, one considered the existence itself of life on this planet. For Permian life can hardly be expected to develop in less than a billion years; yet the irreproachable calendar inherent in the radioactive bones of Viridis insisted that the planet was no more than thirty-five million years old.

V

When Moira's time came, it went hard with her, and Carl forgot to swagger because he could not help. Teague and April took care of her, and Tod stayed with Carl, wishing for the right thing to say and not finding it, wanting to do something for this new strange man with Carl's face, and the unsure hands which twisted each other, clawed the ground, wiped cruelly at the scalp, at the shins, restless, terrified. Through Carl, Tod learned a little more of what he never wanted to know—what it must have been like for Teague when he lost Alma.

Alma's six children were toddlers by then, bright and happy in the only world they had ever known. They had been named for moons—Wynken, Blynken and Nod, Rhea, Callisto and Titan. Nod and Titan were the boys, and they and Rhea had Alma's eyes and hair and sometimes Alma's odd, brave stillness—a sort of suspension of the body while the mind went out to grapple and conquer instead of fearing. If the turgid air and the radiant ground affected them, they did not show it, except perhaps in their rapid development.

They heard Moira cry out. It was like laughter, but it was pain. Carl sprang to his feet. Tod took his arm and Carl pulled it away. "Why can't I do something? Do I have to just *sit* here?"

"Shh. She doesn't feel it. That's a tropism. She'll be all right. Sit down, Carl. Tell you what you can do— you can name them. Think. Think of a nice set of names, all connected in some way. Teague used moons. What are you going to—"

"Time enough for that," Carl grunted. "Tod . . . do you know what I'll . . . I'd be if she—if something happened?"

"Nothing's going to happen."

"I'd just cancel out. I'm not Teague. I couldn't carry it. How does Teague do it? . . ." Carl's voice lapsed to a mumble.

"Names," Tod reminded him. "Seven, eight of 'em. Come on, now."

"Think she'll have eight?"

"Why not? She's normal." He nudged Carl. "Think of names. I know! How many of the old signs of the zodiac would make good names?"

"Don't remember 'em."

"I do. Aries, that's good. Taurus. Gem—no; you wouldn't want to call a child 'Twins.' Leo—that's *fine!*"

"Libra," said Carl, "for a girl. Aquarius, Sagittarius—how many's that?"

Tod counted on his fingers. "Six. Then, Virgo and Capricorn. And you're all set!" But Carl wasn't listening. In two long bounds he reached April, who was just stepping into the compound. She looked tired. She looked more than tired. In her beautiful eyes was a great pity, the color of a bleeding heart.

"Is she all right? Is she?" They were hardly words, those hoarse, rushed things.

April smiled with her lips, while her eyes poured pity. "Yes, yes, she'll be all right. It wasn't too bad."

Carl whooped and pushed past her. She caught his arm, and for all her frailty, swung him around.

"Not yet, Carl. Teague says to tell you first—"

"The babies? What about them? How many, April?"

April looked over Carl's shoulder at Tod. She said, "Three."

Carl's face relaxed, numb, and his eyes went round. "Th—what? Three so far, you mean. There'll surely be more. . . ."

She shook her head.

Tod felt the laughter explode within him, and he clamped his jaws on it. It surged at him, hammered in the back of his throat. And then he caught April's pleading eyes. He took strength from her, and bottled up a great bray of merriment.

Carl's voice was the last fraying thread of hope. "The others died, then."

She put a hand on his cheek. "There were only three. Carl . . . don't be mean to Moira."

"Oh, I won't," he said with difficulty. "She couldn't . . . I mean it wasn't her doing." He flashed a quick, defensive look at Tod, who was glad now he had controlled himself. What was in Carl's face meant murder for anyone who dared laugh.

April said, "Not your doing either, Carl. It's this planet. It must be."

"Thanks, April," Carl muttered. He went to the door, stopped, shook himself like a big dog. He said again, "Thanks," but this time his voice didn't work and it was only a whisper. He went inside.

Tod bolted for the corner of the building, whipped

around it and sank to the ground, choking. He held both hands over his mouth and laughed until he hurt. When at last he came to a limp silence, he felt April's presence. She stood quietly watching him, waiting.

"I'm sorry," he said. "I'm sorry. But . . . it *is* funny."

She shook her head gravely. "We're not on Earth, Tod. A new world means new manners, too. That would apply even on Terra Prime if we'd gone there."

"I suppose," he said, and then repressed another giggle.

"I always thought it was a silly kind of joke anyway," she said primly. "Judging virility by the size of a brood. There isn't any scientific basis for it. Men are silly. They used to think that virility could be measured by the amount of hair on their chests, or how tall they were. There's nothing wrong with having only three."

"Carl?" grinned Tod. "The big ol' swashbuckler?" He let the grin fade. "All right, Ape. I won't let Carl see me laugh. Or you either. All right?" A peculiar expression crossed his face. "What was that you said? April! Men never had hair on their chests!"

"Yes they did. Ask Teague."

"I'll take your word for it." He shuddered. "I can't imagine it unless a man had a tail too. And bony ridges over his eyes."

"It wasn't so long ago that they had. The ridges, anyway. Well—I'm glad you didn't laugh in front of him. You're nice, Tod."

"You're nice too." He pulled her down beside him and hugged her gently. "Bet you'll have a dozen."

"I'll try." She kissed him.

When specimen-hunting had gone as far as it could, classification became the settlement's main enterprise. And gradually, the unique pattern of Viridian life began to emerge.

Viridis had its primitive fish and several of the mollusca, but the fauna was primarily arthropods and reptiles. The interesting thing about each of the three branches was the close relationship between species. It was almost as if evolution took a major step with each generation, instead of bumbling along as on Earth, where certain stages of development are static 'for thousands, millions of years. *Pterodon,* for example, existed in three varieties, the simplest of which showed a clear similarity to *pteronauchis,* the gliding newt. A simple salamander could be shown to be the common ancestor of both the flapping frog and massive *Parametrodon,* and there were strong similarities between this salamander and the worm which fathered the arthropods.

They lived close to the truth for a long time without being able to see it, for man is conditioned to think of evolution from simple to complex, from ooze to animalcule to mollusc to ganoid; amphibid to monotreme to primate to tinker . . . losing the significance of the fact that all these co-exist. Was the vertebrate eel of prehistory a *higher* form of life than his simpler descendant? The whale lost his legs; this men call recidivism, a sort of backsliding in evolution, and treat it as a kind of illegitimacy.

Men are oriented out of simplicity toward the complex, and make of the latter a goal. Nature treats complex matters as expediencies and so is never confused. It is hardly surprising, then, that the Viridis colony took so long to discover their error, for the weight of evidence was in error's favor. There was indeed an unbroken line from the lowest forms of life to the highest, and to assume that they had a common ancestor was a beautifully consistent hypothesis, of the order of accuracy an archer might display in hitting dead center, from a thousand paces, a bowstring with the nock of his arrow.

The work fell more and more on the younger ones. Teague isolated himself, not by edict, but by habit. It was assumed that he was working along his own lines; and then it became usual to proceed without him, until finally he was virtually a hermit in their midst. He was aging rapidly; perhaps it hurt something in him to be surrounded by so much youth. His six children thrived, and, with Carl's three, ran naked in the jungle armed only with their sticks and their speed. They were apparently immune to practically everything Viridis might bring against them, even *Crotalidus'* fangs, which gave them the equivalent of a severe bee-sting (as opposed to what had happened to Moira once, when they had had to reactivate one of the Coffins to keep her alive).

Tod would come and sit with him sometimes, and as long as there was no talk the older man seemed to gain something from the visits. But he preferred to be alone, living as much as he could with memories for which not even a new world could afford a substitute.

Tod said to Carl, "Teague is going to wither up and blow away if we can't interest him in something."

"He's interested enough to spend a lot of time with whatever he's thinking about," Carl said bluntly.

"But I'd like it better if he was interested in something here, now. I wish we could . . . I wish—" But he could think of nothing, and it was a constant trouble to him.

Little Titan was killed, crushed under a great clumsy *Parametrodon* which slid down a bank on him while the child was grubbing for the scarlet cap of the strange red mushroom they had glimpsed from time to time. It was in pursuit of one of these that Moira had been bitten by the *Crotalidus*. One of Carl's children was drowned—just how, no one knew. Aside from these tragedies, life was easy and interesting. The compound began to look more like a *kraal* as they acclimated, for although the adults never adapted as well as the children, they did become far less sensitive to insect bites and the poison weeds which first troubled them.

It was Teague's son Nod who found what was

needed to bring Teague's interest back, at least for a while. The child came back to the compound one day, trailed by two slinking *Felodons* who did not catch him because they kept pausing and pausing to lap up gouts of blood which marked his path. Nod's ear was torn and he had a green-stick break in his left ulna, and a dislocated wrist. He came weeping, weeping tears of joy. He shouted as he wept, great proud noises. Once in the compound he collapsed, but he would not lose consciousness, nor his grip on his prize, until Teague came. Then he handed Teague the mushroom and fainted.

The mushroom was and was not like anything on Earth. Earth has a fungus called *schizophyllum,* not uncommon but most strange. Though not properly a fungus, the red "mushroom" of Viridis had many of the functions of *schizophyllum.*

Schizophyllum produces spores of four distinct types, each of which grows into a genetically distinct, completely dissimilar plant. Three of these are sterile. The fourth produces *schizophyllum.*

The red mushroom of Viridis also produced four distinct heterokaryons or genetically different types, and the spores of one of these produced the mushroom.

Teague spent an engrossing earth-year in investigating the other three.

VI

Sweating and miserable in his integument of flexskin, Tod hunched in the crotch of a finger-tree. His knees were drawn up and his head was down; his arms clasped his shins and he rocked slightly back and forth. He knew he would be safe here for some time— the fleshy fingers of the tree were clumped at the slender, swaying ends of the branches and never turned back toward the trunk. He wondered what it would be like to be dead. Perhaps he would be dead soon, and then he'd know. He might as well be.

The names he'd chosen were perfect and all of a family: Sol, Mercury, Venus, Terra, Mars, Jupiter . . . eleven of them. And he could think of a twelfth if he had to.

For what?

He let himself sink down again into the blackness wherein nothing lived but the oily turning of *what's it like to be dead?*

Quiet, he thought. *No one would laugh.*

Something pale moved on the jungle floor below him. He thought instantly of April, and angrily put the thought out of his mind. April would be sleeping now, having completed the trifling task it had taken her so long to start. Down there, that would be Blynken, or maybe Rhea. They were very alike.

It didn't matter, anyway.

He closed his eyes and stopped rocking. He couldn't see anyone, no one could see him. That was the best way. So he sat, and let time pass, and when a hand lay on his shoulder, he nearly leaped out of the tree. "Damn it, Blynken—"

"It's me. Rhea." The child, like all of Alma's daughters, was large for her age and glowing with health. How long had it been? Six, eight . . . nine Earth years since they had landed.

"Go hunt mushrooms," Tod growled. "Leave me alone."

"Come back," said the girl.

Tod would not answer. Rhea knelt beside him, her arm around the primary branch, her back, with his, against the trunk. She bent her head and put her cheek against his. "Tod."

Something inside him flamed. He bared his teeth and swung a heavy fist. The girl doubled up soundlessly and slipped out of the tree. He stared down at the lax body and at first could not see it for the haze of fury which blew and whirled around him. Then his vision cleared and he moaned, tossed his club down and dropped after it. He caught up the club and whacked off the tree-fingers which probed toward them. He swept up the child and leapt clear, and sank to his knees, gathering her close.

"Rhea, I'm sorry, I'm sorry . . . I wasn't . . . I'm not—*Rhea!* Don't be dead!"

She stirred and made a tearing sound with her throat. Her eyelids trembled and opened, uncovering pain-blinded eyes. "Rhea!"

"It's all right," she whispered, "I shouldn't've bothered you. Do you want me to go away?"

"No," he said, "No." He held her tight. *Why not let her go away?* a part of him wondered, and another part, frightened and puzzled, cried, *No! No!* He had an urgent, half-hysterical need to explain. *Why explain to her, a child? Say you're sorry, comfort her, heal her, but don't expect her to understand.* Yet he said, "I can't go back. There's nowhere else to go. So what can I do?"

Rhea was quiet, as if waiting. A terrible thing, a wonderful thing, to have someone you have hurt wait patiently like that while you find a way to explain. Even if you only explain it to yourself . . . "What could I do if I went back? They—they'll never—they'll laugh at me. They'll all laugh. They're laughing now." Angry again, plaintive no more, he blurted, "April! *Damn* April! She's made a eunuch out of me!"

"Because she had only one baby?"

"Like a savage."

"It's a beautiful baby. A boy."

"A man, a real man, fathers six or eight."

She met his eyes gravely. "That's silly."

"What's happening to us on this crazy planet?" he raged. "Are we evolving backward? What comes next—one of you kids hatching out some amphibids?"

She said only, "Come back, Tod."

"I can't," he whispered. "They'll think I'm . . . that I can't . . ." Helplessly, he shrugged. "They'll laugh."

"Not until you do, and then they'll laugh *with* you. Not at you, Tod."

Finally, he said it, "April won't love me; she'll never love a weakling."

She pondered, holding him with her clear gaze. "You really need to be loved a whole lot."

Perversely, he became angry again. "I can get along!" he snapped.

And she smiled and touched the nape of his neck. "You're loved," she assured him. "Gee, you don't have to be mad about that. I love you, don't I? April loves you. Maybe I love you even more than she does. She loves everything you are, Tod. I love everything you ever were and everything you ever will be."

· He closed his eyes and a great music came to him. A long, long time ago he had attacked someone who came to comfort him, and she had let him cry, and at length she had said . . . not exactly these words, but— it was the same.

"Rhea."

He looked at her. "You said all that to me before."

A puzzled small crinkle appeared between her eyes and she put her fingers on it. "Did I?"

"Yes," said Tod, "but it was before you were even born.

He rose and took her hand, and they went back to the compound, and whether he was laughed at or not he never knew, for he could think of nothing but his full heart and of April. He went straight in to her and kissed her gently and admired his son, whose name was Sol, and who had been born with hair and two tiny incisors, and who had heavy bony ridges over his eyes. . . .

"A fantastic storage capacity," Teague remarked, touching the top of the scarlet mushroom. "The spores are almost microscopic. The thing doesn't seem to want them distributed, either. It positively hoards them, millions of them."

"Start over, please," April said. She shifted the baby in her arms. He was growing prodigiously. "Slowly. I used to know something about biology—or so I thought. But *this*—"

Teague almost smiled. It was good to see. The aging face had not had so much expression in it in five Earth-years. "I'll get as basic as I can, then, and start from there. First of all, we call this thing a mushroom, but it isn't. I don't think it's a plant, though you couldn't call it an animal, either."

"I don't think anybody ever told me the real difference between a plant and an animal," said Tod.

"Oh . . . well, the most convenient way to put it— it's not strictly accurate, but it will do—is that plants make their own food and animals subsist on what others have made. This thing does both. It has roots, but—" he lifted an edge of the skirted stem of the mushroom—"it can move them. Not much, not fast; but if it wants to shift itself, it can."

April smiled, "Tod, I'll give you basic biology any time. Do go on, Teague."

"Good. Now, I explained about the heterokaryons— the ability this thing has to produce spores which grow up into four completely different plants. One is a mushroom just like this. Here are the other three."

Tod looked at the box of plants. "Are they really all from the mushroom spores?"

"Don't blame you," said Teague, and actually chuckled. "I didn't believe it myself at first. A sort of pitcher plant, half full of liquid. A thing like a cactus. And this one. It's practically all underground, like a truffle, although it has these cilia. You wouldn't think it was anything but a few horsehairs stuck in the ground."

"And they're all sterile," Tod recalled.

"They're not," said Teague, "and that's what I

called you in here to tell you. They'll yield if they are fertilized."

"Fertilized how?"

Instead of answering, Teague asked April, "Do you remember how far back we traced the evolution of Viridian life?"

"Of course. We got the arthropods all the way back to a simple segmented worm. The insects seemed to come from another worm, with pseudopods and a hard carapace."

"A caterpillar," Tod interpolated.

"Almost," said April, with a scientist's nicety. "And the most primitive reptile we could find was a little gymnoderm you could barely see without a glass."

"Where did we find it?"

"Swimming around in—oh! In those pitcher plant things!"

"If you won't take my word for this," said Teague, a huge enjoyment glinting between his words, "you'll just have to breed these things yourself. It's a lot of work, but this is what you'll discover.

"An adult gymnoderm—a male—finds this pitcher and falls in. There's plenty of nutriment for him, you know, and he's a true amphibian. He fertilizes the pitcher. Nodules grow under the surface of the liquid inside there—" he pointed "—and bud off. The buds are mobile. They grow into wrigglers, miniature tadpoles. Then into lizards. They climb out and go about the business of being—well, lizards."

"All males?" asked Tod.

"No," said Teague, "and that's an angle I haven't yet investigated. But apparently some males breed with females, which lay eggs, which hatch into lizards, and some find plants to fertilize. Anyway, it looks as if this plant is actually the progenitor of all the reptiles here; you know how clear the evolutionary lines are to all the species."

"What about the truffle with the horsehairs?" asked Tod.

"A pupa," said Teague, and to the incredulous expression on April's face, he insisted, "Really—a pupa. After nine weeks or so of dormance, it hatches out into what you almost called a caterpillar."

And then into all the insects here," said April, and shook her head in wonderment. "And I suppose that cactus-thing hatches out the nematodes, the segmented ones that evolve into arthropods?"

Teague nodded. "You're welcome to experiment," he said again, "but believe me—you'll only find out I'm right: it really happens."

"Then this scarlet mushroom is the beginning of everything here."

"I can't find another theory," said Teague.

"I can," said Tod.

They looked at him questioningly, and he rose and laughed. "Not yet. I have to think it through." He scooped up the baby and then helped April to her feet. "How do you like our Sol, Teague?"

"Fine," said Teague. "A fine boy." Tod knew he was seeing the heavy occipital ridges, the early teeth, and saying nothing. Tod was aware of a faint inward surprise as the baby reached toward April and he handed him over. He should have resented what might be in Teague's mind, but he did not. The beginnings of an important insight welcomed criticism of the child, recognized its hairiness, its savagery, and found these things good. But as yet the thought was too nebulous to express, except by a smile. He smiled, took April's hand, and left.

"That was a funny thing you said to Teague," April told him as they walked toward their quarters.

"Remember, April, the day we landed? Remember—" he made a gesture that took in a quadrant of sky— "Remember how we all felt . . . good?"

"Yes," she murmured. "It was like a sort of compliment, and a reassurance. How could I forget?"

"Yes. Well . . ." He spoke with difficulty but his smile stayed. "I have a thought, and it makes me feel like that. But I can't get it into words," After a thoughtful pause, he added, "Yet."

She shifted the baby. "He's getting so heavy."

"I'll take him." He took the squirming bundle with the deep-set, almost humorous eyes. When he looked up from them, he caught an expression on April's face which he hadn't seen in years. "What is it, Ape?"

"You—*like* him."

"Well, sure."

"I was afraid. I was afraid for a long time that you. . . . he's ours, but he isn't exactly a pretty baby."

"I'm not exactly a pretty father."

"You know how precious you are to me?" she whispered.

He knew, for this was an old intimacy between them. He laughed and followed the ritual: "How precious?"

She cupped her hands and brought them together, to make of them an ivory box. She raised the hands and peeped into them, between the thumbs, as if at a rare jewel, then clasped the magic tight and hugged it to her breast, raising tear-filled eyes to him. "That precious," she breathed.

He looked at the sky, seeing somewhere in it the many peak moments of their happiness when she had made that gesture, feeling how each one, meticulously chosen, brought all the others back. "I used to hate this place," he said. "I guess it's changed."

"You've changed."

Changed how? he wondered. He felt the same, even though he knew he looked older. . . .

The years passed, and the children grew. When Sol was fifteen Earth-years old, short, heavy-shouldered, powerful, he married Carl's daughter Libra. Teague, turning to parchment, had returned to his hermitage from the temporary stimulation of his researches on what they still called "the mushroom." More and more the colony lived off the land and out of the jungle, not because there was any less to be synthesized from their compact machines, but out of preference; it was easier to catch flapping frogs or umbrella-birds and cook them than to bother with machine settings and check-analyses, and, somehow, a lot more fun to eat them, too.

It seemed to them safer, year by year. *Felodon,* unquestionably the highest form of life on Viridis, was growing scarce, being replaced by a smaller, more timid carnivore April called *Vulpidus* (once, for it seemed not to matter much any more about keeping records) and everyone ultimately called "fox," for all the fact that it was a reptile. *Pterodon* was disappearing too, as were all the larger forms. More and more they strayed after food, not famine-driven, but purely for variety; more and more they found themselves welcome and comfortable away from the compound. Once Carl and Moira drifted off for nearly a year. When they came back they had another child—a silent, laughing little thing with oddly long arms and heavy teeth.

The warm days and the glowing nights passed comfortably and the stars no longer called. Tod became a grandfather and was proud. The child, a girl, was albino like April, and had exactly April's deep red eyes. Sol and Libra named her Emerald, a green name and a ground-term rather than a sky-term, as if in open expression of the slow spell worked on them all by Viridis. She was mute—but so were almost all the new children, and it seemed not to matter. They were healthy and happy.

Tod went to tell Teague, thinking it might cheer the old one up a little. He found him lying in what had once been his laboratory, thin and placid and disinterested, absently staring down at one of the arthropodal flying creatures that had once startled them so by zooming into the Coffin chamber. This one had happened to land on Teague's hand, and Teague was laxly waiting for it to fly off again, out through the unscreened window, past the unused sprays, over the faint tumble of rotted spars which had once been a palisade.

"Teague, the baby's come!"

Teague sighed, his tired mind detaching itself from memory episode by episode. His eyes rolled toward Tod and finally he turned his head. "Which one would that be?"

Tod laughed. "My grandchild, a girl. Sol's baby."

Teague let his lids fall. He said nothing.

"Well, aren't you glad?"

Slowly a frown came to the papery brow. "Glad." Tod felt he was looking at the word as he had stared at the arthropod, wondering limply when it might go away. "What's the matter with it?"

"What?"

Teague sighed again, a weary, impatient sound. "What does it look like?" he said slowly, emphasizing each one-syllabled word.

"Like April. Just like April."

Teague half sat up, and blinked at Tod. "You don't mean it."

"Yes, eyes red as—" The image of an Earth sunset flickered near his mind but vanished as too hard to visualize. Tod pointed at the four red-capped "mushrooms" that had stood for so many years in the test-boxes in the laboratory. "Red as those."

"Silver hair," said Teague.

"Yes, beau—"

"All over," said Teague flatly.

"Well, yes."

Teague let himself fall back on the cot and gave a disgusted snort. "A monkey."

"*Teague!*"

"Ah-h-h . . . go 'way," growled the old man. "I long ago resigned myself to what was happening to us here. A human being just can't adapt to the kind of radio-active ruin this place is for us. Your monsters'll breed monsters, and the monsters'll do the same if they can, until pretty soon they just won't breed any more. And that will be the end of that, and good riddance. . . ." His voice faded away. His eyes opened, looking on distant things, and gradually found themselves focused on the man who stood over him in shocked silence. "But the one thing I can't stand is to have somebody come in here saying, 'Oh, joy, oh happy day!'"

"Teague . . ." Tod swallowed heavily.

"Viridis eats ambition; there was going to be a city here," said the old man indistinctly. "Viridis eats humanity; there were going to be people here." He chuckled gruesomely. "All right, all right, accept it if you have to—and you have to. But don't come around here celebrating."

Tod backed to the door, his eyes horror-round, then turned and fled.

VII

April held him as he crouched against the wall, rocked him slightly, made soft unspellable mother-noises to him.

"Shh, he's all decayed, all lonesome and mad," she murmured. "Shh. Shh."

Tod felt half-strangled. As a youth he had been easily moved, he recalled; he had that tightness of the throat for sympathy, for empathy, for injustices he felt the Universe was hurling at him out of its capacious store. But recently life had been placid, full of love and togetherness and a widening sense of membership with the earth and the air and all the familiar things which walked and flew and grew and bred in it. And his throat was shaped for laughter now; these feelings hurt him.

"But he's right," he whispered. "Don't you see? Right from the beginning it . . . it was . . . remember Alma had six children, April? And a little later, Carl

and Moira had three? And you, only one . . . how long
is it since the average human gave birth to only one?"

"They used to say it was humanity's last major mutation," she admitted, "Multiple births . . . these last
two thousand years. But—"

"Eyebrow ridges," he interrupted. "Hair . . . that
skull, Emerald's skull, slanting back like that; did you
see the tusks on that little . . . *baboon* of Moira's?"

"Tod! *Don't!*"

He leaped to his feet, sprang across the room and
snatched the golden helix from the shelf where it had
gleamed its locked symbolism down on them ever since
the landing. "Around and down!" he shouted.
"Around and around and down!" He squatted beside
her and pointed furiously. "Down and down into the
blackest black there is; down into *nothing*." He shook
his fist at the sky. "You see what they do? They find
the highest form of life they can and plant it here and
watch it slide down into the muck!" He hurled the
artifact away from him.

"But it goes up too, round and up. Oh, Tod!" she
cried. "Can you remember them, what they looked
like, the way they flew, and say these things about
them?"

"I can remember Alma," he gritted, "conceiving and
gestating alone in space, while they turned their rays
on her every day. You know *why?*" With the sudden
thought, he stabbed a finger down at her. "To give
her babies a head-start on Viridis, otherwise they'd
have been born normal here; it would've taken another couple of generations to start them downhill,
and they wanted us all to go together."

"No, Tod, no!"

"Yes, April, yes. How much proof do you need?" He
whirled on her. "Listen—remember that mushroom
Teague analyzed? He had to *pry* spores out of it to see
what it yielded. Remember the three different plants
he got? Well, I was just there; I don't know how many
times before I've seen it, but only now it makes sense.

He's got four mushrooms now; do you see? Do you see? Even back as far as we can trace the bugs and newts on this green hell-pit, Viridis won't let anything climb; it must fall."

"I don't—"

"You'll give me basic biology any time," he quoted sarcastically. "Let me tell you some biology. That mushroom yields three plants, and the plants yield animal life. Well, when the animal life fertilized those heterowhatever—"

"Heterokaryons."

"Yes. Well, you don't get animals that can evolve and improve. You get one pitiful generation of animals which breeds back into a mushroom, and there it sits hoarding its spores. Viridis wouldn't let one puny newt, one primitive pupa build! It snatches 'em back, locks 'em up. That mushroom isn't the beginning of everything here—*it's the end!*"

April got to her feet slowly, looking at Tod as if she had never seen him before, not in fear, but with a troubled curiosity. She crossed the room and picked up the artifact, stroked its gleaming golden coils. "You could be right," she said in a low voice. "But that can't be all there is to it." She set the helix back in its place. "They *wouldn't.*"

She spoke with such intensity that for a moment that metrical formation, mighty and golden, rose again in Tod's mind, up and up to the measureless cloud which must be a ship. He recalled the sudden shift, like a genuflection, directed at them, at *him,* and for that moment he could find no evil in it. Confused, he tossed his head, found himself looking out the door, seeing Moira's youngest ambling comfortably across the compound.

"They *wouldn't?*" he snarled. He took April's slender arm and whirled her to the door. "You know what I'd do before I'd father another one like *that?*" He told her specifically what he would do. "A lemur next, hm? A spider, an oyster, a jellyfish!"

April whimpered and ran out. "Know any lullabies to a tapeworm?" he roared after her. She disappeared into the jungle, and he fell back, gasping for breath. . . .

Having no stomach for careful thought nor careful choosing, having Teague for an example to follow, Tod too turned hermit. He could have survived the crisis easily perhaps, with April to help, but she did not come back. Moira and Carl were off again, wandering; the children lived their own lives, and he had no wish to see Teague. Once or twice Sol and Libra came to see him, but he snarled at them and they left him alone. It was no sacrifice. Life on Viridis was very full for the contented ones.

He sulked in his room or poked about the compound by himself. He activated the protein converter once, but found its products tasteless, and never bothered with it again. Sometimes he would stand near the edge of the hilltop and watch the children playing in the long grass, and his lip would curl.

Damn Teague! He'd been happy enough with Sol all those years, for all the boy's bulging eyebrow ridges and hairy body. He had been about to accept the silent, silver Emerald, too, when the crotchety old man had dropped his bomb. Once or twice Tod wondered detachedly what it was in him that was so easily reached, so completely insecure, that the suggestion of abnormality should strike so deep.

Somebody once said, *"You really need to be loved, don't you, Tod?"*

No one would love this tainted thing, father of savages who spawned animals. He didn't deserve to be loved.

He had never felt so alone. *"I'm going to die. But I will be with you too."* That had been Alma. Huh! There was old Teague, tanning his brains in his own sour acids. Alma had believed something or other . . . and what had come of it? That wizened old crab lolling his life away in the lab.

Tod spent six months that way.

"Tod!" He came out of sleep reluctantly, because in sleep an inner self still lived with April where there was no doubt and no fury; no desertion, no loneliness.

He opened his eyes and stared dully at the slender figure silhouetted against Viridis' glowing sky. "April?"

"Moira," said the figure. The voice was cold.

"Moira!" he said, sitting up. "I haven't seen you for a year. More. Wh—"

"Come," she said. "Hurry."

"Come where?"

"Come by yourself or I'll get Carl and he'll carry you." She walked swiftly to the door.

He reeled after her. "You can't come in here and—"

"Come on." The voice was edged and slid out from between clenched teeth. A miserable part of him twitched in delight and told him that he was important enough to be hated. He despised himself for recognizing the twisted thought, and before he knew what he was doing he was following Moira at a steady trot.

"Where are—" he gasped, and she said over her shoulder, "If you don't talk you'll go faster."

At the jungle margin a shadow detached itself and spoke. "Got him?"

"Yes, Carl."

The shadow became Carl. He swung in behind Tod, who suddenly realized that if he did not follow the leader, the one behind would drive. He glanced back at Carl's implacable bulk, and then put down his head and jogged doggedly along as he was told.

They followed a small stream, crossed it on a fallen tree, and climbed a hill. Just as Tod was about to accept the worst these determined people might offer in exchange for a moment to ease his fiery lungs, Moira stopped. He stumbled into her. She caught his arm and kept him on his feet.

"In there," she said, pointing.

"A finger tree."

"You know how to get inside," Carl growled.

Moira said, "She begged me not to tell you, ever. I think she was wrong."

"Who? What is—"

"Inside," said Carl, and shoved him roughly down the slope.

His long conditioning was still with him, and reflexively he sidestepped the fanning fingers which swayed to meet him. He ducked under them, batted aside the inner phalanx, and found himself in the clear space underneath. He stopped there, gasping.

Something moaned.

He bent, fumbled cautiously in the blackness. He touched something smooth and alive, recoiled, touched it again. A foot.

Someone began to cry harshly, hurtfully, the sound exploding as if through clenched hands.

"*April!*"

"I told them not to. . . ." and she moaned.

"April, what is it, what's happened?"

"You needn't . . . be," she said, sobbed a while, and went on, ". . . angry. It didn't live."

"What didn't . . . you mean you . . . April, you—"

"It wouldn't've been a tapeworm," she whispered.

"Who—" he fell to his knees, found her face. "When did you—"

"I was going to tell you that day, that very same day, and when you came in so angry at what Teague told you, I specially wanted to, I thought you'd . . . be glad."

"April, why didn't you come back? If I'd known. . . ."

"You *said* what you'd do if I ever . . . if you ever had another . . . you meant it, Tod."

"It's this place, this Viridis," he said sadly. "I went crazy."

He felt her wet hand on his cheek.

"It's all right. I just didn't want to make it worse for you," April said.

"I'll take you back."

"No, you can't. I've been . . . I've lost a lot of . . . just stay with me a little while."

"Moira should have—"

"She just found me," said April. "I've been alone all the— I guess I made a noise. I didn't mean to. Tod . . . don't quarrel. Don't go into a lot of . . . It's all right."

Against her throat he cried. *"All right!"*

"When you're by yourself," she said faintly, "you think; you think better. Did you ever think of—"

"April!" he cried in anguish, the very sound of her pale, pain-wracked voice making this whole horror real.

"Shh, sh. Listen," she said rapidly, "There isn't time, you know, Tod. Tod, did you ever think of us all, Teague and Alma and Moira and Carl and us, what we are?"

"I know what I am."

"*Shh*. Altogether we're a leader and mother; a word and a shield; a doubter, a mystic. . . ." Her voice trailed off. She coughed and he could feel the spastic jolt shoot through her body. She panted lightly for a moment and went on urgently, "Anger and prejudice and stupidity, courage, laughter, love, music . . . it was all aboard that ship and it's all here on Viridis. Our children and theirs—no matter what they look like, Tod, no matter how they live or what they eat—they have that in them. Humanity isn't just a way of walking, merely a kind of skin. It's what we had together and what we gave Sol. It's what the golden ones found in us and wanted for Viridis. You'll see. You'll see."

"Why Viridis?"

"Because of what Teague said—what you said." Her breath puffed out in the ghost of a laugh. "Basic biology . . . ontogeny follows phylogeny. The human foetus is a cell, an animalcule, a gilled amphibian . . . all up the line. It's there in us; Viridis makes it go backward."

"To what?"

"The mushroom. The spores. We'll be spores, Tod. Together . . . Alma *said* she could be dead, and together with Teague! That's why I said . . . it's all right. This doesn't matter, what's happened. We live in Sol, we live in Emerald with Carl and Moira, you see? Closer, nearer than we've ever been."

Tod took a hard hold on his reason. "But back to spores—why? What then?"

She sighed. It was unquestionably a happy sound. "They'll be back for the reaping, and they'll have us, Tod, all we are and all they worship: goodness and generosity and the urge to build; mercy; kindness."

"They're needed too," she whispered. "And the spores make mushrooms, and the mushrooms make the heterokaryons; and from those, away from Viridis, come the life-forms to breed us—*us,* Tod! into whichever form is dominant. And there we'll be, that flash of old understanding of a new idea . . . the special pressure on a painter's hand that makes him a Rembrandt, the sense of architecture that turns a piano-player into a Bach. Three billion extra years of evolution, ready to help wherever it can be used. On every Earth-type planet, Tod—millions of us, blowing about in the summer wind, waiting to give. . . ."

"Give! Give what Teague is now, rotten and angry?"

"That isn't Teague. That will die off. Teague lives with Alma in their children, and in theirs . . . she *said* she'd be with him!"

"Me . . . what about me?" he breathed. "What I did to you. . . ."

"Nothing, you did nothing. You live in Sol, in Emerald. Living, conscious, alive . . . with me. . . ."

He said, "You mean . . . you could talk to me from Sol?"

I think I might." With his forehead, bent so close to her, he felt her smile. "But I don't think I would. Lying so close to you, why should I speak to an outsider?"

Her breathing changed and he was suddenly terrified. "April, don't die."

"I won't," she said. "Alma didn't." She kissed him gently and died.

It was a long darkness, with Tod hardly aware of roaming and raging through the jungle, of eating without tasting, of hungering without knowing of it. Then there was a twilight, many months long, soft and still, with restfulness here and a promise soon. Then there was the compound again, found like a dead memory, learned again just a little more readily than something new. Carl and Moira were kind, knowing the nature of justice and the limits of punishment, and at last Tod was alive again.

He found himself one day down near the river, watching it and thinking back without fear of his own thoughts, and a growing wonder came to him. His mind had for so long dwelt on his own evil that it was hard to break new paths. He wondered with an awesome effort what manner of creatures might worship humanity for itself, and what manner of creatures humans were to be so worshipped. It was a totally new concept to him, and he was completely immersed in it, so that when Emerald slid out of the grass and stood watching him, he was frightened and shouted.

She did not move. There was little to fear now on Viridis. All the large reptiles were gone, and there was room for the humans, the humanoids, the primates, the . . . children. In his shock the old reflexes played. He stared at her, her square stocky body, the silver hair which covered it all over except for the face, the palms, the soles of the feet. "*A monkey!*" he spat, in

Teague's tones, and the shock turned to shame. He met her eyes, April's deep glowing rubies, and they looked back at him without fear.

He let a vision of April grow and fill the world. The child's rare red eyes helped (there was so little, so very little red on Viridis). He saw April at the spaceport, holding him in the dark shadows of the blockhouse while the sky flamed above them. *We'll go out like that soon, soon, Tod. Squeeze me, squeeze me . . . Ah,* he'd said, *who needs a ship?*

Another April, part of her in a dim light as she sat writing; her hair, a crescent of light loving her cheek, a band of it on her brow; then she had seen him and turned, rising, smothered his first word with her mouth. Another April wanting to smile, waiting; and April asleep, and once April sobbing because she could not find a special word to tell him what she felt for him . . . He brought his mind back from her in the past, from her as she was, alive in his mind, back to here, to the bright mute with the grave red eyes who stood before him, and he said, "How precious?"

The baby kept her eyes on his, and slowly raised her silken hands. She cupped them together to make a closed chamber, looked down at it, opened her hands slightly and swiftly to peer inside, rapt at what she pretended to see; closed her hands again to capture the treasure, whatever it was, and hugged it to her breast. She looked up at him slowly, and her eyes were full of tears, and she was smiling.

He took his grandchild carefully in his arms and held her gently and strongly. Monkey?

"April," he gasped. "Little Ape. Little Ape."

Viridis is a young planet which bears (at first glance) old life-forms. Come away and let the green planet roll around its sun; come back in a while—not long, as astronomical time goes.

The jungle is much the same, the sea, the rolling savannahs. But the life. . . .

Viridis was full of primates. There were blunt-toothed herbivores and long-limbed tree-dwellers, gliders and burrowers. The fish-eaters were adapting the way all Viridis life must adapt, becoming more fit by becoming simpler, or go to the wall. Already the sea-apes had rudimentary gills and had lost their hair. Already tiny forms competed with the insects on their own terms.

On the banks of the wandering rivers, monotremes with opposed toes dredged and paddled, and sloths and lemurs crept at night. At first they had stayed together, but they were soon too numerous for that; and a half dozen generations cost them the power of speech, which was, by then, hardly a necessity. Living was good for primates on Viridis, and became better each generation.

Eating and breeding, hunting and escaping filled the days and the cacophonous nights. It was hard in the beginning to see a friend cut down, to watch a slender silver shape go spinning down a river and know that with it went some of your brother, some of your mate, some of yourself. But as the hundreds became thousands and the thousands millions, witnessing death became about as significant as watching your friend get his hair cut. The basic ids each spread through the changing, mutating population like a stain, crossed and recrossed by the strains of the others, co-existing, eating each other and being eaten and all the while passing down through the generations.

There was a cloud over the savannah, high over the ruins of the compound. It was a thing of many colors and of no particular shape, and it was bigger than one might imagine, not knowing how far away it was.

From it dropped a golden spot that became a thread, and down came a golden mass. It spread and swung, exploded into a myriad of individuals. Some descended on the compound, erasing and changing, lifting, breaking—always careful to kill nothing. Others blanketed the planet, streaking silently through the green aisles, flashing unimpeded through the tangled thickets. They combed the riverbanks and the half-light of hill waves, and everywhere they went they found and touched the mushroom and stripped it of its spores, the compaction and multiplication of what had once been the representatives of a very high reptile culture.

Primates climbed and leaped, crawled and crept to the jungle margins to watch. Eater lay by eaten; the hunted stood on the hunter's shoulder, and a platypoid laid an egg in the open which nobody touched.

Simian forms hung from the trees in loops and ropes, in swarms and beards, and more came all the time, brought by some ineffable magnetism to watch at the hill. It was a fast and a waiting, with no movement but jostling for position, a crowding forward from behind and a pressing back from the slightest chance of interfering with the golden visitors.

Down from the polychrome cloud drifted a mass of the golden beings, carrying with them a huge sleek ship. They held it above the ground, sliced it, lifted it apart, set down this piece and that until a shape began to grow. Into it went bales and bundles, stocks and stores, and then the open tops were covered. It was a much bigger installation than the one before.

Quickly, it was done, and the golden cloud hung waiting.

The jungle was trembling with quiet.

In one curved panel of the new structure, something spun, fell outward, and out of the opening came a procession of stately creatures, long-headed, bright-eyed, three-toed, richly plumed and feathered. They tested their splendid wings, then stopped suddenly, crouched and looking upward.

They were given their obeisance by the golden ones, and after there appeared in the sky the exquisite symbol of a beauty that rides up and up, turns and spirals down again only to rise again; the symbol of that which has no beginning and no end, and the sign of those whose worship and whose work it is to bring to all the Universe that which has shown itself worthy in parts of it.

Then they were gone, and the jungle exploded into killing and flight, eating and screaming, so that the feathered ones dove back into their shelter and closed the door. . . .

And again to the green planet (when the time was right) came the cloud-ship, and found a world full of birds, and the birds watched in awe while they harvested their magic dust, and built a new shelter. In this they left four of their own for later harvesting, and this was to make of Viridis a most beautiful place.

From Viridis, the ship vaulted through the galaxies, searching for worlds worthy of what is human in humanity, whatever their manner of being alive. These they seeded, and of these, perhaps one would produce something new, something which could be reduced to the dust of Viridis, and from dust return.

The Man Who Lost the Sea

In 1959 I left for the West Indies seeking a balmy
climate and a low-rent district. For the first time in my life
I worked eight hours a day, seven days a week on a
regular schedule. And in practically every way it turned
into a disaster. I just couldn't make a story jell. I finally
got going on a space-travel story and ground out words,
one after the other, until I had a start, a middle, a finish.
It was awful—wordy and slow and muzzy.

So literally for months I cut. I cut until the story and I
bled. I cut it from 21,000 words down to 5,000, and at
last called it finished. I showed it to my wife and she
couldn't understand it. I showed it to my mother, who was
alive at the time, and she couldn't understand it. I had
completely lost perspective on it, and I returned to the
States, bloody and very much bowed.

Shortly afterward Bob Mills called and wanted a story
for an All-Star issue of *F&SF*. I told him that all I had was
this, but that if I sent it, I never wanted to see it again. I
did, and he read it, and called back to say it was okay,
he guessed—*but it needed cutting!*

I guess I got a little hysterical. I told him to burn it. But
he bought it, and ran it, and it wound up in that year's

Martha Foley Award Anthology as one of the best short stories of the year. Moral: Don't believe what everybody tells you, even if everybody is your mother.

Say you're a kid, and one dark night you're running along the cold sand with this helicopter in your hand, saying very fast *witchy-witchy-witchy*. You pass the sick man and he wants you to shove off with that thing. Maybe he thinks you're too old to play with toys. So you squat next to him in the sand and tell him it isn't a toy, it's a model. You tell him look here, here's something most people don't know about helicopters. You take a blade of the rotor in your fingers and show him how it can move in the hub, up and down a little, back and forth a little, and twist a little, to change pitch. You start to tell him how this flexibility does away with the gyroscopic effect, but he won't listen. He doesn't want to think about flying, about helicopters, or about you, and he most especially does not want explanations about anything by anybody. Not now. Now, he wants to think about the sea. So you go away.

The sick man is buried in the cold sand with only his head and his left arm showing. He is dressed in a pressure suit and looks like a man from Mars. Built into his left sleeve is a combination time-piece and pressure gauge, the gauge with a luminous blue indicator which makes no sense, the clock hands luminous red. He can hear the pounding of surf and the soft swift pulse of his pumps. One time long ago when he was swimming he went too deep and stayed down too long and came up too fast, and when he came to it was like this: they said, "Don't move, boy. You've got the bends. Don't even *try* to move." He had tried anyway. It hurt. So now, this time, he lies in the sand without moving, without trying.

His head isn't working right. But he knows clearly that it isn't working right, which is a strange thing that happens to people in shock sometimes. Say you were that kid, you could say how it was, because once you woke up lying in the gym office in high school and asked what had happened. They explained how you tried something on the parallel bars and fell on your head. You understood exactly, though you couldn't remember falling. Then a minute later you asked again what had happened and they told you. You understood it. And a minute later . . . forty-one times they told you, and you understood. It was just that no matter how many times they pushed it into your head, it wouldn't stick there; but all the while you *knew* that your head would start working again in time. And in time it did. . . . Of course, if you were that kid, always explaining things to people and to yourself, you wouldn't want to bother the sick man with it now.

Look what you've done already, making him send you away with that angry shrug of the mind (which, with the eyes, are the only things which will move just now). The motionless effort costs him a wave of nausea. He has felt seasick before but he has never *been* seasick, and the formula for that is to keep your eyes on the horizon and stay busy. Now! Then he'd better get busy—now; for there's one place especially not to be seasick in, and that's locked up in a pressure suit. Now!

So he busies himself as best he can, with the seascape, landscape, sky. He lies on high ground, his head propped on a vertical wall of black rock. There is another such outcrop before him, whip-topped with white sand and with smooth flat sand. Beyond and down is valley, salt-flat, estuary; he cannot yet be sure. He is sure of the line of footprints, which begin behind him, pass to his left, disappear in the outcrop shadows, and reappear beyond to vanish at last into the shadows of the valley.

Stretched across the sky is old mourning-cloth, with starlight burning holes in it, and between the holes the black is absolute—wintertime, mountaintop sky-black.

(Far off on the horizon within himself, he sees the swell and crest of approaching nausea; he counters with an undertow of weakness, which meets and rounds and settles the wave before it can break. Get busier. *Now*.)

Burst in on him, then, with the X-15 model. That'll get him. Hey, how about this for a gimmick? Get too high for the thin air to give you any control, you have these little jets in the wingtips, see? and on the sides of the empennage: bank, roll, yaw, whatever, with squirts of compressed air.

But the sick man curls his sick lip: oh, git, kid, git, will you?—that has nothing to do with the sea. So you git.

Out and out the sick man forces his view, etching all he sees with a meticulous intensity, as if it might be his charge, one day, to duplicate all this. To his left is only starlit sea, windless. In front of him across the valley, rounded hills with dim white epaulettes of light. To his right, the jutting corner of the black wall against which his helmet rests. (He thinks the distant moundings of nausea becalmed, but he will not look yet.) So he scans the sky, black and bright, calling Sirius, calling Pleiades, Polaris, Ursa Minor, calling that ... that ... Why, it *moves*. Watch it: yes, it moves! It is a fleck of light, seeming to be wrinkled, fissured, rather like a chip of boiled cauliflower in the sky. (Of course, he knows better than to trust his own eyes just now.) But that movement ...

As a child he had stood on cold sand in a frosty Cape Cod evening, watching Sputnik's steady spark rise out of the haze (madly, dawning a little north of west); and after that he had sleeplessly wound special coils for his receiver, risked his life restringing high antennas, all for the brief capture of an unreadable *tweetle-eep-tweetle* in his earphones from Vanguard, Explorer, Lunik, Discoverer, Mercury. He knew them all (well, some people collect match-covers, stamps) and he knew especially that unmistakable steady sliding in the sky.

This moving fleck was a satellite, and in a moment, motionless, uninstrumented but for his chronometer and his part-brain, he will know which one. (He is grateful beyond expression—without that sliding chip of light, there were only those footprints, those wandering footprints, to tell a man he was not alone in the world.)

Say you were a kid, eager and challengeable and more than a little bright, you might in a day or so work out a way to measure the period of a satellite with nothing but a timepiece and a brain; you might eventually see that the shadow in the rocks ahead had been there from the first only because of the light from the rising satellite. Now if you check the time exactly at the moment when the shadow on the sand is equal to the height of the outcrop, and time it again when the light is at the zenith and the shadow gone, you will multiply this number of minutes by 8—think why, now: horizon to zenith is one-fourth of the orbit, give or take a little, and halfway up the sky is half that quarter—and you will then know this satellite's period. You know all the periods—ninety minutes, two, two-and-a-half hours; with that and the appearance of this bird, you'll find out which one it is.

But if you were that kid, eager or resourceful or whatever, you wouldn't jabber about it to the sick man, for not only does he not want to be bothered with you, he's thought of all that long since and is even now watching the shadows for that triangular split second of measurement. *Now!* His eyes drop to the face of his chronometer: 0400, near as makes no never mind.

He has minutes to wait now—ten? . . . thirty? . . . twenty-three?—while this baby moon eats up its slice of shadowpie; and that's too bad, the waiting, for though the inner sea is calm there are currents below, shadows that shift and swim. Be busy. Be busy. He must not swim near that great invisible ameba, whatever happens: its first cold pseudopod is even now reaching for the vitals.

Being a knowledgeable young fellow, not quite a kid any more, wanting to help the sick man too, you want to tell him everything you know about that cold-in-the-gut, that reaching invisible surrounding implacable ameba. You know all about it—listen, you want to yell at him, don't let that touch of cold bother you. Just know what it is, that's all. Know what it is that is touching your gut. You want to tell him, listen:

Listen, this is how you met the monster and dissected it. Listen, you were skin-diving in the Grenadines, a hundred tropical shoal-water islands; you had a new blue snorkel mask, the kind with face-plate and breathing-tube all in one, and new blue flippers on your feet, and a new blue spear-gun—all this new because you'd only begun, you see; you were a beginner, aghast with pleasure at your easy intrusion into this underwater otherworld. You'd been out in a boat, you were coming back, you'd just reached the mouth of the little bay, you'd taken the notion to swim the rest of the way. You'd said as much to the boys and slipped into the warm silky water. You brought your gun.

Not far to go at all, but then beginners find wet distances deceiving. For the first five minutes or so it was only delightful, the sun hot on your back and the water so warm it seemed not to have any temperature at all and you were flying. With your face under the water, your mask was not so much attached as part of you, your wide blue flippers trod away yards, your gun rode all but weightless in your hand, the taut rubber sling making an occasional hum as your passage plucked it in the sunlit green. In your ears crooned the breathy monotone of the snorkel tube, and through the invisible disk of plate glass you saw wonders. The bay was shallow—ten, twelve feet or so—and sandy, with great growths of brain-, bone-, and fire-coral, intricate waving sea-fans, and fish—such fish! Scarlet and green and aching azure, gold and rose and slate-color studded with sparks of enamel-blue, pink and peach and silver. And that *thing* got into you, that . . . monster.

There were enemies in this otherworld: the sand-colored spotted sea-snake with his big ugly head and turned-down mouth, who would not retreat but lay watching the intruder pass; and the mottled moray with jaws like bolt-cutters; and somewhere around, certainly, the barracuda with his undershot face and teeth turned inward so that he must take away whatever he might strike. There were urchins—the plump white sea-egg with its thick fur of sharp quills and the black ones with the long slender spines that would break off in unwary flesh and fester there for weeks; and file-fish and stone-fish with their poisoned barbs and lethal meat; and the stingaree who could drive his spike through a leg bone. Yet these were not *monsters,* and could not matter to you, the invader churning along above them all. For you were above them in so many ways—armed, rational, comforted by the close shore (ahead the beach, the rocks on each side) and by the presence of the boat not too far behind. Yet you were . . . attacked.

At first it was uneasiness, not pressing, but pervasive, a contact quite as intimate as that of the sea; you were sheathed in it. And also there was the touch—the cold inward contact. Aware of it at last, you laughed: for Pete's sake, what's there to be scared of?

The monster, the ameba.

You raised your head and looked back in air. The boat had edged in to the cliff at the right; someone was giving a last poke around for lobster. You waved

at the boat; it was your gun you waved, and emerging
from the water it gained its latent ounces so that you
sank a bit, and as if you had no snorkel on, you tipped
your head back to get a breath. But tipping your head
back plunged the end of the tube under water; the
valve closed; you drew in a hard lungful of nothing at
all. You dropped your face under; up came the tube;
you got your air, and along with it a bullet of seawater
which struck you somewhere inside the throat. You
coughed it out and floundered, sobbing as you sucked
in air, inflating your chest until it hurt, and the air
you got seemed no good, no good at all, a worthless
devitalized inert gas.

You clenched your teeth and headed for the beach,
kicking strongly and knowing it was the right thing to
do; and then below and to the right you saw a great
bulk mounding up out of the sand floor of the sea.
You knew it was only the reef, rocks and coral and
weed, but the sight of it made you scream; you didn't
care what you knew. You turned hard left to avoid it,
fought by as if it would reach for you, and you
couldn't get air, couldn't get air, for all the unob-
structed hooting of your snorkel tube. You couldn't
bear the mask, suddenly, not for another second, so
you shoved it upward clear of your mouth and rolled
over, floating on your back and opening your mouth
to the sky and breathing with a quacking noise.

It was then and there that the monster well and
truly engulfed you, mantling you round and about
within itself—formless, borderless, the illimitable ameba.
The beach, mere yards away, and the rocky arms of the
bay, and the not-too-distant boat—these you could iden-
tify but no longer distinguish, for they were all one and
the same thing . . . the thing called unreachable.

You fought that way for a time, on your back, dangling the gun under and behind you and straining to
get enough warm sun-stained air into your chest. And
in time some particles of sanity began to swirl in the
roil of your mind, and to dissolve and tint it. The air

pumping in and out of your square-grinned frightened mouth began to be meaningful at last, and the monster relaxed away from you.

You took stock, saw surf, beach, a leaning tree. You felt the new scend of your body as the rollers humped to become breakers. Only a dozen firm kicks brought you to where you could roll over and double up; your shin struck coral with a lovely agony and you stood in foam and waded ashore. You gained the wet sand, hard sand, and ultimately, with two more paces powered by bravado, you crossed high-water mark and lay in the dry sand, unable to move.

You lay in the sand, and before you were able to move or to think, you were able to feel a triumph—a triumph because you were alive and knew that much without thinking at all.

When you *were* able to think, your first thought was of the gun, and the first move you were able to make was to let go at last of the thing. You had nearly died because you had not let it go before; without it you would not have been burdened and you would not have panicked. You had (you began to understand) kept it because someone else would have had to retrieve it—easily enough—and you could not have stood the laughter. You had almost died because They might laugh at you.

This was the beginning of the dissection, analysis, study of the monster. It began then; it had never finished. Some of what you had learned from it was merely important; some of the rest—vital.

You had learned, for example, never to swim farther with a snorkel than you could swim back without one. You learned never to burden yourself with the unnecessary in an emergency: even a hand or a foot might be as expendable as a gun; pride was expendable, dignity was. You learned never to dive alone, even if They laugh at you, even if you have to shoot a fish yourself and say afterward "we" shot it. Most of all, you learned that fear has many fingers, and one of them—a simple one, made of too great a concentration of carbon dioxide in your blood, as from too-rapid breathing in and out of the same tube—is not really fear at all but feels like fear, and can turn into panic and kill you.

Listen, you want to say, listen, there isn't anything wrong with such an experience or with all the study it leads to, because a man who can learn enough from it could become fit enough, cautious enough, foresighted, unafraid, modest, teachable enough to be chosen, to be qualified for—

You lose the thought, or turn it away, because the sick man feels that cold touch deep inside, feels it right now, feels it beyond ignoring, above and beyond anything that you, with all your experience and certainty, could explain to him even if he would listen, which he won't. Make him, then; tell him the cold touch is some simple explainable thing like anoxia, like gladness even: some triumph that he will be able to appreciate when his head is working right again.

Triumph? Here he's alive after . . . whatever it is, and that doesn't seem to be triumph enough, though it was in the Grenadines, and that other time, when he got the bends, saved his own life, saved two other lives. Now, somehow, it's not the same: there seems to be a reason why just being alive afterward isn't a triumph.

Why not triumph? Because not twelve, not twenty, not even thirty minutes is it taking the satellite to complete its eighth-of-an-orbit: fifty minutes are gone, and still there's a slice of shadow yonder. It is this, *this* which is placing the cold finger upon his heart, and he doesn't know why, he doesn't know why, he *will* not know why; he is afraid he shall when his head is working again. . . .

Oh, where's the kid? Where is any way to busy the mind, apply it to something, anything else but the watchhand which outruns the moon? Here, kid: come over here—what you got there?

If you were the kid, then you'd forgive everything

and hunker down with your new model, not a toy, not
a helicopter or a rocket-plane, but the big one, the one
that looks like an overgrown cartridge. It's so big, even
as a model, that even an angry sick man wouldn't call
it a toy. A giant cartridge, but watch: the lower four-
fifths is Alpha—all muscle—over a million pounds
thrust. (Snap it off, throw it away.) Half the rest is
Beta—all brains—it puts you on your way. (Snap it
off, throw it away.) And now look at the polished
fraction which is left. Touch a control somewhere and
see—see? it has wings—wide triangular wings. This is
Gamma, the one with wings, and on its back is a small
sausage; it is a moth with a sausage on its back. The
sausage (click! it comes free) is Delta. Delta is the
last, the smallest: Delta is the way home.

What will they think of next? Quite a toy. Quite a
toy. Beat it, kid. The satellite is almost overhead, the
sliver of shadow going—going—almost gone and . . .
gone.

Check: 0459. Fifty-nine minutes? give or take a few.
Times eight . . . 472 . . . is, uh, 7 hours 52 minutes.

Seven hours fifty-two minutes? Why, there isn't a
satellite round earth with a period like that. In all the
solar system there's only . . .

The cold finger turns fierce, implacable.

The east is paling and the sick man turns to it,
wanting the light, the sun, an end to questions whose
answers couldn't be looked upon. The sea stretches
endlessly out to the growing light, and endlessly, somewhere out of sight, the surf roars. The paling east
bleaches the sandy hilltops and throws the line of footprints into aching relief. That would be the buddy,
the sick man knows, gone for help. He cannot at the
moment recall who the buddy is, but in time he will,
and meanwhile the footprints make him less alone.

The sun's upper rim thrusts itself above the horizon
with a flash of green, instantly gone. There is no
dawn, just the green flash and then a clear white blast
of unequivocal sunup. The sea could not be whiter,

more still, if it were frozen and snow-blanketed. In the west, stars still blaze, and overhead the crinkled satellite is scarcely abashed by the growing light. A formless jumble in the valley below begins to resolve itself into a sort of tent-city, or installation of some kind, with tubelike and sail-like buildings This would have meaning for the sick man if his head were working right. Soon, it would. Will. (Oh . . .)

The sea, out on the horizon just under the rising sun, is behaving strangely, for in that place where properly belongs a pool of unbearable brightness, there is instead a notch of brown. It is as if the white fire of the sun is drinking dry the sea—for look, look! the notch becomes a bow and the bow a crescent, racing ahead of the sunlight, white sea ahead of it and behind it a cocoa-dry stain spreading across and down toward where he watches.

Beside the finger of fear which lies on him, another finger places itself, and another, making ready for that clutch, that grip, that ultimate insane squeeze of panic. Yet beyond that again, past that squeeze when it comes, to be savored if the squeeze is only fear and not panic, lies triumph—triumph, and a glory. It is perhaps this which constitutes his whole battle: to fit himself, prepare himself to bear the utmost that fear could do, for if he can do that, there is a triumph on the other side. But . . . not yet. Please, not yet awhile.

Something flies (or flew, or will fly—he is a little confused on this point) toward him, from the far right where the stars still shine. It is not a bird and it is unlike any aircraft on earth, for the aerodynamics are wrong. Wings so wide and so fragile would be useless, would melt and tear away in any of earth's atmosphere but the outer fringes. He sees then (because he prefers to see it so) that it is the kid's model, or part of it, and for a toy it does very well indeed.

It is the part called Gamma, and it glides in, balancing, parallels the sand and holds away, holds away slowing, then settles, all in slow motion, throwing up graceful sheet-fountains of fine sand from its skids. And it runs along the ground for an impossible distance, letting down its weight by the ounce and stingily the ounce, until *look out* until a skid *look out* fits itself into a bridged crevasse *look out, look out!* and still moving on, it settles down to the struts. Gamma then, tired, digs her wide left wingtip carefully into the racing sand, digs it in hard; and as the wing breaks off, Gamma slews, sidles, slides slowly, pointing her other triangular tentlike wing at the sky, and broadside crushes into the rocks at the valley's end.

As she rolls smashing over, there breaks from her broad back the sausage, the little Delta, which somersaults away to break its back upon the rocks, and through the broken hull spill smashed shards of graphite from the moderator of her power-pile. *Look out! Look out!* and at the same instant from the finally checked mass of Gamma there explodes a doll, which slides and tumbles into the sand, into the rocks and smashed hot graphite from the wreck of Delta.

The sick man numbly watches this toy destroy itself: what will they think of next?—and with a gelid horror prays at the doll lying in the raging rubble of the atomic pile: *don't stay there, man—get away! get away! that's hot, you know?* But it seems like a night and a day and half another night before the doll staggers to its feet and, clumsy in its pressure-suit, runs away up the valleyside, climbs a sand-topped outcrop, slips, falls, lies under a slow cascade of cold ancient sand until, but for an arm and the helmet, it is buried.

The sun is high now, high enough to show the sea is not a sea, but brown plain with the frost burned off it, as now it burns away from the hills, diffusing in air and blurring the edges of the sun's disk, so that in a very few minutes there is no sun at all, but only a glare in the east. Then the valley below loses its shadows, and, like an arrangement in a diorama, reveals the form and nature of the wreckage below: no tent-

city this, no installation, but the true real ruin of
Gamma and the eviscerated hulk of Delta. (Alpha was
the muscle, Beta the brain; Gamma was a bird, but
Delta, Delta was the way home.)

And from it stretches the line of footprints, to and
by the sick man, above to the bluff, and gone with the
sandslide which had buried him there. Whose footprints?

He knows whose, whether or not he knows that he
knows, or wants to or not. He knows what satellite has
(give or take a bit) a period like that (want it exactly?—it's 7.66 hours). He knows what world has
such a night, and such a frosty glare by day. He knows
these things as he knows how spilled radioactives will
pour the crash and mutter of surf into a man's earphones.

Say you were that kid: say, instead, at last, that you
are the sick man, for they are the same; surely then
you can understand why of all things, even while shat-
tered, shocked, sick with radiation calculated (leaving) radiation computed (arriving) and radiation
past all bearing (lying in the wreckage of Delta) you
would want to think of the sea. For no farmer who
fingers the soil with love and knowledge, no poet who
sings of it, artist, contractor, engineer, even child
bursting into tears at the inexpressible beauty of a
field of daffodils—none of these is as intimate with
Earth as those who live on, live with, breathe and drift
in its seas. So of these things you must think; with
these you must dwell until you are less sick and more
ready to face the truth.

The truth, then, is that the satellite fading here is
Phobos, that those footprints are your own, that there
is no sea here, that you have crashed and are killed
and will in a moment be dead. The cold hand ready to
squeeze and still your heart is not anoxia or even fear,
it is death. Now, if there is something more important
than this, now is the time for it to show itself.

The sick man looks at the line of his own footprints,

which testify that he is alone, and at the wreckage below, which states that there is no way back, and at the white east and the mottled west and the paling fleck-like satellite above. Surf sounds in his ears. He hears his pumps. He hears what is left of his breathing. The cold clamps down and folds him round past measuring, past all limit.

Then he speaks, cries out: then with joy he takes his triumph at the other side of death, as one takes a great fish, as one completes a skilled and mighty task, rebalances at the end of some great daring leap; and as he used to say "we shot a fish" he uses no "I":

"God," he cries, dying on Mars, "God, we made it!"

And Now the News . . .

It was 1956, and the beginning of a conscious realization
that to limit science fiction to outer space was just that—a
limitation, and that science fiction has and should have as
limitless a character as poetry; further, that it has a real
function in *inner* space. This in turn led me to a redefinition
of science itself, and to an increasing preoccupation with
humanity not only as the subject of science, but as its
source. It has become my joy to find out what makes it
tick, especially when it ticks unevenly.

One more thing about this story: I had written to a
friend with the complaint that I hadn't an idea in my head,
and needed one urgently. On a cold November morning
my wife and I opened his response. *Twenty-six* story ideas—
a paragraph, a sentence, a suggestion, a situation. Clipped
to the pages was a check with a note: "I have the feeling
your credit is bent." As my wife and I stared at it and
each other—the furnace stopped. That furnace would stop
for only two reasons: the house was warm enough, or we
had just run out of fuel, and it certainly wasn't warm
enough. Right on cue. We both wept.

This story springs from one of the springboards in that
package, and the springboarder's name is Robert A.

Heinlein, and I'm pleased at this opportunity to acknowledge this single favor among the many he has done me
by his writings and by his—well, his being.

═══════════════════════════════

The man's name was MacLyle, which by looking at
you can tell wasn't his real name, but let's say this is
fiction, shall we? MacLyle had a good job in—well—a
soap concern. He worked hard and made good money
and got married to a girl called Esther. He bought a
house in the suburbs and after it was paid for he
rented it to some people and bought a home a little
farther out and a second car and a freezer and a
power-mower and a book on landscaping, and settled
down to the worthy task of giving his kids all the
things he never had.

He had habits and he had hobbies, like everybody
else, and (like everybody else) his were a little different from anybody's. The one that annoyed his wife the
most, until she got used to it, was the news habit, or
maybe hobby. MacLyle read a morning paper on the
8:14 and an evening paper on the 6:10, and the local
paper his suburb used for its lost dogs and auction
sales took up 40 after-dinner minutes. And when he
read a paper he read it, he didn't mess with it. He read
Page 1 first and Page 2 next, and so on all the way
through. He didn't care too much for books but he
respected them in a mystical sort of way, and he used
to say a newspaper was a kind of book, and so would
raise particular hell if a section was missing or in up-
side down, or if the pages were out of line. He also
heard the news on the radio. There were three stations
in town with hourly broadcasts, one on the hour, one
on the half-hour, and one five minutes before the

hour, and he was usually able to catch them all. During these five-minute periods he would look you right in the eye while you talked to him and you'd swear he was listening to you, but he wasn't. This was a particular trial to his wife, but only for five years or so. Then she stopped trying to be heard while the radio talked about floods and murders and scandal and suicide. Five more years, and she went back to talking right through the broadcasts, but by the time people are married ten years, things like that don't matter; they talk in code anyway, and nine tenths of their speech can be picked up anytime like ticker-tape. He also caught the 7:30 news on Channel 2 and the 7:45 news on Channel 4 on television.

Now it might be imagined from all this that MacLyle was a crotchety character with fixed habits and a neurotic neatness, but this was far from the case. MacLyle was basically a reasonable guy who loved his wife and children and liked his work and pretty much enjoyed being alive. He laughed easily and talked well and paid his bills. He justified his preoccupation with the news in a number of ways. He would quote Donne: ". . . any man's death diminishes me, because I am involved in mankind . . ." which is pretty solid stuff and hard to argue down. He would point out that he made his trains and his trains made him punctual, but that because of them he saw the same faces at the same time day after endless day, before, during, and after he rode those trains, so that his immediate world was pretty circumscribed, and only a constant awareness of what was happening all over the earth kept him conscious of the fact that he lived in a bigger place than a thin straight universe with his house at one end, his office at the other, and a railway track in between.

It's hard to say just when MacLyle started to go to pieces, or even why, though it obviously had something to do with all that news he exposed himself to. He began to react, very slightly at first; that is, you could tell he was listening. He'd *shh!* you, and if you tried to finish what you were saying he'd run and stick his head in the speaker grille. His wife and kids learned to shut up when the news came on, five minutes before the hour until five after (with MacLyle switching stations) and every hour on the half-hour, and from 7:30 to 8 for the TV, and during the 40 minutes it took him to read the local paper. He was not so obvious about it when he read his paper, because all he did was freeze over the pages like a catatonic, gripping the top corners until the sheets shivered, knotting his jaw and breathing from his nostrils with a strangled whistle.

Naturally all this was a weight on his wife Esther, who tried her best to reason with him. At first he answered her, saying mildly that a man has to keep in touch, you know; but very quickly he stopped responding altogether, giving her the treatment a practiced suburbanite gets so expert in, as when someone mentions a lawnmower just too damn early on Sunday morning. You don't say yes and you don't say no, you don't even grunt, and you don't move your head or even your eyebrows. After a while your interlocutor goes away. Pretty soon you don't hear these ill-timed annoyances any more than you appear to.

It needs to be said again here that MacLyle was, outside his peculiarity, a friendly and easy-going character. He liked people and invited them and visited them, and he was one of those adults who can really listen to a first-grade child's interminable adventures and really care. He never forgot things like the slow leak in the spare tire or antifreeze or anniversaries, and he always got the stormwindows up in time, but he didn't rub anyone's nose in his reliability. The first thing in his whole life he didn't take as a matter of course was this news thing that started so small and grew so quickly.

So after a few weeks of it his wife took the bull by the horns and spent the afternoon hamstringing every receiver in the house. There were three radios and two TV sets, and she didn't understand the first thing about them, but she had a good head and she went to work with a will and the can-opening limb of a pocket knife. From each receiver she removed one tube, and one at a time, so as not to get them mixed up, she carried them into the kitchen and meticulously banged their bases against the edge of the sink, being careful to crack no glass and bend no pins, until she could see the guts of the tube rolling around loose inside. Then she replaced them and got the back panels on the sets again.

MacLyle came home and put the car away and kissed her and turned on the living-room radio and then went to hang up his hat. When he returned the radio should have been warmed up but it wasn't. He twisted the knobs a while and bumped it and rocked it back and forth a little, grunting, and then noticed the time. He began to feel a little frantic, and raced back to the kitchen and turned on the little ivory radio on the shelf. It warmed up quickly and cheerfully and gave him a clear 60-cycle hum, but that was all. He behaved badly from then on, roaring out the information that the sets didn't work, either of them, as if that wasn't pretty evident by that time, and flew upstairs to the boys' room, waking them explosively. He turned on their radio and got another 60-cycle note, this time with a shattering microphonic when he rapped the case, which he did four times, whereupon the set went dead altogether.

Esther had planned the thing up to this point, but no further, which was the way her mind worked. She figured she could handle it, but she figured wrong. MacLyle came downstairs like a pall bearer, and he was silent and shaken until 7:30, time for the news on TV. The living room set wouldn't peep, so up he went to the boys' room again, waking them just as they were nodding off again, and this time the little guy started to cry. MacLyle didn't care. When he found out there was no picture on the set, he almost started to cry too, but then he heard the sound come in. A TV set has an awful lot of tubes in it and Esther didn't know audio from video. MacLyle sat down in front of the dark screen and listened to the news. *"Everything seemed to be under control in the riot-ridden border country in India,"* said the TV set. Crowd noises and a background of Beethoven's "Turkish March." *"And then—"* Cut music. Crowd noise up: gabble-wurra and a scream. Announcer over: *"Six hours later, this was the scene."* Dead silence, going on so long that MacLyle reached out and thumped the TV set with the heel of his hand. Then, slow swell, Ketelbey's "In a Monastery Garden." *"On a more cheerful note, here are the six finalists in the Miss Continuum contest."* Background music, "Blue Room," interminably, interrupted only once, when the announcer said through a childish chuckle, *". . . and she meant it!"* MacLyle pounded himself on the temples. The little guy continued to sob. Esther stood at the foot of the stairs wringing her hands. It went on for 30 minutes like this. All MacLyle said when he came downstairs was that he wanted the paper—that would be the local one. So Esther faced the great unknown and told him frankly she hadn't ordered it and wouldn't again, which of course led to a full and righteous confession of her activities of the afternoon.

Only a woman married better than fourteen years can know a man well enough to handle him so badly. She was aware that she was wrong but that was quite overridden by the fact that she was logical. It would not be logical to continue her patience, so patience was at an end. That which offendeth thee, cast it out, yea, even thine eye and thy right hand. She realized too late that the news was so inextricably part of her husband that in casting it out she cast him out too. And out he went, while whitely she listened to the rumble of the garage door, the car door speaking its sharp syllables, clear as *Exit* in a play script; the keen of a starter, the mourn of a motor. She said she was glad and went in the kitchen and tipped the useless ivory radio off the shelf and retired, weeping.

And yet, because true life offers few clean cuts, she saw him once more. At seven minutes to three in the morning she became aware of faint music from somewhere; unaccountably it frightened her, and she tiptoed about the house looking for it. It wasn't in the house, so she pulled on MacLyle's trench coat and crept down the steps into the garage. And there, just outside in the driveway, where steel beams couldn't interfere with radio reception, the car stood where it had been all along, and MacLyle was in the driver's seat dozing over the wheel. The music came from the car radio. She drew the coat tighter around her and went to the car and opened the door and spoke his name. At just that moment the radio said ". . . *and now the news*" and MacLyle sat bolt upright and *shh*'d furiously. She fell back and stood a moment in a strange transition from unconditional surrender to total defeat. Then he shut the car door and bent forward, his hand on the volume control, and she went back into the house.

After the news report was over and he had recovered himself from the stab wounds of a juvenile delinquent, the grinding agonies of a derailed train, the terrors of the near-crash of a C-119, and the fascination of a cabinet officer, charter member of the We Don't Trust Nobody Club, saying in exactly these words that there's a little bit of good in the worst of us and a little bit of bad in the best of us, all of which he felt keenly, he started the car (by rolling it down the drive because the battery was almost dead) and drove as slowly as possible into town.

At an all-night garage he had the car washed and greased while he waited, after which the automat was open and he sat in it for three hours drinking coffee, holding his jaw set until his back teeth ached, and making occasional, almost inaudible noises in the back of his throat. At 9:00 he pulled himself together. He spent the entire day with his astonished attorney, going through all his assets, selling, converting, establishing, until when he was finished he had a modest packet of cash and his wife would have an adequate income until the children went to college, at which time the house would be sold, the tenants in the older house evicted, and Esther would be free to move to the smaller home with the price of the larger one added to the basic capital. The lawyer might have entertained fears for MacLyle except for the fact that he was jovial and loquacious throughout, behaving like a happy man—a rare form of insanity, but acceptable. It was hard work but they did it in a day, after which MacLyle wrung the lawyer's hand and thanked him profusely and checked into a hotel.

When he awoke the following morning he sprang out of bed, feeling years younger, opened the door, scooped up the morning paper and glanced at the headlines.

He couldn't read them.

He grunted in surprise, closed the door gently, and sat on the bed with the paper in his lap. His hands moved restlessly on it, smoothing and smoothing until the palms were shadowed and the type hazed. The shouting symbols marched across the page like a parade of strangers in some unrecognized lodge uniform, origins unknown, destination unknown, and the occasion for marching only to be guessed at. He traced the letters with his little finger, he measured the length of a word between his index finger and thumb and lifted them up to hold them before his wondering eyes. Suddenly he got up and crossed to the desk, where signs and placards and printed notes were trapped like a butterfly collection under glass—the breakfast menu, something about valet service, something about checking out. He remembered them all and had an idea of their significance—but he couldn't read them. In the drawer was stationery, with a picture of the building and no other buildings around it, which just wasn't so, and an inscription which might have been in Cyrillic for all he knew. Telegram blanks, a bus schedule, a blotter, all bearing hieroglyphs and runes, as far as he was concerned. A phone book full of strangers' names in strange symbols.

He requested of himself that he recite the alphabet. "A," he said clearly, and "Eh?" because it didn't sound right and he couldn't imagine what would. He made a small foolish grin and shook his head slightly and rapidly, but grin or no, he felt frightened. He felt glad, or relieved—mostly happy anyway, but still a little frightened.

He called the desk and told them to get his bill ready, and dressed and went downstairs. He gave the doorman his parking check and waited while they brought the car round. He got in and turned the radio on and started to drive west.

He drove for some days, in a state of perpetual, cold, and (for all that) happy fright—roller-coaster fright, horror-movie fright—remembering the significance of a stop-sign without being able to read the word STOP across it, taking caution from the shape of a railroad-crossing notice. Restaurants look like restaurants, gas stations like gas stations; if Washington's picture denotes a dollar and Lincoln's five, one doesn't need to read them. MacLyle made out just fine. He drove until he was well into one of those square states with all the mountains and cruised until he recognized the section where, years before he was married, he had spent a hunting vacation. Avoiding the lodge he had used, he took back roads until, sure enough, he came to that deserted cabin in which he had sheltered one night, standing yet, rotting a bit but only around the edges. He wandered in and out of it for a long time, memorizing details because he could not make a list, and then got back into his car and drove to the nearest town, not very near and not very much of a town. At the general store he bought shingles and flour and nails and paint—all sorts of paint, in little cans, as well as big containers of house-paint—and canned goods and tools. He ordered a knockdown windmill and a generator, eighty pounds of modeling clay, two loaf pans and a mixing bowl, and a war-surplus jungle hammock. He paid cash and promised to be back in two weeks for the things the store didn't stock, and wired (because it could be done over the phone) his lawyer to arrange for the predetermined $80 a month which was all he cared to take for himself from his assets. Before he left he stood in wonder before a monstrous piece of musical plumbing called an ophicleide which stood, dusty and majestic, in a corner. (While it might be easier on the reader to make this a French horn or a sousaphone—which would answer narrative purposes quite as well—we're done telling lies here. MacLyle's real name is concealed, his home town cloaked, and his occupation disguised, and dammit it really was a twelve-keyed, 1824, 50-inch, obsolete brass ophicleide.) The storekeeper explained how his great-grandfather had brought it over from the old country and nobody had played it for two generations except an itinerant tuba-player who had turned pale green on the first three notes and put it down as if it was full of percussion caps. MacLyle asked how it sounded and the man told him, terrible. Two weeks later MacLyle was back to pick up the rest of his stuff, nodding and smiling and saying not a word. He still couldn't read, and now he couldn't speak. Even more, he had lost the power to understand speech. He paid for the purchases with a $100 bill and a wistful expression, and then another $100 bill, and the storekeeper, thinking he had turned deaf and dumb, cheated him roundly but at the same time felt so sorry for him that he gave him the ophicleide. MacLyle loaded up his car happily and left. And that's the first part of the story about MacLyle's being in a bad way.

* * *

MacLyle's wife Esther found herself in a peculiar position. Friends and neighbors off-handedly asked her questions to which she did not know the answers, and the only person who had any information at all— MacLyle's attorney—was under bond not to tell her anything. She had not, in the full and legal sense, been deserted, since she and the children were provided for. She missed MacLyle, but in a specialized way; she missed the old reliable MacLyle, and he had, in effect, left her long before that perplexing night when he had driven away. She wanted the old MacLyle back again, not this untrolleyed stranger with the grim and spastic preoccupation with the news. Of the many unpleasant facets of this stranger's personality, one glowed brightest, and that was that he was the sort of man who would walk out the way he did and stay away as long as he had. Ergo, he was that undesirable person just as long as he stayed away, and tracking him down would, if it returned him against his will, return to her only a person who was not the person she missed.

Yet she was dissatisfied with herself, for all that she was the injured party and had wounds less painful than the pangs of conscience. She had always prided herself on being a good wife, and had done many things in the past which were counter to her reason and her desires purely because they were consistent with being a good wife. So as time went on she gravitated away from the "what shall I do?" area into the "what ought a good wife to do?" spectrum, and after a great deal of careful thought, went to see a psychiatrist.

He was a fairly intelligent psychiatrist, which is to say he caught on to the obvious a little faster than most people. For example, he became aware in only four minutes of conversation that MacLyle's wife Esther had not come to him on her own behalf, and further decided to hear her out completely before resolving to treat her. When she had quite finished and he had dug out enough corroborative detail to get the picture, he went into a long silence and cogitated. He matched the broad pattern of MacLyle's case with his reading and his experience, recognized the challenge, the clinical worth of the case, the probable value of the heirloom diamond pendant worn by his visitor. He placed his fingertips together, lowered his fine young head, gazed through his eyebrows at MacLyle's wife Esther, and took up the gauntlet. At the prospect of getting her husband back safe and sane, she thanked him quietly and left the office with mixed emotions. The fairly intelligent psychiatrist drew a deep breath and began making arrangements with another head-shrinker to take over his other patients, both of them, while he was away, because he figured to be away quite a while.

It was appallingly easy for him to trace MacLyle. He did not go near the lawyer. The solid foundation of all skip tracers and Bureaus of Missing Persons, in their *modus operandi,* is the piece of applied psychology which dictates that a man might change his name and his address, but he will seldom—can seldom—change the things he does, particularly the things he does to amuse himself. The ski addict doesn't skip to Florida, though he might make Banff instead of an habitual Mont Tremblant. A philatelist is not likely to mount butterflies. Hence when the psychiatrist found, among MacLyle's papers, some snapshots and brochures, dating from college days, of the towering Rockies, of bears feeding by the roadside, and especially of season after season's souvenirs of a particular resort to which he had never brought his wife and which he had not visited since he married her, it was worth a feeler, which went out in the form of a request to that state's police for information on a man of such-and-such·a description driving so-and-so with out-of-state plates, plus a request that the man not be detained nor warned, but only that he, the fairly intelligent psychiatrist, be notified. He threw out other lines, too, but this is the one that hooked his fish. It was a matter of weeks before a state patrol car happened by MacLyle's favorite general store: after that it was a matter of minutes before the information was in the hands of the psychiatrist. He said nothing to MacLyle's wife Esther except goodby for a while, and this bill is payable now, and then took off, bearing with him a bag of tricks.

He rented a car at the airport nearest MacLyle's hideout and drove a long, thirsty, climbing way until he came to the general store. There he interviewed the proprietor, learning some eighteen hundred items about how bad business could get, how hot it was, how much rain hadn't fallen and how much was needed, the tragedy of being blamed for high mark-ups when anyone with the brains God gave a goose ought to know it cost plenty to ship things out here, especially in the small quantities necessitated by business being so bad and all; and betwixt and between, he learned eight or ten items about MacLyle—the exact location of his cabin, the fact that he seemed to have turned into a deaf-mute who was also unable to read, and that he must be crazy because who but a crazy man would want 84 different half-pint cans of house paint or, for that matter, live out here when he didn't have to?

The psychiatrist got loose after a while and drove off, and the country got higher and dustier and more lost every mile, until he began to pray that nothing would go wrong with the car, and sure enough, ten minutes later he thought something had. Any car that made a noise like the one he began to hear was strictly a shotrod, and he pulled over to the side to worry about it. He turned off the motor and the noise went right on, and he began to realize that the sound was not in the car or even near it, but came from somewhere uphill. There was a mile and a half more of the hill to go, and he drove it in increasing amazement, because that sound got louder and more impossible all the time. It was sort of like music, but like no music currently heard on this or any other planet. It was a solo voice, brass, with muscles. The upper notes, of which there seemed to be about two octaves, were wild and unmusical, the middle was rough, but the low tones were like the speech of these mountains themselves, big up to the sky, hot, and more natural than anything ought to be, basic as a bear's fang. Yet all the notes were perfect—their intervals were perfect—this awful noise was tuned like an electronic organ. The psychiatrist had a good ear, though for a while he wondered how long he'd have any ears at all, and he realized all these things about the sound, as well as the fact that it was rendering one of the more primitive fingering studies from Czerny, Book One, the droning little horror that goes: *do mi fa sol la sol fa mi, re fa sol la ti la sol fa, mi sol la* . . . etcetera, inchworming up the scale and then descending hand over hand.

He saw blue sky almost under his front tires and wrenched the wheel hard over, and found himself in the grassy yard of a made-over prospector's cabin, but that he didn't notice right away because sitting in front of it was what he described to himself, startled as he was out of his professional detachment, as the craziest-looking man he had ever seen.

He was sitting under a parched, wind-warped Engelmann spruce. He was barefoot up to the armpits. He wore the top half of a skivvy shirt and a hat the shape of one of those conical Boy Scout tents when one of the Boy Scouts has left the pole home. And he was playing, or anyway practicing, the ophicleide, and on his shoulders was a little moss of spruce-needles, a small shower of which descended from the tree every time he hit on or under the low B-flat. Only a mouse trapped inside a tuba during band practice can know precisely what it's like to stand that close to an operating ophicleide.

It was MacLyle all right, looming well-fed and filled-out. When he saw the psychiatrist's car he went right on playing, but, catching the psychiatrist's eye, he winked, smiled with the small corner of lip which showed from behind the large cup of the mouthpiece, and twiddled three fingers of his right hand, all he could manage of a wave without stopping. And he didn't stop, either, until he had scaled the particular octave he was working on and let himself down the other side. Then he put the ophicleide down carefully and let it lean against the spruce tree, and got up. The psychiatrist had become aware, as the last stupendous notes rolled away down the mountain, of his extreme isolation with this offbeat patient, of the unconcealed health and vigor of the man, and of the presence of the precipice over which he had almost driven his car a moment before, and had rolled up his window and buttoned the doorlock and was feeling grateful for them. But the warm good humor and genuine welcome on MacLyle's sunburned face drove away fright and even caution, and almost before he knew what he was doing the psychiatrist had the door open and was stooping up out of the car, thinking, merry is a disused word but that's what he is, by God, a merry man. He called him by name but either MacLyle did not hear him or didn't care; he just put out a big warm hand and the psychiatrist took it. He could feel hard flat calluses in MacLyle's hand, and the controlled strength an elephant uses to lift a bespangled child in its trunk; he smiled at the image, because after all MacLyle was not a particularly large man, there was just that feeling about him. And once the smile found itself there it wouldn't go away.

He told MacLyle that he was a writer trying to soak up some of this magnificent country and had just been driving wherever the turn of the road led him, and here he was; but before he was half through he became conscious of MacLyle's eyes, which were in some indescribable way very much on him but not at all on anything he said: it was precisely as if he had stood there and hummed a tune. MacLyle seemed to be willing to listen to the sound until it was finished, and even to enjoy it, but that enjoyment was going to be all he got out of it. The psychiatrist finished anyway and MacLyle waited a moment as if to see if there would be any more, and when there wasn't he gave out more of that luminous smile and cocked his head toward the cabin. MacLyle led the way, with his visitor bringing up the rear with some platitudes about nice place you got here. As they entered, he suddenly barked at that unresponsive back, "Can't you hear me?" and MacLyle, without turning, only waved him on.

They walked into such a clutter and clabber of colors that the psychiatrist stopped dead, blinking. One wall had been removed and replaced with glass panes; it overlooked the precipice and put the little building afloat on haze. All the walls were hung with plain white chenille bedspreads, and the floor was white, and there seemed to be much more light indoors here than outside. Opposite the large window was an oversized easel made of peeled poles, notched and lashed together with baling wire, and on it was a huge canvas, most non-objective, in the purest and most uncompromising colors. Part of it was unquestionably this room, or at least its air of colored confusion here and all infinity yonder. The ophicleide was in the picture, painstakingly reproduced, looking like the hopper of some giant infernal machine, and in the foreground some flowers; but the central figure repulsed him—more, it repulsed everything which surrounded it. It did not look exactly like anything familiar and, in a disturbed way, he was happy about that.

Stacked on the floor on each side of the easel were other paintings, some daubs, some full of ruled lines and overlapping planes, but all in this achingly pure color. He realized what was being done with the dozens of colors of house paint in little cans which had so intrigued the storekeeper.

In odd places around the room were clay sculptures, most mounted on pedestals made of sections of tree-trunks large enough to stand firmly on their sawed ends. Some of the pedestals were peeled, some painted, and in some the bark texture or the bulges or clefts in the wood had been carried right up into the model, and in others clay had been knived or pressed into the bark all the way down to the floor. Some of the clay was painted, some not, some ought to have been. There were free-forms and gollywogs, a marsupial woman and a guitar with legs, and some, but not an overweening number, of the symbolisms which preoccupy even fairly intelligent psychiatrists. Nowhere was there any furniture per se. There were shelves at all levels and of varying lengths, bearing nail-kegs, bolts of cloth, canned goods, tools and cooking utensils. There was a sort of table but it was mostly a workbench, with a vise at one end and at the other, half-finished, a crude but exceedingly ingenious foot-powered potter's wheel.

He wondered where MacLyle slept, so he asked him, and again MacLyle reacted as if the words were not words, but a series of pleasant sounds, cocking his head and waiting to see if there would be any more. So the psychiatrist resorted to sign language, making a pillow of his two hands, laying his head on it, closing his eyes. He opened them to see MacLyle nodding eagerly, then going to the white-draped wall. From behind the chenille he brought a hammock, one end of which was fastened to the wall. The other end he carried to the big window and hung on a hook screwed to a heavy stud between the panes. To lie in that hammock would be to swing between heaven and earth like Mahomet's tomb, with all that sky and scenery virtually surrounding the sleeper. His admiration for this idea ceased as MacLyle began making urgent indications for him to get into the hammock. He backed off warily, expostulating, trying to convey to MacLyle that he only wondered, he just wanted to know; no, no, he wasn't tired, dammit; but MacLyle became so insistent that he picked the psychiatrist up like a child sulking at bed-time and carried him to the hammock. Any impulse to kick and quarrel was quenched by the nature of this and all other hammocks to be intolerant of shifting burdens, and by the proximity of the large window. which he now saw was built leaning outward, enabling one to look out of the hammock straight down a minimum of four hundred and eighty feet. So all right, he concluded, if you say so. I'm sleepy.

So for the next two hours he lay in the hammock watching MacLyle putter about the place, thinking more or less professional thoughts.

He doesn't or can't speak (he diagnosed) : aphasia, motor. He doesn't or can't understand speech: aphasia, sensory. He won't or can't read and write: alexia. And what else?

He looked at all that art—if it *was* art, and any that was, was art by accident—and the gadgetry: the chuntering windmill outside, the sash-weight door-closer. He let his eyes follow a length of clothesline dangling unobtrusively down the leaning centerpost to which his hammock was fastened, and the pulley and fittings from which it hung, and its extension clear across the ceiling to the back wall, and understood finally that it would, when pulled, open two long, narrow horizontal hatches for through ventilation. A small door behind the chenille led to what he correctly surmised was a primitive powder room, built to overhang the precipice, the most perfect no-plumbing solution for that convenience he had ever seen.

He watched MacLyle putter. That was the only word for it, and his actions were the best example of puttering he had ever seen. MacLyle lifted, shifted, and put things down, backed off to judge, returned to lay an approving hand on the thing he had moved. Net effect, nothing tangible—yet one could not say there was no effect, because of the intense satisfaction the man radiated. For minutes he would stand, head cocked, smiling slightly, regarding the half-finished potter's wheel, then explode into activity, sawing, planing, drilling. He would add the finished piece to the cranks and connecting rods already completed, pat it as if it were an obedient child, and walk away, leaving the rest of the job for some other time. With a woodrasp he carefully removed the nose from one of his dried clay figures, and meticulously put on a new one. Always there was this absorption in his own products and processes, and the air of total reward in everything. And there was time, there seemed to be time enough for everything, and always would be.

Here is a man, thought the fairly intelligent psychiatrist, in retreat, but in a retreat the like of which my science has not yet described. For observe: he has reacted toward the primitive in terms of supplying himself with his needs with his own hands and by his own ingenuity, and yet there is nothing primitive in those needs themselves. He works constantly to achieve the comforts which his history has conditioned him to in the past—electric lights, cross-ventilation, trouble-free waste disposal. He exhibits a profound humility in the low rates he pays himself for his labor: he is building a potter's wheel apparently in order to make his own cooking vessels, and, since wood is cheap and clay free, his vessel can only cost him less than engine-turned aluminum by a very low evaluation of his own efforts.

His skills are less than his energy (mused the psychiatrist). His carpentry, like his painting and sculpture, shows considerable intelligence, but only moderate training; he can construct but not beautify, draw but not draft, and reach the artistically pleasing only by not erasing the random shake, the accidental cut; so that real creation in his work is, like any random effect, rare and unpredictable. Therefore his reward is in the area of satisfaction—about as wide a generalization as one can make.

What satisfaction? Not in possessions themselves, for this man could have bought better for less. Not in excellence in itself, for he obviously could be satisfied with less than perfection. Freedom, perhaps, from routine, from dominations of work? Hardly, because for all the complexity of this cluttered cottage, it had its order and its system; the presence of an alarm clock conveyed a good deal in this area. He wasn't dominated by regularity—he used it. And his satisfaction? Why, it must lie in this closed circle, himself to himself, and in the very fact of non-communication!

Retreat . . . retreat. Retreat to savagery and you don't engineer your cross-ventilation or adjust a 500-foot gravity flush for your john. Retreat into infancy and you don't design and build a potter's wheel. Retreat from people and you don't greet a stranger like . . .

Wait.

Maybe a stranger who had something to communicate, or some way of communication, wouldn't be so welcome. An unsettling thought, that. Running the risk of doing something MacLyle didn't like would be, possibly, a little more unselfish than the challenge warranted.

MacLyle began to cook.

Watching him, the psychiatrist reflected suddenly that this withdrawn and wordless individual was a happy one, in his own matrix; further, he had fulfilled all his obligations and responsibilities and was bothering no one.

It was intolerable.

It was intolerable because it was a violation of the prime directive of psychiatry—at least, of that school of psychiatry which he professed, and he was not going to confuse himself by considerations of other, less-tried theories—*It is the function of psychiatry to adjust the aberrate to society, and to restore or increase his usefulness to it.* To yield, to rationalize this man's behavior as balance, would be to fly in the face of science itself; for this particular psychiatry finds its most successful approaches in the scientific method, and it is unprofitable to debate whether or not it is or is not a science. To its practitioner it is, and that's that; it has to be. Operationally speaking, what has been found true, even statistically, must be Truth, and all other things, even Possible, kept the hell out of the tool-box. No known Truth allowed a social entity to secede this way, and, for one, this fairly intelligent psychiatrist was not going to give this—this *suicide* his blessing.

He must, then, find a way to communicate with MacLyle, and when he had found it, he must communicate to him the error of his ways. Without getting thrown over the cliff.

He became aware that MacLyle was looking at him, twinkling. He smiled back before he knew what he was doing, and obeyed MacLyle's beckoning gesture. He eased himself out of the hammock and went to the workbench, where a steaming stew was set out in earthenware bowls. The bowls stood on large plates and were surrounded by a band of carefully sliced tomatoes. He tasted them. They were obviously vine-ripened and had been speckled with a dark-green paste which, after studious attention to its aftertaste, he identified as fresh basil mashed with fresh garlic and salt. The effect was symphonic.

He followed suit when MacLyle picked up his own bowl and they went outside and squatted under the old Engelmann spruce to eat. It was a quiet and pleasant occasion, and during it the psychiatrist had plenty of opportunity to size up his man and plan his campaign. He was quite sure now how to proceed, and all he needed was opportunity, which presented itself when MacLyle rose, stretched, smiled, and went indoors. The psychiatrist followed him to the door and saw him crawl into the hammock and fall almost instantly asleep.

The psychiatrist went to his car and got out his bag of tricks. And so it was that late in the afternoon, when MacLyle emerged stretching and yawning from his nap, he found his visitor under the spruce tree, hefting the ophicleide and twiddling its keys in a perplexed and investigatory fashion. MacLyle strode over

to him and lifted the ophicleide away with a pleasant
I'll-show-you smile, got the monstrous contraption into
position, and ran his tongue around the inside of the
mouthpiece, large as a demitasse. He had barely time
to pucker up his lips at the strange taste there before
his irises rolled up completely out of sight and he collapsed like a grounded parachute. The psychiatrist
was able only to snatch away the ophicleide in time to
keep the mouthpiece from knocking out MacLyle's
front teeth.

He set the ophicleide carefully against the tree and
straightened MacLyle's limbs. He concentrated for a
moment on the pulse, and turned the head to one side
so saliva would not drain down the flaccid throat, and
then went back to his bag of tricks. He came back and
knelt, and MacLyle did not even twitch at the bite of
the hypodermics: a careful blend of the non-soporific
tranquilizers Frenquel, chlorpromazine and Reserpine,
and a judicious dose of scopolamine, a hypnotic.

The psychiatrist got water and carefully sponged
out the man's mouth, not caring to wait out another
collapse the next time he swallowed. Then there was
nothing to do but wait, and plan.

Exactly on schedule, according to the psychiatrist's
wristwatch, MacLyle groaned and coughed weakly.
The psychiatrist immediately and in a firm quiet
voice told him not to move. Also not to think. He
stayed out of the immediate range of MacLyle's un-
focused eyes and explained that MacLyle must trust
him, because he was there to help, and not to worry
about feeling mixed-up or disoriented. "You don't
know where you are or how you got here," he in-
formed MacLyle. He also told MacLyle, who was past
40, that he was 37 years old, but he knew what he was
doing.

MacLyle just lay there obediently and thought
these things over and waited for more information. He
knew he must trust this voice, the owner of which was
here to help him; that he was 37 years old; and his

name. In these things he lay and marinated. The drugs kept him conscious, docile, submissive and without guile. The psychiatrist observed and exulted: oh you azacyclonol, he chanted silently to himself, you pretty piperidyl, handsome hydrochloride, subtle Serpasil . . . Confidently he left MacLyle and went into the cabin where, after due search, he found some decent clothes and some socks and shoes and brought them out and wrapped the supine patient in them. He helped MacLyle across the clearing and into his car, humming as he did so, for there is none so happy as an expert faced with excellence in his specialty. MacLyle sank back into the cushions and gave one wondering glance at the cabin and at the blare of late light from the bell of the ophicleide; but the psychiatrist told him firmly that these things had nothing to do with him, nothing at all, and MacLyle smiled relievedly and fell to watching the scenery. As they passed the general store MacLyle stirred, but said nothing about it. Instead he asked the psychiatrist if the Ardsmere station was open yet, whereupon the psychiatrist could barely answer him for the impulse to purr like a cat: the Ardsmere station, two stops before MacLyle's suburban town, had burned down and been rebuilt almost six years ago; so now he knew for sure that MacLyle was living in a time preceding his difficulties—a time during which, of course, MacLyle had been able to talk. All of this the psychiatrist kept to himself, and answered gravely that yes, they had the Ardsmere station operating again. And did he have anything else on his mind?

MacLyle considered this carefully, but since all the immediate questions were answered—unswervingly, he *knew* he was safe in the hands of this man, whoever he was; he knew (he thought) his correct age and that he was expected to feel disoriented; he was also under a command not to think—he placidly shook his head and went back to watching the road unroll under their wheels. "Fallen Rock Zone," he murmured as they passed a sign. The psychiatrist drove happily down the mountain and across the flats, back to the city where he had hired the car. He left it at the railroad station ("Rail Crossing Road," murmured MacLyle) and made reservations for a compartment on the train, aircraft being too open and public for his purposes and far too fast for the hourly rate he suddenly decided to apply.

They had time for a silent and companionable dinner before train time, and then at last they were aboard.

The psychiatrist turned off all but one reading lamp and leaned forward. MacLyle's eyes dilated readily to the dimmer light, and the psychiatrist leaned back comfortably and asked him how he felt. He felt fine and said so. The psychiatrist asked him how old he was and MacLyle told him, 37, but he sounded doubtful.

Knowing that the scopolamine was wearing off but the other drugs, the tranquilizers, would hang on for a bit, the psychiatrist drew a deep breath and removed the suggestion; he told MacLyle the truth about his age, and brought him up to the here and now. MacLyle just looked puzzled for a few minutes and then his features settled into an expression that can only be described as not unhappy. "Porter," was all he said, gazing at the push-button, and announced that he could read now.

The psychiatrist nodded sagely and offered no comment, being quite willing to let a patient stew as long as he produced essence.

MacLyle abruptly demanded to know why he had lost the powers of speech and reading. The psychiatrist raised his eyebrows a little, smiled one of those "You-tell-me" smiles, and then got up and suggested they sleep on it. He got the porter in to fix the beds and as an afterthought told the man to come back with the evening papers. Nothing can orient a cultural expatriate better than the evening papers. The man did. MacLyle paid no attention to this, one way or the other. He just climbed into the psychiatrist's spare pajamas thoughtfully and they went to bed.

The psychiatrist didn't know if MacLyle had awakened him on purpose or whether the train's slowing had done it, anyway he awoke about three in the morning to find MacLyle standing beside his bunk looking at him fixedly. He noticed, too, that MacLyle's reading lamp was lit and the papers were scattered all over the floor. MacLyle said, "You're some kind of a doctor," in a flat voice.

The psychiatrist admitted it.

MacLyle said, "Well, this ought to make some sense to you. I was skiing out here years ago when I was a college kid. Accident, fellow I was with broke his leg. Compound. Made him comfortable as I could and went for help. Came back, he'd slid down the mountain, thrashing around, I guess. Crevasse, down in the bottom; took two days to find him, three days to get him out. Frostbite. Gangrene."

The psychiatrist tried to look as if he was following this.

MacLyle said, "The one thing I always remember, him pulling back the bandages all the time to look at his leg. Knew it was gone, couldn't keep himself from watching the stuff spread around and upward. Didn't like to; *had* to. Tried to stop him, finally had to help him or he'd hurt himself. Every ten, fifteen minutes all the way down to the lodge, fifteen hours, looking under the bandages."

The psychiatrist tried to think of something to say and couldn't.

MacLyle said, "That Donne, that John Donne I used to spout, I always believed that."

The psychiatrist began to misquote the thing about send not to ask for whom the bell . . .

"Yeah, that, but especially *'any man's death diminishes me, because I am involved in mankind.'* I believed that," MacLyle repeated. "I believed more than that. Not only death. Damn foolishness diminishes me because I am involved. People all the time pushing people around diminishes me. Everybody hungry for a fast buck diminishes me." He picked up a sheet of newspaper and let it slip away; it flapped off to the corner of the compartment like a huge gravemoth. "I was getting diminished to death and I had to watch it happening to me like that kid with the gangrene, so that's why." The train, crawling now, lurched suddenly and yielded. MacLyle's eyes flicked to the window, where neon beer signs and a traffic light were reluctantly being framed. MacLyle leaned close to the psychiatrist. "I just had to get un-involved with mankind before I got diminished altogether, everything mankind did was my fault. So I did and now here I am involved again." MacLyle abruptly went to the door. "And for that, thanks."

The psychiatrist asked him what he was going to do.

"Do?" asked MacLyle cheerfully. "Why, I'm going out there and diminish mankind right back." He was out in the corridor with the door closed before the psychiatrist so much as sat up. He banged it open again and leaned in. He said in the sanest of all possible voices. "Now mind you, doctor, this is only one man's opinion," and was gone. He killed four people before they got him.

The Clinic

Standing on a street corner waiting for the light to change, I noticed the man next to me gesticulating rapidly and with swift precision while he stared intently across the street. Following his gaze, I saw a woman watching him with great attention. When he stopped his gestures, her hands flickered swiftly in response, and they both laughed. They were deaf-mutes, and it came to me then that in this situation they were not handicapped. I was, and so were the dozens of hearing people around us, who could not possibly accomplish such a feat.

So I turned the coin over—as you will see.

The police men and the doctors men and most of the people outside, they all helped me, they were very nice but nobody helped me as many-much as Elena.

De la Torre liked me very nice I think, but number one because what I am is his work. The Sergeant liked me very nice too but inside I think he say not real, not real. He say in all his years he know two for-real amnesiacs but only in police book. Unless me. Some day, he say, some day he find out I not-real amnesiac trying to fool him. De la Torre say I real. Classic case, he say. He say plenty men forget talk forget name forget way to do life-work but *por Dios* not forget buttons forget eating forget every damn thing like me. The Sergeant say yes Doc you would rather find a medical monstrosity than turn up a faker. De la Torre say yes you would rather find out he is a fugitive than a phenomenon, well this just shows you what expert opinion is worth when you get two experts together. He say, one of us has to be wrong.

Is half right. Is both wrong.

If I am a fugitive I must be very intelligent. If I am an amnesiac I could be even intelligenter as a fugitive. Anyway I be intelligent better than any man in the world, as how could conversation as articulo-fluent like this after only six days five hours fifty three minutes?

Is both wrong. I be Némo.

But now comes Elena again, de la Torre is look happy-face, the Sergeant is look watch-face, Elena smile so warm, and we go.

"How are you tonight, Nemo?"

"I am very intelligent."

She laughs. "You can say that again," and then she puts hand on my mouth and more laughs. "No, don't say it again. Another figure of speech. . . . Remember any yet?"

"What state what school what name, all that? No."

"All right." Now de la Torre, he ask me like that and when I no him, he try and try ask some other how. The Sergeant, he ask me like that and when I no him, he try and try ask me the same asking, again again. Elena ask and when I no her, she talk something else. Now she say, "What would you like to do tonight?"

I say, "Go with you whatever."

She say, "Well we'll start with a short beer," so we do.

The short beer is in a room with long twisty blue lights and red lights and a noise-machine looks like two sunsets with bubbles and sounds unhappy out loud. The short beer is wet, high as a hand, color like Elena's eyes, shampoo on top, little bubbles inside. Elena drank then I drink all. Little bubbles make big bubble inside me, big bubble come right back up so roaring that all people look to see, so it is bigger as the noise-machine. I look at people and Elena laugh again. She say, "I guess I shouldn't laugh. Most people don't do that in public, Nemo."

"Was largely recalcitrant bubble and decontrolled," I say. "So what do—keep for intestinals?"

She laugh again and say, "Well, no. Just try to keep it quiet." And now come a man from high long table where so many stand, he has hair on face, low lip flaccid, teeth brown black and gold, he smell as wastefood, first taste of mouth-thermometer, and skin moisture after drying in heavy weavings. He say, "You sound like a pig, Mac, where you think you are, home?"

I look at Elena and I look at he, I say, "Good evening." That what de la Torre say in first speak to peoples after begin night. Elena quick touch arm of mine, say, "Don't pay any attention to him, Nemo." Man bend over, put hand forward and touches it to ear of me with velocity, to make a large percussive effect. Same time bald man run around end of long high table exhibiting wooden device, speaking the prognosis: "Don't start nothing in my place, Purky, or I'll feed you this bung-starter."

I rub at ear and look at man who smells. He say, "Yeah, but you hear this little pig here? Where he think he's at?"

The man with bung-starter device say, "Tell you where you'll be at, you don't behave yourself, you'll be out on the pavement with a knot on your head," and he walk at Purky until Purky move and walk again until Purky is back to old place. I rub on ear and look at Elena and Elena has lip-paint of much bigger red now. No it is not bigger red, it is face skin of more white. Elena say, "Are you all right, Nemo? Did he hurt you?"

I say, "He is destroyed no part. He is create algesia of the middle ear. This is usual?"

"The dirty rat. No, Nemo, it isn't usual. I'm sorry, I'm *so* sorry. I shouldn't've brought you in here. . . . Some day someone'll do the world a favor and knock his block off."

"I have behavior?"

She say, "You what? Oh—did you act right." She gives me diagnostic regard from sides of eyes. "I guess so, Nemo. But . . . you can't let people push you around like that. Come on, let's get out of here."

"But then this is no more short beer, yes?"

"You like it? You want another?"

I touch my larynx. "It localizes a euphoria."

"Does it now. Well, whatever that means, I guess you can have another." She high display two fingers and big bald man gives dispensing of short beer more. I take all and large bubble forms and with concentration I exude it through nostrils quietly and gain Elena's approval and laughter. I say my thanks about the kindlies, about de la Torre and the Sergeant but it is Elena who helps with the large manymuchness.

"Forget it," she say.

"Is figure of speech? Is command?"

She say low-intensity to shampoo on short beer, "I don't know, Nemo. No, I guess I wouldn't want you to forget me." She look up at me and I know she will say again, "You'll never forget your promise, Nemo?" and she say it. And I say, "I not go away before I say, Elena, I going away."

She say, "What's the matter, Nemo? What is it?"

I say, "You think I go away, so I think about I go away too. I like you think about I here. And that not all of it."

"I'm sorry. It's just that I—well, it's important to me, that's all. I couldn't bear it if you just disappeared some day. . . . What else, Nemo?"

I say, "Two more short beer."

We drink the new short beer with no talk and with thinks. Then she say she go powder she nose. She nose have powder but she also have behavior so I no say why. When she go in door-place at back angle, I stand and walk.

I walk to high long table where stand the smelly man Purky, I push on him, he turn around.

He say, "Well look what crawled up! What you want, piggy?"

I say, "Where you block?"

He say, "Where's *what*?" He speak down to me from very tall, but he speak more noise than optimum.

I say, "You block. Block. You know, knock off block. Where you block? I knock off."

Big man who bring short beer, he roar. Purky, he roar. Mens jump back, looking, looking. Purky lift high big bottle, approach it at me swiftly. I move very close swiftlier, impact the neck of Purky by shoulder, squeeze flesh of Purky in and down behind pelvis, sink right thumb in left abdomen of Purky—one-two-three and go away again. Purky still swing down bottle but I not there for desired encounter now. Bottle go down to floor, Purky go down to floor, I walk back to chair, Purky lie twitching, men look at he, men look at me, Purky say "Uh-uh-uh," I sit down.

Elena come out of door running, say "What happened? Nemo . . ." and she look at Purky and all men looking.

I say, "Sorry. Sorry."

"Did you do that, Nemo?"

I make the head-nod, yes.

"Well what are you sorry about?" she say, all pretty with surprise and fierce.

I say, "I think you happy if I knock block off, but not know block. Where is block? I knock off now."

"No you don't!" she say. "You come right along out of here! Nemo, you're dynamite!"

I puzzle. "Is good?"

"Just now, is good."

We go out and big man call, "Hey, how about one on the house, Bomber?"

I puzzle again. Elena say, "He means he wants to give you a drink."

"Short beer?"

Big man put out short beer, I drink all. Purky sit up on floor. I feel big bubble come, I make it roar. I look at Purky. Purky not talk. Elena pull me, we go.

We walk by lakeshore long time. People foot-slide slowly to pulse from mens with air-vibrators, air-column wood, air-column metal, vibrating strings single and sets. "Dancing," Elena say and I say "Nice. Is goodly nice." We have a happy, watching. Pulse fast, pulse slow, mens cry with pulse and vibrations, womens, two at once, cry together. "Singing," Elena say, and the lights move on the dancing, red and yellow-red and big and little blue; clouds shift and change, pulse shift and change, stars come, stars go and the wind, warm. Elena say, "Nemo, honey, do you know what love is?"

I say no.

She look the lake, she look the lights, she wave the arm of her to show all, with the wind and stars; she make her voice like whisper and like singing too and she say, "It's something like this, Nemo. I hope you find out some day."

I say yes, and I have sleepy too. So she take me back to the hospital.

● ● ●

It is the day and de la Torre is tired with me. He fall into chair, wipe the face of he with a small white weaving.

He say, *"Por Dios,* Nemo, I don't figure you at all. Can I be frank with you?"

I say, "Yes," but I know all he be is de la Torre.

He say, "I don't think you're trying. But you must be trying; you couldn't get along so fast without trying. You don't seem to be interested; I have to tell you some things fifty times before you finally get them. Yet you ask questions as if you *were* interested. What are you? What do you want?"

I lift up the shoulders once, quickly, just like de la Torre when he not know.

He say, "You grasp all the complicated things at sight, and ignore the simple ones. You use terms out of *Materia Medica* and use them right, and all the time you refuse to talk anything but a highly individualized pidgin-English. Do you know what I'm talking about?"

I say, "Yes."

He say, *"Do* you? Tell me: what is *Materia Medica?* What is 'Individualized'? What is 'Pidgin-English'?"

I do the shoulders thing.

"So don't tell me you know what I'm talking about."

I turn the head little, raise the one finger like he do sometime, I say, "I do. I do."

"Tell me then. Tell it in your own words. Tell me why you won't learn to talk the way I do."

"No use," I say. Then I say, "No use for me." Then I say, "Not interest me." And still he sit and puzzle at me.

So I try. I say, "De la Torre, I see peoples dancing in the night."

"When? With Elena?"

"Elena, yes. And I see mens make pulse and cries for dancing."

"An orchestra?" I puzzle. He say, "Men with instruments, making noises together?" I make a yes. He say, "Music. That's called music."

I say, "What this?" and I move the arms.

He say, "Violin?"

I say, "Yes.. Make one noise, a new noise, a new noise—one and one and one. Now," I say, "what this?" and I move again.

"Banjo," he say. "Guitar, maybe."

"Make many noise, in set. Make a new set. And a new set. Yes?"

"Yes," he say. "It's played in chords, mostly. What are you getting at?"

I bump on side of head. "You have think word and word and word and you make set. I have think set and set and set."

"You mean I think like a violin, one note at a time, and you think like a guitar, a lot of related notes at a time?" He quiet, he puzzle. "Why do you want to think like that?"

"Is my thinks."

"You mean, that's the way you think? Well, for Pete's sake, Nemo, you'll make it a lot easier to convey your thinks—uh—thoughts if you'll learn to come out with them like other people."

I make the no with the head. "No use for me."

"Look," he say. He blow hard through he nostrils, bang-bang on table, eyes close. He say, "You've got to understand this. I'll give you an example. You know how an automobile engine works?"

I say no.

He grab white card and markstick and start to mark, start to conversation swift, say all fast about they call this a four-cycle engine because its acts in four different phases, the piston goes down, this valve opens, that valve closes, the piston goes up, this makes a fire . . . and a lot, all so swift. "This the intake cycle," and many words. "This is the crankshaft, spark-plug, fuel line, compression stroke . . ." Much and much.

And stops, whump. Points markstick. "Now, you and your thinking in concepts. That's how it works, basically. Don't tell me you got any of that, with any real understanding."

"Don't tell?"

"No, no," he say. He tired, he smile. He say, "Name the four cycles of this engine."

I say, "Suck. Squeeze. Pop. Phooey."

He drop he markstick. A long quiet. He say, "I can't teach you anything."

I say, "I not intelligent?"

He say, "*I* not intelligent."

Is many peoples in eatplace but I by my own with my plate and my thinks, I am alone. Is big roughness impacting on arm, big noise say, "What's your *name?*"

I bend to look up and there is the Sergeant. I say, "Nemo."

He sit down. He look. He make me have think: he like me, he not believe me. He not believe anybody. He say: "Nemo, Nemo. That's not your name."

I do the thing with the shoulders.

He say, "You weren't surprised when I jolted you then. Don't you ever get surprised? Don't you ever get sore?"

I say, "Surprise, no. Sore?"

He say, "Sore, mad, angry."

I have a think. I say, "No."

He say, "Ought to be something that'll shake you up. Hm. . . . They pamper you too much around here, you walking around like Little Eva or Billy Budd or somebody. Sweetness and light. Dr. de la Torre says you're real bright."

"De la Torre real bright."

"Maybe. Maybe." He eyes have like coldness, like so cold nothing move. He say, "That Elena. How you like Elena, Nemo?"

I say, "I like." And I say, "High music, big color-gentle."

He say, "Thought so." He poke sharp into my chest. "Now I'm gonna tell you the truth about your Elena. She's crazy as a coot. She went bad young. She was a mainliner, understand me? She was an addict. She did a lot of things to get money for the stuff. She had to do more'n most of 'em, with a face like that, and it didn't get any prettier. De la Torre pulled her through a cure. He's a good man. Three different times he cured her.

"So one time she falls off again and what do you know, she picks up with a looney just like you. A guy they called George. I figured from the start he was a faker. Showed up wandering, just like you. And she goes for him. She goes for him bigger'n she ever went for anything else, even hash. And he went over the hill one fine day and was never seen again.

"So she's off the stuff, sure. And you know what? The only thing she has any use for is amnesiacs. Yeah, I mean it. You're the sixth in a row. They come in, she sticks with 'em until they get cured or fade. Between times she just waits for the next one.

"And that's your Elena. De la Torre strings along with her because she does 'em good. So that's your light o' love, Nemo boy. A real twitch. If it isn't dope it's dopes. You get cured up, she'll want no part of you. Wise up, fella."

He look at me. He has a quiet time. He say, "God awmighty, you don't give a damn for her after all . . . or maybe you just don't know how to get mad . . . or you didn't understand a word of what I said."

I say, "Every people hurt Elena. Some day Elena be happy, always. Sergeant hurt every people. Sergeant not be happy. Never."

He look at me. Something move in the cold, like lobster on ice; too cold to move much. I say, "Poor Sergeant."

He jump up, he make a noise, not word, he raise a big hand. I look up at him, I say, "Poor Sergeant." He go away. He bump de la Torre who is quiet behind us.

De la Torre say, "I heard that speech of yours, you skunk. I'd clobber you myself if I didn't think Nemo'd done it better already. You'd better keep your big flat feet the hell out of this hospital."

Sergeant run away. De la Torre stand a time, go away. I eat.

It is night by the lake, the moon is burst and leaking yellow to me over the black alive water and Elena by me. I say, "I go soonly."

She breathe, I hear.

I say, "Tree finish, tree die. Sickness finish, sickness gone. House finish, workmens leave. Is right."

"Don't go. Don't go yet, Nemo."

"Seed sprout, child grow, bird fly. Something finish, something change. I finish."

She say, "Not so soon."

"Bury plant? Tie boy to cradle? Nail wings to nest?"

She say, "All right." We sit.

I say, "I promised."

She say, "You kept your promise, Nemo. Thank you." She cry. I watch leaking moon float free, lost light flattening and flattening at the black lake. Light tried, light tried, water would not mix.

Elena say, "What world do you live in, Nemo?"

I say, "My world."

She say, "Yes . . . yes, that's the right answer. You live in your world, I live in my world, a hundred people, a hundred worlds. Nobody lives with me, nobody. Nemo, you can travel from one world to another."

I do the head, yes.

"But just one at a time. I'm talking crazy, but you don't mind. I had a world I don't remember, soft and safe, and then a world that hurt me because I was too stupid to duck when I saw hurt coming. And a world that was better than real where I couldn't stay, but I had to go there . . . and I couldn't stay . . . and I had to go . . . and then I had a world where I thought, just for a little while—*such* a little while—I thought it was a world for me and . . ."

I say, "—and George."

She say, *"You can read my mind!"*

"No!" I say, big; loud. Hurt. I say, "Truly no, not do that, I can't do that."

She touch on my face, say, "It doesn't matter. But George, then, about George . . . I was going to be lost again, and this time forever, and I saw George and spoke right up like a—a—" She shake. "You wouldn't know what I was like. And instead, George was gentle and sweet and he made me feel as if I was . . . well and whole. In all my life nobody ever treated me gently, Nemo, except Dr. de la Torre, and he did it because I was sick. George treated me as if I was healthy and fine, and he . . . admired me for it. Me. And he came to love me like those lights, those lights I showed you, all the colors, slipping among the dancers under the sky. He came to love me so much he wanted to stay with me for ever and ever, and then he went away sometime between a morning and a snowstorm."

The moon is gone up, finished and full, the light left on the water frightened and yearning to it, thinning, breaking and fusing, pointing at the moon, the moon not caring, it finished now.

She say, "I was dead for a long time."

She passes through a think and lets her face be dead until she say, "Dr. de la Torre was so kind, he used to tell me I was a special princess, and I could go anywhere. I went in all the places in the hospital, and I found out a thing I had not known; that I had these hands, these legs, eyes, this body, voice, brains. It isn't much and nobody wants it . . . now . . . but I had it all. And some of those people in there, without all of it, they were happier than I was, brave and good. There's a place with people who have their voices taken out of their throats, Nemo, you know that? And they learn to speak there. You know how they do it? I tell some people this, they laugh, but you won't laugh. You won't laugh, Nemo?"

I am not laugh.

She say, "You know that noise you made when you drank the beer so fast? That's what they do. On purpose. They do it and they practice and practice and work hard, work together. And bit by bit they make a voice that sounds like a voice. It's rough and it's all on one note, but it's a real voice. They talk together and laugh, and have a debating society . . .

"There's a place in there where a man goes in without legs, and comes out dancing, yes twirling and swirling a girl around, her ball-gown a butterfly and he smiling and swift and sure. There's a place for the deaf people, and they must make voices out of nothing too, and ears. They do it, Nemo! And together they understand each other. Outside, people don't understand the deaf. People don't mean to be unkind, but they are. But the deaf understand the deaf, and they understand the hearing as well, better than the hearing understand themselves.

"So one day I met a soldier there, with the deaf. He was very sad at first. Many of the people there are born deaf, but he had a world of hearing behind him. And there was a girl there and they fell in love. Everyone was happy, and one day he went away.

"She cried, she cried so, and when she stopped, it was even worse.

"And Dr. de la Torre went and found the soldier, and very gently and carefully he dug out why he had run away. It was because he was handicapped. It was because he had lost a precious thing. And he wouldn't marry the girl, though he loved her, because she was as she had been born and he felt she was perfect. She was perfect and he was damaged. She was perfect and he was unfit. And that is why he ran away.

"Dr. de la Torre brought him back and they were married right there in the hospital with such fine banquet and dance; and they got jobs there and went to school and now they are helping the others, together . . .

"So then I went into another world, and this is my world; and if I should *know* that it is not a real world I would die.

"My world is here, and somewhere else there are people like us but different. One of the ways they are different is that they need not speak; not words anyway. And something happens to them sometimes, just as it does to us: through sickness, through accident, they lose forever their way of communicating, like our total deaf. But they can learn to speak, just as you and I can learn Braille, or make a voice without a larynx, and then at least they may talk among themselves. And if you are to learn Braille, you should go among the blind. If you are to learn lip-reading you do it best among the deaf. If you have something better than speech and lose it, you must go among a speaking people.

"And that is what I believe, because I must or die. I think George was such a one, who came here to learn to speak so he could rejoin others who also had to learn. And I think that anyone who has no memory of this earth or anything on it, and who must be taught to speak, might be another. They pretend to be amnesiacs so that they will be taught *all* of a language. I think that when they have learned, they understand themselves and those like them, and also the normal ones of their sort, better than anyone, just as the deaf can understand the hearing ones better.

"I think George was such a one, and that he left me because he thought of himself as crippled and of me as whole. He left me for love. He was humble with it.

"This is what I believe and I can't . . ."

She whisper.

" . . . I can't believe it . . . very much . . . longer . . ."

She listen to grief altogether until it tired, and when

she can listen to me I say, "You want me to be George, and stay"

She sit close, she put she wet face on my face and say, "Nemo, Nemo, I wish you could, I do *so* wish you could. But you can't be my George, because I love him, don't you see? You can be my de la Torre, though, who went out and found a man and explained why and brought him back. All he has to know is that when love is too humble it can kill the lovers. . . . Just tell him that, Nemo. When you . . . when you go back."

She look past me at the moon, cold now, and down and out to the water and sky, and she here altogether out of memory and hope-thinks. She say with strong daytime voice, "I talk crazy sometimes, thanks, Nemo, you didn't laugh. Let's have a beer some time."

I wish almost the Sergeant knows where I keep anger. It would please him I have so much. Here in the bare rocks, here in the night, I twist on anger, curl and bite me like eel on spear.

It is night and with anger, I alone in cold hills, town and hospital a far fog of light behind. I stand to watch it the ship and around it, those silents who watch me, eight of them, nine, all silent.

This is my anger: that they are silent. They share all thinks in one thinking instant, each with one other, each with all others. All I do now is talk. But the silents, there stand by ship, share and share all thinks, none talks. They wait, I come. They have pity.

They have manymuch pity, so I angry.

Then I see my angry is envy, and envy never teach to dance a one-legged man. Envy never teach the lipreading.

I see that and laugh at me, laugh but it sting my eyes.

"Hello!"

One comes to me, not silent, but have conversation! Surprise. I say, "Good evening."

He shake hand of me, say, "We thought you were not going to come." His speak slow, very strong, steadily.

I say, "I ready. I surprise you have talk."

He say, "Oh, I spent some time here. I studied very carefully. I have come back to live here."

I say, "You conversation goodly. I have learn talk idea, good enough. You have word and word and word, like Earth peoples. Good. Why you come returning?"

He look my face, very near, say, "I did not like it at home. When you go back there, everyone will be kind. But they will have their own lives to live, and there is not much they can share with you any more. You will be blind among the seeing, deaf among those who hear. But they will be kind, oh yes: very kind."

Then he look back at the silents, who stand watching. He say, "But here, I speak among the speaking, and it is a better sharing than even a home planet gone all silent." He point at watchers. He laugh. He say, "We speak together in a way they have never learned to speak, like two Earth mutes gesticulating together in a crowd. It is as if we were the telepaths and not they—see them stare and wonder!"

I laugh too. "Not need to telepath here!"

He say, "Yes, on Earth we can be blind with the blind, and we will never miss our vision. While I was here I was happy to share myself by speaking. When I went home I could share only with other . . . damaged . . . people. I had to go home to find out that I did not feel damaged when I was here, so I came back."

I look to ship, to wondering silents. I say, "What name you have here?"

He say, "They called me George."

I think, I have message for you: Elena dying for you. I say, "Elena waiting for you."

He make large shout and hug on me and run. I cry, "Wait! wait!" He wait, but not wanting. I say, "I learn talk like you, word and word, and one day find Elena for me too."

He hit on me gladly, say, "All right. I'll help you."

We go down hill togetherly, most muchly homelike. Behind, ship wait, ship wait, silents watch and wonder. Then ship load up with all pity I need no more, scream away up to stars.

I have a happy now that I get sick lose telepathy come here learn talk find home, *por Dios*.

. . . and my fear is great . . .

This is one of my favorite stories. It appeared a long time ago in a hardcover collection, which (like most such) disappeared fairly soon, and when the collection went into paperback, this story was dropped. It was a convention at the time to fill up tables of contents with as many titles as possible, and the longer stories filled up the book with fewer titles. A great many went to limbo because of that, and it is gratifying to have this one back in the light.

I've been a "wordaholic" all my life, reveling in the texture and feel and shape and music of words; and outside of Whitman's "I Sing the Body Electric," I know of no more exquisite and moving passage than "The Irish Girl's Lament," included in this story, and also the title-giver. I found it in an essay by W. B. Yeats called "What Modern Poetry?" in which he decried artifice and artificiality in poetry, and said that the best poetry, the real poetry, came from the lips and hearts of the people, speaking in their own idiom. He quoted this lament as an example, affirming that he did not write it; it is not his. Therefore I cannot acknowledge it as his, but can only express my gratitude to him for leading me to such a treasure.

He hefted one corner of the box high enough for him to get his knuckle on the buzzer, then let it sag. He stood waiting, wheezing. The door opened.

"Oh! You *didn't* carry it up five flights!"

"No, huh?" he grunted, and pushed inside. He set the groceries down on the sink top in the kitchenette and looked at her. She was sixty-something and could have walked upright under his armpit with her shoes on.

"That old elevator . . ." she said. "Wait. Here's something."

He wiped sweat out of his eyes and sensed her approach. He put out his hand for the coin but it wasn't a coin. It was a glass. He looked at it, mildly startled. He wished it were beer. He tasted it, then gulped it down. Lemonade.

"Slow-ly, slow-ly," she said, too late. "You'll get heat cramps. What's your name?" Her voice seemed to come from a distance. She seemed, in an odd way, to stand at a distance as well. She was small as a tower is small on the horizon.

"Don," he grunted.

"Well, Donny," she said, "sit down and rest."

He had said, "Don," not "Donny." When he was in rompers he was "Donny." He turned to the door. "I got to go."

"Wait a bit."

He stopped without turning.

"That's a beautiful watch for a boy like you."

"I like it."

"May I see it?"

Breath whistled briefly in his nostrils. She had her fingers lightly on the heel of his hand before he could express any more annoyance than that.

Grudgingly, he raised his arm and let her look.

"Beautiful. Where did you get it?"

He looked at her, surlily. "In a store."

Blandly she asked, "Did you buy it?"

He snatched his hand away. He swiped nervously,

twice, with a hooked index finger at his upper lip. His eyes were slits. "What's it to you?"

"Well, did you?"

"Look, lady. I brought your groceries and I got my lemonade. It's all right about the watch, see? Don't worry about the watch. I got to go now."

"You stole it."

"Whaddaya—crazy? I didn't steal no watch."

"You stole that one."

"I'm gettin' outa here." He reached for the knob.

"Not until you tell me about the watch."

He uttered a syllable and turned the knob. The door stayed closed. He twisted, pulled, pushed, twisted again. Then he whirled, his back thudding against the door. His gangly limbs seemed to compact. His elbows came out, his head down. His teeth bared like an animal's. "Hey, what is this?"

She stood, small and chunky and straight, and said in her far-away voice, "Are you going to tell me?" Her eyes were a milky blue, slightly protruding, and unreadable.

"You lemme out, hear?"

She shook her head.

"You better lemme out," he growled. He took two steps toward her. "Open that door."

"You needn't be frightened. I won't hurt you."

"Somebuddy's goin' to get hurt," he said.

"Not—another—step," she said without raising her voice.

He released an ugly bark of nervous laughter and took the other step. His feet came forward and upward and his back slammed down on the floor. For a moment he lay still, then his eyelids moved slowly up and down and up again while for a moment he gave himself over to the purest astonishment. He moved his head forward so that he could see the woman. She had not moved.

He sat up, clenching his jaw against pain, and scuttled backward to the door. He helped himself rise with the doorpost, never taking his eyes off her. "Jesus, I slipped."

"Don't curse in this house," she said—just as mild, just as firm.

"I'll say what I damn please!"

Wham! His shoulders hit the floor again. His eyes were closed, his lips drawn back. He lifted one shoulder and arched his spine. One long agonized wheeze escaped through his teeth like an extrusion.

"You see, you didn't slip," said the woman. "Poor child. Let me help you."

She put her strong, small hand on his left biceps and another between his shoulder-blades. She would have led him to a chair but he pulled away.

"I'm awright," he said. He said it again, as if unconvinced, and, "What'd you . . . do?"

"Sit down," she said solicitously. He cowered where he was. "Sit down," she said again, no more sharply, but there was a difference.

He went to the chair. He sidled along the wall, watching her, and he did not go very fast, but he went. He sank down into it. It was a very low chair. His long legs doubled and his knees thrust up sharply. He looked like a squashed grasshopper. He panted.

"About the watch," she prompted him.

He panted twice as fast for three breaths and whimpered. "I don't want no trouble, lady, just lemme go, huh?"

She pointed at his wrist.

"Awright, you want the watch?" Hysterically he stripped it off and dangled it toward her. "Okay? Take it." His eyes were round and frightened and wary. When she made no move he put the watch on her ancient gateleg table. He put his palms on the seat of the chair and his feet walked two paces doorward, though he did not rise, but swiveled around, keeping his face to her, eager, terrified.

"Where did you get it?"

He whimpered, wordless. He cast one quick, hungry

look at the door, tensed his muscles, met her gaze again, and slumped. "You gonna turn me in?"

"Of course not!" she said with more force than she had used so far.

"You're goin' to, all the same."

She simply shoook her head, and waited.

He turned, finally, picked up the watch, snapped the flexible gold band. "I swiped it—off Eckhart," he whispered.

"Who?"

"Eckhart on Summit Av-noo. He lives behind the store. It was just laying there, on the counter. I put a box of groceries on it and snagged it out from under. You gonna tell?"

"Well, Donny! Don't you feel better, now you've confessed?"

He looked up at her through his eyebrows, hesitated. "Yeah."

"Is that the truth, Donny?"

"Uh-huh." Then, meeting those calm, imponderable eyes, he said, "Well, no. I dunno, lady. I dunno. You got me all mixed up. Can I go now?"

"What about the watch?"

"I don't want it no more."

"I want you to take it back where you got it."

"*What?*" He recoiled, primarily because in shock he had raised his voice and the sound of it frightened him. "Je— shucks, lady, you want him to put me in the can?"

"My name is Miss Phoebe, not 'lady.' No, Donny, I think you'll do it. Just a moment."

She sat at a shaky escritoire and wrote for a moment, while he watched. Presently, "Here," she said. She handed him the sheet. He looked at her and then at the paper.

Dear Mr. Eckhart,
Inside the clasp of this watch your name and address is stamped.

Would you be good enough to see that it gets to its rightful owner?

Yours very truly,
(Miss) Phoebe Watkins

She took it out of his hand, folded it. She put the watch in an envelope, folded that neatly into a square, dropped it in a second envelope with the note, sealed it and handed it to Don.

"You—you're givin' it right back to me!"

"Am I?"

He lowered his eyes, pinched the top edge of the envelope, pulled it through his fingers to crease the top edge sharply. "I know. You're gonna phone him. You're gonna get me picked up."

"You would be no good to me in the reformatory, Donny."

He looked quickly at her eyes, one, then the other. "I'm gonna be some good to you?"

"Tomorrow at four, I want you to come to tea," she said abruptly.

"To what?"

"To tea. That means wash your face and hands, put on a tie and don't be late."

Wash your face and hands. Nobody had dared to order him around like that for years. And yet, instead of resentment, something sharp and choking rose up in his throat. It was not anger. It was something which, when swallowed, made his eyes wet. He frowned and blinked hard.

"You'd better go," she said, before he could accept or refuse, "before the stores close." She didn't even say which stores.

He rose. He pulled his shoulderblades together and his back cracked audibly. He winced, shambled to the door and stood waiting—not touching it, head down, patient—like a farm horse before a closed gate.

"What is it, Donny?"

"Ain'tcha gonna unlock it?"

"It was never locked."

For a long moment he stood frozen, his back to her, his eyes down. Then he put a slow hand to the knob, turned it. The door opened. He went out, almost but not quite pausing at the threshold, almost but not quite turning to look back. He closed the door quietly and was gone.

She put her groceries away.

He did not come at four o'clock.

He came at four minutes before the hour, and he was breathing hard.

"Come in, Donny!" She held the door for him. He looked over his shoulder, down the corridor, at the elevator gates and the big window where feathery trees and the wide sky showed, and then he came into the room. He stood just inside, watching her as she moved to the kitchenette. He looked around the room, looking for policemen, perhaps, for bars on the windows.

There was nothing in the room but its old-not-antique furniture, the bow-legged occasional chair with the new upholstery which surely looked as old as it had before it was redone; there was the gateleg table, now bearing a silver tea-service with a bit of brass showing at the shoulder of the hot-water-pot, and a sugar-bowl with delicate tongs which did not match the rest of the set. There was the thin rug with its nap quite swept off, and the dustless books; there was the low chair where he had sat before with its tassled antimacassars on back and arms.

"Make yourself at home," said her quiet voice, barely competing, but competing easily with the susurrus of steam that rose from the kettle.

He moved a little further in and stopped awkwardly. His Adam's apple loomed mightily over the straining button of his collar. His tie was blue and red, and he wore a horrendous sport-jacket, much too small, with a violent yellow-and-gray tweed weave. His trousers were the color of baked earth, and had as much crease as his shoes had shine, and their soles had more polish than the uppers. But he'd scrubbed his face almost raw, and his hair was raked back so hard that his forehead gleamed like scoured porcelain.

When she faced him he stood his ground and said abruptly, before she could tell him to sit down, "I din' wanna come."

"Didn't you?"

"Well, I did, but I wasn' gonna."

"Why did you come, then?"

"I wuz scared not to."

She crossed the room with a large platter of little sandwiches. There were cheese and Spam and egg salad and liverwurst. They were not delicacies; they were food. She put it down next to a small store-bought chocolate cake and two bowls of olives, one ripe, one green, neither stuffed.

She said, "You had nothing to be afraid of."

"No, huh?" He wet his lips, took a deep breath. The rehearsed antagonism blurted out. "You done something to me yesterday I don't know what it was. How I know I ain't gonna drop dead if I don't show up or somep'n like that?"

"I did nothing to you, child!"

"Somebuddy sure as h— sure did."

"You did it to yourself."

"*What?*"

She looked at him. "Angry people don't live very long, Donny, did you know? But sometimes—" Her eyes fell to her hand on the table, and his followed. With one small age-mottled finger she traced around the table's edge, from the far side around one end. "—Sometimes it takes a long time to hurt them. But the hurt can come short and quickly, like *this!*" and she drew her finger straight across from side to side.

Don looked at the table as if something were written on it in a strange language. "Awight, but you made it do that."

"Come and sit down," she said.

But he hadn't finished. "I took the watch back."

"I knew you would."

"Well, okay then. Thass what I come to tell you. That's what you wanted me for, isn't it?"

"I asked you to *tea*. I didn't want to bully you and I didn't want to discuss that silly watch—that matter is closed. It was closed yesterday. Now *do* come and sit down."

"Oh," he said. "I get it. You mean sit down *or else*."

She fixed her eyes on his and looked at him without speaking and without any expression at all until his gaze dropped. "Donny, go and open the door."

He backed away, felt behind him for the knob. He paused there, tense. When she nodded he opened it.

"You're free to go whenever you like. But before you do, I want you to understand that there are a lot of people I could have tea with. I haven't asked anyone but you. I haven't asked the grocery boy or the thief or any of the other people you seem to be sometimes. Just *you*."

He pulled the door to and stood yanking at his bony knuckles. "I don't know about none of that," he said confusedly. He glanced down between his ribs and his elbow at the doorknob. "I just din' want you to think you hadda put on no feedbag to fin' out did I take the watch back."

"I could have telephoned to Mr. Eckhart."

"Well, din't you?"

"Certainly not. There was no need. Was there?"

He came and sat down.

"Sugar?"

"Huh? Yeah—yeah."

"Lemon, or cream?"

"You mean I can have whichever?"

"Of course."

"Then both."

"Both? I think perhaps the cream would curdle."

"In lemon ice cream it don't."

She gave him cream. He drank seven cups of tea, ate all the sandwiches and most of the cake. He ate quickly, not quite glancing over his shoulder to drive away enemies who might snatch the food. He ate with a hunger that was not of hours or days, but the hunger of years. Miss Phoebe patiently passed and refilled and stoked and served until he was done. He loosened his belt, spread out his long legs, wiped his mouth with one sleeve and his brow with the other, closed his eyes and sighed.

"Donny," she said when his jaws had stopped moving, "have you ever been to a bawdy house?"

The boy literally and immediately fell out of his chair. In this atmosphere of doilies and rectitude he could not have been more jolted by a batted ball on his mountainous Adam's apple. He floundered on the carpet, bumped the table, slopped her tea, and crawled back into his seat with his face flaming.

"No," he said, in a strangled voice.

She began then to talk to him quite calmly about social ills of many kinds. She laid out the grub and smut and greed and struggle of his own neighborhood streets as neatly and as competently as she had laid the tea-table.

She spoke without any particular emphasis of the bawdy house she had personally closed up, after three reports to the police had no effect. (She had called the desk-sergeant, stated her name and intentions, and had asked to be met at the house in twenty minutes. When the police got there she had the girls lined up and two-thirds of their case-histories already written.) She spoke of playgrounds and civil defense, of pool-rooms, dope-pushers, candy-stores with beer-taps in the soda-fountains and the visiting nurse service.

Don listened, fairly humming with reaction. He had seen all the things she mentioned, good and bad. Some he had not understood, some he had not thought about, some he wouldn't dream of discussing in mixed company. He knew vaguely that things were better than they had been twenty, fifty, a hundred years ago, but he had never before been face to face with one of those who integrate, correlate, extrapolate this progress, who dirty their hands on this person or that in order to work for people.

Sometimes he bit the insides of his cheeks to keep from laughing at her bluntness and efficiency—he wished he could have seen that desk-sergeant's *face!*— or to keep from sniggering self-consciously at the way unmentionables rolled off her precise tongue. Sometimes he was puzzled and lost in the complexities of the organizations with which she was so familiar. And sometimes he was slackjawed with fear for her, thinking of the retribution she must surely be in the way of, breaking up rackets like that. But then his own aching back would remind him that she had ways of taking care of herself, and a childlike awe would rise in him.

There was no direct instruction in anything she said. It was purely description. And yet, he began to feel that in this complex lay duties for him to perform. Exactly what they might be did not emerge. It was simply that he felt, as never before, a functioning part, rather than an excrescence, of his own environment.

He was never to remember all the details of that extraordinary communion, nor the one which immediately followed; for somehow she had stopped speaking and there was a long quiet between them. His mind was so busy with itself that there seemed no break in this milling and chewing of masses of previously unregarded ideas.

For a time she had been talking, for a time she did not talk, and in it all he was completely submerged. At length she said, "Donny, tell me something ugly."

"What do you mean ugly?" The question and its answer had flowed through him almost without contact; had she not insisted, he would have lapsed into his busy silence.

"Donny, something that you know about that you've done. Anything at all. Something you've seen."

It was easy to turn from introspection to deep recalls. "Went to one of those summer camps that there paper runs for kids. I wus about seven, I guess."

"Donny," she said, after what may have been a long time, "go on."

"Wasps," he said, negotiating the divided sibilant with some difficulty. "The ones that make paper nests." Suddenly he turned quite pale. "They stung me, it was on the big porch. The nurse, she came out an' hugged me and went away and came back with a bottle, ammonia it was, and put it on where I was stung." He coughed. "Stuff stunk, but it felt fine. Then a counsellor, a big kid from up the street, he came with a long stick. There was a ol' rag tied on the end, it had kerosene on it. He lit it up with a match, it burned all yellow and smoky. He put it up high by them paper nests. The wasps, they come out howlin', they flew right into the fire. When they stopped comin' he pushed at the nest and down it come.

"He gone on to the next one, and down the line, twelve, fifteen of them. Every time he come to a new one the wasps they flew into the fire. You could see the wings go, not like burning, not like melting, sort of *fzzz!* they gone. They fall. They fall all over the floor, they wiggle around, some run like ants, some with they legs burned off they just go around in one place like a phonograph.

"Kids come from all over, watching bugeyed, runnin' around the porch, stampin' on them wasps with their wings gone, they can't sting nobody. Stamp on 'em and squeal and run away an' run back and stamp some more. I'm back near the door, I'm bawlin'. The nurse is squeezin' me, watchin' the wasps, wipin' the ammonia on me any old place, she's not watchin' what she's doin'.

"An' all the time the fire goes an' goes, the wasps fly at it, never once a dumb damn wasp goes to see who's at the other end of the stick. An' I'm there with the nurse, bawlin'. *Why am I bawlin'?*" It came out a deep, basic demand.

"You must have been stung quite badly," said Miss Phoebe. She was leaning forward, her strange unlovely eyes fixed on him. Her lower lip was wet.

"Nah! Three times, four . . ." He struggled hard to fit rich sensation to a poverty of words. "It was me, see. I guess if I got stung every wasp done it should get killed. Maybe burned even. But them wasps in the nest-es, they din't sting nobody, an' here they are all . . . all *brave,* that's what, brave, comin' and fallin' and comin' and fallin' and gettin' squashed. Why? Fer *me,* thass why! Me, it was me, I hadda go an' holler because I got stung an' make all that happen." He screwed his eyes tight shut and breathed as if he had been running. Abruptly his eyes opened very wide and he pressed himself upward in his chair, stretching his long bony neck as if he sat in rising water up to his chin. "What am I talkin' about, wasps? We wasn't talkin' about no wasps. How'd we get talkin' like this?"

She said, "It's all part of the same thing." She waited for him to quiet down. He seemed to, at last. "I asked you to tell me something ugly, and you did. Did it make you feel better?"

He looked at her strangely. *Wasn't there something—oh, yes. Yesterday, about the watch. She made him tell and then asked if he didn't feel better. Was she getting back to that damn watch? I guess not,* he thought, and for some reason felt very ashamed. "Yeah, I feel some better." He looked into himself, found that what he had just said was true, and started in surprise. "Why should that be?" he asked, and it was the first time in his whole life he had asked such a question.

"There's two of us carrying it now," she explained.

He thought, and then protested, "There was twenty people there."

"Not one of them knew why you were crying."

Understanding flashed in him, bloomed almost to revelation. "God damn," he said softly.

This time she made no comment. Instead she said, "You learned something about bravery that day, didn't you?"

"Not until . . . now."

She shrugged. "That doesn't matter. As long as you understand, it doesn't matter how long it takes. Now, if all that happened just to make you understand something about bravery, it isn't an ugly thing at all, is it?"

He did not answer, but his very silence was a response.

"Perhaps one day you will fly into the fire and burn your wings and die, because it's all you can do to save something dear to you," she said softly. She let him think about that for a moment and then said, "Perhaps you will be a flame yourself, and see the brave ones fly at you and lose their wings and die. Either way, you'd know a little better what you were doing, because of the wasps, wouldn't you?"

He nodded.

"The playgrounds," she said, "the medicines, the air-raid watching, the boys' clubs, everything we were discussing . . . each single one of them kills something to do its work, and sometimes what is killed is very brave. It isn't easy to know good from evil."

"*You* know," he blurted.

"Ah," she said, "but there's a reason for that. You'd better go now, Donny."

Everything she had said flew to him as she spoke it, rested lightly on him, soaked in while he waited, and in time found a response. This was no exception. When he understood what she had said he jumped up, guiltily covering the thoughtful and receptive self with self-consciousness like a towel snatched up to cover nakedness.

"Yeah I got to, what time is it?" he muttered. "Well," he said, "yeah. I guess I should." He looked about him as if he had forgotten some indefinable thing, turned and gave her a vacillating smile and went to the door. He opened it and turned. Silently and with great difficulty his mouth moved. He pressed the lips together.

"Good-by, Donny."

"Yeah. Take it easy," he said.

As he spoke he saw himself in the full-length mirror fixed to the closet door. His eyes widened. It was himself he saw there—no doubt of that. But there was no sharpcut, seam-strained sports jacket, no dull and tattered shoes, no slickeddown hair, smooth in front and down-pointing shag at the nape. In the reflection, he was dressed in a dark suit. The coat matched the trousers. The tie was a solid color, maroon, and was held by a clasp so low down that it could barely be seen in the V of the jacket. The shoes gleamed, not like enamel but like the sheen of a new black-iron frying pan.

He gasped and blinked, and in that second the reflection told him only that he was what he was, flashy and clumsy and very much out of place here. He turned one long scared glance on Miss Phoebe and bolted through the door.

Don quit his job at the market. He quit jobs often, and usually needed no reason, but he had one this time. The idea of delivering another package to Miss Phoebe made him sweat, and the sweat was copious and cold. He did not know if it was fear or awe or shame, because he did not investigate the revulsion. He acknowledged it and acted upon it and otherwise locked the broad category labeled "Miss Phoebe" in the most guarded passages of his mind.

He was, unquestionably, haunted. Although he refused to acknowledge its source, he could not escape what can only be described as a sense of function. When he sharked around the pool-halls to pick up some change—he carried ordinary seaman's papers, so could get a forty-cent bed at the Seaman's Institute—

he was of the nonproductive froth on the brackish edges of a backwater, and he knew it acutely.

When he worked as helper in a dockside shop, refurbishing outdated streetcars to be shipped to South America, his hand was unavoidably a link in a chain of vision and enterprise starting with an idea and ending with a peasant who, at this very moment, walked, but who would inevitably ride. Between that idea and that shambling peasant were months and miles and dollars, but the process passed through Don's hands every time they lifted a wrench, and he would watch them with mingled wonder and resentment.

He was a piece of nerve-tissue becoming aware of the proximity of a ganglion, and dimly conscious of the existence, somewhere, of a brain. His resentment stemmed from a nagging sense of loss. In ignorance he had possessed a kind of freedom—he'd have called it loneliness while he had it—which in retrospect filled him with nostalgia. He carried his inescapable sense of *belonging* like a bundle of thorns, light but most irritating. It was with him in drunkenness and the fights, the movies and the statistical shoutings of the baseball season. He never slept, but was among those who slept. He could not laugh without the realization that he was among the laughers. He no longer moved in a static universe, or rested while the world went by, for his every action had too obvious a reaction. Unbidden, his mind made analogies to remind him of this invert-unwanted duality.

The street, he found, pressed upward to his feet with a force equal to his weight. A new job and he approached one another with an equal magnetism, and he lost it or claimed it not by his effort or lack of it, but by an intricate resultant compounded of all the forces working with him matched against those opposed.

On going to bed he would remove one shoe, and wake from a reverie ten minutes later to find with annoyance that he had sat motionless all that time to contemplate the weight of the shoe versus the upward force of the hand that held it. No birth is painless, and the stirrings of departure from a reactive existence are most troubling, since habit opposes it and there is no equipment to define the motivating ambition.

His own perceptions began to plague him. There had been a time when he was capable of tuning out that which did not concern him. But whatever it was that was growing within him extended its implacable sense of kinship to more areas than those of human endeavor. *Why*, he would ask himself insistently, *is the wet end of a towel darker than the dry end? What do spiders do with their silk when they climb up a single strand? What makes the brows of so many big executives tilt downward from the center?*

He was not a reader, and though he liked to talk, his wharf-rat survival instinct inhibited him from talking "different" talk, which *is* what his "different" questions would be, for one does not expose oneself to the sharp teeth of raillery.

He found an all-night cafe where the talk was as different as the talkers could make it; where girls who were unsure of their difference walked about with cropped hair and made their voices boom, and seedy little polyglots surreptitiously ate catsup and sugar with their single interminable cup of coffee; where a lost man could exchange his broken compass for a broken oar.

He went there night after night, sitting alone and listening, held by the fact that many of these minds were genuinely questing. Armed with his strange understanding of opposites, he readily recognized those on one side or the other of forces which most naturally oppose one another, but since he could admire neither phrasing nor intensity for their own sakes, he could only wonder at the misery of these children perched so lonesomely on their dialectical seesaws, mourning the fact that they did not get off the ground while refusing to let anyone get on the other end.

Once he listened raptly to a man with a bleeding ear who seemed to understand the things he felt, but instead of believing many things, this man believed in nothing. Don went away, sad, wondering if there were anyone anywhere who cared importantly that when you yawn, an Italian will ask you if you're hungry while a Swede will think you need sleep; or that only six parallel cuts on a half-loaf of bread will always get you seven slices.

So for many months he worked steadily so that his hands could drain off tensions and let him think. When he had worked through every combination and permutation of which he was capable, he could cast back and discover that all his thoughts had stemmed from Miss Phoebe. His awe and fear of her ceased to exist when he decided to go back, not to see her, but to get more material.

A measure of awe returned, however, when he phoned. He heard her lift the receiver, but she did not say "Hello." She said, "Why, Don! How are you?"

He swallowed hard and said, "Good, Miss Phoebe."

"Four o'clock tomorrow," she said, and hung up.

He put the receiver back carefully and stood looking at the telephone. He worked the tip of the finger-stop under his thumbnail and stood for a long time in the booth, carefully cleaning away the thin parenthesis of oily grime which had defied his brush that morning. When it was gone, so was his fright, but it took a long time. *I've forgotten it all right*, he thought, *but oh, my aching back!*

Belatedly he thought, *Why, she called me Don, not Donny.*

He went back to the cafe that night, feeling a fine new sense of insulation. He had so much to look forward to that searches could wait. And like many a searcher before him, he found what he was looking for as soon as he stopped looking. It was a face that could not have drawn him more if it had been luminous, or leaf-green. It was a face with strong and definite lines, with good pads of laughter-muscles under the cheek-bones, and eye-sockets shaped to catch and hold laughter early and long. Her hair was long and seemed black, but its highlights were not blue but red. She sat with six other people around a large table, her eyes open and sleeping, her mouth lax and miserable.

He made no attempt to attract her attention, or to join the group. He simply watched her until she left, which was some three or four hours later. He followed her and so did another man. When she turned up the steps of a brownstone a few blocks away the man followed her, and was halfway up the steps when she was at the top, fumbling for a key. When Don stopped, looking up, the man saw him and whirled. He blocked Don's view of the girl. To Don he was not a person at all, but something in the way.

Don made an impatient, get-out-of-the-way gesture with his head, and only then realized that the man was at bay, terrified, caught red-handed. His eyes were round and he drooled. Don stood, looking upward, quite astonished, as the man sidled down, glaring, panting, and suddenly leaped past him and pelted off down the street.

Don looked from the shadowed, dwindling figure to the lighted doorway. The girl had both hands on the side of the outer, open doorway and was staring down at him with bright unbelief in her face. "Oh, dear God," she said.

Don saw that she was frightened, so he said, "It's all right." He stayed where he was.

She glanced down the street where the man had gone and found it empty. Slowly, she came toward Don and stopped on the third step above him. "Are you an angel?" she asked. In her voice was a childlike eagerness and the shadow of the laughter that her face was made for.

Don made a small, abashed sound. "Me? Not me."

She looked down the street and shuddered. "I

thought I didn't care any more *what* happened," she said, as if she were not speaking to him at all. Then she looked at him. "Anyway, thanks. Thanks. I don't know what he might've . . . if you . . ."

Don writhed under her clear, sincere eyes. "I didn't do nothing." He backed off a pace. "What do you mean, am I a angel?"

"Didn't you ever hear about a guardian angel?"

He had, but he couldn't find it in himself to pursue such a line of talk. He had never met anyone who talked like this. "Who was that guy?"

"He's crazy. They had him locked up for a long time, he hurt a little girl once. He gets like that once in a while."

"Well, you want to watch out," he said.

She nodded gravely. "I guess I care after all," she said. "I'll watch out."

"Well, take it easy," he said.

She looked quickly at his face. His words had far more dismissal in them than he had intended, and he suddenly felt miserable. She turned and slowly climbed the steps. He began to move away because he could think of nothing else to do. He looked back over his shoulder and saw her in the doorway, facing him. He thought she was going to call out, and stopped. She went inside without speaking again, and he suddenly felt very foolish. He went home and thought about her all night and all the next day. He wondered what her name was.

When he pressed the buzzer, Miss Phoebe did not come to the door immediately. He stood there wondering if he should buzz again or go away or what. Then the door opened. "Come in, Don."

He stepped inside, and though he thought he had forgotten about the strange mirror, he found himself looking for it even before he saw Miss Phoebe's face. It was still there, and in it he saw himself as before, with the dark suit, the quiet tie, the dull, clean-buffed shoes. He saw it with an odd sense of disappointment, for it had given him such a wondrous shock before, but now reflected only what a normal mirror would, since he was wearing such a suit and tie and shoes, but wait—the figure in the reflection carried something and he did not. A paper parcel . . . a wrapped bunch of flowers; not a florist's elaboration, but tissue-wrapped jonquils from a subway peddler. He blinked, and the reflection was now quite accurate again.

All this took place in something over three seconds. He now became aware of a change in the room, *it's—oh, the light*. It had been almost glary with its jewel-clean windows and scrubbed white woodwork, but now it was filled with mellow orange light. Part of this was sunlight struggling through the inexpensive blinds, which were drawn all the way down. Part was something else he did not see until he stepped fully into the room and into the range of light from the near corner. He gasped and stared, and, furiously, he felt tears rush into his eyes so that the light wavered and ran.

"Happy birthday, Don," said Miss Phoebe severely.

Don said, "Aw." He blinked hard and looked at the little round cake with its eighteen five-and-dime candles. "Aw."

"Blow them out quickly," she said. "They run."

He bent over the cake.

"Every one, mind," she said. "In one breath."

He blew. All the candles went out but one. He had no air left in his lungs, and he looked at the candle in purple panic. In a childlike way, he could not bring himself to break the rules she had set up. His mouth yawped open and closed like that of a beached fish. He puffed his cheeks out by pushing his tongue up and forward, leaned very close to the candle, and released the air in his mouth with a tiny explosive pop. The candle went out.

"Splendid. Open the blinds for me like a good boy."

He did as he was asked without resentment. As she

plucked the little sugar candle-holders out of the cake, he said, "How'd you know it was my birthday?"

"Here's the knife. You must cut it first, you know."

He came forward. "It's real pretty. I never had no birthday cake before."

"I'm glad you like it. Hurry now. The tea's just right."

He busied himself, serving and handing and receiving and setting down, moving chairs, taking sugar. He was too happy to speak.

"Now then," she said when they were settled. "Tell me what you've been up to."

He assumed she knew, but if she wanted him to say, why, he would. "I'm a typewriter mechanic now," he said. "I like it fine. I work nights in big offices and nobody bothers me none. How've you been?"

She did not answer him directly, but her serene expression said that nothing bad could ever happen to her. "And is that all? Just work and sleep?"

"I been thinkin'," he said. He looked at her curiously. "I thought a lot about what you said." She did not respond. "I mean about everything working on everything else, an' the wasps and all." Again she was silent, but now there was response in it.

He said, "I was all mixed up for a long time. Part of the time I was mad. I mean, like you're working for a boss who won't let up on you, thinks he owns you just because you work there. Used to be I thought about whatever I wanted to, I could stop thinkin' like turnin' a light off."

"Very apt," she remarked. "It was exactly that."

He waited while this was absorbed. "After I was here I couldn't turn off the light; the switch was busted. The more I worked on things, the more mixed up they got." In a moment he added, "For a while."

"What things?" she asked.

"Hard to say," he answered honestly. "I never had nobody to tell me much, but I had some things pretty straight. It's wrong to swipe stuff. It's right to do what they tell you. It's right to go to church."

"It's right to worship," she interjected. "If you can worship in a church, that's the best place to do it. If you can worship better in another place, then that's where you should go instead."

"*That's* what I mean!" he barked, pointing a bony finger like a revolver. "You say something like that, so sure and easy, an' all the—the fences go down. Everything's all in the right box, see, an' you come along and shake everything together. You don't back off from nothing. You say what you want about anything, an' you let me say anything I want to you. Everything I ever thought was right or wrong could be wrong or right. Like those wasps dyin' because of me, and you say they maybe died *for* me, so's I could learn something. Like you sayin' I could be a wasp or a fire, an' still know what was what . . . I'll get mixed up again if I go on talkin' about it."

"I think not," she said, and he felt very pleased. She said, "It's in the nature of things to be 'shaken all together,' as you put it. A bird brings death to a worm and a wildcat brings death to the bird. Can we say that what struck the worm and the bird was evil, when the wildcat's kittens took so much good from it? Or if the murder of the worm is good, can we call the wildcat evil?"

"There isn't no . . . no *altogether* good or bad, huh."

"Now, that is a very wrong thing to say," she said with soft-voiced asperity.

"You gone an' done it again!" he exclaimed.

She did not smile with him. "There is an absolute good and an absolute evil. They cannot be confused with right and wrong, or building and destroying as we know them, because, like the cat and the worm, those things depend on whose side you take. Don, I'm going to show you something very strange and wonderful."

She went to her little desk and got pencil and paper.

She drew a circle, and within it she sketched in an S-shaped line. One side of this line she filled in with quick short strokes of her pencil:

"This," she said, as Don pored over it, "is the most ancient symbol known to man. It's called 'yin and yang.' 'Yin' is the Chinese term for darkness and earth. 'Yang' means light and sky. Together they form the complete circle—the universe, the cosmos—everything. Nothing under heaven can be altogether one of these things or the other. The symbol means light and dark. It means birth and death. It is everything which holds together and draws down, with everything that pours out and disperses. It is male and female, hope and history, love and hate. It's—everything there is or could be. It's why you can't say the murder of a worm by a bird is good or evil."

"This here yin an' yang's in everything we do, huh."

"Yes."

"It's God an' the Devil then."

"*Good* and *evil*." She placed her hand over the entire symbol. "God is all of it."

"Well, all right!" he exclaimed. "So it's like I said. There ain't a 'altogether good' and a 'altogether bad'. Miss Phoebe, how you know you're right when you bust up some pusher's business or close a joint?"

"There's a very good way of knowing, Don. I'm very glad you asked me that question." She all but beamed at him—she, who hardly ever even smiled. "Now listen carefully. I am going to tell you something which it took me many years to find out. I am going to tell you because I do not see why the young shouldn't use it.

"Good and evil are active forces—almost like living things. I said that nothing under heaven can be completely one of these things or the other, and it's true. But, Don—good and evil come to us from *somewhere*. They reach this cosmos as living forces, constantly replenished—from *somewhere*. It follows that there is a Source of good and a Source of evil . . . or call them light and dark, or birth and death if you like."

She put her finger on the symbol. "Human beings, at least with their conscious wills, try to live here, in the yang part. Many find themselves on the dark side, some cross and recross the borderline. Some set a course for themselves and drive it straight and true, and never understand that the border itself turns and twists and will have them in one side and then the other.

"In any case, these forces are in balance, and they must remain so. But as they are living, vital forces, there must be those who willingly and purposefully work with them."

With his thumbnail he flicked the paper. "From this, everything's so even-steven you'd never know who you're working for."

"Not true, Don. There are ways of knowing."

He opened his lips and closed them, turned away, shaking his head.

"You may ask me, Don," she said.

"Well, okay. You're one of 'em. Right?"

"Perhaps so."

"Perhaps *nothing*. You knocked me flat on my noggin twice in a row an' never touched me. You're—you're somethin' special, that's for sure. You even knew about my birthday. You know who's callin' when the phone rings."

"There are advantages."

"All right then, here's what I'm gettin' to, and I

don't want you to get mad at me. What I want to
know is, why ain't you rich?"

"What do you mean by *rich?*"

He kicked the table-leg gently. "Junk," he said. He
waved at the windows. "Everybody's got venetian
blinds now. Look there, cracks in the ceiling 'n' you'll
get a rent rise if you complain, long as it ain't leakin'.
You know, if I could do the things you do, I'd have me
a big house an' a car. I'd have flunkies to wash dishes
an' all like that."

"I wouldn't be rich if I had all those things, Don."

He looked at her guardedly. He knew she was capable of a preachment, though he had been lucky so far.
"Miss Phoebe," he said respectfully, "You ain't goin'
to tell me the—uh—inner riches is better'n a fishtail
Cadillac."

"I'll ask *you,*" she said patiently. "Would you want
a big house and servants and all those things?"

"Well, *sure!*"

"Why?"

"Why? Well, because, because—well, that's the way
to live, that's all."

"Why is it the way to live?"

"Well, anyone can see why."

"Don, answer the question! Why is that the way to
live?"

"Well," he said. He made a circular gesture and put
his hand down limply. He wet his lips. "Well, because
you'd have what you wanted." He looked at her hope-
fully and realized he'd have to try again. "You could
make anyone do what you wanted."

"Ah," she said. "Why would you want to do that?"

"So you wouldn't have to do your own work."

"Aside from personal comfort—why would you
want to be able to tell other people what to do?"

"You tell me," he said with some warmth.

"The answers are in you if you'll only look, Don.
Tell me: Why?"

He considered. "I guess it'd make me feel good."

"Feel good?"

"The boss. The Man. You know. I say jump, they jump."

"Power?"

"Yeah, that's it, power."

"Then you want riches so you'll have a sense of power."

"You're in."

"And you wonder why I don't want riches. Don, I've *got* power. Moreover, it was given me and it's mine. I needn't buy it for the rest of my life."

"Well, now . . ." he breathed.

"You can't imagine power in any other terms than cars and swimming pools, can you?"

"Yes I can," he said instantly. Then he grinned and added, "But not yet."

"I think that's more true than you know," she said, giving him her sparse smile. "You'll come to understand it."

They sat in companionable silence. He picked up a crumb of cake icing and looked at it. "Real good cake," he murmured, and ate it. Almost without change of inflection, he said, "I got a real ugly one to tell you."

She waited, in the responsive silence he was coming to know so well.

"Met a girl last night."

He was not looking at her and so did not see her eyes click open, round and moist. He hooked his heel in the chair rung and put his fist on the raised knee, thumb up. He lowered his head until the thumb fitted into the hollow at the bridge of his nose. Resting his head precariously there, rolling it slightly from time to time as if he perversely enjoyed the pressure and the ache, he began to speak. And if Miss Phoebe found surprising the leaps from power to birthday cake to a girl to what happened in the sewer, she said nothing.

"Big sewer outlet down under the docks at Twenty-seventh," he said. "Wuz about nine or ten, playing

there. Kid called Renzo. We were inside the pipe; it
was about five feet high, and knee-deep in storm water. Saw somethin' bobbin' in the water, got close
enough to look. It was the hind feet off a dead rat, a
great big one, and *real* dead. Renzo, he was over by
the outlet tryin' to see if he could get up on a towboat
out there, and I thought it might be fine if I could
throw the rat on his back on account he didn't have
no shirt on. I took hold of the rat's feet and pulled,
but that rat, he had his head stuck in a side-pipe somehow, an' I guess he swole some too. I guess I said something and Renzo he come over, so there was nothin'
for it then but haul the rat out anyway. I got a good
hold and yanked, an' something popped an' up he
came. I pulled 'im right out of his skin. There he was
wet an' red an' bare an' smellin' a good deal. Renzo,
he lets out a big holler, laughin', I can still hear it in
that echoey pipe. I'm standin' there like a goofball,
starin' at this rat. Renzo says, 'Hit'm quick, Doc, or
he'll never start breathin'!' I just barely got the idea
when the legs come off the rat an' it fell in the water
with me still holdin' the feet."

It was very quiet for a while. Don rocked his head,
digging his thumb into the bridge of his nose. "Renzo
and me we had a big fight after. He tol' everybody I
had a baby in the sewer. He tol' 'em I's a firstclass
stork. They all started to call me Stork, I hadda fight
five of 'em in two days before they cut it out.

"Kid stuff," he said suddenly, too loudly, and sat
upright, wide-eyed, startled at the sound. "I know it
was kid stuff, I can forget it. But it won't . . . it won't
forget."

Miss Phoebe stirred, but said nothing.

Don said, "Girls. I never had nothing much to do
with girls, kidded 'em some if there was somebody
with me started it, and like that. Never by myself. I
tell you how it is, it's—" He was quiet for a long moment. His lips moved as if he were speaking silently,
words after words until he found the words he wanted.

He went on in precisely the same tone, like an interrupted tape recorder.

"—Like this, I get so I like a girl a whole lot, I want to get close to her, I think about her like any fellow does. So before I can think much about it, let alone *do* anything, zing! I'm standin' in that stinkin' sewer, Renzo's yellin' 'Hit'm quick, Doc,' an' all the rest of it." He blew sharply from his nostrils. "The better a girl smells," he said hoarsely, "the worse it is. So I think about girls, I think about rats, I think about babies, it's Renzo and me and that echo. Laughin'," he mumbled, "him laughin'.

"I met a girl last night," he said clearly. "I don't want ever to think about like that. I walked away. I don't know what her name is. I want to see her some more. I'm afraid. So that's why."

After a while he said, "That's why I told you."

And later, "You were a big help before, the wasps." As he spoke he realized that there was no point in hurrying her; she had heard him the first time and would wait until she was ready. He picked up another piece of icing, crushed it, tossed the pieces back on the plate.

"You never asked me," said Miss Phoebe, "about the power I have, and how it came to me."

"Din't think you'd say. I wouldn't, if I had it. This girl was—"

"Study," said Miss Phoebe. "More of it than you realize. Training and discipline and, I suppose, a certain natural talent which," she said, fixing him sternly with her eyes as he was about to interrupt, "I am sure you also have. To a rather amazing degree. I have come a long way, a long hard way, and it isn't so many years ago that I first began to feel this power . . . I like to think of you with it, young and strong and . . . and good, growing greater, year by year. Don, would you like the power? Would you work hard and patiently for it?"

He was very quiet. Suddenly he looked up at her. "What?"

She said—and for once the control showed—"I thought you might want to answer a question like that."

He scratched his head and grinned. "Gee, I'm sorry, Miss Phoebe, but for that one second I was thinkin' about . . . something else, I guess. Now," he said brightly, "what was it you wanted to know?"

"What was this matter you found so captivating?" she asked heavily. "I must say I'm not used to talking to myself, Don."

"Ah, don't jump salty, Miss Pheobe," he said contritely. "I'll pay attention, honest. It's just that I—you din't say *one* word about what I told you. I guess I was tryin' to figure it out by myself if you wasn't goin' to help."

"Perhaps you didn't wait long enough."

"Oh." He looked at her and his eyes widened. *"Oh!* I never thought of that. Hey, go ahead, will you? He drew his knees together and clasped them, turned to face her fully.

She nodded with a slightly injured satisfaction. "I asked you, Don, if you'd like the kind of power I have, for yourself."

"Me?" he demanded, incredulously.

"You. And I also asked you if you would work hard and patiently to get it. Would you?"

"Would I! Look, you don't really think, I mean, I'm just a—"

"We'll see," she said.

She glanced out the window. Dusk was not far away. The curtains hung limp and straight in the still air. She rose and went to the windows, drew the blinds down. The severe velour drapes were on cranes. She swung them over the windows. They were not cut full enough to cover completely, each window admitted a four-inch slit of light. But that side of the building was in shadow, and she turned back to find Don blinking in deep obscurity. She went back to her chair.

"Come closer," she said. "No, not that way—facing me. That's it. Your back to the window. Now, I'm going to cover my face. That's because otherwise the light would be on it; I don't want you to look at me or at anything but what you find inside yourself." She took a dark silk scarf from the small drawer in the end of the gateleg table. "Put your hands out. Palms down. So." She dropped the scarf over her face and hair, and felt for his hands. She slipped hers under his, palms upward, and leaned forward until she could grasp his wrists. "Hold mine that way too. Good. Be absolutely quiet."

He was.

She said, "There's something the matter. You're all tightened up. And you're not close enough. Don't move! I mean, in your mind . . . ah, I see. You'll have your questions answered. Just trust me." A moment later she said, "That's *much* better. There's something on your mind, though, a little something. Say it, whatever it is."

"I was thinkin', this is a trapeze grip, like in the circus."

"So it is! Well, it's a good contact. Now, don't think of anything at all. If you want to speak, well, do; but nothing will be accomplished until you no longer feel like talking.

"There is a school of discipline called yoga," she said quietly. "For years I have studied and practiced it. It's a lifetime's work in itself, and still it's only the first part of what I've done. It has to do with the harmony of the body and the mind, and the complete control of both. My breathing will sound strange to you. Don't be frightened, it's perfectly all right."

His hands lay heavily in hers. He opened his eyes and looked at her but there was nothing to see, just the black mass of her silk-shrouded head and shoulders in the dim light. Her breathing deepened. As he became more and more aware of other silences, her

breathing became more and more central in his attention. He began to wonder where she was putting it all;
an inhalation couldn't possibly continue for so long,
like the distant hiss of escaping steam. And when it
dwindled, the silence was almost too complete, for too
long: no one could hold such a deep breath for as long
as that! And when at last the breath began to come
out again, it seemed as if the slow hiss went on longer
even than the inhalation. If he had wondered where
she was putting it, he now wondered where she was
getting it.

And at last he realized that the breathing was not
deep at all, but shallow in the extreme; it was just that
the silence was deeper and her control greater than he
had imagined. His hands—

"It tingles. Like electric," he said aloud.

His voice did not disturb her in the least. She made
no answer in any area. The silence deepened, the darkness deepened, the tingling continued and grew . . .
not grew; it spread. When he first felt it, it had lived
in a spot on each wrist, where it contacted hers. Now it
uncoiled, sending a thin line of sensation up into his
forearms and down into his hands. He followed its
growth, fascinated. Around the center of each palm
the tingling drew a circle, and sent a fine twig of feeling growing into his fingers, and at the same time he
could feel it negotiating the turn of his elbows.

He thought it had stopped growing, and then realized that it had simply checked its twig-like creeping,
and was broadening: the line in his arms and fingers
was becoming a band, a bar of feeling. It crossed his
mind that if this bothered him at all he could pull his
hands away and break the contact, and that if he did
that Miss Phoebe would not resent it in any way. And,
since he knew he was free to do it, knew it without
question, he was not tempted. He sat quietly, wonder-
struck, tasting the experience.

With a small silent explosion there were the tingling, hair-thin lines of sensation falling like distant

fireworks through his chest and abdomen, infusing his loins and thighs and the calves of his legs. At the same time more of them crept upward through his neck and head, flared into and around his ears, settled and boiled and shimmered through his lobes and cheeks, curled and clasped the roots of his eyelids. And again there was the feeling of the lines broadening, fusing one with the other as they swelled. Distantly he recognized their ultimate; they would grow inward and outward until they were a complete thing, bounded exactly by everything he was, every hair, every contour, every thought and function.

He opened his eyes, and the growth was not affected. The dark mass of Miss Phoebe's head was where it had been, friendly and near and reassuring. He half-smiled, and the sparkling delicate little lines of feeling on his lips yielded to the smile, played in it like infinitesimal dolphins, gave happy news of it to all the other threads, and they all sang to his half-smile and gave him joy. He closed his eyes comfortably, and cheerful filaments reached for one another between his upper and lower lashes.

An uncountable time passed. Time now was like no time he knew of, drilling as it always had through event after event, predictable and dictatorial to rust, springtime, and the scissoring hands of clocks. This was a new thing, not a suspension, for it was too alive for that. It was different, that's all, different the way this feeling was, and now the lines and bands and bars were fused and grown, and he was filled . . . he was, himself, of a piece with what had once been the tingling of a spot on his wrist.

It was a feeling, still a feeling, but it was a substance too, Don-sized, Don-shaped. A color . . . no, it wasn't a color, but if it had been a color it was beginning to glow and change. It was glowing as steel glows in the soaking-pits, a color impossible to call black because it is red inside; and now you can see the red, and now the red has orange in it, and now in the orange is yellow, and when white shows in the yellow you may no longer look, but still the radiation beats through you, intensifying . . . not a color, no; this thing had no color and no light, but if it had been a color, this would have been its spectral growth.

And this was the structure, this the unnameable *something* which now found itself alive and joyous. It was from such a peak that the living thing rose as if from sleep, became conscious of its own balance and strength, and leaped heavenward with a single cry like all the satisfying, terminal resolving chords of all music, all uttered in a wingbeat of time.

Then it was over, not because it was finished, like music or a meal, but because it was perfect—like foam or a flower caught in the infrangible amber of memory. Don left the experience without surfeit, without tension, without exhaustion. He sat peacefully with his hands in Miss Phoebe's, not dazzled, not numb, replenished in some luxurious volume within him which kept what it gained for all of life, and which had an infinite capacity. But for the cloth over her face and the odd fact that their hands were dripping with perspiration, they might just that second have begun. It may even have been that second.

Miss Phoebe disengaged her hands and plucked away the cloth. She was smiling—really smiling, and Don understood why she so seldom smiled, if this were the expression she used for such experiences.

He answered the smile, and said nothing, because about perfect things nothing can be said. He went and dried his hands and then pulled back the drapes and raised the blinds while she straightened the chairs.

"The ancients," said Miss Phoebe, "recognized four elements: earth, air, fire and water. This power can do anything those four elements can do." She put down the clean cups, and went to get her crumb brush. "To start with," she added.

He placed the remark where it would soak in, and picked up a piece of icing from the cake plate. This time he ate it. "Why is a wet towel darker than a dry one?"

"I—why, I hadn't thought," she said. "It is, now that you mention it. I'm sure I don't know why, though."

"Well, maybe you know this," he said. "Why I been worrying about it so much?"

"Worrying?"

"You know what I mean. That and why most motors that use heat for power got to have a cooling system, and why do paper towels tear where they ain't perf'rated, and a zillion things like that. I never used to."

"Perhaps it's . . . yes, I know. Of *course!*" she said happily. "You're getting a—call it a kinship with things. A sense of interrelationship."

"Is that good?"

"I think it is. It means I was right in feeling that you have a natural talent for what I'm going to teach you."

"It takes up a lot of my time," he grumbled.

"It's good to be alive all the time," she said. She poured. "Don, do you know what a revelation is?"

"I heard of it."

"It's a sudden glimpse of the real truth. You had one about the wasps."

"I had it awful late."

"That doesn't matter. You had it, that's the important thing. You had one with the rat, too."

"I did?"

"With the wasps you had a revelation of sacrifice and courage. With the rat—well, you know yourself what effect it has had on you."

"I'm the only one I know has no girl," he said.

"That is exactly it."

"Don't tell me it's s'posed to be that way!"

"For you, I—I'd say so."

"Miss Phoebe, I don't think I know what you're talkin' about."

She looked at her teacup. "I've never been married."

"Me too," he said somberly. "Wait, is that what you—"

"Why do people get married?"

"Kids."

"Oh, that isn't all."

He said, with his mouth full, "They wanna be together, I guess. Team up, like. One pays the bills, the other runs the joint."

"That's about it. Sharing. They want to share. You know the things they share."

"I heard," he said shortly.

She leaned forward. "Do you think they can share anything like what we've had this afternoon?"

"*That* I never heard," he said pensively.

"I don't wonder. Don, your revelation with the rat is as basic a picture of what is called 'original sin' as anything I have ever heard."

"Original sin." he said thoughtfully. "That's about Adam an'—no, wait. I remember. Everybody's supposed to be sinful to start with because it takes a sin to get'm started."

"Once in a while," she said, "it seems as if you know so few words because you don't need them. That was beautifully put. Don, I think that awful thing that happened to you in the sewer was a blessing. I think it's a good thing, not a bad one. It might be bad for someone else, but not for you. It's kept you as you are, so far. I don't think you should try to forget it. It's a warning and a defense. It's a weapon against the 'yin' forces. You are a very special person, Don. You were made for better things than—than others."

"About the wasps," he said. "As soon as you started to talk I begun to feel better. About this, I don't feel better." He looked up to the point where the wall met the ceiling and seemed to be listening to his own last phrase. He nodded definitely. "I don't feel better. I feel worse."

She touched his arm. It was the only time she had

made such a gesture. "You're strong and growing and you're just eighteen." Her voice was very kind. "It would be a strange thing indeed if a young man your age didn't have his problems and struggles and tempta—I mean, battles. I'm sorry I can't resolve it for you, Don. I wish I could. But I know what's right. Don't I, Don, don't I?"

"Every time," he said glumly. "But I . . ." His gaze became abstracted.

She watched him anxiously. "Don't think about her," she whispered. "Don't. You don't have to. Don, do you know that what we did this afternoon was only the very beginning, like the first day of kindergarten?"

His eyes came back to her, bright.

"Yeah, huh. Hey, Miss Phoebe, how about that."

"When would you like to do some more?"

"Now?"

"Bless you, no! We both have things to do. And besides, you have to think. You know it takes time to think."

"Yeah, okay. When?"

"A week."

"Don't worry about me, I'll be here. Hey, I'm gonna be late for work."

He went to the door. "Take it easy," he said.

He went out and closed the door but before the latch clicked he pushed it open again. He crossed the room to her.

He said. "Hey, thanks for the birthday cake. It was . . ." His mouth moved as he searched. "It was a good birthday cake." He took her hand and shook it heartily. Then he was gone.

Miss Phoebe was just as pink as the birthday cake. To the closed door she murmured, "Take it easy."

Don was in a subway station two nights later, waiting for an express. The dirty concrete shaft is atypical and mysterious at half-past four in the morning. The platforms are unlittered and deserted, and there is a complete absence of the shattering roar and babble and bustle for which these urban entrails are built. An approaching train can be heard starting and running and stopping sometimes ten or twelve minutes before it pulls in, and a single set of footfalls on the mezzanine above will outlast it. The few passengers waiting seem always to huddle together near one of the wooden benches, and there seems to be a kind of inverse square law in operation, for the closer they approach one another the greater the casual unnoticing manners they affect, though they will all turn to watch someone walking toward them from two hundred feet away. And when angry voices bark out, the effect is more shocking than it would be in a cathedral.

A tattered man slept uneasily on the bench. Two women buzz-buzzed ceaselessly at the other end. A black-browed man in gray tweed strode the platform, glowering, looking as if he were expected to decide on the recall of the Ambassador to the Court of St. James by morning.

Don happened to be looking at the tattered man, and the way the old brown hat was pulled down over the face (it could have been a headless corpse, and no one would have been the wiser) when the body shuddered and stirred. A strip of stubbled skin emerged between the hat and the collar, and developed a mouth into which was stuffed a soggy collection of leaf-mold which may have been a cigar butt yesterday. The man's hand came up and fumbled around for the thing. The jaws worked, the lips smacked distastefully. The hand pushed the hatbrim up only enough to expose a red eye, which glared at the butt. The hat fell again, and the hand pitched the butt away.

At this point the black-browed man hove to, straddle-legged in front of the bench. He opened his coat and hooked his thumbs in the armholes of his waistcoat. He tilted his head back, half-closed his eyes, and sighted through the cleft on his chin at the huddled creature on the bench. "You!" he grated, and everyone swung around to stare at him. He thumped the sleeping man's ankle with the side of his foot. "You!" Everyone looked at the bench.

. The tattered man said "Whuh-wuh-wuh-wuh," and smacked his lips. Suddenly he was bolt upright, staring.

"You!" barked the black-browed man. He pointed to the butt. "Pick that up!"

The tattered man looked at him and down at the butt. His hand strayed to his mouth, felt blindly on and around it. He looked down again at the butt and dull recognition began to filter into his face. "Oh, sure, boss, sure," he whined. He cringed low, beginning to stoop down off the bench but afraid to stop talking, afraid to turn his gaze away from the danger point. "I don't make no trouble for anybody, mister, not me, honest I don't," he wheedled. "A feller gets down on his luck, you know how it is, but I never make trouble, mister . . ."

"Pick it up!"

"Oh sure, sure, right away, boss."

That was when Don, to his amazement, felt himself approaching the black-browed man. He tapped him on the shoulder.

"Mister," he said. He prayed that his tight voice would not break. "Mister, make *me* pick it up, huh?"

"*What?*"

Don waved at the tattered man. "A two-year-old kid could push him around. So what are you proving, you're a big man or something? Make *me* pick up the butt, you're such a big man."

"Get away from me," said the black-browed man. He took two quick paces backward. "I know what you are, you're one of those subway hoodlums."

Don caught a movement from the corner of his eye. The tattered man had one knee on the platform, and was leaning forward to pick up the butt. "Get away from that," he snapped, and kicked the butt onto the local tracks.

"Sure, boss, sure, I don't want no . . ."

"Get away from me, both of you," said the black-browed man. He was preparing for flight. Don suddenly realized that he was afraid—afraid that he and the tattered man might join forces, or perhaps even that they had set the whole thing up in advance. He laughed. The black-browed man backed into a pillar. And just then a train roared in, settling the matter.

Something touched Don between the shoulder-blades and he leaped as if it had been an icepick. But it was one of the women. "I just had to tell you, that was very brave. You're a fine young man," she said. She sniffed in the direction of the distant tweed-clad figure and marched to the train. It was a local. Don watched it go, and smiled. He felt good.

"Mister, you like to save my life, you did. I don't want no trouble, you unnerstan', I never do. Feller gets down on his luck once in a wh—"

"Shaddup!" said Don. He turned away and froze. Then he went back to the man and snatched off the old hat. The man cringed.

"I know who you are. You just got back from the can. You got sent up for attackin' a girl."

"I ain't done a *thing*," whispered the man. "Gimme back my hat, please, mister?"

Don looked down at him. He should walk away, he ought to leave this hulk to rot, but his questing mind was against him. He threw the hat on the man's lap and wiped his fingers on the side of his jacket. "I saw you stayin' out of trouble three nights ago on Mulberry Street. Followin' a girl into a house there."

"It was you chased me," said the man. "Oh God." He tucked himself up on the bench in a uterine position and began to weep.

"Cut that out," Don snarled. "I ain't hit you. If I wanted I coulda thrown you in front of that train, right?"

"Yeah, instead you saved me f'm that killer," said

the man brokenly. "Y'r a prince, mister. Y'r a real prince, that's what you are."

"You goin' to stay away from that girl?"

"*Your girl?* Look, I'll never even walk past her house no more. I'll kill anybody looks at her."

"Never mind that. Just *you* stay away from her."

The express roared in. Don rose and so did the man. Don shoved him back to the bench. "Take the next one."

"Yeah, sure, anything you say. Just you say the word."

Don thought, *I'll ask him what it is that makes it worth the risk, chance getting sent up for life just for a thing like that.* Then, *No,* he thought. *I think I know why.*

He got on the train.

He sat down and stared dully ahead. *A man will give up anything, his freedom, his life even, for a sense of power. How much am I giving up? How should I know?*

He looked at the advertisements. "Kulkies are better." "The better skin cream." He wondered if anyone ever wanted to know what these things were better *than.* "For that richer, creamier, safer lather." "Try Miss Phoebe for that better, more powerful power."

He wondered, and wondered . . .

Summer dusk, all the offices closed, the traffic gone, no one and nothing in a hurry for a little while. Don put his back against a board fence where he could see the entrance, and took out a toothpick. She might be going out, she might be coming home, she might be home and not go out, she might be out and not come home. He'd stick around.

He never even got the toothpick wet.

She stood at the top of the steps, looking across at him. He simply looked back. There were many things he might have done. Rushed across. Waved. Done a time-step. Looked away. Run. Fallen down.

But he did nothing, and the single fact that filled

his perceptions at that moment was that as long as she stood there with russet gleaming in her black hair, with her sad, sad cups-for-laughter eyes turned to him, with the thin summer cloak whipping up and falling to her clean straight body, why there was nothing he could do.

She came straight across to him. He broke the toothpick and dropped it, and waited. She crossed the sidewalk and stopped in front of him, looking at his eyes, his mouth, his eyes. "You don't even remember me."

"I remember you all right."

She leaned closer. The whites of her eyes showed under her pupils when she did that, like the high crescent moon in the tropics that floats startlingly on its back. These two crescents were twice as startling. "I don't think you do."

"Over there." With his chin he indicated her steps. "The other night."

It was then, at last, that she smiled, and the eyes held what they were made for. "I saw him again."

"He try anything?"

She laughed. "He *ran!* He was afraid of me. I don't think anybody was ever afraid of me."

"I am."

"Oh, that's the silliest—" She stopped, and again leaned toward him. "You mean it, don't you?"

He nodded.

"Don't ever be afraid of me," she said gravely, "not *ever*. What did you do to that man?"

"Nothin'. Talked to him."

"You didn't hurt him?"

He nodded.

"I'm glad," she said. "He's sick and he's ugly and he's bad, too, I guess, but I think he's been hurt enough. What's your name?"

"Don."

She counted on her fingers. "Don is a Spanish grandee. Don is putting on clothes. Don is the sun coming up in the morning. Don is . . . is the opposite of up.

You're a whole lot of things, Don." Her eyes widened. "You laughed!"

"Was that wrong?"

"Oh, *no!* But I didn't know you ever laughed."

"I watched you for three hours the other night and *you* didn't laugh. You didn't even talk."

"I would've talked if I'd known you were there. Where were you?"

"That all night joint. I followed you."

"Why?"

He looked at his shoeshine. With his other foot, he carefully stepped on it.

"Why did you follow me? Were you going to talk to me?"

"No!" he said. "No, by God, I wasn't. I wouldn'ta."

"Then why did you follow me?"

"I liked looking at you. I liked seeing you walk." He glanced across at the brownstone steps. "I didn't want anything to happen to you, all alone like that."

"Oh, I didn't care."

"That's what you said that night."

The shadow that crossed her face crossed swiftly, and she laughed. "It's all right now."

"Yeah, but what was it?"

"Oh," she said. Her head moved in an impatient gesture, but she smiled at the sky. "There was nothing and nobody. I left school. Daddy was mad at me. Kids from school acted sorry for me. Other kids, the ones you saw, they made me tired. I was tired because they were the same way all the time about the same things all the time, and I was tired because they kept me up so late."

"What did you leave school for?"

"I found out what it was for."

"It's for learning stuff."

"It isn't," she said positively. "It's for learning how to learn. And I know that already. I can learn anything. Why did you come here today?"

"I wanted to see you. Where were you going when you came out?"

"Here," she said, tapping her foot. "I saw you from the window. I was waiting for you. I was waiting for you yesterday too. What's the matter?"

He grunted.

"Tell me, tell me!"

"I never had a girl talk to me like you do."

"Don't you like the way I talk?" she asked anxiously.

"Oh for Pete's sake it ain't that!" he exploded. Then he half-smiled at her. "It's just I had a crazy idea. I had the idea you always talk like this. I mean, to anybody."

"I don't, I don't!" she breathed. "Honestly, you've got to believe that. Only you. I've always talked to you like this."

"What do you mean always?"

"Well, everybody's got somebody to talk to, all their life. You know what they like to talk about and when they like to say nothing, when you can be just silly and when they'd rather be serious and important. The only thing you don't know is their face. For that you wait. And then one day you see the face, and then you have it all."

"You ain't talkin' about *me*?"

"Yes I am."

"Look," he said. He had to speak between heartbeats. He had never felt like this in his whole life before. "You could be—takin' a—*awful* chance."

She shook her head happily.

"Did you ever think maybe everybody ain't like that?"

"It doesn't matter. I am."

His face pinched up. "Suppose I just walked away now and never saw you again."

"You wouldn't."

"But suppose."

"Why then I—I'd've had this. Talking to you."

"Hey, you're crying!"

"Well," she said, "there you were, walking away."

"You'd've called me back though."

She turned on him so quickly a tear flew clear off her face and fell sparkling to the back of his hand. Her eyes blazed. "Never that!" she said between her teeth. "I want you to stay, but if you want to go, you go, that's all. All *I* want to do is make you want to stay. I've managed so far . . ."

"How many minutes?" he teased.

"Minutes? Years," she said seriously.

"The—somebody you talked to, you kind of made him up, huh?"

"I suppose."

"How could he ever walk away?"

"Easiest thing in the world," she said. "Somebody like that, they're somebody to live up to. It isn't always easy. You've been very patient," she said. She reached out and touched his cheek.

He snatched her wrist and held it, hard. "You know what I think," he said in a rough whisper, because it was all he had. "I think you're out of your goddam head."

She stood very straight with her eyes closed. She was trembling.

"What's your name, anyway?"

"Joyce."

"I love you too, Joyce. Come on, I want you to meet a friend of mine. It's a long ride on the subway and I'll tell you all about it."

He tried hard but he couldn't tell her all of it. For some of it there were no words at all. For some of it there were no words he could use. She was attentive and puzzled. He bought flowers from a cart, just a few—red and yellow rosebuds.

"Why flowers?"

He remembered the mirror. That was one of the things he hadn't been able to talk about. "It's just what you do," he said, "bring flowers."

"I bet she loves you."

"Whaddya mean, she's pushin' sixty!"

"All the same," said Joyce, "if she does she's not going to like me."

They went up in the elevator. In the elevator he kissed her.

"What's the matter, Don?"

"If you want to crawl around an' whimper like a puppy-dog," he whispered, "if you feel useful as a busted broom-handle and worth about two wet sneezes in a hailstorm—this is a sense of power?"

"I don't understand."

"Never mind."

In the corridor he stopped. He rubbed a smudge off her nose with his thumb. "She's sorta funny," he said. "Just give her a little time. She's quite a gal. She looks like Sunday school and talks the same way but she knows the score. Joyce, she's the best friend I ever had."

"All right all right all *right!* I'll be good."

He kissed where the smudge had been.

"Come on."

One of Miss Phoebe's envelopes was stuck to the door by its flap. On it was his name.

They looked at one another and then he took the envelope down and got the note from it.

Don:

I am not at home. Please phone me this evening.

P. W.

"Don, I'm *sorry!*"

"I shoulda phoned. I wanted to surprise her."

"Surprise her? She knew you were coming."

"She didn't know you were coming. Damn it anyway."

"Oh it's all right," she said. She took his hand. "There'll be other times. Come on. What'll you do with those?"

"The flowers? I dunno. Want 'em?"

"They're hers," said Joyce.

He gave her a puzzled look. "I got a lot of things to get used to. What do you mean when you say somethin' that way?"

"Almost exactly what I say."

He put the flowers against the door and they went away.

The phone rang four times before Miss Phoebe picked it up. "It is far too late," she said frigidly, "for telephone calls. You should have called earlier, Don. However, it's just as well. I want you to know that I am *very* displeased with you. I have given you certain privileges, young man, but among them is not that of calling on me unexpectedly."

"Miss—"

"Don't interrupt. In addition, I have never indicated to you that you were free to—"

"But Miss Ph—"

"—to bring to my home any casual acquaintance you happen to have scraped up in heaven knows where—"

"Miss *Phoebe!* Please! I'm in *jail.*"

"—and invade my—you are *what?*"

"Jail, Miss Phoebe, I got arrested."

"Where are you now?"

"County. But you don't need—"

"I'm coming right down," said Miss Phoebe.

"No, Miss Phoebe, I didn't call you for that. You go back to b—"

Miss Phoebe hung up.

Miss Phoebe strode into the County Jail with grim familiarity, and before her, red tape disappeared like confetti in a blast-furnace. Twelve minutes after she arrived she had Don out of his cell and into a private room, his crisp new jail-record card before her, and was regarding him with a strange expression of wooden ferocity.

"Sit there," she said, as the door clicked shut behind an awed and reverberating policeman.

Don sat. He was rumpled and sleepy, angry and hurt, but he smiled when he said, "I never thought you'd come. I never expected that, Miss Phoebe."

She did not respond. Instead she said coldly, "Indeed? Well, young man, the matters I have to discuss will not wait." She sat down opposite him and picked up the card.

"Miss Phoebe," he said, "could you be wrong about what you said about me and girls . . . that original sin business, and all? I'm all mixed up, Miss Phoebe. I'm all mixed up!" In his face was a desperate appeal.

"Be quiet," she said sternly. She was studying the card. "This," she said, putting the card down on the table with a dry snap, "tells a great deal, but says nothing. Public nuisance, indecent exposure, suspicion of rape, impairing the morals of a minor, resisting an officer, and destruction of city property. Would you care to explain this—this catalogue to me?"

"What you mean, tell you what happened?"

"That is what I mean."

"Miss Phoebe, where is she? What they done with her?"

"With whom? You mean the girl? I do not know; moreover, it doesn't concern me and it should no longer concern you. Didn't she get you into this?"

"I got her into it. Look, could you find out, Miss Phoebe?"

"I do not know what I will do. You'd better explain to me what happened."

Again the look of appeal, while she waited glacially. He scratched his head hard with both hands at once. "Well, we went to your house."

"I am aware of that."

"Well, you wasn't home so we went out. She said

take her father's car. I got a license; it was all right. So we went an' got the car and rode around. Well, we went to a place an' she showed me how to dance some. We went somewheres else an' ate. Then we parked over by the lake. Then, well, a cop come over and poked around an' made some trouble an' I got mad an' next thing you know here we are."

"I asked you," said Miss Phoebe evenly, "what happened?"

"Aw-w." It was a long-drawn sound, an admixture of shame and irritation. "We were in the car an' this cop came pussy-footin' up. He had a big flashlight *this* long. I seen him comin'. When he got to the car we was all right. I mean, I had my arm around Joyce, but that's all."

"What *had* you been doing?"

"Talkin', that's all, just talkin', and . . ."

"And what?"

"Miss Phoebe," he blurted, "I always been able to say anything to you I wanted, about anything. Listen, I *got* to tell you about this. That thing that happened, the way it is with me and girls because of the rat, well, it just wasn't there with Joyce, it was nothin', it was like it never happened. Look, you and me, we had that thing with the hands; it was . . . I can't say it, you know how good it was. Well, with Joyce it was somepin' different. It was like I could fly. I never felt like that before. Miss Phoebe, I had too much these last few days, I don't know what goes on . . . you was right, you was always right, but this I had with Joyce, that was right too, and they can't both be right." He reached across the table, not quite far enough to touch her. The reaching was in his eyes and his voice.

Miss Phoebe stiffened a spine already straight as a bowstring. "I have asked you a simple question and all you can do is gibber at me. *What happened in that car?*"

Slowly he came back to the room, the hard chair, the bright light, Miss Phoebe's implacable face. "That cop," he said. "He claimed he seen us. Said he was goin' to run us in, I said what for, he said carryin' on like that in a public place. There was a lot of argument. Next thing you know he told Joyce to open her dress, he said when it was the way he seen it before he'd let me know. Joyce she begun to cry an' I tol' her not to do it, an' the cop said if I was goin' to act like that he would run us in for *sure*. You know, I got the idea if she'd done it he'da left us alone after?

"So I got real mad, I climbed out of the car, I tol' him we ain't done nothin', he pushes me one side, he shines the light in on Joyce. She squinchin' down in the seat, cryin', he says, 'Come on, you, you know what to do.' I hit the flashlight. I on'y meant to get the light off her, but I guess I hit it kind of hard. It came up and clonked him in the teeth. Busted the flashlight too. That's the city property I destroyed. He started to cuss and I tol' him not to. He hit me and opened the car door an' shoved me in. He got in the back an' took out his gun and tol' me to drive to the station house." He shrugged. "So I had to. That's all."

"It is not all. You have not told me what you did before the policeman came."

He looked at her, startled. "Why, I—we—" His face flamed, "I love her," he said, with difficulty, as if he spoke words in a new and troublesome tongue. "I mean I . . . do, that's all."

"What did you do?"

"I kissed her."

"What else did you do?"

"I—" He brought up one hand, made a vague circular gesture, dropped the hand. He met her gaze. "Like when you love somebody, that's all."

"Are you going to tell me exactly what you did, or are you not?"

"Miss Phoebe . . ." he whispered, "I ain't never seen you look like that."

"I want the whole filthy story," she said. She leaned forward so far that her chin was only a couple of

inches from the table top. Her protruding, milky eyes
seemed to whirl, then it was as if a curtain over them
had been twitched aside, and they blazed.

Don stood up. "Miss Phoebe," he said. "Miss Phoebe
. . ." It was the voice of terror itself.

Then a strange thing happened. It may have been
the mere fact of his rising, of being able, for a moment, to stand over her, look down on her. "Miss
Phoebe," he said, "there—ain't—no—filthy—story."

She got up and without another word marched to
the door. As she opened it the boy raised his fists. His
wrists and forearms corded and writhed. His head
went back, his lungs filled, and with all his strength
he shouted the filthiest word he knew. It had one syllable, it was sibilant and explosive, it was immensely
satisfying.

Miss Phoebe stopped, barely in balance between one
pace and the next, momentarily paralyzed. It was like
the breaking of the drive-coil on a motion picture pro-
jector.

"They locked her up," said Don hoarsely. "They
took her away with two floozies an' a ole woman with
DT's. She ain't never goin' to see me again. Her ole
man'll kill me if he ever sets eyes on me. You were all
I had left. Get the hell out of here . . ."

She reached the door as it was opened from the other
side by a policeman, who said, "What's goin' on here?"

"Incorrigible," Miss Phoebe spat, and went out. They
took Don back to his cell.

The courtroom was dark and its pew-like seats were
almost empty. Outside it was raining, and the statue of
Justice had a broken nose. Don sat with his head in his
hands, not caring about the case then being heard, not
caring about his own, not caring about people or
things or feelings. For five days he had not cared
about the white-washed cell he had shared with the
bicycle thief; the two prunes and weak coffee for
breakfast, the blare of the radio in the inner court; the

day in, day out screaming of the man on the third tier
who hoarsely yelled, "I din't do it I din't do it I din't
do . . ."

His name was called and he was led or shoved—he
didn't care which—before the bench. A man took his
hand and put it on a book held by another man who
said something rapidly. "I do," said Don. And then
Joyce was there, led up by a tired kindly old fellow
with eyes like hers and an unhappy mouth. Don
looked at her once and was sure she wasn't even trying
to recognize his existence. If she had left her hands at
her sides, she was close enough for him to have
touched one of them secretly, for they stood side by
side, facing the judge. But she kept her hands in front
of her and stood with her eyes closed, with her whole
face closed, her lashes down on her cheeks like little
barred gates.

The cop, the lousy cop was there too, and he reeled
off things about Don and things about Joyce that were
things they hadn't done, couldn't have done, wouldn't
do . . . he cared about that for a moment, but as he
listened it seemed very clear that what the cop was saying was about two other people who knew a lot about
flesh and nothing about love; and after that he
stopped caring again.

When the cop was finished, the kindly tired man
came forward and said that he would press no charges
against this young man if he promised he would not
see his daughter again until she was twenty-one. The
judge pushed down his glasses and looked over them
at Don. "Will you make that promise?"

Don looked at the tired man, who turned away. He
looked at Joyce, whose eyes were closed. "Sure," he
told the judge.

There was some talk about respecting the laws of
society which were there to protect innocence, and
how things would be pretty bad if Don ever appeared
before that bench again, and next thing he knew he
was being led through the corridors back to the jail,

where they returned the wallet and fountain pen they had taken away from him, made him sign a book, unlocked three sets of doors and turned him loose. He stood in the rain and saw, half a block away, Joyce and her father getting into a cab.

About two hours later one of the jail guards came out and saw him. "Hey, boy. You like it here?"

Don pulled the wet hair out of his eyes and looked at the man. and turned and walked off without saying anything.

"Well, hello!"

"Now you get away from me, girl. You're just going to get me in trouble and I don't want no trouble."

"I won't make any trouble for you, really I won't. Don't you want to talk to me?"

"Look, you know me, you heard about me. Hey, you been sick?"

"No."

"You look like you been sick. I was sick a whole lot. Fellow down on his luck, everything happens. Here comes the old lady from the delicatessen. She'll see us."

"That's all right."

"She'll see you, she knows you, she'll see you talkin' to me. I don't want no trouble."

"There won't be any trouble. Please don't be afraid. I'm not afraid of you."

"I ain't scared of you either but one night that young fellow of yours, that tall skinny one, he said he'll throw me under a train if I talk to you."

"I have no fellow."

"Yes you have, that tall skin—"

"Not any more. Not any more . . . talk to me for a while. Please talk to me."

"You sure? You sure he ain't . . . you ain't . . ."

"I'm sure. He's gone, he doesn't write, he doesn't care."

"You been sick."

"No, no, no, no!—I want to tell you something: if

ever you eat your heart out over something, hoping
and wishing for it, dreaming and wanting it, doing
everything you can to make yourself fit for it, and then
that something comes along, know what to do?"

"I do' wan' no trouble . . . yea, grab it!"

"No. *Run!* Close your eyes and turn your back and
run away. Because wanting something you've never
had hurts, sometimes, but not as much as having it
and then losing it."

"I never had *nothing*."

"You did so. And you were locked up for years."

"I didn't have it, girl. I used it. It wasn't mine."

"You didn't lose it, then—ah, I *see!*"

"If a cop comes along he'll pinch me just because
I'm talkin' to you. I'm just a bum, I'm down on my
luck, we can't stand out here like this."

"Over there, then. Coffee."

"I ain't got but four cents."

"Come on. I have enough."

"What'sa matter with you, you want to talk to a
bum like me!"

"Come on, come on . . . listen, listen to this:

" 'It is late last night the dog was speaking of you; the
snipe was speaking of you in her deep marsh. It is you
are the lonely bird throughout the woods; and that
you may be without a mate until you find me.

" 'You promised me and you said a lie to me, that
you would be before me where the sheep are flocked. I
gave a whistle and three hundred cries to you; and I
found nothing there but fleeting lamb.

" 'You promised me a thing that was hard for you, a
ship of gold under a silver mast; twelve towns and a
market in all of them, and a fine white court by the
side of the sea.

" 'You promised me a thing that is not possible; that
you would give me gloves of the skin of a fish; that
you would give me shoes of the skin of a bird, and a
suit of the dearest silk in Ireland.

" 'My mother said to me not to be talking with you,
to-day or to-morrow or on Sunday. It was a bad time
she took for telling me that, it was shutting the door
after the house was robbed . . .

" 'You have taken the east from me, you have taken
the west from me, you have taken what is before me
and what is behind me; you have taken the moon, you
have taken the sun from me, and my fear is great you
have taken God from me.'

". . . That's something I remembered. I remember, I
remember everything."

"That's a lonesome thing to remember."

"Yes . . . and no one knows who she was. A man
called Yeats heard this Irish girl lamenting, and took
it down."

"I don't know, I seen you around, I never saw you
like this, you been sick."

"Drink your coffee and we'll have another cup."

Dear Miss Phoebe:
   Well dont fall over with surprise to get a letter from
me I am not much at letter writing to any body and I
never thot I would wind up writing to you.
   I know you was mad at me and I guess I was mad at
you too. Why I am writing this is I am trying to figure
out what it was all about. I know why I was mad I was
mad because you said there was something dirty about
what I did. Mentioning no names. I did not do nothing dirty and so thats why I was mad.
   But all I know about you Miss Phoebe is you was
mad I dont know why. I never done nothing to you I
was ascared to in the first place and anyway I thot you
was my friend. I thot anytime there was something on
my mind I could not figure it out, all I had to do was
to tell you. This one time I was in more trouble then I
ever had in my entire. All you did you got mad at me.
   Now if you want to stay mad at me thats your bus-

nis but I wish you would tell me why. I wish we was freinds again but okay if you dont want to.

Well write to me if you feel like it at the Seamans Institute thats where I am picking up my mail these days I took a ride on a tank ship and was sick most of the time but thats life.

I am going to get a new fountan pen this one wont spell right (joke). So take it easy yours truly Don.

Don came out of the Seaman's Institute and stood looking at the square. A breeze lifted and dropped, carrying smells of fish and gasoline, spices, sea-salt, and a slight chill. Don buttoned up his pea-jacket and pushed his hands down into the pockets. Miss Phoebe's letter was there, straight markings on inexpensive, efficient paper, the envelope torn almost in two because of the way he had opened it. He could see it in his mind's eye without effort.

My Dear Don:

Your letter came as something of a surprise to me. I thought you might write, but not that you would claim unawareness of the reasons for my feelings toward you.

You will remember that I spent a good deal of time and energy in acquainting you with the nature of Good and the nature of Evil. I went even further and familiarized you with a kind of union between souls which, without me, would have been impossible to you. And I feel I made quite clear to you the fact that a certain state of grace is necessary to the achievement of these higher levels of being.

Far from attempting to prove to me that you were a worthy pupil of the teachings I might have given you, you plunged immediately into actions which indicate that there is a complete confusion in your mind as to Good and Evil. You have grossly defiled yourself, almost as if you insisted upon being unfit. You engaged in foul and carnal practices which make a mockery of the pure meetings of the higher selves which once were possible to you.

You should understand that the Sources of the power I once offered you are ancient and sacred and not to be taken lightly. Your complete lack of reverence for these antique matters is to me the most unforgivable part of your inexcusable conduct. The Great Thinkers who developed these powers in ancient times surely meant a better end for them than that they be given to young animals.

Perhaps one day you will become capable of understanding the meaning of reverence, obedience, and honor to ancient mysteries. At that time I would be interested to hear from you again.

> Yours very truly,
> (Miss) Phoebe Watkins.

Don growled deep in his throat. Subsequent readings would serve to stew all the juices from the letter; one reading was sufficient for him to realize that in the note was no affection and no forgiveness. He remembered the birthday cake with a pang. He remembered the painful hot lump in his throat when she had ordered him to wash his face; she had *cared* whether he washed his face or not.

He went slowly down to the street. He looked older; he felt older. He had used his seaman's papers for something else besides entree to a clean and inexpensive dormitory. Twice he had thought he was near that strange, blazing loss of self he had experienced with Miss Phoebe, just in staring at the living might of the sea. Once, lying on his back on deck in a clear moonless night, he had been sure of it. There had been a sensation of having been *chosen* for something, of having been fingertip-close to some simple huge fact, some great normal coalescence of time and distance, a fusion and balance, like yin and yang, in all things. But it had escaped him, and now it was of little assistance to him to know that his sole authority in such things considered him as disqualified.

"Foul an' carnal practices," he said under his breath. *Miss Phoebe,* he thought, *I bet I could tell you a thing or two about 'reverence, obedience an' honor to ancient mysteries.'* In a flash of deep understanding, he saw that those who hold themselves aloof from the flesh are incapable of comprehending this single fact about those who do not: only he who is free to take it is truly conscious of what he does when he leaves it alone.

Someone was in his way. He stepped aside and the man was still in the way. He snapped out of his introspection and brought his sight back to earth, clothed in an angry scowl.

For a moment he did not recognize the man. He was still tattered, but he was clean and straight, and his eyes were clear. It was obvious that he felt the impact of Don's scowl, he retreated a short pace, and with the step were the beginnings of old reflexes; to cringe, to flee. But then he held hard, and Don had to stop.

"Y'own the sidewalk?" Don demanded. "Oh—it's you."

"I got to talk to you," the man said in a strained voice.

"I got nothin' to talk to you about," said Don. "Get back underground where you belong. Go root for cigar butts in the subway."

"It's about Joyce," said the man.

Don reached and gathered together the lapels of the man's old jacket. "I told you once to stay away from her. That means don't even talk about her."

"Get your hands off me," said the man evenly.

Don grunted in surprise, and let him go.

The man said, "I had somepin' to tell you, but now you can go to hell."

Don laughed. "What do you know! What are you—full of hash or somethin'?"

The man tugged at the lapels and moved to pass Don. Don caught his arm. "Wait. What did you want to tell me?"

The man looked into his face. "Remember you said you was going to kill me, I get near her?"

"I remember."

"I seen her this morning. I seen her yesterday an' four nights last week."

"The hell you did!"

"You got to get that through your head 'fore I tell you anything."

Don shook his head slowly. "This beats anything I ever seen. What happened to you?"

As if he had not heard, the man said, "I found out what ship you was on. I watched the papers. I figured you'd go to the Institoot for mail. I been waitin' three hours."

Don grabbed the thin biceps. "Hey. Is somethin' wrong with Joyce?"

"You give a damn?"

"Listen," said Don, "I can still break your damn neck."

The man simply shrugged.

Baffled, Don said, between his teeth, "Talk. You said you wanted to talk—go ahead."

"Why ain't you wrote to her?"

"What's that to you?"

"It's a whole lot to her."

"You seem to know a hell of a lot.

"I told you I see her all the time," the man pointed out.

"She must talk a lot."

"To me," said the man, closing his eyes, "a whole lot."

"She wouldn't want to hear from me," Don said. Then he barked, "What are you tryin' to tell me? You and her—what are *you* to her? You're not messin' with her, comin' braggin' to me about it?"

The man put a hand on Don's chest and pushed

him away. There was disgust on his face, and a strange dignity. "Cut it out," he said. "Look, I don't like you. I don't like doin' what I'm doin' but I got to. Joyce, she's been half crazy, see. I don't know why she started to talk to me. Maybe she just didn't care any more, maybe she felt so bad she wanted to dive in a swamp an' I was the nearest thing to it. She been talkin' to me, she . . . smiles when she sees me. She'll eat with me, even."

"You shoulda stayed away from her," Don mumbled uncertainly.

"Yeah, maybe. And suppose I did, what would she do? If she didn't have me to talk to, maybe it would be someone else. Maybe someone else wouldn't . . . be as . . . leave her . . ."

"You mean, take care of her," said Don softly.

"Well, if you want to call it that. Take up her time, anyway, she can't get into any other trouble." He looked at Don beseechingly. "I ain't never laid a hand on her. You believe that?"

Don said, "Yeah, I believe that."

"You going to see her?"

Don shook his head.

The man said in a breathy, shrill voice, "I oughta punch you in the mouth!"

"Shaddup," said Don miserably. "What you want me to see her for?"

Suddenly there were tears in the weak blue eyes. But the voice was still steady. "I ain't got nothin'. I'll never have nothin'. This is all I can do, make you go back. Why won't you go back?"

"She wouldn't want to see me," said Don, "after what I done."

"You better go see her," whispered the man. "She thinks she ain't fit to live, gettin' you in jail and all. She thinks it was her fault. She thinks you feel the same way. She even . . . she even thinks that's right. You dirty rotten no-good lousy—" he cried. He suddenly raised his fists and hit his own temples with them, and made a bleating sound. He ran off toward the waterfront.

Don watched him go, stunned to the marrow. Then he turned blindly and started across the street. There was a screeching of brakes, a flurry of movement, and he found himself standing with one hand on the front fender of a taxi.

"Where the hell you think you're goin'?"

Stupidly, Don said, "What?"

"What's the matter with you?" roared the cabby.

Don fumbled his way back to the rear door. "A lot, a whole lot," he said as he got in. "Take me to 37 Mulberry Street," he said.

It was three days later, in the evening, when he went to see Miss Phoebe.

"Well!" she said when she opened to his ring.

"Can I come in?"

She did not move. "You received my letter?"

"Sure."

"You understood . . ."

"I got the idea."

"There were—ah—certain conditions."

"Yeah," said Don. "I got to be capable of understandin' the meaning of reverence, obedience, an' honor to certain ancient mysteries."

"Have you just memorized it, or do you feel you really are capable?"

"Try me."

"Very well." She moved aside.

He came in, shoving a blue knitted cap into his side pocket. He shucked out of the pea-jacket. He was wearing blue slacks and a black sweater with a white shirt and blue tie. He was as different from the scrubbed schoolboy neatness of his previous visit as he was from the ill-fit flashiness of his first one. "How've you been?"

"Well, thank you," she answered coolly. "Sit down."

They sat facing one another. Don was watchful, Miss Phoebe wary.

"You've . . . grown," said Miss Phoebe. It was made not so much as a statement, but as an admission.

"I did a lot," said Don. "Thought a lot. You're so right about people in the world that work for—call it yin an' yang—an' know what they're doin', why they're doin' it. All you got to do is look around you. Read the papers."

She nodded. "Do you have any difficulty in determining which side these people are on?"

"No more."

"If that's true," she said, "it's wonderful." She cleared her throat. "You've seen that—that girl again."

"I couldn't lie."

"Are you willing to admit that beastliness is no substitute for the true meeting of minds?"

"Absolutely."

"Well!" she said. "This *is* progress!" She leaned forward suddenly. "Oh, Don, that wasn't for you. Not you! You are destined for great things, my boy. You have no idea."

"I think I have."

"And you're willing to accept my teaching?"

"Just as much as you'll teach me."

"I'll make tea," she said, almost gaily. She rose and as she passed him she squeezed his shoulder. He grinned.

When she was in the kitchenette he said, "Fellow in my neighborhood just got back from a long stretch for hurting a little girl."

"Oh?" she said. "What is his name?"

"I don't know."

"Find out," she said. "They have to be watched."

"Why?"

"Animals," she said, "wild animals. They have to be caught and caged, to protect society."

He nodded. The gesture was his own, out of her range. He said, "I ate already. Don't go to no trouble."

"Very well. Just some cookies." She emerged with the tea service. "It's good to have you back. I'm rather surprised. I'd nearly given you up."

He smiled. "Never do that."

She poured boiling water from the kettle into the teapot and brought it out. "You're almost like a different person."

"How come?"

"Oh, you—you're much more self-assured." She looked at him searchingly. "More complete. I think the word for it is 'integrated.' Actually, I can't seem to . . . to . . . Don, you're not hiding anything from me, are you?"

"Me? Why, how could I do that?"

She seemed troubled. "I don't know." She gave him a quick glance, almost spoke, then shook her head slightly.

"What's the matter? I do something wrong?"

"No, oh no."

They were quiet until the tea was steeped and poured.

"Miss Phoebe . . ."

"What is it?"

"Just what did you think went on in that car before we got arrested?"

"Isn't that rather obvious?"

"Well," he said, with a quick smile, "to me, yeah. I was there."

"You can be cleansed," she said confidently.

"Can I now! Miss Phoebe, I just want to get this clear in my mind. I think you got the wrong idea, and I'd like to straighten you out. I didn't go the whole way with that girl."

"You didn't?"

He shook his head.

"Oh," she said. "The policeman got there in time after all."

He put down his teacup very carefully. "We had lots of time. What I'm telling you is we just didn't."

"Oh," she said. "Oh!"

"What's the matter, Miss Phoebe?"

"Nothing," she said, tensely. "Nothing. This . . . puts a different complexion on things."

"I sort of thought you'd be glad."

"But of course!" She whirled on him. "You are telling me the truth, Don?"

"You can get in an' out of County," he reminded her. "There's records of her medical examination there that proves it, you don't believe me."

"Oh," she said, "oh dear." Suddenly her face cleared. "Perhaps I've underestimated you. What you're telling me is that you . . . you didn't *want* to, is that it? But you said that the old memory of the rat left you when you were with her. Why didn't you—*why?*"

"Hey—easy, take it easy! You want to know why, it was because it wasn't the time. What we had would last, it would keep. We din't have to grab."

"You . . . really felt that way about her?"

He nodded.

"I had no idea," she said in a stunned whisper. "And afterward . . . did you . . . do you still . . ."

"You can find out, can't you? You know ways to find out what I'm thinking."

"I can't," she cried. "I can't! Something has happened to you. I can't get in, it's as if there were a steel plate between us!"

"I'm sorry," he said with grave cheerfulness.

She closed her eyes and made some huge internal effort. When she looked up, she seemed quite composed. "You are willing to work with me?"

"I want to."

"Very well. I don't know what has happened—and I must find out, even if I have to use . . . drastic measures."

"Anything you say, Miss Phoebe."

"Lie down over there."

"On that? I'm longer than it is!" He went to the

little sofa and maneuvered himself so that at least his shoulder-blades and head were horizontal. "Like so?"

"That will do. Make yourself just as comfortable as you can." She threw a tablecloth over the lampshade and turned out the light in the kitchenette. Then she drew up a chair near his head, out of his visual range. She sat down.

It got very quiet in the room. "You're sleepy, you're so sleepy," she said softly. "You're sl—"

"No I ain't," he said briskly.

"Please," she said, "fall in with this. Just let your mind go blank and listen to me."

"Okay."

She droned on and on. His eyes half-closed, opened, then closed all the way. He began to breathe more slowly, more deeply.

". . . And sleep, sleep, but hear my voice, hear what I am saying, can you hear me?"

"Yes," he said heavily.

"Lie there and sleep, and sleep, but answer me truthfully, tell me only the truth, the truth, answer me, whom do you love?"

"Joyce."

"You told me you restrained yourself the night you were arrested. Is this true?"

"Yes."

Miss Phoebe's eyes narrowed. She wet her lips, wrung her hands.

"The union you had with me, that flight of soul, was that important to you?"

"Yes."

"Would you like to do more of it?"

"Yes."

"Don't you realize that it is a greater, more intimate thing than any union of the flesh?"

"Yes."

"Am I not the only one with whom you can do it?"

"No."

Miss Phoebe bit her lip. "Tell the truth, the truth," she said raggedly. "Who else?"

"Joyce."

"Have you ever done it with Joyce?"

"Not yet."

"Are you sure you can?"

"I'm sure."

Miss Phoebe got up and went into the kitchenette. She put her forehead against the cool tiles of the wall beside the refrigerator. She put her fingertips on her cheeks, and her hands contracted suddenly, digging her fingers in, drawing her flesh downward until her scalding, tight-shut eyes were dragged open from underneath. She uttered an almost soundless whimper.

After a moment she straightened up, squared her shoulders and went noiselessly back to her chair. Don slumbered peacefully.

"Don, go on sleeping. Can you hear me?"

"Yes."

"I want you to go down deeper and deeper and deeper, down and down to a place where there is nothing at all, anywhere, anywhere, except my voice and everything I say is true. Go down, down, deep, deep . . ." On and on she went, until at last she reached down and gently rolled back one of his eyelids. She peered at the eye, nodded with satisfaction.

"Stay down there, Don, stay there."

She crouched in the chair and thought, hard. She knew of the difficulty of hypnotically commanding a subject to do anything repugnant to him. She also knew, however, that it is a comparatively simple matter to convince a subject that a certain person is a pillow and then fix the command that a knife must be thrust into that pillow.

She pieced and fitted, and at last, "Don, can you hear me?"

His voice was a bare whisper, slurred, "Yes . . ."

"The forces of evil have done a terrible thing to Joyce, Don. When you see her again she will look as before. She will speak and act as before. But she is different. The real Joyce has been taken away. A substitute has been put in her place. The substitute is dangerous. You will know, when you see her. You will not trust her. You will not touch her. You will share nothing with her. You will put her aside and have nothing to do with her.

"But the real Joyce is alive and well, although she was changed. I saved her. When she was replaced by the substitute, I took the real Joyce and made her a part of me. So now when you talk to Miss Phoebe you are talking to Joyce, when you touch Miss Phoebe you are touching Joyce, when you kiss and hold and love Miss Phoebe you will be loving Joyce. Only through Miss Phoebe can you know Joyce, and they are one and the same. And you will never call Joyce by name again. Do you understand?"

"Miss . . . Phoebe is . . . Joyce now . . ."

"That's right."

Miss Phoebe was breathing hard. Her mouth was wet.

"You will remember none of this deep sleep, except what I have told you. Don," she whispered, "my dear, my dear . . ."

Presently she rose and threw the cloth off the lampshade. She felt the teapot; it was still quite hot. She emptied the hot-water pot and filled it again from the kettle. She sat down at the tea-table, covered her eyes, and for a moment the only sound in the room was her deep, slow, controlled breathing as she oxygenated her lungs.

She sat up, refreshed, and poured tea. "Don! Don! Wake up, Don!"

He opened his eyes and stared unseeingly at the ceiling. Then he raised his head, sat up, shook himself.

"Goodness!" said Miss Phoebe. "You're getting positively absent-minded. I like to be answered when I speak to you."

"Whuh? Hm?" He shook himself again and rose.

"Sorry, Miss Phoebe. Guess I sorta . . . did you ask me something?"

"The tea, the tea," she said with pleasant impatience. "I've just poured."

"Oh," he said. "Good."

"Don," she said, "we're going to accomplish so *very* much."

"We sure are. And we'll do it a hell of a lot faster with your help."

"I beg—*what?*"

"Joyce and me," he said patiently. "The things you can do, that planting a reflection in a mirror the way you want it, and knowing who's at the door and on the phone and all . . . we can sure use those things."

"I—I'm afraid I don't . . ."

"Oh God, Miss Phoebe, don't! I hate to see you cut yourself up like this!"

"You were faking."

"You mean just now, the hypnosis routine? No I wasn't. You had me under all right. It's just that it won't stick with me. Everything worked but the commands."

"That's—impossible!"

"No it ain't. Not if I had a deeper command to remember 'em—and disregard 'em."

"Why didn't I think of that?" she said tautly. "*She* did it!"

He nodded.

"She's evil, Don, can't you see? I was only trying to save—"

"I know what you were tryin' to save," he interrupted, not unkindly. "You're in real good shape for a woman your age, Miss Phoebe. This power of yours, it keeps you going. Keeps your glands going. With you, that's a problem. With us, now, it'll be a blessing. Pity you never thought of that."

"Foul," she said, "how perfectly foul . . ."

"No it ain't!" he rapped. "Look, maybe we'll all get a chance to work together after all, and if we do, you'll get an idea what kind of chick Joyce is. I hope that happens. But mind you, if it don't, we'll get along. We'll do all you can do, in time."

"I'd *never* cooperate with evil!"

"You went and got yourself a little mixed up about that, Miss Phoebe. You told me yourself about yin an' yang, how some folks set a course straight an' true an' never realize the boundary can twist around underneath them. You asked me just tonight was I sure which was which, an' I said yes. It's real simple. When you see somebody with power who is usin' it for what yang stands for—good, an' light, an' all like that, you'll find he ain't usin' it for himself."

"I wasn't using it for myself!"

"No, huh?" He chuckled. "Who was it I was goin' to kiss an' hold just like it was Joyce?"

She moaned and covered her face. "I just wanted to keep you pure," she said indistinctly.

"Now that's a thing you got to get straightened out on. That's a big thing. Look here." He rose and went to the long bookcase. Through her fingers, she watched him. "Suppose this here's all the time that has passed since there was anything like a human being on earth." He moved his hand from one end of the top shelf to the other. "Maybe way back at the beginning they was no more 'n smart monkeys, but all the same they had whatever it is makes us human beings. These forces you talk about, they were operatin' then just like now An' the cave men an' the savages an' all, hundreds an' hundreds of years, they kept developing until we got humans like us.

"All right. You talk about ancient mysteries, your yoga an' all. An' this tieup with virgins. Look, I'm going to show you somepin. You an' all your studyin' and copyin' the ancient secrets, you know how ancient they were? I'll show you." He put out his big hand and put three fingers side by side on the "modern" end of the shelf.

"Those three fingers covers it—down to about four-

teen thousand years before Christ. Well, maybe the
thing did work better without sex. But only by
throwin' sex into study instead of where it was meant
to go. Now you want to free yourself from sex in your
thinkin', there's a much better way than that. You do
it like Joyce an' me. We're a bigger unit together than
you ever could be by yourself. An' we're not likely to
get pushed around by our glands, like you. No offense,
Miss Phoebe . . . so there's your *really* ancient mystery.
Male an' female together; there's a power for you.
Why you s'pose people in love get to fly so high, get to
feel like gods?" He swept his hand the full length of
the shelf. "A *real* ancient one."

"Wh-where did you learn all this?" she whispered.

"Joyce. Joyce and me, we figured it out. Look, she's
not just any chick. She quit school because she learns
too fast. She gets everything right now, this minute, as
soon as she sees it. All her life everyone around her
seems to be draggin' their feet. An' besides, she's like a
kid. I don't mean childish, I don't mean simple, I
mean like she believes in something even when there's
no evidence around for it, she keeps on believing until
the evidence comes along. There must be a word for
that."

"Faith," said Miss Phoebe faintly.

He came and sat down near her. "Don't take it so
hard, Miss Phoebe," he said feelingly. "It's just that
you got to stand aside for a later model. If anybody's
going to do yang work in a world like this, they got to
get rid of a lot of deadwood. I don't mean you're deadwood. I mean a lot of your ideas are. Like that fellow
was in jail about the little girl, you say *watch 'im!* one
false move an' back in the cage he goes. And all that
guy wanted all his life was just to have a couple people around him who give a damn, 'scuse me, Miss
Phoebe. He never had that, so he took what he could
get from whoever was weaker'n him, and that was only
girls. You should see him now, he's goin' to be our best
man."

"You're a child. You can't undertake work like this. You don't know the powers you're playing with."

"Right. We're goin' to make mistakes. An' that's where you come in. Are you on?"

"I—don't quite—"

"We want your help," he said, and bluntly added, "but if you can't help, don't hinder."

"You'd want to work with me after I . . . Joyce, Joyce will hate me!"

"Joyce ain't afraid of you." Her face crumpled. He patted her clumsily on the shoulder. "Come on, what do you say?"

She sniffled, then turned red-rimmed, protruding eyes up to him. "If you want me. I'd have to . . . I'd like to talk to Joyce."

"Okay. JOYCE!"

Miss Phoebe started. "She—she's not—*oh!*" she cried as the doorknob turned. She said, "It's locked."

He grinned. "No it ain't."

Joyce came in. She went straight to Don, her eyes on his face, searching, and did not look around her until her hand was in his. Then she looked down at Miss Phoebe.

"This here, this is Joyce," Don said.

Joyce and Miss Phoebe held each other's eyes for a long moment, tense at first, gradually softening. At last Miss Phoebe made a tremulous smile.

"I'd better make some tea," she said, gathering her feet under her.

"I'll help," said Joyce. She turned her face to the tea-tray, which lifted into the air and floated to the kitchenette. She smiled at Miss Phoebe. "You tell me what to do."

The Ultimate Egoist

This is a very early one—one of the first I ever sold—and that must be very clear to the critical sophisticates among you. Yet there is a wonderful freshness about the ignorance of a beginning writer, who has yet to learn the fine points of plot and characterization, and the technicalities of 'crisis" and "climax" and "denouement" and all that, and tumbles ahead, writing any damn thing that comes into his head.

This was fun to do. So much of what I have written may have been illuminating and instructive (especially to the author), but it wasn't joyful. This is.

So I was holding forth as usual, finding highly audible reasons for my opinion of myself. I could do that with Judith. She was in love with me, and women in love are funny that way. You can tell them anything about yourself, and as long as it's a buildup they'll believe it. If they can't they'll try.

We were walking down to the lake for a swim. What got me started in this vein—should I say "vain"?—was the fact that Judith looked so wonderful. She was a brunette who was a redhead when she was close by, which she usually was, and turned blonde when the sun hit her. Lovely. Her transparent skin seemed proof that her flesh was rose ivory all the way through, and she had long green eyes. She moved like a hawk tilting against the wind and she loved me. Wonderful. Since I was thinking about wonderful things I just naturally began talking about myself, and Judith held my hand and skipped along beside me and agreed with everything I said, which was as it should be.

"Let me put it this way," I declaimed. "The world and the universe are strictly as I see them. I see no fallacy in the supposition that if I disbelieve in any given object, theory, or principle, it does not exist."

"You've never seen Siam, darling," said Judith. "Does that mean that Siam does not exist?" She was not disagreeing with me, but she knew how to keep me talking. That was all right because we enjoyed hearing me talk.

"Oh, Siam can exist if it wants," I said generously, "providing I have no reason to doubt its existence."

"Ah," she said. She hadn't exactly heard all this before because I expressed myself with a high degree of originality. There were so many ins and outs to my faceted personality that I found my ego quite inexhaustible. Judith giggled.

"Suppose you really and truly doubted Siam, Woodie."

"That would be tough on the Siamese."

She laughed outright, and I joined her, because if I had not she would have been laughing *at* me, and that would have been unthinkable.

"Darling," she said, pulling my head down so she

could bite my ear, "you're marvelous. Do you mean to tell me in so many words that you created all this—these old trees, that sprouted so many years before you were born; the stars and that nice, warm old sun, and the flow of sap, and life itself—wasn't that quite a job, honey?"

I looked at her blankly. "Not at all. Truly, darling. I have never seen nor heard nor read anything to disprove my conviction that this universe is my product, and mine alone. Look—I exist. I can take that as a basic fact. I observe that I have a particular form; hence there must be a physical environment to suit it."

"How about the possibility that your exquisite form might be the *result* of your physical environment?"

"Don't interrupt," I said patiently. "Don't be sarcastic and above all don't be heretical. Now.

"Since my existence requires a certain set of circumstances, those circumstances must necessarily exist to care for me. The fact that part of these circumstances are century-old trees and ageless heavenly bodies is a matter of little importance except insofar as it is a credit to the powers of my fertile imagination."

"*Whew!*" She let go my hand. "You're strong."

"Thank you, darling. Do you see my point?"

"In theory, O best beloved. My, my, how you do go on. But—what's to prevent my thinking that the universe is a figment of *my* imagination?"

"Nothing. It would be a bit fantastic, of course, in the face of my certain knowledge that it's my creation."

"I'll be damned," she said. She could say things like that—and worse—because she looked so young and sweet that most people simply wouldn't believe it was she who spoke. "I'll be *very* bedamned," she said, and added under her breath a sentence containing the word "insufferable." I imagine she was talking about the weather.

* * *

We walked along, and she plucked a leaf of sassafras and chewed on it. The leaf was the kind of green against her lips that showed how red her lips were against her cheeks. "Wouldn't it be funny," she said after a bit, "if all that nonsense you drool were true, and things just stopped *being* when you doubted them?"

"Please!" I said sharply, changing my bathing trunks from my right hand to my left so I could raise a more admonitory forefinger at her. "Nonsense? Drool? Explain yourself, Judith!"

"Oh, stop it!" she shouted, quite taking me aback. "I love you, Woodie," she went on more quietly, "but I think you're a conceited ass. Also, you talk too much. Let's sing songs or something."

"I do not feel like singing songs or something," I said coldly, "while you are so hysterically unfair. You can't disprove a thing I've said."

"And you can't prove it. Please. Woodie—I don't want to fight. This is a summer vacation and we're going swimming today and I love you and I agree with everything you say. I think you're marvelous. Now for Heaven's sake *will* you talk about something else for a change?"

"I can't prove it, hm-m-m?" I said darkly.

She clapped two slim hands to her head and said in a monotone, "The moon is made of green cheese. It isn't but if it did happen to be and you found it out, it certainly would be. I am going out of my mind. I am going to gnash my teeth and paw the air and froth at the mouth and you make me SICK!"

"Your reasoning is typically feminine," I told her, "Spectacular but highly inaccurate. My point is this." I ignored her moans. "Since I am the creator of all things"—I made an inclusive gesture—"I can also be their destroyer. A case in point—we'll take that noble old spruce over there. I don't believe in it. It does not exist. It is but another figment of my imagination, one without a rational explanation. I do not see it any more because it is not there. It could not be there: it's a physical and psychic impossibility. It—" At last I yielded to her persistent yanking on my elbow.

"Woodie! Oh— Woodie . . . it's gone! Th-that tree; it's . . . oh, Woodie! I'm scared! What happened?"

She pointed wordlessly at the new clearing in the copse.

"I dunno. I—" I wet my lips and tried again. "My God," I said quietly. "Oh, my God." I was shaking and stone-cold, there in the sun, and my throat was tight. Judith had bruised my arm with her nails; I felt it sharply when she let me go and stood back from me. It wasn't the disappearance of a thousand board feet of good spruce that bothered me particularly. After all, it wasn't my tree. But—oh, my God!

I looked at Judith and was suddenly conscious that she was about to run away from me. I put out my arms, and she ran into them instead. She cried then. We both knew then who—what—I was; neither of us could admit it. But anyway, she cried . . . you know, I was quite a fellow. The miracle of growth was my invention, and the air was warm and the sky blue for me, and the moon was silver and the sun golden, all for me alone. The earth would quake beneath my feet if I so chose, and a supernova was but a flash in my brainpan. And yet when Judith cried in my arms I just did not know what to do. We sat together on a rock beside the road and she cried because she was scared and I patted her shoulder and felt perfectly rotten. I was scared too.

What was real? I dropped my fingers to the stone and stroked its mossy coolth. Something that was all legs scuttled out from under my fingertips. I glanced down at it. It was red-brown and shiny and rather horrible. What peculiar ideas I did have at times!

The stone, for instance. It didn't *have* to be there. It wasn't necessary to me, save as a minor element in a pretty bit of scenery that I appreciated. I might just as well not—

"Uff," said Judith, and bit her lip as she plumped down on the bare earth where that stone had been.

"Judith," I said weakly as I climbed to my feet and helped her up. "That was a—a trick."

"I didn't like it," she said furiously. "Ooooh."

"I didn't do anything," I said plaintively. "I just . . . It just . . ."

She rubbed her lip. "I know, I know. Let's see you put it back, smart man. Go ahead! Don't look so helpless! Go *on!*"

I tried. I tried with everything I had, and you know, I couldn't put it back? Truly. It wasn't there, that's all. You've got to have some belief in a thing before you can so much as imagine it; you have to allow for its possibility. That stone was gone, and gone for good. It was terrifying. It was something more inevitable, more completely final, than death.

Afterward we walked along together. Judith clung to my hand all the way down to the lake. She was considerably shaken. Oddly, I wasn't. This thing was like a birthmark with me. I hadn't quite realized I was this way until that day; and then I just had the feeling, "I'll be damned, it's true after all."

It was true, and as time went on I realized more and more what was going to happen because of it. I was so certain that I couldn't even worry about it. For your own peace of mind, I'd try not to get into the same frame of mind, if I were you. I know what I am talking about, because I am you, being as to how you are all figments of my imagination. A strange and wonderful imagination . . .

So there we were down at the lake, and as long as I was with Judith I was all right. She kept me from thinking about anything but her own magnificent self, and that was what was required to maintain the status quo. Anything I doubted had no chance to exist. I couldn't doubt Judith. Not then I couldn't. Ah, what a beauty she was! . . . too bad about Judith.

I stood there watching her dive. She was a wonder. Only girl I ever knew personally who could do a two-and-a-half off a twelve-foot board. Maybe she could fly like that because she was half angel. I noticed Monte Carleau looking at her too, through his expensive polarized sun glasses. I went over to him and took the glasses away from him.

I didn't like Monte. I guess I envied him that long brown chassis of his, and his blue-black hair. I can admit things like that now.

"Hey!" he barked, grabbing for the specs. "What's the huge idea?"

I put on the glasses and watched Judith, who was poised for a cutaway, up there on the twelve-foot, and I talked to Monte over my shoulder. "I don't like you," I told him. "I don't like your staring at Judith. And I don't like to see you wearing glasses on account of I feel like poking you every time I see you and I'd hate to hit a guy with glasses on."

Judith did her cutaway and it was perfect. Then Monte grabbed me and twisted me around. He was thirty pounds heavier than I and one of those guys who takes credit to himself for being what he was born. "Gettin' big, hey?" he barked. "Little ol' Woodie, a tough guy after all these years! What's that twist see in you anyway? She sure shows bad taste."

"—and I don't like a guy that fights with his mouth," I said as if I hadn't been interrupted. I could just see Monte Carleau lying flat on his back with a busted jaw.

As a matter of fact I did see Monte Carleau lying flat on his back with a busted jaw. I shrugged and walked over to where Judith was climbing out of the water.

"What happened to the glamor-boy?" she asked, seeing the crowd gathering around the writhing figure on the bank.

"Oh—he just overlooked a possibility."

"Woodie—you didn't hit him?"

"Nup."

"Another—trick, Woodie?"

I didn't answer. She watched me for a moment, standing near, smelling of wet wool and wonder. She looked down at her nails, drew a deep breath and shrugged. She saw the glasses and reached for them.

She put them on and looked out across the lake, and gasped at the way the polarized glass killed the glare. "That *is* something. How does it work?" she asked in the tone that women in love use, and which signifies, "You know this as well as everything else, you great, big, clever brute, you."

I said vaguely, "Oh, it's something about making the light-waves all vibrate in one plane. I dunno."

"It hardly seems possible."

"No," I said. I'm pretty simple about things like that, anyway. As far as I was concerned it wasn't possible . . .

"Ouch!" she said. "Ouch. I was looking at that patch on the lake where all that sun glare is, and the glasses killed it, and all of a sudden it was there, just as if I hadn't had the glasses on at all . . . Woodie! Did you—?" She snatched off the glasses and stared at me with her eyes very wide.

I didn't say anything. Just tried to think about something else.

"You've ruined a good pair of sunglasses," she said.

"I've ruined an industry, I'm afraid."

She twitched the glasses into the lake and crinkled up the smoothness over her eyes. "Woodie—this was funny for a while. I—think . . . oh darling, I m so scared."

I spread my hands. "I can't—*help* it, honey. Honestly. It's just that—uh—since I figured something out up the trail there, anything I don't believe just . . . isn't. Just *can't be!*"

She looked at me while she shook her head, so that her long green eyes slid back and forth. "I don't like it. I don't like it at all, Woodie."

"Can't be helped."

"Let's go back," she said suddenly, and went to the dressing cabins.

I didn't worry much about Judith for a while after that. There were too many other things to worry about.

I was looking at some pictures in a magazine one day, and ran across the picture of an albino catfish which had a profile like a shrimp and a complexion like a four-color cosmetic ad. Weirdest thing I ever saw, and I couldn't be expected to believe it. A week later I read in the paper that the genus Clariidae had disappeared from the earth, simultaneously and with no apparent explanation—not only from its natural habitat, but from aquaria all over the world. I got quite a shock from that. You can imagine.

Good thing I've got a matter-of-fact sort of mind. Suppose I had been highly imaginative, now, like those characters who write for magazines. I might have believed in any old thing! "Ghosties and ghoulies and lang-leggedy beasties, and things that go boomp i' th' nicht—" as they put it in Scotland. People who believe in those things do see them, come to think of it. Maybe everybody's like me, only they don't realize it. I hoped, at the time, that nobody ever would. Another like me could certainly complicate things. I've made enough of a hash of it. A nice, churned-up, illimitably negative hash.

It didn't matter what the circumstances were in those next days, I drove a hard bargain with the fates. I could accept things—anything—unless something gave me cause to doubt. For quite a while I didn't realize where this was leading me; than I saw that every recognized fact must wind up in incredulity. Take a fact; reason from it; sooner or later you'll run up against something a little hard to take. My particular egocentricity led me to disbelieve, completely, anything I could not fully understand. For a lightweight like me that made my skepticism pretty inclusive after a while!

What I did was to get away from that summer resort—and Judith. She was the sort to stick to a man, no matter what. I wanted to find out "what."

She didn't want me to go. She was definite about it. "Something's happened to you, Woodie," she said quietly as she systematically threw out all the clothes I put in my suitcase, just as systematically as I put them in. "I told you before I don't like it. Isn't that enough to make you stop it?"

"I'm not doing anything I can stop," I said.

"I would stop," she said illogically, "if you asked *me* to."

"I told you, darling—I'm not doing anything. Things happen, that's all."

"Matter," she said suddenly, planting herself in front of me, "can be neither created nor destroyed."

I sighed and sat down on the edge of the bed. She immediately sat beside, on, and around me. "You been reading books," I said.

"Well, what about it? You're worried because things happen. You made a rock vanish. But you can't destroy matter. It has to turn into energy or something. So you just couldn't have done it."

"But I did."

"That doesn't matter. It isn't logic," she said, in a *quod erat demonstrandum* tone.

"You're overlooking one thing, irresistible creature," I said, pushing her away from me, "and that is the fact that I don't believe that precept about the indestructibility of matter, and never did. Therefore matter can be destroyed. Matter's just a figment of my imagination, anyway."

She opened and closed her lovely mouth twice and then said, "But in school—"

"*Damn* school!" I snapped. "Do I have to prove it to you?" I looked about the room for demonstration material, but couldn't see anything offhand I could do without. I was traveling light. My eyes fell on her low-heeled pumps. "Look—you've lost your shoes some place, I'll wager."

"I have not. I—*eek!*"

"—and your socks—"

"Woodie!"

"And that cute little blue beret—"

"Woodie, if you—"

"—what! No sunsuit?"

I suppose I went too far. As far as that was concerned, I should have realized that she didn't need one. As for those—well, how was I supposed to know she didn't use 'em? . . . I think that this was the only time I ever consciously did anything constructive with my creative imagination. Once somebody gave me a shapeless, hooded, scratchy burnoose from North Africa. It wasn't pretty, and it wasn't comfortable, but it was the most all-fired enveloping garment ever devised by the mind of man. But she didn't deserve this kind of treatment. When I thought "Cover up" I thought "Burnoose" automatically . . .

She clutched it around her. Now, get this. She didn't say "You're a beast." Or "heel." Or "Schlemiel." She said "I think you're wonderful, Woodie." And she ran out, crying.

I sat there for a long time and then I finished my packing.

When I got back to the city and into my room I felt much better. The way I was now, I had to have things around me that I knew and was used to. They lent solidity to a quivering old universe. As long as they stood firm, the universe was safe.

My room was pretty nice. If you came to see me, we could drink coffee, if you didn't mind getting up every time I reached for the sugar. Small. The carpet was on the wall and there was a Navajo rug on the floor. Couple of pastels and a nice charcoal of Judith. Indirect lighting, which meant a disk of black cardboard hanging by rubber bands from the otherwise unshaded bulb. Books. Bed. A radio that was going twenty-four hours a day.

Why should there be only twenty-four hours in a day?

I throttled the thought before it got anywhere.

I switched on both lights, the radio, and the hot-plate under my coffee brewer. That humming noise was the meter turning like a phonograph playing the "Landlord's Blues" (the utilities were included in the three fifty a week).

While I was hanging up my coat, Drip burst in, bellowing "Hiyah, Woodie? Hiyah, pal, back huh. What happened, huh?"

I closed the closet, spun around and gave him the old one-two on the mouth and chin, planted a foot in his stomach, and kicked him out in the hall. Opposite my door is what was first a crack, then a dent, now a hollow, where the Drip had continually hit it, I didn't have anything against him, but I'd asked him, I'd asked him time and time again, to knock before he came in.

As soon as I had the door closed he bumped timidly upon it.

"Who is it?"

"Me?"

I opened up. "Oh. Hello, Drip."

He came in and started his greetings and salutations all over again. Poor old Drip. He'd been pushed around by half the population from Eastport to Sandy Hook, and if he minded it, it never showed. He had a voice which was squeaky without being high, a curving stance that was apprehensive rather than round-shouldered, a complexion which was more pink than healthy, shoulders which were much broader than they were strong, and an untruthful aggressive chin. The guy was whacked but harmless.

He once asked me what I thought of him and I said, "You're the Creator's transition between a hypothesis and a theory." He's still trying to figure it out . . . if he's where he can figure anything.

Drip was useful, though. I don't care who you are, if you are with the Drip, you feel superior. So he was useful. The fact that he felt correspondingly inferior was his hard luck. It was no one's fault that he pushed an eight-ball ahead of him through life. Certainly not his.

He talked like this:

"Gee? Woodie? It's good to see you again? What are you going to do. Go back to work. Without? Finishing your vacation. Gee? Something must have. Did you fight. With Judith? Gosh . . . everything happens to you?"

"Do you want some coffee and stop crossquestioning me," I said.

"I'm sorry." The phrase was a reflex with him.

"What've you been doing with yourself, Drip?"

"Nothing? Nothing? Why are you. *Back*, Woodie?"

"Well, I'll tell you." I scratched my head. "Oh, hell. Never mind. Drip, I'm going to grab an oil can."

"Sh-ship out. On a tanker again? Oh, Woodie, you can't. *Do* that? I thought you'd quit going to sea."

"I can do anything," I said with conviction. "I'm— jittery around here, thassall."

He looked at the Arabian prayer-rug on the wall and the way it was reflected in the big mirror across the room. "If you go, could I have your room," he whispered as if he were asking me to die for him.

"No, boy. I want you to come with me."

"What?" he screamed. "Me. On a ship. Oh? No! Nono*no!*"

Looking at Drip putting sugar in his coffee, I felt suddenly sorry for him. I wanted to help him. I wanted him to share the exultance I had known in the days before I met Judith and dropped the anchor.

"Sure. Why not, Drip? I hit my first ship when I was sixteen, and I got treated all right."

"Oh, yes," he said without sarcasm, "you can do all

sorts of things. Not me? I could never do the things you've done?"

"Nuts," I said. Being with Drip always did one of two things: made me think how wonderful I was, or how pathetic he was. This was the latter case. In trying to help him out a little, I completely forgot my new potentialities. That's where I made my mistake. "Look," I said, "why is it that you're afraid of the ghost of your own shadow? I think it's because you refuse to make the effort to overcome your fear. If you're afraid of the dark, turn the light out, if you're afraid of falling, jump off a roof—just a little garage roof some place. If you're afraid of women, stick around them. And if you're afraid to ship out, for gosh sakes come along with me. I'll get a quartermaster's job and you can be ordinary seaman on my watch. I'll show you the ropes. But on any account, face your fear."

"That's the way you do things, isn't it?" he said almost adoringly.

"Well, sure. And you could if you tried. Come on, Drip. Make an effort."

His forehead wrinkled up and he said, "You don't know the kind of things I'm afraid of."

"Name 'em!"

"You'd laugh."

"No!" "Well, like now, there's a—a—right outside the door. Oh, it's horrible!"

I got up and opened the door. "There's nothing there but some dirt that should have been swept up three days ago."

"You see?" he said. "You want me to see things your way and you can't begin to see the things I see." And he began to cry.

I put my hand on his shoulder. "Drip. Cut it out. I can see everything you can. I can—" Why—of *course* I could! Drip was a part of—of everything. His ideas, his way of thought was a part of everything. Why not see what he saw? "Drip, I'll see things the way you do.

I *will!* I'll see everything with your eyes. I'll show you!"

And immediately the room began to shake itself; things wavered uncomfortably; then I realized that Drip was astigmatic. I also realized with a powerful shock that I had been nearly color blind, compared with the vividness with which he saw things. *Whew!*

Then I became conscious of the terrors—the million unidentifiable fears with which the poor dope had been living, day and night.

The ceiling was going to crush me. The floor was going to rise up and strike me. There was something in the closet, and it would jump out at me any second. I was going to swell inside my clothes and choke to death—I was going to go blind any day now—I was going to be run over if I went outside, suffocate if I stayed in. My appendix was going to burst some night when I was alone and I would die in agony. I was going to catch some terrible disease. People hated me. And laughed . . . I was alone. I was on the outside looking in. I was on the inside looking on. I hated myself.

Gradually the impact of the thing faded while the horror grew. I glanced at Drip; he was still crying into his coffee, but at least he was not trembling. I was trembling . . . poor, scared, morbid, dismal Drip was, in that moment, a tower of strength.

I must have stood there for quite a while, pulling out of it. I had to *do* something! I couldn't shrink against Drip! I had my self-respect to think of. I—

"Wh-what was that you said about . . . outside the door?"

He started, looked up at me, pointed wordlessly at the door. I reached out and opened it.

It was out there, crunched in a corner in the dimness, waiting for someone to come along. I slammed the door and leaned against it, mopping my forehead with my sleeve.

"Is it out there?" whispered Drip.

I nodded. "It's . . . covered with mouths," I gasped. "It's all *wet!*"

He got up and peeked out. Then he laughed. "Oh, that's just the little one. He won't hurt you. Wait till you see the others. Gee? Woodie. You're the first one who ever saw them, besides me. Come on? I'll show you more."

He got up and went out, waiting just outside for me. I realized now why he had always refused to precede me through a door. When he went out he trod on a writhing thing and killed it so it would not creep up my legs. I realized that I must have done it for him many times in the past without realizing it.

We came to the top of the stairs. They wound away from under my feet. They looked fragile. They looked dangerous. But it seemed all right as long as he led the way. He had a certain control over the thousands of creeping, crawling, fluttering things around us. He passed the little landing and something tentacular melted into the wall. Little slimy things slid out from under his feet and reappeared just behind mine. I pressed very close to him, crushed by the power of hate which oozed from them.

When we reached his room, which was just above mine, he put his hand on the doorknob and turned to me. "We have to burst in," he whispered, "there's a big one that hides here. We can frighten him away if we come suddenly. Otherwise he might not know we were inside. And if he found us in there he would. Eat us?"

Drip turned the knob silently and hurled the door open. A livid mass of blood and blackness that filled the whole room shrank into itself, melting down like ice in a furnace. When it was in midair, and about the size of a plum, it dropped squashily to the floor and rolled under the bed. "You see," said Drip with conviction. "If we went in quietly we would shrink down? With it?"

"My God!" I said hoarsely. "Let's get out of here!"

"Oh, it's all right," he said almost casually. "As long as we know exactly what time it is, he can't come back until we go." I understood now why Drip had his wall covered with clocks.

I was going to sink down on a chair because I felt a little weak, but I noticed that the seat of the straight-back he had—it was red plush—was quivering. I pointed to it.

"What? Oh, don't mind that," said Drip. "I think it's stuffed with spiders. They haven't bitten anyone yet, but soon they will. Burst the seat. And swarm all over the room?"

I looked at him. "This is hor—Drip! What are you grinning about?"

"Grinning. I'm sorry? You see, I never saw anyone frightened before by my things?"

"*Your* things?"

"Certainly. I made them up."

I have never been so furious. That he should terrify me—*me*—with figments of his phobiacal imagination; make me envy him for knowing his way about his terrifying world; put me in an inferior position—it was unthinkable! It was—impossible!

"Why did you make them up?" I asked him with frozen intensity.

His answer, of all things in the fluid universe, was the most rational. I have thought of it since. He said:

"I made them up because I was afraid of things. Ever since I could remember. So I didn't know what it was I was afraid of, and I had to make up something to fear. If I didn't do that I *would go crazy* . . ."

I backed away from him, mouthing curses, and the lines of the room straightened out as I regained my own point of view. The colors dulled to my old familiar tones, and Drip, that improbable person, that hypothesis, faded out, lingering a moment like a double exposure, and then vanished.

I went downstairs. Drip was better off nonexistent, I

thought as I tuned out a jam session. He was a subversive influence in this—my universe. He was as horrible a figment of imagination as was that thing in the hall of his. And just as unbelievable . . . I got me Tchaikovsky's B minor concerto on the radio because that's the way I felt, and I lay down on the bed. Jive would have driven me morbid, because Drip had been a hep-cat, and I didn't want to think of him somehow.

Footsteps came soft-shoeing up the corridor and stopped outside my door. "Woodie—"

"Oh, damn," I said. "Come in, Judith."

She passed the knob from one hand to the other as she entered, looking at me.

"I must be quite a guy to have such a lovely shadow."

"Every man in the world seems to be after me," she said, "and I'm stupid enough to follow you. I came back to say goodbye."

"Where are you going?"

"No place."

"Where am I going?"

"You've already gone."

"I . . . Where?"

"Here. From the camp. You forgot to kiss me before you left. You can't get away with that."

"Oh." I got up and kissed her. "Now why did you follow me?"

"I was afraid."

"What; that I'd jump a ship?"

She nodded. "That and . . . I dunno. I was afraid, thassall."

"I promised you I'd stay ashore, didn't I?"

"You're such an awful liar," she reminded me without malice.

"Heh!" I said. "Always?"

"As long as I've known you—"

"I love you."

"—except when you say that. Woodie, that's one thing I *have* to be sure of."

"I know how it is, insect." I let her go and reached for my hat. "Let's eat."

I remember that meal. It was the last meal I ate on earth. Minestrone, chicken cacciatore and black coffee at a little Italian kitchen. And over the coffee I explained it to her again, the thing that had happened to me.

"Woodie, you're impossible!"

"Could be. Could be. I've found a lot of things impossible in the last couple of days. They don't exist anymore. Drip, for instance."

"Drip? What happened?"

I told her. She began putting on her hat.

"Wait," I said. "I haven't finished my coffee."

"Do you realize what you're telling me? Woodie, if you're wrong about all this, you don't know it—you believe it—and you're insane. If you're right—you *murdered* that boy!"

"I did nothing of the kind. I did nothing of any kind. Damn it, darling, I know this is a little hard to take. But the universe is my dream, and that's . . . all. Drip couldn't have existed—you told me that yourself when you first met him."

"That was strictly a gag," she said, and stood up.

"Where are you going?"

"I don't know." She sounded tired. "Anywhere . . . away from you, Woodie. Let me know when you've got all this out of your head. I've never heard anything so . . . Oh, well. And anyway, there's a natural explanation for everything that's happened."

"Sure. I've given you one and you won't believe it."

She threw up her hands in what I saw was very real disgust. I caught her hand as she turned away. "Judith!" She stood there not looking at me, not trying to get away, simply not *caring*. "You don't mean this, Judy kid. You can't. You're the only thing I can believe in now."

"When you 'dreamed' me up, Woodie, you let me have too much discernment to stay in love with a . . . a lunatic," she said quietly. She slipped her hand out of mine and went away from there.

I sat still for a long time watching tomato sauce seep into a piece of Italian bread. "When it gets to that pore in the bread," I told myself, "she'll come back." A little later, "When it gets to the crust—" It took quite a while, and she still didn't come back. I tried to laugh it off, but laughing hurt my face. I paid my way out and drifted down the street. I found me a ginmill and I got good . . . and . . . plastered.

Listen, winged things. Listen, things that delight in liveness and greenness. I am sorry I created you, I am sorry I dreamed of you, watched you grow, watched you die and die and live again to see your ultimate death. You were made of laughter and of the warmth in my heart. You were made of the light of the sun I made. You and shy creatures, and strong and beautiful things and people, and music, and richness, and magic, and the beat of hearts; you are gone because I was awakened. Forgive me, my glorious phantasms!

I knew what to start on. It's called Habañera Seco and they brew it in Guatemala and it's smooth like scotch and strong like vodka and worse all around than absinthe. If you can't stand to mix these—and who can?—you can't drink Habañera . . .

One drink and I felt better. Two, much better. Three, and I was back where I started from. Four, I started getting dismal. Seven, I was definitely morbid. Great stuff. Far as I was concerned, the woes of the world were in a bottomless bottle, and it was my duty and desire to empty the bottle and buy another. Judith was gone, and without Judith there was no sun any more, and nothing for it to shine on. Everything was over, I said dramatically to myself; and, by God, I'd see that a good job was done of it. I staggered out and leaned against the door post, looking up the street.

"Wake up, Woodie," I quavered, "It's all over now. It's all done. There's nothing left any more, anywhere,

anywhere. A life is an improbable louse on a sterile sphere. A man is a monster and a woman is a wraith! I am not a man but a consciousness asleep, and now I wake! Now I wake!" I pushed away from the door post and began screaming, "Wake! Wake!"

Just how it happened I can't say. Things slipped and slid out of existence. There was no violence, nothing fell; everything went out of focus and left me alone in an element which was deep and thick and the essence of solitude. What struck coldly into me was something I saw just before I . . . went. It was Judith. She was running down the street toward me with her arms out, and a smile keeping tears from running all the way down her face. She had come back after all, but the thing couldn't be stopped now. My dream was gone!

I and that thick element expanded soundlessly to the limits of my dream, the universe, and where we passed, mighty suns and nebulae joined the nothingness of us. I rode again in a place where there is no time, where I had been before I dreamed up a universe. I thought about it then, how birds and rocks and wars and loveliness and choking exultance had been figments of my proud imagination.

Only now can I dare to face that ultimate question, that last, deep, inclusive conception . . .

. . . for if all things in a universe were but peopling a dream, and if they could not exist when their existence was doubted, then it is possible that I myself am a mere figment of my imagi

The Skills of Xanadu

Wishful thinking . . . I yearn to live on Xanadu, and wear their garment, and join with them in their marvelous life-style.

Well, I can't live there and I can't live as they do, but I can do the next best thing: to infect locked-up minds with the idea of freedom in highly contagious ways.

Dr. Toni Morrison, novelist, essayist, and educator, gave a commencement address at Bard College in 1979 in which she said (among many other powerful things) that your freedom is worthless unless you use it to free someone else, and that happiness is not happiness unless it makes others happy.

I never set down in a simple declarative sentence the theme of my Xanadu story, and now a truly great human being has done it for me.

And the Sun went nova and humanity fragmented and fled; and such is the self-knowledge of humankind that it knew it must guard its past as it guarded its being, or it would cease to be human; and such was its pride in itself that it made of its traditions a ritual and a standard.

The great dream was that wherever humanity settled, fragment by fragment by fragment, however it lived, it would continue rather than begin again, so that all through the universe and the years, humans would be humans, speaking as humans, thinking as humans, aspiring and progressing as humans; and whenever human met human, no matter how different, how distant, he would come in peace, meet his own kind, speak his own tongue.

Humans, however, being humans—

Bril emerged near the pink star, disliking its light, and found the fourth planet. It hung waiting for him like an exotic fruit. (And was it ripe, and could he ripen it? And what if it were poison?) He left his machine in orbit and descended in a bubble. A young savage watched him come and waited by a waterfall.

"Earth was my mother," said Bril from the bubble. It was the formal greeting of all humankind, spoken in the Old Tongue.

"And my father," said the savage, in an atrocious accent.

Watchfully, Bril emerged from the bubble, but stood very close by it. He completed his part of the ritual. "I respect the disparity of our wants, as individuals, and greet you."

"I respect the identity of our needs, as humans, and greet you. I am Wonyne," said the youth, "son of Tanyne, of the Senate, and Nina. This place is Xanadu, the district, on Xanadu, the fourth planet."

"I am Bril of Kit Carson, second planet of the Sumner System, and a member of the Sole Authority," said the newcomer, adding, "and I come in peace."

He waited then, to see if the savage would discard

any weapons he might have, according to historic protocol. Wonyne did not; he apparently had none. He wore only a cobwebby tunic and a broad belt made of flat, black, brilliantly polished stones and could hardly have concealed so much as a dart. Bril waited yet another moment, watching the untroubled face of the savage, to see if Wonyne suspected anything of the arsenal hidden in the sleek black uniform, the gleaming jackboots, the metal gauntlets.

Wonyne said only, "Then, in peace, welcome." He smiled. "Come with me to Tanyne's house and mine, and be refreshed."

"You say Tanyne, your father, is a Senator? Is he active now? Could he help me to reach your center of government?"

The youth paused, his lips moving slightly, as if he were translating the dead language into another tongue. Then, "Yes. Oh, yes."

Bril flicked his left gauntlet with his right fingertips and the bubble sprang away and up, where at length it would join the ship until it was needed. Wonyne was not amazed—probably, thought Bril, because it was beyond his understanding.

Bril followed the youth up a winding path past a wonderland of flowering plants, most of them purple, some white, a few scarlet, and all jeweled by the waterfall. The higher reaches of the path were flanked by thick soft grass, red as they approached, pale pink as they passed.

Bril's narrow black eyes flickered everywhere, saw and recorded everything: the easy-breathing boy's spring up the slope ahead, and the constant shifts of color in his gossamer garment as the wind touched it; the high trees, some of which might conceal a man or a weapon; the rock outcroppings and what oxides they told of; the birds he could see and the birdsongs he heard which might be something else.

He was a man who missed only the obvious, and there is so little that is obvious.

Yet he was not prepared for the house; he and the boy were halfway across the parklike land which surrounded it before he recognized it as such.

It seemed to have no margins. It was here high and there only a place between flower beds; yonder a room became a terrace, and elsewhere a lawn was a carpet because there was a roof over it. The house was divided into areas rather than rooms, by open grilles and by arrangements of color. Nowhere was there a wall. There was nothing to hide behind and nothing that could be locked. All the land, all the sky, looked into and through the house, and the house was one great window on the world.

Seeing it, Bril felt a slight shift in his opinion of the natives. His feeling was still one of contempt, but now he added suspicion. A cardinal dictum on humans as he knew them was: *Every man has something to hide.* Seeing a mode of living like this did not make him change his dictum: he simply increased his watchfulness, asking: *How do they hide it?*

"Tan! Tan!" the boy was shouting. "I've brought a friend!"

A man and a woman strolled toward them from a garden. The man was huge, but otherwise so like the youth Wonyne that there could be no question of their relationship. Both had long, narrow, clear gray eyes set very wide apart, and red—almost orange—hair. The noses were strong and delicate at the same time, their mouths thin-lipped but wide and good-natured.

But the woman—

It was a long time before Bril could let himself look, let himself believe that there was such a woman. After his first glance, he made of her only a presence and fed himself small nibbles of belief in his eyes, in the fact that there could be hair like that, face, voice, body. She was dressed, like her husband and the boy, in the smoky kaleidoscope which resolved itself, when the wind permitted, into a black-belted tunic.

"He is Bril of Kit Carson in the Sumner System," babbled the boy, "and he's a member of the Sole Authority and it's the second planet and he knew the greeting and got it right. So did I," he added, laughing. "This is Tanyne, of the Senate, and my mother Nina."

"You are welcome, Bril of Kit Carson," she said to him; and unbelieving in this way that had come upon him, he took away his gaze and inclined his head.

"You must come in," said Tanyne cordially, and led the way through an arbor which was not the separate arch it appeared to be, but an entrance.

The room was wide, wider at one end than the other, though it was hard to determine by how much. The floor was uneven, graded upward toward one corner, where it was a mossy bank. Scattered here and there were what the eye said were white and striated gray boulders; the hand would say they were flesh. Except for a few shelf- and tablelike niches on these and in the bank, they were the only furniture.

Water ran frothing and gurgling through the room, apparently as an open brook; but Bril saw Nina's bare foot tread on the invisible covering that followed it down to the pool at the other end. The pool was the one he had seen from outside, indeterminately in and out of the house. A large tree grew by the pool and leaned its heavy branches toward the bank, and evidently its wide-flung limbs were webbed and tented between by the same invisible substance which covered the brook, for they formed the only cover overhead yet, to the ear, felt like a ceiling.

The whole effect was, to Bril, intensely depressing, and he surprised himself with a flash of homesickness for the tall steel cities of his home planet.

Nina smiled and left them. Bril followed his host's example and sank down on the ground, or floor, where it became a bank, or wall. Inwardly, Bril rebelled at the lack of decisiveness, of discipline, of clear-cut limitation inherent in such haphazard design as this. But he was well trained and quite prepared, at first, to keep his feelings to himself among barbarians.

"Nina will join us in a moment," said Tanyne.

Bril, who had been watching the woman's swift movements across the courtyard through the transparent wall opposite, controlled a start. "I am unused to your ways and wondered what she was doing," he said.

"She is preparing a meal for you," explained Tanyne.

"Herself?"

Tanyne and his son gazed wonderingly. "Does that seem unusual to you?"

"I understood the lady was wife to a Senator," said Bril. It seemed adequate as an explanation, but only to him. He looked from the boy's face to the man's. "Perhaps I understand something different when I use the term 'Senator.'"

"Perhaps you do. Would you tell us what a Senator is on the planet Kit Carson?"

"He is a member of the Senate, subservient to the Sole Authority, and in turn leader of a free Nation."

"And his wife?"

"His wife shares his privileges. She might serve a member of the Sole Authority, but hardly anyone else—certainly not an unidentified stranger."

"Interesting," said Tanyne, while the boy murmured the astonishment he had not expressed at Bril's bubble, or Bril himself. "Tell me, have you not identified yourself, then?"

"He did, by the waterfall," the youth insisted.

"I gave you no proof," said Bril stiffly. He watched father and son exchange a glance. "Credentials, written authority." He touched the flat pouch hung on his power belt.

Wonyne asked ingenuously, "Do the credentials say you are *not* Bril of Kit Carson in the Sumner System?"

Bril frowned at him and Tanyne said gently, "Wonyne, take care." To Bril, he said, "Surely there are many differences between us, as there always are between different worlds. But I am certain of this one similarity: the young at times run straight where wisdom has built a winding path."

Bril sat silently and thought this out. It was probably some sort of apology, he decided, and gave a single sharp nod. Youth, he thought, was an attenuated defect here. A boy Wonyne's age would be a soldier on Carson, ready for a soldier's work, and no one would be apologizing for him. Nor would he be making blunders. *None!*

He said, "These credentials are for your officials when I meet with them. By the way, when can that be?"

Tanyne shrugged his wide shoulders. "Whenever you like."

"The sooner the better."

"Very well."

"Is it far?"

Tanyne seemed perplexed. "Is what far?"

"Your capital, or wherever it is your Senate meets."

"Oh, I see. It doesn't meet, in the sense you mean. It is always in session, though, as they used to say. We—"

He compressed his lips and made a liquid, bisyllabic sound, then he laughed. "I do beg your pardon," he said warmly. "The Old Tongue lacks certain words, certain concepts. What is your word for—er—the-presence-of-all-in-the-presence-of-one?"

"I think," said Bril carefully, "that we had better go back to the subject at hand. Are you saying that your Senate does not meet in some official place, at some appointed time?"

"I—" Tan hesitated, then nodded. "Yes, that is true as far as it—"

"And there is no possibility of my addressing your Senate in person?"

"I didn't say that." Tan tried twice to express the thought, while Bril's eyes slowly narrowed. Tan suddenly burst into laughter. "Using the Old Tongue to tell old tales and to speak with a friend are two different things," he said ruefully. "I wish you would learn our speech. Would you, do you suppose? It is rational and well based on what you know. Surely you have another language besides the Old Tongue on Kit Carson?"

"I honor the Old Tongue," said Bril stiffly, dodging the question. Speaking very slowly, as if to a retarded child, he said, "I should like to know when I may be taken to those in authority here, in order to discuss certain planetary and interplanetary matters with them."

"Discuss them with me."

"You are a Senator," Bril said, in a tone which meant clearly: *You are only a Senator.*

"True," said Tanyne.

With forceful patience, Bril asked, "And what is a Senator here?"

"A contact point between the people of his district and the people everywhere. One who knows the special problems of a small section of the planet and can relate them to planetary policy."

"And whom does the Senate serve?"

"The people," said Tanyne, as if he had been asked to repeat himself.

"Yes, yes, of course. And who, then, serves the Senate?"

"The Senators."

Bril closed his eyes and barely controlled the salty syllable which welled up inside him. "Who," he inquired steadily, "is your Government?"

The boy had been watching them eagerly, alternately, like a devotee at some favorite fast ball game. Now he asked, "What's a Government?"

Nina's interruption at that point was most welcome to Bril. She came across the terrace from the covered area where she had been doing mysterious things at a long work-surface in the garden. She carried an enormous tray—guided it, rather, as Bril saw when she came closer. She kept three fingers under the tray and one behind it, barely touching it with her palm. Either the transparent wall of the room disappeared as she approached, or she passed through a section where there was none.

"I do hope you find something to your taste among these," she said cheerfully, as she brought the tray down to a hummock near Bril. "This is the flesh of birds, this of small mammals, and, over here, fish. These cakes are made of four kinds of grain, and the white cakes here of just one, the one we call milk-wheat. Here is water, and these two are wines, and this one is a distilled spirit we call warm-ears."

Bril, keeping his eyes on the food, and trying to keep his universe from filling up with the sweet fresh scent of her as she bent over him, so near, said, "This is welcome."

She crossed to her husband and sank down at his feet, leaning back against his legs. He twisted her heavy hair gently in his fingers and she flashed a small smile up at him. Bril looked from the food, colorful as a corsage, here steaming, there gathering frost from the air, to the three smiling, expectant faces and did not know what to do.

"Yes, this is welcome," he said again, and still they sat there, watching him. He picked up the white cake and rose, looked out and around, into the house, through it and beyond. Where could one go in such a place?

Steam from the tray touched his nostrils and saliva filled his mouth. He was hungry, but. . . .

He sighed, sat down, gently replaced the cake. He tried to smile and could not.

"Does none of it please you?" asked Nina, concerned.

"I can't eat here!" said Bril; then, sensing something in the natives that had not been there before, he added, "thank you." Again he looked at their controlled faces. He said to Nina, "It is very well prepared and good to look on."

"Then eat," she invited, smiling again.

This did something that their house, their garments, their appallingly easy ways—sprawling all over the place, letting their young speak up at will, the shameless admission that they had a patois of their own—that none of these things had been able to do. Without losing his implacable dignity by any slightest change of expression, he yet found himself blushing. Then he scowled and let the childish display turn to a flush of anger. He would be glad, he thought furiously, when he had the heart of this culture in the palm of his hand, to squeeze when he willed; then there would be an end to these hypocritical amenities and they would learn who could be humiliated.

But these three faces, the boy's so open and unconscious of wrong, Tanyne's so strong and anxious for him, Nina's—that face, that face of Nina's—they were all utterly guileless. He must not let them know of his embarrassment. If they had planned it, he must not let them suspect his vulnerability.

With an immense effort of will, he kept his voice low; still, it was harsh. "I think," he said slowly, "that we on Kit Carson regard the matter of privacy perhaps a little more highly than you do."

They exchanged an astonished look, and then comprehension dawned visibly on Tanyne's ruddy face. "You don't eat together!"

Bril did not shudder, but it was in his word: "No."

"Oh," said Nina, "I'm *so* sorry!"

Bril thought it wise not to discover exactly what she was sorry about. He said, "No matter. Customs differ. I shall eat when I am alone."

"Now that we understand," said Tanyne, "go ahead. Eat."

"But they *sat* there!

"Oh," said Nina, "I wish you spoke our other language; it would be so easy to explain!" She leaned forward to him, put out her arms, as if she could draw meaning itself from the air and cast it over him.

"Please try to understand, Bril. You are very mistaken about one thing—we honor privacy above almost anything else."

"We don't mean the same thing when we say it," said Bril.

"It means aloneness with oneself, doesn't it? It means to do things, think or make or just *be*, without intrusion."

"So?" replied Wonyne happily, throwing out both hands in a gesture that said *quod erat demonstrandum.* "Go on then—eat! We won't look!" and helped the situation not at all.

"Wonyne's right," chuckled the father, "but, as usual, a little too direct. He means we can't look, Bril. If you want privacy, *we can't see you.*"

Angry, reckless, Bril suddenly reached to the tray. He snatched up a goblet, the one she had indicated as water, thumbed a capsule out of his belt, popped it into his mouth, drank and swallowed. He banged the goblet back on the tray and shouted, "Now you've seen all you're going to see."

With an indescribable expression, Nina drifted upward to her feet, bent like a dancer and touched the tray. It lifted and she guided it away across the courtyard.

"All right," said Wonyne. It was precisely as if someone had spoken and he had acknowledged. He lunged out, following his mother.

What *had* been on her face?

Something she could not contain; something rising to that smooth surface, about to reveal outlines, break through . . . anger? Bril hoped so. Insult? He could, he supposed, understand that. But—laughter? *Don't make it laughter,* something within him pleaded.

"Bril," said Tanyne.

For the second time, he was so lost in contemplation of the woman that Tanyne's voice made him start.

"What is it?"

"If you will tell me what arrangements you would like for eating, I'll see to it that you get them."

"You wouldn't know how," said Bril bluntly. He threw his sharp, cold gaze across the room and back. "You people don't build walls you can't see through, doors you can close."

"Why, no, we don't." As always, the giant left the insult and took only the words.

I bet you don't, Bril said silently, *not even for*—and a horrible suspicion began to grow within him. "We of Kit Carson feel that all human history and development are away from the animal, toward something higher. We are, of course, chained to the animal state, but we do what we can to eliminate every animal act as a public spectacle." Sternly, he waved a shining gauntlet at the great open house. "You have apparently not reached such an idealization. I have seen how you eat; doubtless you perform your other functions so openly."

"Oh, yes," said Tanyne. "But with this—" he pointed"—it's hardly the same thing."

"With what?"

Tanyne again indicated one of the boulderlike objects. He tore off a clump of moss—it was real moss—and tossed it to the soft surface of one of the boulders. He reached down and touched one of the gray streaks. The moss sank into the surface the way a pebble will in quicksand, but much faster.

"It will not accept living animal matter above a certain level of complexity," he explained, "but it instantly absorbs every molecule of anything else, not only on the surface but for a distance above."

"And that's a—a—where you—"

Tan nodded and said that that was exactly what it was.

"But—anyone can see you!"

Tan shrugged and smiled. "How? That's what I meant when I said it's hardly the same thing. Of eating, we make a social occasion. But this—" he threw another clump of moss and watched it vanish—"just isn't observed." His sudden laugh rang out and again he said, "I wish you'd learn the language. Such a thing is so easy to express."

But Bril was concentrating on something else. "I appreciate your hospitality," he said, using the phrase stiltedly, "but I'd like to be moving on." He eyed the boulder distastefully. "And very soon."

"As you wish. You have a message for Xanadu. Deliver it, then."

"To your Government."

"To our Government. I told you before, Bril—when you're ready, proceed."

"I cannot believe that you represent this planet!"

"Neither can I," said Tanyne pleasantly. "I don't. Through me, you can speak to forty-one others, all Senators."

"Is there no other way?"

Tanyne smiled. "Forty-one other ways. Speak to any of the others. It amounts to the same thing."

"And no higher government body?"

Tanyne reached out a long arm and plucked a goblet from a niche in the moss bank. It was chased crystal with a luminous metallic rim.

"Finding the highest point of the government of Xanadu is like finding the highest point on this," he said. He ran a finger around the inside of the rim and the goblet chimed beautifully.

"Pretty unstable," growled Bril.

Tanyne made it sing again and replaced it; whether that was an answer or not, Bril could not know.

He snorted, "No wonder the boy didn't know what Government was."

"We don't use the term," said Tanyne. "We don't need it. There are few things here that a citizen can't handle for himself; I wish I could show you how few. If you'll live with us a while, I will show you."

He caught Bril's eye squarely as it returned from another disgusted and apprehensive trip to the boulder, and laughed outright. But the kindness in his voice as he went on quenched Bril's upsurge of indignant fury, and a little question curled up: *Is he managing me?* But there wasn't time to look at it.

"Can your business wait until you know us, Bril? I tell you now, there is no centralized Government here, almost no government at all; we of the Senate are advisory. I tell you, too, that to speak to one Senator is to speak to all, and that you may do it now, this minute, or a year from now—whenever you like. I am telling you the truth and you may accept it or you may spend months, years, traveling this planet and checking up on me; you'll always come out with the same answer."

Noncommittally, Bril said, "How do I know that what I tell you is accurately relayed to the others?"

"It isn't relayed," said Tan frankly. "We all hear it simultaneously."

"Some sort of radio?"

Tan hesitated, then nodded. "Some sort of radio."

"I won't learn your language," Bril said abruptly. "I can't live as you do. If you can accept those conditions, I will stay a short while."

"Accept? We *insist!*" Tanyne bounded cheerfully to the niche where the goblet stood and held his palm up. A large, opaque sheet of a shining white material rolled down and stopped. "Draw with your fingers," he said.

"Draw? Draw what?"

"A place of your own. How you would like to live, eat, sleep, everything."

"I require very little. None of us on Kit Carson do."

He pointed the finger of his gauntlet like a weapon, made a couple of dabs in the corner of the screen to test the line, and then dashed off a very creditable parallelepiped. "Taking my height as one unit, I'd want this one-and-a-half long, one-and-a-quarter high. Slit vents at eye level, one at each end, two on each side, screened against insects—"

"We have no preying insects," said Tanyne.

"Screened anyway, and with as near an unbreakable mesh as you have. Here a hook suitable for hanging a garment. Here a bed, flat, hard, with firm padding as thick as my hand, one-and-one-eighth units long, one-third wide. All sides under the bed enclosed and equipped as a locker, impregnable, and to which only I have the key or combination. Here a shelf one-third by one-quarter units, one-half unit off the floor, suitable for eating from a seated posture.

"One of—those, if it's self-contained and reliable," he said edgily, casting a thumb at the boulderlike convenience. "The whole structure to be separate from all others on high ground and overhung by nothing—no trees, no cliffs, with approaches clear and visible from all sides; as strong as speed permits; and equipped with a light I can turn off and a door that only I can unlock."

"Very well," said Tanyne easily. "Temperature?"

"The same as this spot now."

"Anything else? Music? Pictures? We have some fine moving—"

Bril, from the top of his dignity, snorted his most eloquent snort. "Water, if you can manage it. As to those other things, this is a dwelling, not a pleasure palace."

"I hope you will be comfortable in this—in it," said Tanyne, with barely a trace of sarcasm.

"It is precisely what I am used to," Bril answered loftily.

"Come, then."

"What?"

The big man waved him on and passed through the arbor. Bril, blinking in the late pink sunlight, followed him.

On the gentle slope above the house, halfway between it and the mountaintop beyond, was a meadow of the red grass Bril had noticed on his way from the waterfall. In the center of this meadow was a crowd of people, bustling like moths around a light, their flimsy, colorful clothes flashing and gleaming in a thousand shades. And in the middle of the crowd lay a coffin-shaped object.

Bril could not believe his eyes, then stubbornly would not, and at last, as they came near, yielded and admitted it to himself: this was the structure he had just sketched.

He walked more and more slowly as the wonder of it grew on him. He watched the people—children, even—swarming around and over the little building, sealing the edge between roof and wall with a humming device, laying screen on the slit-vents. A little girl, barely a toddler, came up to him fearlessly and in lisping Old Tongue asked for his hand, which she clapped to a tablet she carried.

"To make your keys," explained Tanyne, watching the child scurry off to a man waiting at the door.

He took the tablet and disappeared inside, and they could see him kneel by the bed. A young boy overtook them and ran past, carrying a sheet of the same material the roof and walls were made of. It seemed light, but its slightly rough, pale-tan surface gave an impression of great toughness. As they drew up at the door, they saw the boy take the material and set it in position between the end of the bed and the doorway. He aligned it carefully, pressing it against the wall, and struck it once with the heel of his hand, and there was Bril's required table, level, rigid, and that without braces and supports.

"You seemed to like the looks of some of this, anyway." It was Nina, with her tray. She floated it to the new table, waved cheerfully and left.

"With you in a moment," Tan called, adding three singing syllables in the Xanadu tongue which were, Bril concluded, an endearment of some kind; they certainly sounded like it. Tan turned back to him, smiling.

"Well, Bril, how is it?"

Bril could only ask, "Who gave the orders?"

"You did," said Tan, and there didn't seem to be any answer to that.

Already, through the open door, he could see the crowd drifting away, laughing, and singing their sweet language to each other. He saw a young man scoop up scarlet flowers from the pink sward and hand them to a smiling girl, and unaccountably the scene annoyed him. He turned away abruptly and went about the walls, thumping them and peering through the vents. Tanyne knelt by the bed, his big shoulders bulging as he tugged at the locker. It might as well have been solid rock.

"Put your hand there," he said, pointing, and Bril clapped his gauntlet to the plate he indicated.

Sliding panels parted. Bril got down and peered inside. It had its own light, and he could see the buff-colored wall of the structure at the back and the heavy filleted partition which formed the bed uprights. He touched the panel again and the doors slid silently shut, so tight that he could barely see their meeting.

"The door's the same," said Tanyne. "No one but you can open it. Here's water. You didn't say where to put it. If this is inconvenient . . ."

When Bril put his hand near the spigot, water flowed into a catch basin beneath. "No, that is satisfactory. They work like specialists."

"They are," said Tanyne.

"Then they have built such a strange structure before?"

"Never."

Bril looked at him sharply. This ingenuous barbarian surely could not be making a fool of him by design! No, this must be some slip of semantics, some shift in meaning over the years which separated each of them from the common ancestor. He would not forget it, but he set it aside for future thought.

"Tanyne," he asked suddenly, "how many are you in Xanadu?"

"In the district, three hundred. On the planet, twelve, almost thirteen thousand."

"We are one and a half billion," said Bril. "And what is your largest city?"

"City," said Tanyne, as if searching through the files of his memory. "Oh—city! We have none. There are forty-two districts like this one, some larger, some smaller."

"Your entire planetary population could be housed in one building within one city on Kit Carson. And how many generations have your people been here?"

"Thirty-two, thirty-five, something like that."

"We settled Kit Carson not quite six Earth centuries ago. In point of time, then, it would seem that yours is the older culture. Wouldn't you be interested in how we have been able to accomplish so much more?"

"Fascinated," said Tanyne.

"You have some clever little handicrafts here," Bril mused, "and a quite admirable cooperative ability. You could make a formidable thing of this world, if you wanted to, and if you had the proper guidance."

"Oh, could we really?" Tanyne seemed very pleased.

"I must think," said Bril somberly. "You are not what I—what I had supposed. Perhaps I shall stay a little longer than I had planned. Perhaps while I am learning about your people, you in turn could be learning about mine."

"Delighted," said Tanyne. "Now is there anything else you need?"

"Nothing. You may leave me."

His autocratic tone gained him only one of the big man's pleasant, open-faced smiles. Tanyne waved his hand and left. Bril heard him calling his wife in ringing baritone notes, and her glad answer. He set his mailed hand against the door plate and it slid shut silently.

Now what, he asked himself, *got me to do all that bragging?* Then the astonishment at the people of Xanadu rose up and answered the question for him.

What manner of people are specialists at something they have never done before?

He got out his stiff, polished, heavy uniform, his gauntlets, his boots. They were all wired together, power supply in the boots, controls and computers in the trousers and belt, sensory mechs in the tunic, projectors and field loci in the gloves.

He hung the clothes on the hook provided and set the alarm field for anything larger than a mouse any closer than thirty meters. He dialed a radiation dome to cover his structure and exclude all spy beams or radiation weapons. Then he swung his left gauntlet on its cable over to the table and went to work on one small corner.

In half an hour, he had found a combination of heat and pressure that would destroy the pale brown board, and he sat down on the edge of the bed, limp with amazement. You could build a spaceship with stuff like this.

Now he had to believe that they had it in stock sizes exactly to his specifications, which would mean warehouses and manufacturing facilities capable of making up those and innumerable other sizes; or he had to believe that they had machinery capable of making what his torches had just destroyed, in job lots, right now.

But they didn't have any industrial plant to speak of, and if they had warehouses, they had them where the Kit Carson robot scouts had been unable to detect them in their orbiting for the last fifty years.

Slowly he lay down to think.

To acquire a planet, you locate the central government. If it is an autocracy, organized tightly up to the peak, so much the better; the peak is small and you kill it or control it and use the organization. If there is no government at all, you recruit the people or you exterminate them. If there is a plant, you run it with overseers and make the natives work it until you can train your own people to it and eliminate the natives.

If there are skills, you learn them or you control those who have them. All in the book; a rule for every eventuality, every possibility.

But what if, as the robots reported, there was high technology and no plant? Planetwide cultural stability and almost no communications?

Well, nobody ever heard of such a thing, so when the robots report it, you send an investigator. All he has to find out is how they do it. All he has to do is to parcel up what is to be kept and what eliminated when the time comes for an expeditionary force.

There's always one clean way out, thought Bril, putting his hands behind his head and looking up at the tough ceiling. Item, one Earth-normal planet, rich in natural resources, sparsely populated by innocents. You can always simply exterminate them.

But not before you find out how they communicate, how they cooperate, and how they specialize in skills they never tried before. How they manufacture superior materials out of thin air in no time.

He had a sudden heady vision of Kit Carson equipped as these people were, a billion and a half universal specialists with some heretofore unsuspected method of intercommunication, capable of building cities, fighting wars, with the measureless skill and split-second understanding and obedience with which this little house had been built.

No, these people must not be exterminated. They must be used. Kit Carson had to learn their tricks. If the tricks were—he hoped not!—inherent in Xanadu and beyond the Carson abilities, then what would be the next best thing?

Why, a cadre of the Xanadu, scattered through the cities and armies of Kit Carson, instantly obedient, instantly trainable. Instruct one and you teach them all; each could teach a group of Kit Carson's finest. Production, logistics, strategy, tactics—he saw it all in a flash.

Xanadu might be left almost exactly as is, except for its new export—aides de camp.

Dreams, these are only dreams, he told himself sternly. *Wait until you know more. Watch them make impregnable hardboard and anti-grav tea trays . . .*

The thought of the tea tray made his stomach growl. He got up and went to it. The hot food steamed, the cold was still frosty and firm. He picked, he tasted. Then he bit. Then he gobbled.

Nina, that Nina . . .

No, they can't be exterminated, he thought drowsily, not when they can produce such a woman. In all of Kit Carson, there wasn't a cook like that.

He lay down again and dreamed, and dreamed until he fell asleep.

They were completely frank. They showed him everything, and it apparently never occurred to them to ask him why he wanted to know. Asking was strange, because they seemed to lack that special pride of accomplishment one finds in the skilled potter, metalworker, electronician, an attitude of: "Isn't it remarkable that I can do it!" They gave information accurately but impersonally, as if anyone could do it.

And on Xanadu, anyone could.

At first, it seemed to Bril totally disorganized. These attractive people in their indecent garments came and went, mingling play and work and loafing, without apparent plan. But their play would take them through a flower garden just where the weeds were, and they would take the weeds along. There seemed to be a group of girls playing jacks right outside the place where they would suddenly be needed to sort some seeds.

Tanyne tried to explain it: "Say we have a shortage of something—oh, strontium, for example. The shortage itself creates a sort of vacuum. People without anything special to do feel it; they think about strontium. They come, they gather it."

"But I have seen no mines," Bril said puzzledly.

"And what about shipping? Suppose the shortage is here and the mines in another district?"

"That never happens any more. Where there are deposits, of course, there are no shortages. Where there are none, we find other ways, either to use something else, or to produce it without mines."

"Transmute it?"

"Too much trouble. No, we breed a freshwater shellfish with a strontium carbonate shell instead of calcium carbonate. The children gather them for us when we need it."

He saw their clothing industry—part shed, part cave, part forest glen. There was a pool there where the young people swam, and a field where they sunned themselves. Between times, they went into the shadows and worked by a huge vessel where chemicals occasionally boiled, turned bright green, and then precipitated. The black precipitate was raised from the bottom of the vessel on screens, dumped into forms and pressed.

Just how the presses—little more than lids for the forms—operated, the Old Tongue couldn't tell him, but in four or five seconds the precipitate had turned into the black stones used in their belts, formed and polished, with a chemical formula in Old Tongue script cut into the back of the left buckle.

"One of our few superstitions," said Tanyne. "It's the formula for the belts—even a primitive chemistry could make them. We would like to see them copied, duplicated all over the Universe. They are what we are. Wear one, Bril. You would be one of us, then."

Bril snorted in embarrassed contempt and went to watch two children deftly making up the belts, as easily, and with the same idle pleasure, as they might be making flower necklaces in a minute or two. As each was assembled, the child would strike it against his own belt. All the colors there are would appear each time this happened, in a brief, brilliant, cool flare. Then the belt, now with a short trim of vague tongued light, was tossed in a bin.

Probably the only time Bril permitted himself open astonishment on Xanadu was the first time he saw one of the natives put on this garment. It was a young man, come dripping from the pool. He snatched up a belt from the bank and clasped it around his waist, and immediately the color and substance flowed up and down, a flickering changing collar for him, a moving coruscant kilt.

"It's alive, you see," said Tanyne. "Rather, it is not nonliving."

He put his fingers under the hem of his own kilt and forced his fingers up and outward. They penetrated the fabric, which fluttered away, untorn.

"It is not," he said gravely, "altogether material, if you will forgive an Old Tongue pun. The nearest Old Tongue term for it is 'aura.' Anyway, it lives, in its way. It maintains itself for—oh, a year or more. Then dip it in lactic acid and it is refreshed again. And just one of them could activate a million belts or a billion—how many sticks can a fire burn?"

"But why wear such a thing?"

Tanyne laughed. "Modesty." He laughed again. "A scholar of the very old times, on Earth before the Nova, passed on to me the words of one Rudofsky: 'Modesty is not so simple a virtue as honesty.' We wear these because they are warm when we need warmth, and because they conceal some defects some of the time—surely all one can ask of any human affectation."

"They are certainly not modest," said Bril stiffly.

"They express modesty just to the extent that they make us more pleasant to look at with than without them. What more public expression of humility could you want than that?"

Bril turned his back on Tanyne and the discussion. He understood Tanyne's words and ways imperfectly to begin with, and this kind of talk left him bewildered, or unreached, or both.

He found out about the hardboard. Hanging from

the limb of a tree was a large vat of milky fluid—the paper, Tan explained, of a wasp they had developed, dissolved in one of the nucleic acids which they synthesized from a native weed. Under the vat was a flat metal plate and a set of movable fences. These were arranged in the desired shape and thickness of the finished panel, and then a cock was opened and the fluid ran in and filled the enclosure. Thereupon two small children pushed a roller by hand across the top of the fences. The white lake of fluid turned pale brown and solidified, and that was the hardboard.

Tanyne tried his best to explain to Bril about that roller, but the Old Tongue joined forces with Bril's technical ignorance and made the explanation incomprehensible. The coating of the roller was as simple in design, and as complex in theory, as a transistor, and Bril had to let it go at that, as he did with the selective analysis of the boulderlike "plumbing" and the antigrav food trays (which, he discovered, had to be guided outbound, but which "homed" on the kitchen area when empty).

He had less luck, as the days went by, in discovering the nature of the skills of Xanadu. He had been quite ready to discard his own dream as a fantasy, an impossibility—the strange idea that what any could do, all could do. Tanyne tried to explain; at least, he answered every one of Bril's questions.

These wandering, indolent, joyful people could pick up anyone's work at any stage and carry it to any degree. One would pick up a flute and play a few notes, and others would stroll over, some with instruments and some without, and soon another instrument and another would join in, until there were fifty or sixty and the music was like a passion or a storm, or afterlove or sleep when you think back on it.

And sometimes a bystander would step forward and take an instrument from the hands of someone who was tiring, and play on with all the rest, pure and harmonious; and, no, Tan would aver, he didn't think they'd ever played that particular piece of music before, those fifty or sixty people.

It always got down to *feeling,* in Tan's explanations. "It's a *feeling* you get. The violin, now; I've heard one, we'll say, but never held one. I watch someone play and I understand how the notes are made. Then I take it and do the same, and as I concentrate on making the note, and the note that follows, it comes to me not only how it should sound, but how it should *feel*—to the fingers, the bowing arm, the chin and collarbone. Out of those feelings comes the feeling of how it feels to be making such music.

"Of course, there are limitations," he admitted, "and some might do better than others. If my fingertips are soft, I can't play as long as another might. If a child's hands are too small for the instrument, he'll have to drop an octave or skip a note. But the feeling's there, when we think in that certain way.

"It's the same with anything else we do," he summed up. "If I need something in my house, a machine, a device, I won't use iron where copper is better; it wouldn't *feel* right for me. I don't mean feeling the metal with my hands; I mean thinking about the device and its parts and what it's for. When I think of all the things I could make it of, there's only one set of things that feels right to me."

"So," said Bril then. "And that, plus this—this competition between the districts, to find all elements and raw materials in the neighborhood instead of sending for them—that's why you have no commerce. Yet you say you're standardized—at any rate, you all have the same kind of devices, ways of doing things."

"We all have whatever we want and we make it ourselves, yes," Tan agreed.

In the evenings, Bril would sit in Tanyne's house and listen to the drift and swirl of conversation or the floods of music, and wonder; and then he would guide his tray back to his cubicle and lock the door and eat and brood. He felt at times that he was under an attack with weapons he did not understand, on a field which was strange to him.

He remembered something Tanyne had said once, casually, about men and their devices: "Ever since there were human beings, there has been conflict between Man and his machines. They will run him or he them; it's hard to say which is the less disastrous way. But a culture which is composed primarily of men has to destroy one made mostly of machines, or be destroyed. It was always that way. We lost a culture once on Xanadu. Didn't you ever wonder, Bril, why there are so few of us here? And why almost all of us have red hair?"

Bril had, and had secretly blamed the small population on the shameless lack of privacy, without which no human race seems to be able to whip up enough interest in itself to breed readily.

"We were billions once," said Tan surprisingly. "We were wiped out. Know how many were left? *Three!*"

That was a black night for Bril, when he realized how pitiable were his efforts to learn their secret. For if a race were narrowed to a few, and a mutation took place, and it then increased again, the new strain could be present in all the new generations. He might as well, he thought, try to wrest from them the secret of having red hair. That was the night he concluded that these people would have to go; and it hurt him to think that, and he was angry at himself for thinking so. That, too, was the night of the ridiculous disaster.

He lay on his bed, grinding his teeth in helpless fury. It was past noon and he had been there since he awoke, trapped by his own stupidity, and ridiculous, ridiculous. His greatest single possession—his dignity—was stripped from him by his own carelessness, by a fiendish and unsportsmanlike gadget that—

His approach alarm hissed and he sprang to his feet in an agony of embarrassment, in spite of the strong opaque walls and the door which only he could open.

It was Tanyne; his friendly greeting bugled out and

mingled with birdsong and the wind. "Bril! You there?"

Bril let him come a little closer and then barked through the vent. "I'm not coming out." Tanyne stopped dead, and even Bril himself was surprised by the harsh, squeezed sound of his voice.

"But Nina asked for you. She's going to weave today; she thought you'd like—"

"No," snapped Bril. "Today I leave. Tonight, that is. I've summoned my bubble. It will be here in two hours. After that, when it's dark, I'm going."

"Bril, you can't. Tomorrow I've set up a sintering for you; show you how we plate—"

"No!"

"Have we offended you, Bril? Have I?"

"No." Bril's voice was surly, but at least not a shout.

"What's happened?"

Bril didn't answer.

Tanyne came closer. Bril's eyes disappeared from the slit. He was cowering against the wall, sweating.

Tanyne said, "Something's happened, something's wrong. I . . . feel it. You know how I feel things, my friend, my good friend, Bril."

The very thought made Bril stiffen in terror. Did Tanyne know? Could he?

He might, at that. Bril damned these people and all their devices, their planet and its sun and the fates which had brought him here.

"There is nothing in my world or in my experience you can't tell me about. You know I'll understand," Tanyne pleaded. He came closer. "Are you ill? I have all the skills of the surgeons who have lived since the Three. Let me in."

"No!" It was hardly a word; it was an explosion.

Tanyne fell back a step. "I beg your pardon, Bril. I won't ask again. But—tell me. Please tell me. I must be able to help you!"

All right, thought Bril, half hysterically, *I'll tell you and you can laugh your fool red head off. It won't matter once we seed your planet with Big Plague.* "I can't come out. I've ruined my clothes."

"Bril! What can that matter? Here, throw them out; we can fix them, no matter what it is."

"No!" He could just see what would happen with these universal talents getting hold of the most compact and deadly armory this side of the Sumner system.

"Then wear mine." Tan put his hands to the belt of his black stones.

"I wouldn't be seen dead in a flimsy thing like that. Do you think I'm an exhibitionist?"

With more heat (it wasn't much) than Bril had ever seen in him, Tanyne said, "You've been a lot more conspicuous in those winding sheets you've been wearing than you ever would be in this."

Bril had never thought of that. He looked longingly at the bright nothing which flowed up and down from the belt, and then at his own black harness, humped up against the wall under its hook. He hadn't been able to bear the thought of putting them back on since the accident happened, and he had not been this long without clothes since he'd been too young to walk.

"What happened to your clothes, anyway?" Tan asked sympathetically.

Laugh, thought Bril, *and I'll kill you right now and you'll never have a chance to see your race die.* "I sat down on the—I've been using it as a chair; there's only room for one seat in here. I must have kicked the switch. I didn't even feel it until I got up. The whole back of my—" Angrily he blurted, "Why doesn't that ever happen to you people?"

"Didn't I tell you?" Tan said, passing the news item by as if it meant nothing. Well, to him it probably was nothing. "The unit only accepts nonliving matter."

"Leave that thing you call clothes in front of the door," Bril grunted after a strained silence. "Perhaps I'll try it."

Tanyne tossed the belt up against the door and

strode away, singing softly. His voice was so big that even his soft singing seemed to go on forever.

But eventually Bril had the field to himself, the birdsong and the wind. He went to the door and away, lifted his seatless breeches sadly and folded them out of sight under the other things on the hook. He looked at the door again and actually whimpered once, very quietly. At last he put the gauntlet against the door-plate, and the door, never designed to open a little way, obediently slid wide. He squeaked, reached out, caught up the belt, scampered back and slapped at the plate.

"No one saw," he told himself urgently.

He pulled the belt around him. The buckle parts knew each other like a pair of hands.

The first thing he was aware of was the warmth. Nothing but the belt touched him anywhere and yet there was a warmth on him, soft, safe, like a bird's breast on eggs. A split second later, he gasped.

How could a mind fill so and not feel pressure? How could so much understanding flood into a brain and not break it?

He understood about the roller which treated the hardboard; it was a certain way and no other, and he could feel the rightness of that sole conjecture.

He understood the ions of the mold press that made the belts, and the life analog he wore as a garment. He understood how his finger might write on a screen, and the vacuum of demand he might send out to have this house built so, and so, and exactly so; and how the natives would hurry to fill it.

He remembered without effort Tanyne's description of the *feel* of playing an instrument, making, building, molding, holding, sharing, and how it must be to play in a milling crowd beside a task, moving randomly and only for pleasure, yet taking someone's place at vat or bench, furrow or fishnet, the very second another laid down a tool.

He stood in his own quiet flame, in his little coffin

cubicle, looking at his hands and knowing without question that they would build him a model of a city on Kit Carson if he liked, or a statue of the soul of the Sole Authority.

He knew without question that he had the skills of this people, and that he could call on any of those skills just by concentrating on a task until it came to him how the right way (for him) would *feel*. He knew without surprise that these resources transcended even death; for a man could have a skill and then it was everyman's, and if the man should die, his skill still lived in everyman.

Just by concentrating—that was the key, the key way, the keystone to the nature of this device. A device, that was all—no mutations, nothing "extrasensory" (whatever that meant); only a machine like other machines. You have a skill, and a feeling about it; I have a task. Concentration on my task sets up a demand for your skill; through mine, I receive. Then I perform; and what bias I put upon that performance depends on my capabilities. Should I add something to that skill, then mine is the higher, the more complete; the *feeling* of it is better, and it is I who will transmit next time there is a demand.

And he understood the authority that lay in this new aura, and it came to him then how his home planet could be welded into a unit such as the universe had never seen. Xanadu had not done it, because Xanadu had grown randomly with its gift, without the preliminary pounding and shaping and milling of authority and discipline.

But Kit Carson! Carson with all skills and all talents shared among all its people, and overall and commanding, creating that vacuum of need and instant fulfillment, the Sole Authority and the State. It must be so (even though, far down, something in him wondered why the State kept so much understanding away from its people), for with this new depth came a solemn new dedication to his home and all it stood for.

Trembling, he unbuckled the belt and turned back its left buckle. Yes, there it was, the formula for the precipitate. And now he understood the pressing process and he had the flame to strike into new belts and make them live—by the millions, Tanyne had said, the billions.

Tanyne had said . . . why had he never said that the garments of Xanadu were the source of all their wonders and perplexities?

But had Bril ever asked?

Hadn't Tanyne begged him to take a garment so he could be one with Xanadu? The poor earnest idiot, to think he could be swayed away from Carson this way! Well, then, Tanyne and his people would have an offer, too, and it would all be even; soon they could, if they would join the shining armies of a new Kit Carson.

From his hanging black suit, a chime sounded. Bril laughed and gathered up his old harness and all the fire and shock and paralysis asleep in its mighty, compact weapons. He slapped open the door and sprang to the bubble which waited outside, and flung his old uniform in to lie crumpled on the floor, a broken chrysalis. Shining and exultant, he leaped in after it and the bubble sprang away skyward.

Within a week after Bril's return to Kit Carson in the Sumner System, the garment had been duplicated, and duplicated again, and tested.

Within a month, nearly two hundred thousand had been distributed, and eighty factories were producing round the clock.

Within a year, the whole planet, all the millions, were shining and unified as never before, moving together under their Leader's will like the cells of a hand.

And then, in shocking unison, they all flickered and dimmed, every one, so it was time for the lactic acid dip which Bril had learned of. It was done in panic, without test or hesitation; a small taste of this luminous subjection had created a mighty appetite. All was well for a week—

And then, as the designers in Xanadu had planned, all the other segments of the black belts joined the first meager two in full operation.

A billion and a half human souls, who had been given the techniques of music and the graphic arts, and the theory of technology, now had the others: philosophy and logic and love; sympathy, empathy, forbearance, unity in the idea of their species rather than in their obedience; membership in harmony with all life everywhere.

A people with such feelings and their derived skills cannot be slaves. As the light burst upon them, there was only one concentration possible to each of them—to be free, and the accomplished feeling of being free. As each found it, he was an expert in freedom, and expert succeeded expert, transcended expert, until (in a moment) a billion and a half human souls had no greater skill than the talent of freedom.

So Kit Carson, as a culture, ceased to exist, and something new started there and spread through the stars nearby.

And because Bril knew what a Senator was and wanted to be one, he became one.

In each other's arms, Tanyne and Nina were singing softly, when the goblet in the mossy niche chimed.

"Here comes another one," said Wonyne, crouched at their feet. "I wonder what will make *him* beg, borrow or steal a belt."

"Doesn't matter," said Tanyne, stretching luxuriously, "as long as he gets it. Which one is he, Wo—that noisy mechanism on the other side of the small moon?"

"No," said Wonyne. "That one's still sitting there squalling and thinking we don't know it's there. No, this is the force-field that's been hovering over Fleetwing District for the last two years."

Tanyne laughed. "That'll make conquest number eighteen for us."

"Nineteen," corrected Nina dreamily. "I remember because eighteen was the one that just left and seventeen was that funny little Bril from the Sumner System. Tan, for a time that little man loved me." But that was a small thing and did not matter.

The Dark Room

I would like to state here and now that the above was not
my title; there is a room in the story but at no time is it
dark, nor is darkness of any particular significance to the
story. I called it "Alien Bee," which is probably not the
best possible title for it either, but a better one, I think, than
the one the editor chose. Anyway, I am keeping his title
for bibliographical purposes.

Written in 1953, this story is one of my first efforts to
develop different styles. Anyone with any verbal facility
can develop a style, polish and perfect it until it becomes
that writer's special trademark, and you can come a long
way in the writing business by doing that. However, like
any specialization, it can inhibit and even imprison you, so
that all the characters speak like each other and like the
author. The writers I admire most—Samuel R. Delany, to
name a single one—are masters of many styles, not just one,
and no one will ever write one-paragraph pastiches or
lampoons of his work.

So here is a hard-heeling, fast-paced, brawling, macho
Sturgeon story. And if it turns out that you don't like this
kind of person—well, neither do I.

The world ended at that damn party of Beck's.

At least if it had fallen into the sun, or if it had collided with a comet, it would have been all right with me. I mean, I'd have been able to look at that fellow in the barber chair, and that girl on the TV screen, and somebody fresh from Tasmania, and I'd have been able to say, "Ain't it hell, neighbor?" and he would've looked at me with sick eyes, feeling what I felt about it.

But this was much worse. Where you sit and look around, that's the center of the whole universe. Everything you see from there circles around you, and you're the center. Other people share a lot of it, but they're circling around out there too. The only one who comes right in and sits with you, looking out from the same place, is the one you love. That's your world. Then one night you're at a party and the one you love disappears with a smooth-talking mudhead; you look around and they're gone; you worry and keep up the bright talk; they come back and the mudhead calls you "old man" and is too briskly polite to you, and she—she won't look you in the eye. So the center of the universe is suddenly one great big aching nothing, nothing at all—it's the end of your world. The whole universe gets a little shaky then, with nothing at its center.

Of course, I told myself, this is all a crazy suspicion, and you, Tom Conway, ought to hang your head and apologize. This sort of thing happens to people, but not to us. Women do this to their husbands, but Opie doesn't do this to me—does she, *does she?*

We got out of there as soon as I could manage it without actually pushing Opie out like a wheelbarrow. We left party noises behind us, and I remember one deep guttural laugh especially that I took extremely personally, though I knew better. It was black dark outside, and we had to feel the margins of the path through our soles before our eyes got accustomed to the night. Neither of us said anything. I could almost sense the boiling, bottled-up surging agony in Opie, and I knew she felt it in me, because we always felt things in each other that way.

Then we were through the arched gateway in the hedge and there was concrete sidewalk under us instead of gravel. We turned north toward where the car was parked and I glanced quickly at her. All I could see was the turn of her throat, curved a bit more abruptly than usual because of the stiff, controlled way she was holding her head.

I said to myself, something's happened here and it's bad. Well, I'll have to ask her. I know, I thought, with a wild surge of hope, I'll ask her what happened; I'll ask her if it was the worst possible thing, and she'll say no, and then I'll ask her if it's the next worse, and so on, until when I get to it I'll be able to say things aren't so bad after all.

So I said, "You and that guy, did you—" and all the rest of it, in words of one syllable. The thing I'm grateful to her about is that she didn't let one full second of silence go by before she answered me.

She said, "Yes."

And that was the end of the world.

The end of the world is too big a thing to describe in detail. It's too big a thing to remember clearly. The next thing that happened, as far as I can recall, is that there was gravel under my feet again and party noises ahead of me, and Opie sprinting past me and butting me in the chest to make me stop. "Where are you going?" she gasped.

I pushed her but she bounded right back against me. "Get out of the way," I said, and the sound of my voice surprised me.

"Where are you going?" she said again.

"Back there," I said. "I'm going to kill him."

"Why?"

I didn't answer that because there wasn't room inside me for such a question, but she said, "He didn't do it by himself, Tom. I was . . . I probably did more than he did. Kill me."

I looked down at the faint moon-glimmer that told where her face was. I whispered, because my voice wouldn't do anything else, "I don't want to kill you, Opie."

She said, with an infinite weariness, "There's less reason to kill him. Come on. Let's go—" I thought she was going to say "home," and winced, but she realized as much as I did that the word didn't mean anything anymore. "Let's go," she said.

When the world ends it doesn't do it once and finish with the business. It rises up and happens again, sometimes two or three times in a minute, sometimes months apart but for days at a time. It did it to me again then, because the next thing I can remember is driving the car. Next to me where Opie used to sit was just a stretch of seat-cushion. Where there used to be a stretch of seat-cushion, over next to the right-hand door, Opie sat.

Back there in the path Opie had asked me a one-word question, and in me there was no room for it. Now, suddenly, there was no room in me for anything else. The word burst out of me, pressed out by itself. *"Why?"*

Opie sat silently. I waited until I couldn't stand it any longer and then looked over at her. A streetlight fled past and the pale gold wash of it raced across her face. She seemed utterly composed, but her eyes were too wide, and I sensed that she'd held them that way long enough for the eyeballs to dry and hurt her. "I asked you why," I snarled.

"I heard you," she said gently. "I'm just trying to think."

"You don't know why?"

She shook her head.

I looked straight through the windshield again and wrenched the wheel. I'd damned near climbed a bank. I was going too fast, too. I knew she'd seen it coming, and she hadn't moved a muscle to stop it. I honestly don't think she cared just then.

I got the car squared away and slowed down a little. "You've got to know why. A person doesn't just—just go ahead and—and do something without a reason."

"I did," she said in that too-tired voice.

I'd already said that people don't just do things that way, so there was no point in going over it again. Which left me nothing further to say. Since she offered nothing more, we left it like that.

A couple of days later Hank blew into my office. He shut the door, which people don't usually do, and came over and half-sat on the desk, swinging one long leg. "What happened?" he said.

Hank is my boss, a fine guy, and Opie's brother.

"What happened to who?" I asked him. I was as casual as a guy can be who is rudely being forced to think about something he's trying to wall up.

He wagged his big head. "No games, Tom. What happened?"

I quit pretending. "So that's where she is. Home to mother, huh?"

"Have you been really interested in where she is?"

"Cut it out, Hank. This 'have you hurt my little sister, you swine' routine isn't like you."

He had big amber eyes like Opie's, and it was just as hard to tell what flexed and curled behind them. Finally he said, "You know better than that. You and Opie are grownups and usually behave like grownups."

"We're not now?"

"I don't know. Tom, I'm not trying to protect Opie. Not from you. I know you both too well."

"So what *are* you trying to do?"

"I just want to know what happened."

"Why?" I rapped. There it was again: why, why, why.

He scratched his head. "Not to get sloppy about it, I want to know because I think that you and Opie are the two finest bipeds that ever got together to make a fine combo. I have one of these logical minds. A fact plus a fact plus a force gives a result. If you know all the facts, you can figure the result. I've been thinking for a lot of years that I know all the facts about both of you, everything that matters. And this—this just doesn't figure. Tom, what happened?"

He was beginning to annoy me. "Ask Opie," I spat. It sounded ugly. Why not? It was ugly.

Hank swung the foot and looked at me. I suddenly realized that this guy was miserable. "I did ask her," he said in a choked voice.

I waited.

"She told me."

That rocked me. "She told you what?"

"What happened. Saturday night, at Beck's party."

"She told you?" I couldn't get over that. "What in time made her tell you?"

"I made her. She held out for a long while and then let me have it, in words of one syllable. I guess it was to shut me up."

I put my head in my hands. It made a difference to have someone else in on it. I didn't know whether I cared for the difference or not.

I jumped up then and yelled at him. "So you know what happened and you came bleating in here what happened, what happened! Why ask me, if you know?"

"You got me wrong, Tom," he said. His voice was so soft against my yelling that it stopped me like a cut throat. "Yeah, I know what she did. What I want to know is what happened to make her do it."

I didn't say anything.

"Have you talked to anyone about it?" he wanted to know.

I shook my head.

He spread his hands. "Talk to me about it."

When I didn't move, he leaned closer. "What do you say, Tom?"

"I say," I breathed, "that I got work to do. We have a magazine to get out. This is company time, remember?"

He got up off the desk right away. Did you ever listen to someone walk away from you when you weren't looking at him, and know by his footsteps that he was hurt and angry?

He opened the door and hesitated. "Tom . . ."

"What?"

"If you've got nothing to do this evening . . . call me. I'll come over."

I glared at him. "Fat chance."

He didn't say anything else. Just went away. I sat there staring at the open door. Here was a guy bragging how much he knew about me. Thinking I'd want to call him, talk to him.

Fat chance.

I didn't call him, either. Not until after eight o'clock. His phone didn't get through the first ring. He must have been sitting with his hand on it. "Hank?" I said.

He said, "I'll be right over," and hung up.

I had drinks ready when he got there. He came in saying, the stupid way people do, "How are you?"

"I'm dead," I said. I was, too. No sleep for two nights; dead tired. No Opie in the house. Dead. Dead inside.

He sat down and had sense enough to say nothing. When I could think of something to say, it was, "Hank, I'm not going to say anything about Opie that sounds lousy. But I have to check, I have to be sure. Just what did she tell you?"

He sighed and said what Opie had done. What she had done to me, to a marriage. She'd told him, all right. He said it and, "Better drink your drink, Tom."

I drank it. I needed to. Then I looked at him. "Now that's on the record, what do you do about it?"

Hank didn't say anything. I covered my face and rocked back and forth. "I guess this happens to lots of guys, their wives making it with someone else. Sometimes it breaks them up, sometimes it doesn't. How do they live when it doesn't?"

Hank just fiddled with a table lighter. I picked up my empty glass and looked at it and all of a sudden the stem broke in two. Red blood began welling out. Hank yelped and came to me with his handkerchief. He tied it around my wrist and pulled it so tight it hurt. "Why is it so important that Opie and I get back together, Hank? To you, I mean?"

He gave me a strange look and went into the bathroom. I heard him rummaging around in the medicine chest. "There's more in it than you and Opie, Tom," he called out. He came back in with bandages. "I guess you're so full of this that it's around you every way you look, but there are other things going on in the world, honest."

"I guess there are, but they don't seem to matter."

"Hold still," he said. "This'll hurt." He stuck the iodine on my cut. It hurt like hell and I wished all hurts were as easy to take. He said, "Something awful funny is going on at Beck's."

"What happened to me is funny?" I said.

"Shut up. You know what I mean." He finished the bandage and went to the bar. "Well, maybe you don't. Look, how long have you known Beck?"

"Years."

"How well?"

"As well as you can know a guy you went to school with, roomed with, lent money to and had lunch with four times a week for eight-nine years."

"Ever notice anything odd about him?"

"No. Not Beck. The original predictable boy. Right-wing Republican, solid-color tie, independent income, thinks 'Rustle of Spring' is opera, drinks vermouth-and-soda in hot weather and never touches a martini until 4 P.M. Likes to have people around, all kinds of people. The wackier the better. But he never did, said, or thought a wacky thing in his life."

"Never? You did say never?"

"Never. Except—"

"Except?"

I looked at the bandage he had made. Very neat. "That rumpus room of his. What got into him to fix it up that way I'll never know. I almost dropped dead when I saw it."

"Why?"

"Have you been there?"

He nodded. Something uncoiled back of his eyes, and it reminded me so much of Opie that I grunted the way a man does when he walks into a wagon-tongue in the dark. I took a good pull at the glass he'd brought and hung on to the subject, hard. "So you've been there. Does that look like the setup of a man who's surrounded himself all his life with nothing more modern than Dutch Queen Anne?"

He didn't say anything.

"I tell you I *know*. I think Beck would ride around in a Victorian brougham if it wouldn't make him conspicuous. He hates to be conspicuous as much as he hates modern furniture."

"A room can't get more 'modern' than that one," said Hank.

"Foam rubber and chromium," I said reminiscently. "Fireplace of black marble; high-gloss black Formica on the table-tops. Wall-to-wall broadlooms and free-form scatter-rugs. Fluorescents, all in coves, yet. The bookcase looks like a bar; the bar looks like a legitimate flight of steps."

"Maybe he's a masochist, making himself unhappy in a house furnished the way he hates it."

"He's no masochist, unless you figure the painful company of some of the weirdies he invites to his parties. And he doesn't live in a *house* furnished in Science Fiction Modern. He lives in a house with alternate Chinese Chippendale and that Dutch Queen Anne I was talking about. Only that room, that one rumpus room, is modern; and what he did it for I'll never know. It must have cost him a young fortune."

"It cost him what you might call a middle-aged fortune," Hank said bluntly. "I got the figures."

I snapped out of the mild reminiscences. "Have you now! Hank, what's the burning interest in Beck and his decor?"

Hank got up, stretched, sat down again and leaned forward with such earnestness and urgency that I drew back. "Tom, suppose I could prove that it wasn't her fault at all?"

I thought about it. Finally, between my teeth, I said, "If you could really prove that, I know one mudhead that would get thoroughly killed."

"There'll be none of that talk," he rapped. I squinted up at him and decided not to protest. He really meant it. He went on, "You have *got* to understand exactly what I mean." He paused to chew words before he let them out, then said, "I don't want you to get up any wild hopes. I'm not going to be able to prove Opie didn't . . . didn't do what she said she did Saturday night. She did it, and that's that. Shut up, now, Tom—don't say it! Not to me. She's my sister; do you think I'm enjoying this?" When I simmered down a bit, Hank said, "All I think I can prove is that what happened was completely beyond her control, and that she's completely innocent in terms of intention, even if she is guilty in terms of action."

"I'd like that," I said, with all my heart. "I'd like that just fine. Only it's hardly the kind of thing you can really prove." I double-took it. "What are you talking about?" I demanded angrily. "You mean she was hypnotized?"

"I do not," he said positively. "No amount of hypnotism would make her do something she didn't want to do, and I'm working on the premise that she didn't want to."

"Dope, then?"

"I don't think so. Did she look doped to you?"

"No." I thought back carefully. "Besides, I never

heard of a drug that could do that to a woman that quickly and leave no after-effects."

"There is none, and if there were it wasn't used on her."

"Cut out the guessing games then, and tell me what it was!"

He looked at me and his face changed. "Sorry," he said softly. "I can't. I don't know. But I mean to find out."

"You better say more," I said, dazed. "You lost me back there some place."

"You know where Klaus was picked up?"

I started. "The atom spy? No. What's that got to do with it?"

"Maybe a lot," said Hank. "Just a hunch I've got. Anyway, they got him at one of Beck's parties."

"I'll be damned," I breathed. "I didn't know that."

"Most people don't. It was one-two-three-hush. There was a Central Intelligence agent there and Klaus walked over to him and spilled the whole thing. The agent got him out of there and arrested him, then checked his story. It checked all right. Do you know *Cry for Clara?*"

"Do I know it? I wish I'd never heard it. Seventeen weeks on the 'Hit Parade,' and squalling out of every radio and every record store and juke-box in creation. Do I know it?"

"Know who wrote it?"

"No."

"Guy called Willy Simms. Never wrote a song before, never wrote one since."

"So?"

"He did the first draft at one of Beck's parties."

"I don't see what that has to do with—"

He interrupted me. "The hen fight that put two nice deep fingernail gouges across Marie Munro's million-dollar face happened at Beck's. A school-teacher did it—an otherwise harmless old biddy who'd never even seen a Munro picture and hadn't even spoken to The Face that evening. The man who—"

"Wait a minute, wait a min—" I started, but he wouldn't wait.

"The man who killed that preacher on Webb Street two weeks ago—remember?—did it with Beck's poker, which he threw out of Beck's rumpus room window like a damn javelin. That hilarious story—I heard you telling it yourself—about the pansy breeder at the Flower Show.

"Don't tell me that one came from Beck's." I grinned in spite of myself.

"It did. Because of someone's remark that nobody knows where dirty stories originate. And *bing*, that one was originated on the spot." He paused. "By Lila Falsehaven."

"Lila? You mean the white-haired old granny who writes children's books?" I drank on that. That was too fine. "Hank, what are you getting at with all this?"

Hank pulled on an earlobe. "All these things I mentioned—all different, all happening to different kinds of people. I think there's a lowest common denominator."

"You've already told me that; they all happened at Beck's parties."

"The thing I'm talking about *makes* things happen at Beck's parties."

"Aw, for Pete's sake. Coincidence. . . ."

"Coincidence hell!" he rumbled. "Can't you understand that I've known about this thing for a long time now? I'm not telling you all these things occurred to me just since Opie . . . uh . . . since last Saturday night. I'm telling you that what Opie did is another one of those things."

I grunted thoughtfully. "Lowest common denominator. . . . Heck, the main thing all those people have in common is that they have nothing in common."

"That's right," Hank nodded. "That seems to be

Beck's rule-of-thumb: always mix them up. A rich one, a talented one, a weird one, a dull one."

"Makes for a good party," I said stupidly.

He had the good sense not to pick that one up. Good party. Swell party. Opie. . . . No, I wouldn't think about it. I said, "What's this all about, anyway? Why worry so much about Beck? It's his business who he invites. Strange things happen—sure, they'd happen at your house if you filled it up with characters."

"Here's what it's about. I want you to go back there and find out what that lowest common denominator is."

"Why?"

"For the magazine, maybe. It depends. Anyhow, kid, that's an assignment."

"Stick it," I said. "I'm not going back there."

"Why not?"

"That's the stupidest question yet!"

"Tom," he said gently. "Getting riled up won't help. I really want to know why you don't want to go back. Is it the place you can't stand, or the idea of seeing Opie there?"

"I don't mind the place," I said sullenly.

He was so pleased I was astonished. "Then you can go back. She will never go there again."

"You sound real positive."

"I am. Things happen at Beck's parties. But if they happen to you, you don't go back."

"I don't get it."

"Neither do I. But that's one of the things I want you to find out about."

"Hank, this is crazy!"

"Sure it's crazy. And you're just the man for the job."

"Why, especially?"

"Because you know Beck better than most people. Because you have something personal at stake. Because you're a good reporter. And—well, because you're so damn normal."

I didn't feel normal. I said, "If you're so interested in Beck and his shindigs, why don't you chase the story down yourself? You seem to know what to look for."

When he didn't answer, I looked up. He had turned his back. After a while he said, "I'm one of the ones who can't go back."

I thought that over. "You mean something happened to you?"

"Yes, something happened to me," he snarled in angry mimicry. "And that part of it you can skip."

For the first time I felt that little nubbin of intrigue that bites me when I'm near a really hot story. "So you've taken care of my Saturday nights. What am I supposed to do the rest of the week?"

"You've been around the magazine long enough not to ask me how to do your work. I just mentioned a lot of people. Go find out why they did the things they did." And all of a sudden he stalked to the door, scooped up his hat, growled a noise that was probably "Goodnight," and left.

I went to see Lila Falsehaven. It was no trouble at all to get her address from Kiddy-Joy Books, Inc. She invited me to tea when I called her up. Tea, no less. Me. Tom Conway.

She was a real greeting-card grandma. Steel-rimmed specs with the thickest part at the lower edges. Gleaming, perfect, even false teeth. A voice that reminded you of a silver plate full of warm spice cookies. And on the table between us, a silver plate full of warm spice cookies. "Cream?" she said. "Or lemon?"

"Straight."—"I mean, neither, thank you. This place looks just like the place where the Lila Falsehaven books are written."

"Thank you," she said, inclining her neat little head. She passed me tea in a convoluted bone-china cup I could have sneezed off a mantel at forty paces. "I've been told before that my books and my home and my appearance are those of the perfect grandmother. I've never had a child, you know. But I believe I've more grandchildren than anyone who ever lived." She delivered up an intricate old laugh like intricate old lace.

I tasted the tea. People should drink more tea. I put down the little cup and leaned back and smiled at her. "I like it here."

She blushed like a kid and smiled back. "And now—what can I do for you? Surely that wicked magazine of yours doesn't want a story by me. Or even about me."

"It's not a wicked magazine," I said loyally. "Just true-to-life. We call them as we see them."

"Some truths," she said gently, "are better left uncalled."

"You really believe that?"

"I really do," she said.

"But the world isn't what your grandchildren read about in your books."

"My world is," she said with conviction.

I had come here for something, and now was the time to get it. I shook my head. "Not completely. Some of your world has flower shows with pansies in them."

She didn't make a sound. She closed her eyes, and I watched her smooth old skin turn to ivory and then to paper. I waited. At last her eyes opened again. She looked straight at me, lifted one hand, then the other, spread them apart and placed each on the carven chair-arms. I looked at the hands, and saw each in turn relax as if by a deep effort of will. Her eyes drew me right up out of my chair. Deep in them was a spark, as hot, as bright, and quite as clean as a welding arc. The whole sweet room held its breath.

"Mr. Conway," she said in a voice that was very faint and very distinct, "I believe in truth as I believe in innocence and in beauty, so I shall not lie to you. I understand now that you came here to find out if I was really the one who contrived that filthy anecdote.

I was. But if you came to find out why I did it, or
what is in me that made it possible, I cannot help you.
I'm sorry. If I knew, if I only knew, perhaps I'd tell
you. Now you'd better go."

"But—"

Then I found out that the clean bright fire so deep
in her eyes could repel as well as attract, and I was in
the doorway with my hat in my hand. I said, "I'm
sor—" but the way she looked, the way she sat there
looking at me without moving, made it impossible for
me to speak or bow, or do anything but just get out. I
knew I'd never be back, too, and that was a shame.
She's a nice person. She lives in a nice place.

The whole thing was spoiled, and I felt lousy.
Lousy.

My press card got me as far as Col. Briggs, and the
memory of the time I got Briggs out of a raided stag
party just after the war got me the rest of the way. If it
hadn't been for those two items, I'd never have seen
Klaus. The death house was damn near as hard to get
into as it was to get out of.

They gave me ten minutes and left me alone with
him, though there was a guard standing where he
could see in. Klaus did not look as if he'd have
brought out the silver tea service even if he had one.
All he did when I came in was to say the name of the
magazine under his breath, and said that way it sounds
pretty dirty. I sat down on the bunk beside him and
he got right up off it. I didn't say anything, and after
a while that bothered him. I don't suppose anyone did
that to him, ever.

"Well, what is it? What do you want?" he snarled
finally.

"You'd never guess," I said.

"Am I guilty? Yes. Did I know what I was doing?
Yes. Is it true that I just want to see this crummy human race blown off this crummy planet as soon as possible? Yes. Am I sorry? Yes—that I got caught. Otherwise—no." He shrugged. "That's my whole story, you

know it, everybody knows it. I've been scooped dry and the bottom scraped. Why can't you guys leave me alone?"

"There's still something I'd like to know, though."

"Don't you read the papers?" he asked. "Once I got nabbed I had no secrets."

"Look," I said, "this guy Stevens—" Stevens was the Central Intelligence man who had dragged him in.

"Yeah, Stevens," Klaus snorted. "Our hero. I not only put him on page one—he's on boxes of breakfast cereal. You *really* got to be a hero to get on corn flakes."

"He wasn't a hero," I said. "He didn't know you from Adam and didn't care until you spilled to him."

Klaus stopped his pacing and slowly turned toward me. "Do you believe that?"

"Why not? That's what happened."

He came and sat beside me, looking at me as if I had turned into a two-headed giraffe. "You know, I've told that to six million different people and you're the first one who ever believed it. What did you say your name was? If you don't mind my asking."

"Conway," I said.

"I'm glad you came," he said. For him, that was really something.

He shoved back so he could lean aganist the wall and gave me a cigarette. "What do you want to know?"

"Why you did it."

He looked at me angrily, and I added quickly, "Not about the atom secrets. About the spill."

The angry look went away, but he didn't say anything. I pushed a bit. "You never made another mistake. Nobody in history ever operated as quietly and cleverly as you did. No one in the world suspected you, and as far as I've been able to discover no one was even about to. So you suddenly find yourself at a party with a C.I.A. man, walk over, and sing. Why?"

He thought about it. "It was a good party," he said,

after a bit. Then, "I guess I figured the game had gone on long enough, that's all."

I snorted.

"What's that for?" he wanted to know.

"You don't really believe that."

"I don't?"

"You don't," I said positively. "That's just something you figured out after it happened. What I want to know is what went on in your head before it happened."

"You know a hell of a lot about how I think," he said sneeringly.

"Sure I do," I said, and when he was quiet, I added, "Don't I?"

"Yeah," he growled. "Yeah." He closed his eyes to think about it, and then said, "You just asked me the one thing I don't know. One second I was sitting there enjoying myself, and the next I was backing that goon-boy into the corner and telling him about my life of sin. It just seemed a good idea at the time."

The guard came then to let me out. "Thanks for coming," Klaus said.

"That's all right. You're sure you can't tell me?"

"Yes, I'm sure."

"Shall I come back? Maybe after you think about it for a while. . . ."

He shook his head. "Wouldn't do no good," he said positively. "I know, because I haven't thought about anything else much since it happened. But I'm glad somebody believes it, anyway."

"So long. Drop me a note if you figure it out."

I don't know if he ever did. They burned him a few days later. I never got a note.

I grabbed another name from the list I'd run up. Willy Simms. Song writer.

I went into a music shop and asked the man if he had a record of *Cry for Clara*. He looked as if he'd found root beer in a bock bottle. "Still?" he breathed with a sort of weary amazement, and went and got the record.

"Look," I told him, "I think this platter is the most awful piece of candy corn that ever rolled out of the Alley." I don't often explain myself to people, but I couldn't have even a total stranger think I liked it.

He leaned across the counter. "Did you know," he said in a much friendlier tone of voice, "that Guy Lombardo is cutting it this week?"

I shared his tired wonder for a long moment, and then got out of there.

One and three-quarter million copies sold and still moving, and yet Willy Simms still lived in a place with four flights of stairs up to it. I found the door and leaned against the frame for a while, blowing hard. When the spots went away from my eyes, I knocked. A wrinkled little man opened the door.

"Is Willy Simms here?"

He looked at me and down at the flat record envelope I held. "What's that?"

"Cry for Clara," I said. He took it out of my hand and asked me how much I paid for it. I told him. He held the door open with his foot, scooped up a handful of change from an otherwise empty bookshelf, and counted out the price into my hand. Then he broke the record in two on his thigh, put the pieces together and broke them again, and slung them into the fireplace at his right. "I'm Willy Simms," he said. "Come on in."

I went in and stood just inside. I didn't know what this little prune would do next. I said, "My name's Tom—"

"Drop your hat there," he said. He crossed the room.

"I just dropped in to—"

"Drink?" he asked.

Since I never say no to that, and didn't have to say yes because he was already pouring, I just waited.

He came smiling with a glass. He had good teeth.

"Bourbon," he said. "A man's drink. Knew the minute I saw you you were a bourbon man."

I very much prefer rye. I said, "Once in a while—"

"Sure," he said. "Nothing like Bourbon. Sit down."

"Mr. Simms," I said.

"Willy. Nobody ever called me mister. Used to be I wasn't worth a 'mister.' Now I'm too good for it." He salvaged his modesty as he said this with a warm grin. "Maybe you think I shouldn't of busted your record."

"Well," I smiled, "I thought it a bit strange."

"I don't have a copy here and I won't let one in. Two reasons," he barked, making a V with shiny-dry, bony fingers. "First, I don't like it. What I specially don't like is the way people try to make me sit and listen to it and tell me how good this part is and that part, and where did I ever get the idea of going from the sub-dominant into an unrelated minor. Yeah, that's what one of them wanted to know."

"I remember that part," I said. "It's—"

"Second," said Willy Simms, "every time I bust one of those records it reminds me I can afford to do it, and I like to be reminded."

"Yeah," I said. "That's—"

"Besides," he said, "any time I bust one, the party walks out of here and buys another. It ain't the royalty, you understand. It's the score I'm running up. They tell me it'll sell two and a quarter million."

"Two and a—"

"You've finished your drink," he said. He took it out of my hand and filled it again. I wished it was rye, raised it to him and then sipped. "Willy," I began.

"I never wrote a song before," Willy said.

"Yes," I answered. "So I—"

"And I'm going to tell you something I ain't told nobody else. I'm going to tell it to you, and from now on, I just decided, I'm going to tell everybody."

He leaned toward me excitedly. I realized that he was boiled. I knew instinctively that it hadn't made any difference in him; he was probably this way cold sober too. He was obviously waiting for me to say something, but by this time I didn't want to spoil anything.

"So I'll tell you first, and it's this: I'm never going to write another song, either."

"But you've just begun to—"

"There's a good reason for it," he said. "Since you ask me, I'll tell you. I ain't going to write another song because I can't. It ain't that I don't read or write music. They say Leadbelly couldn't read music either. And it ain't that I don't want to. I want to, all right. But did you ever hear the old saying lightning never strikes twice in the same place?"

That I could match. "Sure, and they say it's always darkest before the dawn, too, but that doesn't—"

"The real reason," said Willy Simms, "is this." He paused dramatically. "I'm tone deaf. I couldn't carry a chord in a keyster. Do you see a piano here, or even a harmonica?"

"Listen," I said, "no one who was tone deaf could have—"

"Lightning," he said gravely. "It struck, that's all. Way down inside me was one little crumb called *Cry for Clara*, and the lightning struck and drove it out. But there was just the one little crumb there, and now there is no more."

"Shucks," I said. "Maybe—"

"And I could be wrong even about that," he said morosely. "I don't really believe even the little crumb was there. What I actually did just can't be done, not by me, anyway. Like a lobster writing a book. Like a phonograph playing a pizza pie. Like us not having another drink."

He demonstrated the impossibility of his last remark. I said, "There are certain things a man can do and certain things—"

"Like a trip back to one of Beck's parties," he said.

"Some things just can't happen." He glowered at me suddenly. "You don't happen to be a friend of this Beck? This is the guy made me hate myself."

"Me? Why, I—"

"If you were, I'd throw you right down hose stairs out there, big as you are." He half rose, and for a split second I was genuinely alarmed. He was one of those people who, in speaking of anger, acts it out, pulsing temples, narrowed eyes and all. But he sank back and recovered his disarming smile. "I been doing all the talking. What was it you came to see me about?"

I opened my mouth, and hesitated. To my amazement, he waited. "I just dropped up to sort of. . . ." I paused. He nodded encouragingly. "To find out about—" I began, then stopped.

"I see everybody," he confided. "Some people, now, they pick and choose who comes in. Not me."

I was at the door with my hat, which I'd picked up on the way. "Thanks for the dr—"

"Well, don't rush off."

I searched valiantly for the one word which might serve me, and found it. "Goodbye," I said, and whipped through the door. I could hear Willy Simms' muffled voice through the panel: "All right, I'll finish your drink if you're in such a damn hurry."

All the way down the stairs I could hear him, though I could no longer distinguish his words. Once he laughed. I got to the sidewalk and turned left. There was a man standing by a tree a few yards down the street, curbing a dog. "Hey," I said.

He turned toward me, raising his eyebrows. "Who—me?"

I tapped his shoulder with my left index finger. "New York would have the largest telephone book in the world," I said, "if they didn't have to break it into five sections."

He said, "Huh?"

"Don't mind me," I told him, "I just wanted to see if I could say a whole sentence all the way through." I tipped my hat and walked on. At the corner I looked back. He was still standing there, staring at me. When he saw me turn he called, "Whaddaya—wise?" I just waved at him and went home.

"Beck," I said into the phone, "I want to see you."

"Sure," he said. "You're coming over Saturday, aren't you?"

"Uh . . . yes. But I want to see you before that."

"It'll wait," he said easily.

"No, it won't," I said. There must have been something special in my voice because he asked me if anything was the matter.

"I don't know, Beck," I said honestly. "I mean, something is, but I don't know what." I had an idea suddenly. "Beck, can I bring someone to the party?"

"You know you can, Tom. Anyone you like."

"My brother-in-law Hank."

There was a long silence at the other end. Then, in a slightly strained voice, Beck said, "Why him?"

"Why not?"

The silence again. Then, as if he had had a brain-wave, Beck said easily, "No reason. If he wants to come, bring him."

"Thanks. Now, about seeing you before. How about tonight?"

"Tom, I'd love to, but I'm tied up. It'll wait till Saturday, won't it?"

"No," I said. "Tomorrow?"

"I'm out of town tomorrow. I'm really very sorry, Tom."

Abruptly, I said, "It's about the lowest common denominator."

"What?"

"Your parties," I said patiently. "The people who go to them."

He laughed suddenly. "The one thing they have in common is that they have nothing in common."

"That I know," I said. "I meant the people who used to go to your parties and don't any more."

The silence, but much shorter this time. "I'm looking at my book," he said. "Maybe I could squeeze in a few minutes with you tomorrow."

"What time?" I said, keeping the humorless grin out of my voice.

"Two o'clock. Kelly's all right?"

"At the bar. I'll be there, Beck, and thanks."

I hung up and scratched my chin. Lowest common denominator?

Hank's phrase, that was. Hank. The guy who'd put me on to this weird business. The guy who'd told me that if things happened to you at Beck's parties, you didn't go back. The guy who said *he* was never going back.

And wouldn't say why.

Well, if I had anything to do with it he'd be back.

Opie, Lila Falsehaven, Klaus, Willy Simms, Hank. Each had done something they shouldn't—maybe *couldn't* was the word—have done. Each would not—could not?—go back. Sometimes the thing was just silly, like Lila Falsehaven's dirty story. Sometimes it was deadly, like Klaus's crazy break.

Well, I told myself, keep plugging at it. Get enough case histories and a basic law will show itself. Avogadro worked up a fine theory about the behavior of gas molecules because he had enough molecules to work with. Sociologists struggle toward theories without enough numbers to work with, and they make some sort of progress. If I worked hard enough and lived long enough, maybe I could pile up a couple hundred million case histories of people who didn't go to Beck's parties any more, and come out with an answer.

Meanwhile, I'd better talk to Hank.

This time I went to his office and closed the door. He picked up the phone and said, "Sue, don't ring this thing until I tell you. . . . I know, I *know*. I don't care.

Tell him to wait." Then he just lounged back and looked at me.

"Hank," I said, "about this assignment. How much are you willing to help me?"

"All the way."

"Okay," I said. "Saturday night you have a date."

"I have? Where?

"Beck's."

He sat upright, his eyes still on my face. "No."

"That's what you mean by 'all the way'?" I asked quietly.

"I said I'd help you. Me going there—that wouldn't help anything. Besides, Beck wouldn't hold still for it."

"Beck told me to bring you."

"The hell he did!"

"Look, Hank, when I tell you—"

"Okay, okay, cool down, will you? I'm not calling you a liar." He pulled at his lip. "Tell me exactly what you said about it and what he said. As near as you can remember it."

I thought back. "I asked him if I could bring someone and he said sure. Then I mentioned your name and he—well, sort of hesitated. So I wanted to know why not, and he came off it right away. Said 'If he wants to come, bring him.' "

"The foxy little louse!" Hank said from between clenched teeth.

"What's the matter?"

Hank got up, smacked his fist into his palm. "He meant exactly what he said, Tom. Bring me—if I want to come. Conversely, if I don't want to come, don't bring me. I don't want to, Tom."

"Not even in the process of 'going all the way' to help me?" I asked sarcastically.

He said tightly. "That's right." I must have looked pretty grim, because he tried to explain. "If I could be sure it would break the case, Tom, I'd do it no matter what. If you can convince me that that one single act on my part is all you need, why, I'm your boy. Can you do that?"

"No," I said in all honesty. "It might help like crazy, though. All right," I conceded reluctantly. "If you don't want to go, you won't, and that's that. Now—short of that, will you help?"

"Absolutely," he said relievedly.

Then I aimed a forefinger at him and barked. "Okay. Then you'll tell me what happened to you there, and why you won't go back. You'll tell me now, and you won't even try to wriggle out of it."

It got real quiet in the office then. Hank's eyes half-closed, and I had seen that sleepy look before. Every time I had, somebody had gotten himself rather badly hurt.

"I should have known better," he said after a while, "than to put a real reporter on something that concerned me. You really want that information?"

I nodded.

"Tom," he said, and his voice was almost a lazy yawn, "I'm going to punch you right in the middle of your big fat mouth."

"For asking you a businesslike question that you made my business?"

"Not exactly," Hank said. "I'm going to tell you, and you're going to laugh, and when you laugh I'm going to let you have it."

"I haven't laughed at any of this yet," I said.

"And you still want to know."

I just waited.

"All right," he said. He came around his desk, balled up his fist, and eyed my face carefully. "I went to one of Beck's parties, and right in the middle of the proceedings I wet my pants."

I bit down hard on the insides of my cheeks, but I couldn't hold it. I let out a joyful whoop. Then I caromed off the water cooler, slid eight feet on the side of my head, and brought up against the wall. A great cloud of luminous fog rolled in, swirled, then gradually began to clear. I sat up. There was blood on my mouth and chin. Hank was standing over me, looking very sad. He dropped a clean handkerchief where I could reach it. I used it, then got my feet under me.

"Damn it, Tom, I'm sorry," he said. The way he said it I believed him. "But you shouldn't've laughed. I told you you shouldn't."

I went to the deskside chair and sat down. Hank drew me some water and brought it over. "Dip the handkerchief," he ordered. "Tom, this'll make more sense to you when you have a chance to think it over. Why don't you cut out?"

"I don't have to, I guess," I said with difficulty. "I guess if a thing like that happened to. . . ."

"If it happened," Hank said soberly, "it wouldn't be funny, and God help the man who laughed at it. It would shake your confidence like nothing else could. You'd think of it suddenly in a bus, at a board-meeting, in the composing room. You'd think of it when you were tramping up and down the office dictating. You'd remember that when it happened it came without warning and there was nothing you could do about it until it was over. It would be the kind of thing that just couldn't happen—and forever after you'd be afraid of its happening again."

"And the last place in the world you'd go back to is the place where it happened."

"I'd go through hell first," he said, his voice thick, like taking a vow. "And . . . just to cap it, that damned Beck—"

"He laughed?"

"He did not," said Hank viciously. "All he did was meet me at the door when I was escaping, and tell me I'd do just as well not to come again. He was polite enough, I guess, but he meant it."

I dunked the handkerchief again and leaned over the glass desktop, where I could see my reflection. I mopped at my chin. "This Beck," I said. "He certainly makes sure. Hank, all the other people who used to go to Beck's and don't any more . . . do you suppose Beck told them all not to come back?"

"I never thought of it. Probably so. Except maybe Klaus. He wasn't going anywhere after what he did."

"I saw Willy Simms," I told him. "He acted mad at Beck, and said something about going there again being as impossible as writing another song. He's tone deaf, you know."

"I didn't know. What about Miss Falsehaven? Did you see her?"

"She wouldn't be seen dead in the place. She's half crazy with the memory of what she did. To you or me, that would be nothing. To her it was the end of the world."

The end of the world. The end of the world. "Hank, I'm just dimly beginning to understand what you meant about . . . Opie. That what she did wasn't her doing." Suddenly, shockingly—I believe I was more startled than Hank—I bellowed, "But it was in her to do it! There had to be that one grain of—of whatever it took!"

"Maybe, maybe . . . ," he said gently. "I'd like to think not, though. I'd like to think there is something there at Beck's that puts the bee in people's bonnets. An alien bee, one that couldn't under any other circumstances exist with that person." He blushed. "I'd feel better if I could prove that."

"I got to get out of here. I'm meeting Beck," I said, after a glance at his desk clock.

"Are you now?" He sat down again. "Give him my regards."

I started out. "Tom—"

"Well?"

"I'm sorry I had to hit you. I had to. See?"

"Sure I see," I said, and when I grinned it hurt. "If I didn't see, they'd be mixing a cast for your busted back by now." I went out.

Beck was waiting for me when I rushed into Kelly's. I picked up his drink and started back to the corner.

"Not a table," he bleated, following me. "I have a train to catch, Tom. I told you that."

"Come on," I said. "This won't take but a minute." He came, grumbling, and he let me maneuver him into the upholstered corner of a booth. I sat down where he'd have to climb over me if the conversation should make him too impulsive.

"Sorry I'm late, Beck. But I'm glad you're in a hurry. I won't have to beat about the bush."

"What's on your mind?" he said, irritatingly looking at his watch and, for a moment, closing his eyes as he calculated the minutes.

"Where's your money come from?" I asked bluntly.

"Why, it—well, really, Tom. You've never—I mean—" He shifted gears and began to get stuffy. "I'm not used to being catechized about my personal affairs, old man. We are old friends, yes, but after all—"

"Shove it," I said. "I'm the boy who knew you when, remember? We roomed together in college, and unless my memory fails me it was State College, as near to being a public school as you can find these days. We had three neckties and one good blanket between us for more than two years, and skipped forty-cent lunches for date money. That wasn't so long ago, Beck. You graduated into pushing a pen for an insurance company—right? And when you left it you never took another job. But here you are with a big ugly house full of big ugly furniture, a rumpus room by Hilton out of Tropics, and a passion for throwing big noisy parties every week."

"May I ask," he said between his protruding front teeth, "why you are so suddenly interested?"

"You look more than ever like a gopher," I said detachedly, figuring it wouldn't hurt to make him mad. He always blurts things when he's mad enough. "Now, Beck—working around a magazine like ours, we get a lot of advance stuff about things that are about to break. I'm just trying to do you a favor, son."

"I don't see—"

"How would you make out," I asked, "if they dragged out your income tax returns for the last four years and balanced them against your real property?"

"I'd make out nicely," he said smugly. "If you must know, my income comes from investments. I've done very well indeed."

"What did you use for capital in the first place?"

"That's really none of your business, Tom," he said briskly, and I almost admired him for the way he stood up to me. "But I might remind you that you need very little capital to enter the market, and if you can buy low and sell high just a few times in a row, you don't have to worry about capital."

"You're not a speculator, Beck," I snorted, "Not *you!* Why I never figured you had the sense to pour pith out of a helmet. Who's your tipster?"

For some reason, that hit him harder than anything else I'd said. "You're being very annoying," he said prissily, "and you're going to make me miss my train. I'll have to leave now. I don't know what's gotten into you, Tom. I don't much care for this kind of thing, and I'm sure I don't know what this is all about."

"I'll go with you," I said, "and explain the whole thing."

"You needn't bother," he snapped. He got up, and so did I. I let him out from behind the table and followed him to the door. The hat check girl rummaged around and found a pigskin suitcase for him. I took it from her before he could get a hand on it. "Give me that!" he yelled.

"Don't stand here and argue," I said urgently. "You'll be late." I barreled on out to the curb and whistled. I whistle pretty well. Cabs stopped three blocks in every direction. I shoved him into the nearest one and climbed in after him. "You know you could never catch a cab like I can," I said. "I just want to help."

"Central Depot," Beck said to the driver. "Tom, what are you after? I've never seen you like this."

"Just trying to help," I said. "A lot of people starting to talk about you, Beck."

He paled. "Really?"

"Oh, yes. What do you expect: hidden income, big parties that anyone can come to, and all?"

"Lot of people have parties."

"Nobody talks about them afterward the way they do about yours."

"What are they saying, Tom?" He hated to be conspicuous.

"Why did you tell Willy Simms never to show his face at your house again?" It was a shot in the dark, but the bell rang.

"I think I was quite reasonable with him," Beck protested. "He talks all the time, and he bored me. He bored everybody, every time he came."

"He still talks all the time," I said mysteriously, and dropped that part of it. Beck began to squirm. "Personally, I think you get something from the people who come to those brawls. And once you've gotten it, you drop them."

Beck leaned forward to speak to the driver, but for some reason his voice wouldn't work. He coughed and tried again. "Faster, driver."

"So what I want to know is, what do you get from those people, and how do you get it?"

"I don't know what you mean, and I don't see how any of this concerns you."

"Something happened to my wife last Saturday."

"Oh," he said. "Oh, dear." Then, "Well, what do you suppose I got from her?"

I put my hands behind me, lifted up, and sat on them. "I know you awful well," I grated, "which fact just saved your life. You don't mean what you just said, old man, do you?"

He went quite white. "Oh, good heavens, Tom, no! No! It was what you said before—that I got something out of every one of these people. I'm more sorry than I can say about—about Opie—I couldn't help it, you know, I was busy, there was a lot to do, there always is. . . . No, Tom, I didn't mean that the way you thought."

He didn't, either. Not Beck. There were some things that were just not in Beck's department. I took a deep, head-clearing breath and asked, "Why did you tell Hank not to come back?"

"I'd rather not say exactly," he said, pleading and sincere. "It was for his own benefit, though. He . . . er . . . made rather a fool of himself. I thought it would be a kindness if he could be angry at me instead of at himself."

I gave him a long careful look. He had never been very smart, but he had always been as glib as floor wax. The cab turned into the station ramp just then, so I came up with the big question. "Beck, does everybody who goes to your parties sooner or later make a fool of himself?"

"Oh dear no," he said, and I think if he had not been looking at his watch and worrying, he would never have said what came out. "Some people are immune."

The cab stopped and he got out. "I'll take it," I said when his hand went for his pocket. "You better run." I hung my head out the window, watching him, waiting, wondering if it would come, even after all this. And it came.

From fifty feet away he called over his shoulder, "See you Saturday, Tom!"

"Kelly's," I told the cabbie, and settled back.

So. I couldn't make Beck so mad he'd exclude me from one of his parties—and somehow or other the rich and dumb and smart and stupid and ugly and big and famous and nowhere people who came there became prone to making fools of themselves—and Beck got something out of it when they did—and what did he want out of me? And what did he mean by "some people are immune"? Immune . . . that was a peculiar word to use. Immune. There was something in that house—in that room—that made people do things that—Wait a minute. Hank and Miss Falsehaven and, if you wanted to be broad about it, Opie—they had indeed made fools of themselves. But the guy who killed the preacher with Beck's poker—and Klaus the spy—that wasn't what you'd call foolishness. And then Willy Simms. Is the creation of a hit song foolishness?

Lowest common denominator . . .

I paid off the cab and went in to Kelly's to double the drink I'd missed because Beck had been in such a hurry. I was drinking the second one when some simple facts fell into place.

The next best thing to knowing what the answer is is to know where it is. Beck was on his way out of town.

There was only one single thing that connected all these crazy facts: Beck's rumpus room.

A good thing I have credit at Kelly's. I flew out of there so fast I forgot to leave anything on the bar. Except a half shot of rye.

It wasn't quite dark when I reached Beck's, but that didn't matter. The house was set well back in its mid-city three acres. High board fences guarded the sides, and a thick English privet hid it from the street. Once I'd slipped through the gate and onto the lawn, I might as well have been underground. The house was one of those turn-of-the-century horrors, not quite chalet, not quite manse, with a little more gingerbread than the moderns like and a little less than the Victorians drooled about. It had gables and turrets and rooms scattered on slightly different levels, so that the windows looked like the holes on an IBM card.

I hefted the package I'd picked up at the hardware store on the way and, sticking close to the north hedge, worked my way cautiously around to the back.

One glance told me I couldn't do business there. The house was built at the very back of its property,

and behind it ran a small street or a large alley, whichever you like. The back of the house hung over it like
a cliff, and there was traffic and neighbors across the
way. No, it would have to be a side. I cursed, because I
knew the rumpus room faced the back with its huge
picture windows of one-way glass; then I remembered
that the room was air-conditioned; the windows
wouldn't open and couldn't be cut because they were
certainly double-pane jobs.

I tried two ground-floor windows, but they were
locked. Another was open, but barred. Then nothing
but a bare, windowless stretch. On a hunch I approached it, through the flower bed at its base. And
sure enough, just at chest-height, hidden behind a
phalanx of hollyhocks, was a small window.

I got out the penlite flash I'd just bought and
peered in. The window was locked with one of those
burglar-proof cast-steel locks that screws a rubber fer-
rule up against the frame. I was pleased. I got out the
can of aquarium cement and worked the stuff into a
cone, which I placed against the glass. Then I got out
the glass cutter and scribed around the cone. I rapped
the cut circle once, and with a snap it broke out, with
the cone of putty holding it. I reached down and laid
putty and glass on the window-sill, unscrewed the
burglarproof lock, opened the window and climbed in.
With my putty-knife I carefully removed the broken
pane, and cracked it and the circle into small enough
pieces to wrap up in the brown paper from the parcel
I carried. I measured the frame and cut the one spare
piece of window glass I'd brought along, and installed
it using the aquarium cement. The stuff's black and
doesn't glare at you the way clean, new putty does. I
cleaned the new pane inside and out, shut and locked
the window, and carefully swept the sill and the floor
under it. I dumped the sweepings into my jacket
pocket and stowed the tools here and there in my
jacket and pants. So now nobody ever had to know I'd
been here.

I was in a large storage closet which turned out to belong to the butler's pantry. That led to the kitchen, and that to the dining room, and now I knew where I was. I went into the front hall and down toward the back of the house. The door to the rumpus room was closed. On this side it was all crudded up with carven wainscoting; golden oak and Ionic columns. It was a sliding door; I rolled it back and on the other side it was a flat slab of birch to match the shocking modern of the rumpus room. Again I had that strange feeling of wonderment about Beck and his single peculiarity.

I shut the door and crossed the dim room to the picture windows. There I touched the button that closed the heavy drapes. There was a faint hum and they began to move. As they did, all but sourceless light began to grow in the room, until when they met the room was filled with a pervasive golden glow.

And standing in the middle of the rug which I had just crossed, standing yards away from any door and a long way from any furniture, was a girl.

The shock of it was almost physical. And for a split second I thought my eyes registered a dazzle, like the subjective after-glow of a lightning flash. Then I got hold of myself and met her long, level, green-eyed gaze.

If a woman can be strong and elfin at once, she was. Her hair was blue-black with a strange reddish light in it. Her skin was too flawless, like something in a wax museum, but for all that it was real and warm-looking. She was smiling, and I could see how her teeth met edge to edge in that rarity, the perfect bite. Her lowcut dress was of a heavy gold and purple brocade, and she must have had a dozen petticoats under it. Sixteenth century—seventeenth century? In *this* room?

"That was nice," she said.

"It was?" I said stupidly.

"Yes, but it didn't last. I suppose you're immune."

"Depends," I said, looking at the neckline of her dress. Then I remembered Beck's strange remark.

She said, "You're not supposed to be here. Not all alone."

"I could say the same for you. But since we're both here, we're not alone."

"I'm not," she said. "But you are." And she laughed. "You're Conway."

"Oh. He told you about me, did he? Well, he never said a word about you."

"Of course not. He wouldn't dare."

"Do you live here?"

She nodded. "I've always lived here."

"What do you mean always? Beck's been here three—yes, it's four years now. And you've been here all this time?"

She nodded. "Since before that."

"I'll be damned," I said. "Good for Beck. I thought he didn't like women."

"He doesn't need to." I saw her gaze stray over my shoulder and fix on something behind me. I whirled. Clinging to the drape was a spider as big as a Stetson hat. I didn't know whether it was going to jump or what. With the same motion which began when I turned, I snatched up a heavy ashstand made of links of chain welded together. Before I could heave it the girl was beside me, holding it with both hands. "Don't," she said. "You'll break the window and people will come. I want you to stay here for a while."

"But the—"

"It isn't real," she said. I looked and the spider was gone. I turned back to her. "What the hell goes on here?"

She sighed. "That wasn't so good," she said. "You were supposed to be frightened. But you just got angry at it. Why weren't you frightened?"

"I am now," I said, glancing at the drapes. "I guess I get mad first and scared later. What's the idea? You put that thing there, didn't you?"

She nodded.

"What for?"

"I was hungry."

"I don't get you."

"I know."

She moved to the divan, rustling wonderfully as she walked. She subsided into the foam rubber, patted the seat next to her. I crossed slowly. You don't have to know what a thing's all about to like it. I sat beside her.

She cast her eyes down and smoothed her skirt. It was as if she were waiting for something.

I didn't give her long to wait. I pulled her to me and clawed at the back of her dress. It slipped downward easily just as my cheek encountered the heavy stubble on hers.

The heavy—

With a shout I sprang back, goggle-eyed. There on the couch sprawled a heavy-set man with bad teeth and a four-day beard. He roared with rich baritone laughter.

You don't have to understand a situation to dislike it. I stepped forward and let loose with my Sunday punch. It travels from my lower rib to straight ahead, and by the time it gets where it's going it has all of me behind it. But this time it didn't get anywhere. My elbow crackled from the strain as my fist connected with nothing at all. But from the seat of the divan came a large black cat. It leaped to the floor and streaked across the room. I fell heavily onto the divan, bounced off, and rushed the animal. It doubled back at the end of the room, eluded my grasping fingers easily, and the next thing I knew it was climbing the drapes, hand over hand.

Yes, hands; the cat had three-fingered hands and an opposed thumb.

When it got up about fifteen feet it tucked itself into a round ball and—I think *spun* is the word for it. I shook my head to clear it and looked again. There was no sign of the animal; there was only a speaker baffle I had not noticed before.

Speaker baffle?

Anyone who knows ultramodern knows there's a convention against speakers or lights showing. Everything has to be concealed or to look like something else.

"That," said the speaker in a sexless, toneless voice, "was more like it."

I backed away and sank down on the divan, where I could watch the baffle.

"Even if you are immune, I can get something out of you."

I said, "How do you mean immune?"

"There is nothing you wouldn't do," said the impersonal voice. "Now, when I make somebody do something he *can't* do—then I feed. All I can do with you is make you mad. Even then, you're not mad at yourself at all. Just the girl or the spider or whatever else."

I suddenly realized the speaker wasn't there any more. However, a large spotted snake was on the rug near my feet. I dived on it, found in my hand the ankle of the girl I had seen before. I backed off and sat down again. "See?" she said in her velvet voice. "You don't even scare much now."

"I won't scare at all," I said positively.

"I suppose not," she said regretfully. Then she brightened. "But it's almost Saturday. *Then* I'll feed."

"What are you, anyhow?"

She shrugged. "You haven't a name for it. How could a thing like me have a name anyhow? I can be anything I like."

"Stay this way for a while." I looked her up and down. "I like you fine this way. Why don't you come over here and be friendly?"

She stepped back a pace, shaking her head.

"Why not? It wouldn't matter to you."

"That's right. I won't though. You see, it wouldn't matter to you."

"I don't get you."

She said patiently, "In your position, some men

wouldn't want me. Some would in spite of themselves, and when they found out what I was—or what I *wasn't*—they'd hate themselves for it. That I could use," she crooned, and licked her full lips. "But you— you want me the way I am right now, and it doesn't matter in the least to you that I might be reptile, insect, or just plain hypocrite, as long as you got what you want."

"Wait a minute—this feeding. You feed on—hate?"

"Oh, no. Look, when a human being does something he's incapable of, like—oh, that old biddy who clawed the pretty actress—there's a glandular reaction set up that's unlike any other. All humans have a drive to live and a drive to die—a drive to build and a drive to destroy. In most people they're shaken down pretty well. But what I do is to give them a big charge of one or the other, so the two parts are thrown into conflict. That conflict creates a—call it a field, an aura. That's what feeds me. Now do you see?"

"Sort of like the way a mosquito injects a dilutant into the blood." I looked at her. "You're a parasite."

"If you like," she said detachedly. "So are you, if you define parasitism as sustaining oneself from other life-forms."

"Now tell me about the immunity."

"Oh, that. Very annoying. Like being hungry and finding you have nothing but canned food and no opener. You know it's there but you can't get to it. It's quite simple. You're immune because you're capable of anything—anything at all."

"Like Superman?"

She curled her lip. "You? No, I'm sorry."

"What then?"

She was thoughtful. "Do you remember asking me what I was? Well, down through your history there have been a lot of names for such as I. All wrong, of course. But the one that's used most often is *conscience*. A man's natural conscience tells him when he's done wrong. But any time you see a case of a man's conscience working on him, trying to destroy him—you can bet one of us has been around. Any time you see a man doing something utterly outside all his background and conditioning—you can be sure one of us is there with him."

I was beginning to understand a whole lot of things. "Why are you telling me all this?"

"Why not? I like to talk, same as you do. It can't do any harm. No one would believe you. After a while you yourself won't believe anything I've told you. Humans *can't* believe in things that have no set size or shape or weight or behavior. If an extra fly buzzes around your table; if your morning-glory vine has a new shoot it lacked ten minutes ago—you wouldn't believe it. These things happen around all humans all the time, and they never notice. They explain everything in terms of what they already believe. Since they never believe in anything remotely resembling us, we are free to pass and repass in front of their silly eyes, feeding when and where we want. . . ."

"You can't get away with it. Humans will catch up with you," I blurted. "Humans are learning to think in new ways. Did you ever hear of non-Euclidean geometry? Do you know anything about non-Aristotelian systems?"

She laughed. "We know about them. But by the time they are generally accepted, we'll no longer be parasites. We'll be symbiotes. Some of us already are. I am."

"Symbiotes? You mean you depend on another life-form?"

"And it depends on me."

"What does?"

She indicated the incongruous room. "Your silly friend Beck, of course. Some of the people who are attracted to the feeding-grounds here are operators—very shrewd. The last thing in the world they would ever do is to pass on investment secrets to anyone. I see to it that they tell Beck. And oh, *how* they regret it!

How *foolish* they feel! And how I feed! In exchange, Beck brings them here."

"I *knew* he couldn't do it by himself!" I said. "Now tell me—why does he have me hanging around here all the time?"

"My doing." She looked at me coolly. "One day I'm going to eat you. One day I'll find that can-opener. I'll learn how to slam a door on you, or pound you with a flatiron, and I'll eat you like candy."

I laughed at her. "You'll have to find something I'll regret doing first."

"There has to be something." She yawned. "I have to work up a new edge to my appetite," she said lazily. "Go away."

"She's wrong," Hank said, when I'd finished telling him the story. He'd galloped over to my place when I called and just let me talk.

"Wrong how?"

"She said it was impossible for a human to believe this. Well, by God I do."

"I think I do myself," I said. Then, "Why?"

"Why?" Hank repeated. He gave a thoughtful pull to his lower lip. "Maybe it's just because I want to believe in any theory that keeps Opie clean—that makes what she did really out of character."

"Opie," I said. "Yes."

He gave me a swift look. "Something I've been thinking about, Tom. That night it happened—with Opie, I mean. . . ."

"Spill it if it bothers you," I said, recognizing the expression.

"Thanks, Tom. Well . . . no matter what Opie was suffering from, no matter how . . . uh . . . willing she might have been—these things take time. You can see them happening."

"So?"

"*Where were you when that guy started making passes at her?*"

I thought. I started to smile, cut it off. Then I got mad. "I don't remember."

"Yes you do. Where were you, Tom?"

"Around."

"You weren't even in the room."

"I wasn't?"

"No."

"Who told you?"

"You did," he said. He began to get that sleepy look. "You're a lousy liar, Tom. When you duck a question, you're saying yes. Who was the babe, Tom?"

"I don't know."

"*What?*"

"I said I don't know," I said sullenly. "Just a babe."

"Oh. You didn't ask her her name."

"Guess not."

"And you raised all that fuss about Opie."

"You leave Opie out of this!" I blazed. "There's a big difference."

"You ought to be hung by your thumbs," he said pityingly. "But I guess it isn't your fault." He snorted. "No wonder that parasite of Beck's can't reach you. You don't do anything you regret because you never regret anything you do. Not one thing!"

"Well, why not?" I jumped to my feet. "Listen, Hank, I'm alive, see. I'm alive all over. Everybody I know is killing off this part of themselves, that part of themselves—parts that get hungry get starved, they die. Don't drink this, don't look at that, don't eat the other, when all the time something in you is hungry for these things. It's easily fed—and once it's fed it's quiet. I'm alive, damn it, and I mean to stay alive!"

Hank went to the door. "I'm getting out of here," he said in a shaking voice. "I got to think of my sister. I don't want you to get hurt. She might not forgive me."

He slammed the door. I kicked the end-table and busted a leg off it. The door opened again. Hank said,

"I'm going with you to Beck's Saturday night. I'll pick you up here. Don't leave until I get here."

The front door at Beck's stood wide, as it always did on Saturdays. There was nothing to stop Hank or any other "graduate" from walking right in. Unless the something was inside those people. Hank sure felt it; I could tell by the way he jammed his hands in his pockets and sauntered through the door. He looked so relaxed, but he radiated tension.

It was the usual unusual type of party. Beck self-effacingly rode herd on about nineteen of the goofiest assortment of people ever collected—since last week. A famous lady economist. An alderman. A pimply Leftist. A brace of German tourists, binoculars and all. A dazed-looking farmer in store-clothes. Somebody playing piano. Somebody looking adoringly at the piano-player—she obviously didn't play. Somebody else looking disgustedly at the piano-player. He obviously did play.

When we came in, Beck hurried over, chortling greetings, which dried up completely when he recognized Hank. "Hank," he gasped. "Really, old man, I think—"

"Hiya, Beck," Hank said. "Been quite a while." He walked out into the room and to the bar in the far corner. Beck gawped like a beached haddock. "Tom," Beck said, "you shouldn't have taken a chance like—"

"I'm just as thirsty as he is," I told him, and followed Hank.

I got a rye. "Hank."

"What?" His eyes were on the crowd.

"When are you going to quit the silent treatment and tell me what you have in mind?"

He looked at me, and the strain he was under must have been painful. "Hey," I said, "take it easy. Nothing's going to happen to you. Our hungry little friend here is an epicure. I don't think she's interested in anything but the first rush of anguish she kicks up. You're old stuff."

"I know," he muttered. "I know . . . I guess." He wiped his forehead. "Do you see her?"

"No," I said. "But then, how would I know her if I did see her? Maybe she's not in the room."

"I think she is," he said. "I think she's stuck here."

"That's a thought. Hey! Her specialty is the incongruous—right? The out-of-character. Well, that's what this room is all about."

He nodded. "That's what I mean. And that's what I'm going to check on, but for sure. Here."

He moved close to the bar and to me, and quickly and secretly passed me something chunky and flat. "Hank!" I whispered. "A gun! What—"

"Take it. I have one too. Follow my cue when the time comes."

I don't like guns. But it was in my pocket before I could make any more talk. I wondered if Hank had gone off his rocker. "Bullets wouldn't make no nevermind to her."

"They aren't for her," he said, watching the crowd again.

"But—"

"Shut up. Tom," he asked abruptly, "does somebody always do something crazy at these shindigs? Every time?"

I remembered about the "investment" tips, the number of quiet, unnoticed times people must have done things in this room that caused them humiliation, regret. "Maybe so, Hank."

"Early or late in the proceedings?"

"That I don't know, Hank. I really don't."

"I can't wait," he muttered. "I can't risk it. Maybe it only feeds once. Here I go," he said clearly.

I called to him, but he put his chin down between his collarbones and went to the piano. I flashed a look around. I remember Beck's face watching Hank was white and strained.

Hank climbed right up on the piano, one foot on the bench, one foot on the keys, both big feet on the exquisite finish of the top. The pianist faltered and stopped. The ardent girl watching him squeaked. People looked. People rushed to finish a sentence while they turned. Others didn't even notice. After all—those parties of Beck's. . . .

"Parasite!" Hank bellowed. And do you know, four-fifths of that crowd practically snapped to attention.

"He's not immune," Hank said. He was talking, apparently, to the place where the wall met the ceiling. "Here's your can-opener, parasite. Listen to me."

He paused, and in the sudden embarrassed silence Beck's voice came shakingly, stretched and gasping. "Get off there, you hear? Get—"

Hank pulled out his gun. "Shut up, Beck." Beck sat right down on the floor. Hank lifted his big head. "All he wants to do is live. He'd hate to die. But how do you suppose he'd feel if he killed himself?"

There shouldn't be silences like that. But it didn't last long. Somebody whimpered. Somebody shuffled. And then, in that voice I had heard here before, on the crazy day I saw the spider and the cat with hands, I heard a single syllable.

Starve a man for a day and a half, then put a piece of charcoal-crusted, juicy-pink steak in his mouth. Set out glasses of a rough red wine, and secretly substitute a vintage burgundy in one man's glass. Drop a silky mink over the shoulders of a shabby girl as she stands in front of a mirror. Do any of these things and you'll hear that sound, starting suddenly, falling in pitch, turning to a sigh, then a breath.

"M-m-m-m-m . . . !"

"You won't have long to take it, but it doesn't take long, does it?" asked Hank.

I thought, what the hell is he talking about? Who? And then I pulled the gun out of my pocket.

Now I've got to talk about how much can run through a man's mind, how fast. In the time it took to raise the gun and aim it and pull the trigger, I thought:

It's Tom Conway he's been talking about to the parasite.

Hank wants the parasite to take me.

It's the parasite, not Hank, not I, who is raising this gun, aiming it.

This is Hank's way to avenge himself on me. And why vengeance? Only because I think differently from him. Doesn't Hank know that to me my thinking is right and needs no excuse?

And it's a stupid vengeance, because it's on Opie's behalf, and surely Opie wouldn't want it; certainly it can't benefit her.

The gun was aimed at my temple and I pulled the trigger.

I'm alive, I'm alive all over. Everybody has to die sometime, but oh, the stupid, stupid, sick realization that you did it to yourself! That you let yourself be killed, that you let your own finger tighten on the trigger.

A gunshot is staccato, sharp, short. This was different. This was a sound that started with a gunshot but sustained itself; it was a roar, it filled the world. It roared and roared while the room hazed over, spun, turned on its side as my cheek thumped the carpet. The roar went on and on while the light faded, and through it I could hear their screams, and Hank's voice, distant but clear. "Everybody out! This place is going to blow sky-high." "Fire!" he shouted a second later "Fire!" And, *"Beck, damn you, help me with Tom."*

Nothing then but a sense of time passing, then cool air, darkness, and a moment of lucidity I saw too clearly, heard too well. Everything hurt. The roar was still going on as a background, I heard the gunshot, tasted it bitterly, saw it as a flickering aurora in and of everything around me, smelled it acrid and sharp and felt it. I was on the gravel path, and frightened people poured out of the house.

"Stay with him!" Hank roared, and my head was cradled on Beck's trembling knees.

"But there is no fire—no fire," Beck quavered.

And Hank was a black bulk in blackness, and his voice was distant as he raced to the bushes. "Wait," he said. "Wait." He stooped back there, and there was a dull explosion inside the house, and another, and white light showed in the downstairs windows, turned to yellow, flickered and grew.

Hank came back. "There's a fire," he said.

Beck screamed. "You'll kill it!" He tried to rise. Hank caught his shirt and held him down.

"Yes, I'll kill it, you Judas!"

"You don't understand," Beck cried, "I can't live without it."

"Go back to your insurance company job. Make your own way, and don't harvest better people than yourself to feed monsters." Flames shot from the second-story windows. "But if you really can't live without it—die," said Hank, and then he shouted, "Is everybody out?"

"All accounted for," called a voice. I remember thinking then that if they had counted heads and all were safe—who was that screaming in the fire?

After that even the roar stopped.

First pain, and then enough light to filter through my closed lids. I tried to move my right hand and failed. I opened my eyes and saw the cast on my right forearm. I turned my head.

"Tom?"

I looked up at the speaking blur. Then it wasn't a blur, it was Hank.

"You're all right now, Tom. You're home. My house."

I turned from him and looked at the ceiling, the window, then back to him. "You tried to kill me," I said.

He shook his head. "I used you for bait. I had to know if it was in that room. I had to know if it would feed. I had to know what it could do, what it would do. I tried to shoot the gun out of your hand. I missed, and hit your forearm. It's broken. Your bullet creased your scalp. It was awful close, Tom."

"Suppose I'd killed myself?"

He said, "Bait is expendable."

"You booby-trapped the house, didn't you?"

"After your blow-by-blow instruction in burglary, it was no trouble."

"You tried to kill me," I said.

"I didn't," he said with finality.

I wondered—I really wondered—why what I had done was that important. And it was as if Hank read my mind. "It's because of the difference between you and Opie," he said. "Superficially, you and Opie did exactly the same thing that night.

"But Opie's own feelings about it will cost her something for the rest of her life. And you didn't even remember who you were with."

I lay there like a block of wood. Hank went away. Maybe I slept. Next thing I knew, Opie was there, kneeling by the bed.

"Tom," she said brokenly. "Oh, Tom. I wish I were dead. Tom," she said, "I'll spend the rest of my life making it up to you. . . ."

I thought, I wish that thing, whatever it was, hadn't died in the fire. I know what I am now, I thought. I'm immune. And knowing that gives me enough anguish to feed the likes of you for a thousand years.

Yesterday Was Monday

"Where do you get your crazy ideas?"

Every writer gets this question in various inflections, some of them downright insulting. Where this idea came from is a mystery; why I set about writing it is another. Everything I have said about *The Ultimate Egoist* applies to this one too: I was a beginner, I was unpracticed, I was eager—ready to write everything that came into my head. Often I would write myself into situations in which I had no idea where I was going or what might happen before the end. I do not recommend this as a technique; but if it does happen and you find a way out, you have written a story that doesn't "telegraph" to the reader what the ending will be. If the author doesn't know, the reader can't.

This is one of those. And also: it was fun to do.

Harry Wright rolled over and said something spelled "Bzzzzhha-a-aw!" He chewed a bit on a mouthful of

dry air and spat it out, opened one eye to see if it
really would open, opened the other and closed the
first, closed the second, swung his feet onto the floor,
opened them again and stretched. This was a daily occurrence, and the only thing that made it remarkable
at all was that he did it on a Wednesday morning,
and—

Yesterday was Monday.

Oh, he knew it was Wednesday all right. It was
partly that, even though he knew yesterday was Monday, there was a gap between Monday and now; and
that must have been Tuesday. When you fall asleep
and lie there all night without dreaming, you know,
when you wake up, that time has passed. You've done
nothing that you can remember; you've had no particular thoughts, no way to gauge time, and yet you
know that some hours have passed. So it was with
Harry Wright. Tuesday had gone wherever your eight
hours went last night.

But he hadn't slept through Tuesday. Oh no. He
never slept, as a matter of fact, more than six hours at
a stretch, and there was no particular reason for him
doing so now. Monday was the day before yesterday;
he had turned in and slept his usual stretch, he had
awakened, and it was Wednesday.

It *felt* like Wednesday. There was a Wednesdayish
feel to the air.

Harry put on his socks and stood up. He wasn't
fooled. He knew what day it was. "What happened to
yesterday?" he muttered. "Oh—yesterday was Monday." That sufficed until he got his pajamas off.
"Monday," he mused, reaching for his underwear,
"was quite a while back, seems as though." If he had
been the worrying type, he would have started then
and there. But he wasn't. He was an easygoing sort,
the kind of man that gets himself into a rut and stays
there until he is pushed out. That was why he was an
automobile mechanic at twenty-three dollars a week;
that's why he had been one for eight years now, and

would be from now on, if he could only find Tuesday and get back to work.

Guided by his reflexes, as usual, and with no mental effort at all, which was also usual, he finished washing, dressing, and making his bed. His alarm clock, which never alarmed because he was of such regular habits, said, as usual, six twenty-two when he paused on the way out, and gave his room the once-over. And there was a certain something about the place that made even this phlegmatic character stop and think.

It wasn't finished.

The bed was there, and the picture of Joe Louis. There were the two chairs sharing their usual seven legs, the split table, the pipe-organ bedstead, the beige wallpaper with the two swans over and over and over, the tiny corner sink, the tilted bureau. But none of them were finished. Not that there were any holes in anything. What paint there had been in the first place was still there. But there was an odor of old cut lumber, a subtle, insistent air of building, about the room and everything in it. It was indefinable, inescapable, and Harry Wright stood there caught up in it, wondering. He glanced suspiciously around but saw nothing he could really be suspicious of. He shook his head, locked the door and went out into the hall.

On the steps a little fellow, just over three feet tall, was gently stroking the third step from the top with a razor-sharp chisel, shaping up a new scar in the dirty wood. He looked up as Harry approached, and stood up quickly.

"Hi," said Harry, taking in the man's leather coat, his peaked cap, his wizened, bright-eyed little face. "Whatcha doing?"

"Touch-up," piped the little man. "The actor in the third floor front has a nail in his right heel. He came in late Tuesday night and cut the wood here. I have to get it ready for Wednesday."

"This is Wednesday," Harry pointed out.

"Of course. Always has been. Always will be."

Harry let that pass, started on down the stairs. He had achieved his amazing bovinity by making a practice of ignoring things he could not understand. But one thing bothered him—

"Did you say that feller in the third floor front was an actor?"

"Yes. They're all actors, you know."

"You're nuts, friend," said Harry bluntly. "That guy works on the docks."

"Oh yes—that's his part. That's what he acts."

"No kiddin'. An' what does he do when he isn't acting?"

"But he— Well, that's all he does do! That's all any of the actors do!"

"Gee— I thought he looked like a reg'lar guy, too," said Harry. "An actor? 'Magine!"

"Excuse me," said the little man, "but I've got to get back to work. We mustn't let anything get by us, you know. They'll be through Tuesday before long, and everything must be ready for them."

Harry thought: this guy's crazy nuts. He smiled uncertainly and went down to the landing below. When he looked back the man was cutting skillfully into the stair, making a neat little nail scratch. Harry shook his head. This was a screwy morning. He'd be glad to get back to the shop. There was a '39 sedan down there with a busted rear spring. Once he got his mind on that he could forget this nonsense. That's all that matters to a man in a rut. Work, eat, sleep, pay day. Why even try to think anything else out?

The street was a riot of activity, but then it always was. But not quite this way. There were automobiles and trucks and buses around, aplenty, but none of them were moving. And none of them were quite complete. This was Harry's own field; if there was anything he didn't know about motor vehicles, it wasn't very important. And through that medium he began to get the general idea of what was going on.

Swarms of little men who might have been twins of

the one he had spoken to were crowding around the cars, the sidewalks, the stores and buildings. All were working like mad with every tool imaginable. Some were touching up the finish of the cars with fine wire brushes, laying on networks of microscopic cracks and scratches. Some, with ball peens and mallets, were denting fenders skillfully, bending bumpers in an artful crash pattern, spider-webbing safety-glass windshields. Others were aging top dressing with high-pressure, needlepoint sandblasters. Still others were pumping dust into upholstery, sandpapering the dashboard finish around light switches, throttles, chokes, to give a finger-worn appearance. Harry stood aside as a half dozen of the workers scampered down the street bearing a fender which they riveted to a 1930 coupé. It was freshly bloodstained.

Once awakened to this highly unusual activity, Harry stopped, slightly open-mouthed, to watch what else was going on. He saw the same process being industriously accomplished with the houses and stores. Dirt was being laid on plate-glass windows over a coat of clear sizing. Woodwork was being cleverly scored and the paint peeled to make it look correctly weather-beaten, and dozens of leather-clad laborers were on their hands and knees, poking dust and dirt into the cracks between the paving blocks. A line of them went down the sidewalk, busily chewing gum and spitting it out; they were followed by another crew who carefully placed the wads according to diagrams they carried, and stamped them flat.

Harry set his teeth and muscled his rocking brain into something like its normal position. "I ain't never seen a day like this or crazy people like this," he said, "but I ain't gonna let it be any of my affair. I got my job to go to." And trying vainly to ignore the hundreds of little, hard-working figures, he went grimly on down the street.

When he got to the garage he found no one there but more swarms of stereotyped little people climbing over the place, dulling the paint work, cracking the cement flooring, doing their hurried, efficient little tasks of aging. He noticed, only because he was so familiar with the garage, that they were actually *making* the marks that had been there as long as he had known the place. "Hell with it," he gritted, anxious to submerge himself into his own world of wrenches and grease guns. "I got my job; this is none o' my affair."

He looked about him, wondering if he should clean these interlopers out of the garage. Naw—not his affair. He was hired to repair cars, not to police the joint. Long as they kept away from him—and, of course, animal caution told him that he was far, far outnumbered. The absence of the boss and the other mechanics was no surprise to Harry; he always opened the place.

He climbed out of his street clothes and into coveralls, picked up a tool case and walked over to the sedan, which he had left up on the hydraulic rack yester— that is, Monday night. And that is when Harry Wright lost his temper. After all, the car was his job, and he didn't like having anyone else mess with a job he had started. So when he saw his job—his '39 sedan—resting steadily on its wheels over the rack, which was down under the floor, and when he saw that the rear spring was repaired, he began to burn. He dived under the car and ran deft fingers over the rear wheel suspensions. In spite of his anger at this unprecedented occurrence, he had to admit to himself that the job had been done well. "Might have done it myself," he muttered.

A soft clank and a gentle movement caught his attention. With a roar he reached out and grabbed the leg of one of the ubiquitous little men, wriggled out from under the car, caught his culprit by his leather collar, and dangled him at arm's length.

"What are you doing to my job?" Harry bellowed. The little man tucked his chin into the front of his shirt to give his windpipe a chance, and said, "Why, I was just finishing up that spring job."

"Oh. So you were just finishing up on that spring job," Harry whispered, choked with rage. Then, at the top of his voice, "Who told you to touch that car?"

"Who told me? What do you— Well, it just had to be done, that's all. You'll have to let me go. I must tighten up those two bolts and lay some dust on the whole thing."

"You must *what?* You get within six feet o' that car and I'll twist your head offn your neck with a Stillson!"

"But— It has to be done!"

"You won't do it! Why, I oughta—"

"Please let me go! If I don't leave that car the way it was Tuesday night—"

"When was Tuesday night?"

"The last act, of course. Let me go, or I'll call the district supervisor!"

"Call the devil himself. I'm going to spread you on the sidewalk outside; and heaven help you if I catch you near here again!"

The little man's jaw set, his eyes narrowed, and he whipped his feet upward. They crashed into Wright's jaw; Harry dropped him and staggered back. The little man began squealing, "Supervisor! Supervisor! Emergency!"

Harry growled and started after him; but suddenly, in the air between him and the midget workman, a long white hand appeared. The empty air was swept back, showing an aperture from the garage to blank, blind nothingness. Out of it stepped a tall man in a single loose-fitting garment literally studded with pockets. The opening closed behind the man.

Harry cowered before him. Never in his life had he seen such noble, powerful features, such strength of purpose, such broad shoulders, such a deep chest. The man stood with the backs of his hands on his hips, staring at Harry as if he were something somebody forgot to sweep up.

"That's him," said the little man shrilly. "He is trying to stop me from doing the work!"

"Who are you?" asked the beautiful man, down his nose.

"I'm the m-mechanic on this j-j— Who wants to know?"

"Iridel, supervisor of the district of Futura, wants to know."

"Where in hell did you come from?"

"I did not come from hell. I came from Thursday."

Harry held his head. "What *is* all this?" he wailed. "Why is today Wednesday? Who are all these crazy little guys? What happened to Tuesday?"

Iridel made a slight motion with his finger, and the little man scurried back under the car. Harry was frenzied to hear the wrench busily tightening bolts. He half started to dive under after the little fellow, but Iridel said, "Stop!" and when Iridel said, "Stop!" Harry stopped.

"This," said Iridel calmly, "is an amazing occurrence." He regarded Harry with unemotional curiosity. "An actor on stage before the sets are finished. Extraordinary."

"What stage?" asked Harry. "What are you doing here anyhow, and what's the idea of all these little guys working around here?"

"You ask a great many questions, actor," said Iridel. "I shall answer them, and then I shall have a few to ask you. These little men are stage hands— I am surprised that you didn't realize that. They are setting the stage for Wednesday. Tuesday? That's going on now."

"Arrgh!" Harry snorted. "How can Tuesday be going on when today's Wednesday?"

"Today isn't Wednesday, actor."

"Huh?"

"Today is Tuesday."

Harry scratched his head. "Met a feller on the steps this mornin'—one of these here stage hands of yours. He said this was Wednesday."

"It *is* Wednesday. Today is Tuesday. Tuesday is today. 'Today' is simply the name for the stage set which happens to be in use. 'Yesterday' means the set that has just been used; 'Tomorrow' is the set that will be used after the actors have finished with 'today.' This is Wednesday. Yesterday was Monday; today is Tuesday. See?"

Harry said, "No."

Iridel threw up his long hands. "My, you actors are stupid. Now listen carefully. This is Act Wednesday, Scene 6:22. That means that everything you see around you here is being readied for 6:22 a.m. on Wednesday. Wednesday isn't a time; it's a place. The actors are moving along toward it now. I see you still don't get the idea. Let's see . . . ah. Look at that clock. What does it say?"

Harry Wright looked at the big electric clock on the wall over the compressor. It was corrected hourly and highly accurate, and it said 6:22. Harry looked at it amazed. "Six tw— but my gosh, man, that's what time I left the house. I walked here, an' I been here ten minutes already!"

Iridel shook his head. "You've been here no time at all, because there is no time until the actors make their entrances."

Harry sat down on a grease drum and wrinkled up his brains with the effort he was making. "You mean that this time proposition ain't something that moves along all the time? Sorta—well, like a road. A road don't go no place— You just go places along it. Is that it?"

"That's the general idea. In fact, that's a pretty good example. Suppose we say that it's a road; a highway built of paving blocks. Each block is a day; the actors move along it, and go through day after day. And our job here—mine and the little men—is to . . . well, pave that road. This is the clean-up gang here. They are fixing up the last little details, so that everything will be ready for the actors."

Harry sat still, his mind creaking with the effects of this information. He felt as if he had been hit with a lead pipe, and the shock of it was being drawn out infinitely. This was the craziest-sounding thing he had ever run into. For no reason at all he remembered a talk he had had once with a drunken aviation mechanic who had tried to explain to him how the air flowing over an airplane's wings makes the machine go up in the air. He hadn't understood a word of the man's discourse, which was all about eddies and chords and cambers and foils, dihedrals and the Bernouilli effect. That didn't make any difference; the things flew whether he understood how or not; he knew that because he had seen them. This guy Iridel's lecture was the same sort of thing. If there was nothing in all he said, how come all these little guys were working around here? Why wasn't the clock telling time? Where was Tuesday?

He thought he'd get that straight for good and all. "Just where is Tuesday?" he asked.

"Over there," said Iridel, and pointed. Harry recoiled and fell off the drum; for when the man extended his hand, it *disappeared!*

Harry got up off the floor and said tautly, "Do that again."

"What? Oh— Point toward Tuesday? Certainly." And he pointed. His hand appeared again when he withdrew it.

Harry said, "My gosh!" and sat down again on the drum, sweating and staring at the supervisor of the district of Futura. "You point, an' your hand—ain't," he breathed. "What direction is that?"

"It is a direction like any other direction," said Iridel. "You know yourself there are four directions—forward, sideward, upward, and"—he pointed again, and again his hand vanished—"*that* way!"

"They never tole me that in school," said Harry. "Course, I was just a kid then, but—"

Iridel laughed. "It is the fourth dimension—it is *duration*. The actors move through length, breadth, and height, anywhere they choose to within the set. But there is another movement—one they can't control—and that is duration."

"How soon will they come . . . eh . . . here?" asked Harry, waving an arm. Iridel dipped into one of his numberless pockets and pulled out a watch. "It is now eight thirty-seven Tuesday morning," he said. "They'll be here as soon as they finish the act, and the scenes in Wednesday that have already been prepared."

Harry thought again for a moment, while Iridel waited patiently, smiling a little. Then he looked up at the supervisor and asked, "Hey—this 'actor' business—what's that all about?"

"Oh—that. Well, it's a play, that's all. Just like any play—put on for the amusement of an audience."

"I was to a play once," said Harry. "Who's the audience?"

Iridel stopped smiling. "Certain— Ones who may be amused," he said. "And now I'm going to ask you some questions. How did you get here?"

"Walked."

"You *walked* from Monday night to Wednesday morning?"

"Naw— From the house to here."

"Ah— But how did you get to Wednesday, six twenty-two?"

"Well I— Damfino. I just woke up an' came to work as usual."

"This is an extraordinary occurrence," said Iridel, shaking his head in puzzlement. "You'll have to see the producer."

"Producer? Who's he?"

"You'll find out. In the meantime, come along with me. I can't leave you here; you're too close to the play. I have to make my rounds anyway."

Iridel walked toward the door. Harry was tempted to stay and find himself some more work to do, but when Iridel glanced back at him and motioned him out, Harry followed. It was suddenly impossible to do anything else.

Just as he caught up with the supervisor, a little worker ran up, whipping off his cap.

"Iridel, sir," he piped, "the weather makers put .006 of one percent too little moisture in the air on this set. There's three sevenths of an ounce too little gasoline in the storage tanks under here."

"How much is in the tanks?"

"Four thousand two hundred and seventy-three gallons, three pints, seven and twenty-one thirty-fourths ounces."

Iridel grunted. "Let it go this time. That was very sloppy work. Someone's going to get transferred to Limbo for this."

"Very good, sir," said the little man. "Long as you know we're not responsible." He put on his cap, spun around three times and rushed off.

"Lucky for the weather makers that the amount of gas in that tank doesn't come into Wednesday's script," said Iridel. "If anything interferes with the continuity of the play, there's the devil to pay. Actors haven't sense enough to cover up, either. They are liable to start whole series of miscues because of a little thing like that. The play might flop and then we'd all be out of work."

"Oh," Harry oh-ed. "Hey, Iridel—what's the idea of that patchy-looking place over there?"

Iridel followed his eyes. Harry was looking at a corner lot. It was tree-lined and overgrown with weeds and small saplings. The vegetation was true to form around the edges of the lot, and around the path that ran diagonally through it; but the spaces in between were a plane surface. Not a leaf nor a blade of grass grew there; it was naked-looking, blank, and absolutely without any color whatever.

"Oh, that," answered Iridel. "There are only two characters in Act Wednesday who will use that path. Therefore it is as grown-over as it should be. The rest of the lot doesn't enter into the play, so we don't have to do anything with it."

"But— Suppose someone wandered off the path on Wednesday," Harry offered.

"He'd be due for a surprise, I guess. But it could hardly happen. Special prompters are always detailed to spots like that, to keep the actors from going astray or missing any cues."

"Who are they—the prompters, I mean?"

"Prompters? G.A.'s—Guardian Angels. That's what the script writers call them."

"I heard o' them," said Harry.

"Yes, they have their work cut out for them," said the supervisor. "Actors are always forgetting their lines when they shouldn't, or remembering them when the script calls for a lapse. Well, it looks pretty good here. Let's have a look at Friday."

"Friday? You mean to tell me you're working on Friday already?"

"Of course! Why, we work years in advance! How on earth do you think we could get our trees grown otherwise? Here—step in!" Iridel put out his hand, seized empty air, drew it aside to show the kind of absolute nothingness he had first appeared from, and waved Harry on.

"Y-you want me to go in there?" asked Harry diffidently.

"Certainly. Hurry, now!"

Harry looked at the section of void with a rather weak-kneed look, but could not withstand the supervisor's strange compulsion. He stepped through.

And it wasn't so bad. There were no whirling lights, no sensations of falling, no falling unconscious. It was just like stepping into another room—which is what had happened. He found himself in a great round chamber, whose roundness was touched a bit with the indistinct. That is, it had curved walls and a domed roof, but there was something else about it. It seemed to stretch off in that direction toward which Iridel had so astonishingly pointed. The walls were lined with an amazing array of control machinery—switches and ground-glass screens, indicators and dials, knurled knobs, and levers. Moving deftly before them was a crew of men, each looking exactly like Iridel except that their garments had no pockets. Harry stood wide-eyed, hypnotized by the enormous complexity of the controls and the ease with which the men worked among them. Iridel touched his shoulder. "Come with me," he said. "The producer is in now; we'll find out what is to be done with you."

They started across the floor. Harry had not quite time to wonder how long it would take them to cross that enormous room, for when they had taken perhaps a dozen steps they found themselves at the opposite wall. The ordinary laws of space and time simply did not apply in the place.

They stopped at a door of burnished bronze, so very highly polished that they could see through it. It opened and Iridel pushed Harry through. The door swung shut. Harry, panic-stricken lest he be separated from the only thing in this weird world he could begin to get used to, flung himself against the great bronze portal. It bounced him back, head over heels, into the middle of the floor. He rolled over and got up to his hands and knees.

He was in a tiny room, one end of which was filled by a colossal teakwood desk. The man sitting there regarded him with amusement. "Where'd you blow in from?" he asked; and his voice was like the angry bee sound of an approaching hurricane.

"Are you the producer?"

"Well, I'll be darned," said the man, and smiled. It seemed to fill the whole room with light. He was a big man, Harry noticed; but in this deceptive place, there was no way of telling how big. "I'll be most verily darned. An actor. You're a persistent lot, aren't you? Building houses for me that I almost never go into. Getting together and sending requests for better parts. Listening carefully to what I have to say and then ignoring or misinterpreting my advice. Always asking for just one more chance, and when you get it, messing that up too. And now one of you crashes the gate. What's your trouble, anyway?"

There was something about the producer that bothered Harry, but he could not place what it was, unless it was the fact that the man awed him and he didn't know why. "I woke up in Wednesday," he stammered, "and yesterday was Tuesday. I mean Monday. I mean—" He cleared his throat and started over. "I went to sleep Monday night and woke up Wednesday, and I'm looking for Tuesday."

"What do you want me to do about it?"

"Well—couldn't you tell me how to get back there? I got work to do."

"Oh—I get it," said the producer. "You want a favor from me. You know, someday, some one of you fellows is going to come to me wanting to give me something, free and for nothing, and then I am going to drop quietly dead. Don't I have enough trouble running this show without taking up time and space by doing favors for the likes of you?" He drew a couple of breaths and then smiled again. "However—I have always tried to be just, even if it is a tough job sometimes. Go on out and tell Iridel to show you the way back. I think I know what happened to you; when you made your exit from the last act you played in, you somehow managed to walk out behind the wrong curtain when you reached the wings. There's going to be a prompter sent to Limbo for this. Go on now—beat it."

Harry opened his mouth to speak, thought better of it and scuttled out the door, which opened before him. He stood in the huge control chamber, breathing hard. Iridel walked up to him.

"Well?"

"He says for you to get me out of here."

"All right," said Iridel. "This way." He led the way to a curtained doorway much like the one they had used to come in. Beside it were two dials, one marked in days, and the other in hours and minutes.

"Monday night good enough for you?" asked Iridel.

"Swell," said Harry.

Iridel set the dials for 9:30 p.m. on Monday. "So long, actor. Maybe I'll see you again some time."

"So long," said Harry. He turned and stepped through the door.

He was back in the garage, and there was no curtained doorway behind him. He turned to ask Iridel if this would enable him to go to bed again and do Tuesday right from the start, but Iridel was gone.

The garage was a blaze of light. Harry glanced up at the clock— It said fifteen seconds after nine-thirty. That was funny; everyone should be home by now except Slim Jim, the night man, who hung out until four in the morning serving up gas at the pumps outside. A quick glance around sufficed. This might be Monday night, but it was a Monday night he hadn't known.

The place was filled with the little men again!

Harry sat on the fender of a convertible and groaned. "Now what have I got myself into?" he asked himself.

He could see that he was at a different place-in-time from the one in which he had met Iridel. There, they had been working to build, working with a precision and nicety that was a pleasure to watch. But here—

The little men were different, in the first place. They were tired-looking, sick, slow. There were scores of overseers about, and Harry winced with one of the little fellows when one of the men in white lashed out with a long whip. As the Wednesday crews worked, so the Monday gangs slaved. And the work they were doing was different. For here they were breaking down, breaking up, carting away. Before his eyes,

Harry saw sections of paving lifted out, pulverized, toted away by the sackload by lines of trudging, browbeaten little men. He saw great beams upended to support the roof, while bricks were pried out of the walls. He heard the gang working on the roof, saw patches of roofing torn away. He saw walls and roof both melt away under that driving, driven onslaught, and before he knew what was happening he was standing alone on a section of the dead white plain he had noticed before on the corner lot.

It was too much for his overburdened mind; he ran out into the night, breaking through lines of laden slaves, through neat and growing piles of rubble, screaming for Iridel. He ran for a long time, and finally dropped down behind a stack of lumber out where the Unitarian church used to be, dropped because he could go no farther. He heard footsteps and tried to make himself smaller. They came on steadily; one of the overseers rounded the corner and stood looking at him. Harry was in deep shadow, but he knew the man in white could see in the dark.

"Come out o' there," grated the man. Harry came out.

"You the guy was yellin' for Iridel?"

Harry nodded.

"What makes you think you'll find Iridel in Limbo?" sneered his captor. "Who are you, anyway?"

Harry had learned by this time. "I'm an actor," he said in a small voice. "I got into Wednesday by mistake, and they sent me back here."

"What for?"

"Huh? Why— I guess it was a mistake, that's all."

The man stepped forward and grabbed Harry by the collar. He was about eight times as powerful as a hydraulic jack. "Don't give me no guff, pal," said the man. "Nobody gets sent to Limbo by mistake, or if he didn't do somethin' up there to make him deserve it. Come clean, now."

"I didn't do nothin'." Harry wailed. "I asked them

the way back, and they showed me a door, and I went through it and came here. That's all I know. Stop it, you're choking me!"

The man dropped him suddenly. "Listen, babe, you know who I am? Hey?" Harry shook his head. "Oh—you don't. Well, I'm Gurrah!"

"Yeah?" Harry said, not being able to think of anything else at the moment.

Gurrah puffed out his chest and appeared to be waiting for something more from Harry. When nothing came, he walked up to the mechanic, breathed in his face. "Ain't scared, huh? Tough guy, huh? Never heard of Gurrah, supervisor of Limbo an' the roughest, toughest son of the devil from Incidence to Eternity, huh?"

Now Harry was a peaceable man, but if there was anything he hated, it was to have a stranger breathe his bad breath pugnaciously at him. Before he knew it had happened, Gurrah was sprawled eight feet away, and Harry was standing alone rubbing his left knuckles—quite the more surprised of the two.

Gurrah sat up, feeling his face. "Why, you . . . you hit me!" he roared. He got up and came over to Harry. "You hit me!" he said softly, his voice slightly out of focus in amazement. Harry wished he hadn't—wished he was in bed or in Futura or dead or something. Gurrah reached out with a heavy fist and—patted him on the shoulder. "Hey," he said, suddenly friendly, "you're all right. Heh! Took a poke at me, didn't you? Be damned! First time in a month o' Mondays anyone ever made a pass at me. Last was a feller named Orton. I killed 'im." Harry paled.

Gurrah leaned back against the lumber pile. "Dam'f I didn't enjoy that, feller. Yeah. This is a hell of a job they palmed off on me, but what can you do? Breakin' down—breakin' down. No sooner get through one job, workin' top speed, drivin' the boys till they bleed, than they give you the devil for not bein' halfway through another job. You'd think I'd been in the business long enough to know what it was all about, after more than eight hundred an' twenty million acts, wouldn't you? Heh. Try to tell *them* that. Ship a load of dog houses up to Wednesday, sneakin' it past backstage nice as you please. They turn right around and call me up. 'What's the matter with you, Gurrah? Them dog houses is no good. We sent you a list o' worn-out items two acts ago. One o' the items was dog houses. Snap out of it or we send someone back there who can read an' put you on a toteline.' That's what I get—act in and act out. An' does it do any good to tell 'em that my aide got the message an' dropped dead before he got it to me? No. Uh-uh. If I say anything about that, they tell me to stop workin' 'em to death. If I do that, they kick because my shipments don't come in fast enough."

He paused for breath. Harry had a hunch that if he kept Gurrah in a good mood it might benefit him. He asked, "What's your job, anyway?"

"Job?" Gurrah howled. "Call this a job? Tearin' down the sets, shippin' what's good to the act after next, junkin' the rest?" He snorted.

Harry asked, "You mean they use the same props over again?"

"That's right. They don't last, though. Six, eight acts, maybe. Then they got to build new ones and weather them and knock 'em around to make 'em look as if they was used."

There was silence for a time. Gurrah, having got his bitterness off his chest for the first time in literally ages, was feeling pacified. Harry didn't know how to feel. He finally broke the ice. "Hey, Gurrah— How'm I goin' to get back into the play?"

"What's it to me? How'd you— Oh, that's right, you walked in from the control room, huh? That it?"

Harry nodded.

"An' how," growled Gurrah, "did you get inta the control room?"

"Iridel brought me."

"Then what?"

"Well, I went to see the producer, and—"

"Th' *producer!* Holy— You mean you walked right in and—" Gurrah mopped his brow. "What'd he say?"

"Why—he said he guessed it wasn't my fault that I woke up in Wednesday. He said to tell Iridel to ship me back."

"An' Iridel threw you back to Monday." And Gurrah threw back his shaggy head and roared.

"What's funny," asked Harry, a little peeved.

"Iridel," said Gurrah. "Do you realize that I've been trying for fifty thousand acts or more to get something on that pretty ol' heel, and he drops you right in my lap. Pal, I can't thank you enough! He was supposed to send you back into the play, and instead o' that you wind up in yesterday! Why, I'll blackmail him till the end of time!" He whirled exultantly, called to a group of bedraggled little men who were staggering under a cornerstone on their way to the junkyard. "Take it easy, boys!" he called. "I got ol' Iridel by the short hair. No more busted backs! No more snotty messages! *Haw haw haw!*"

Harry, a little amazed at all this, put in a timid word, "Hey—Gurrah. What about me?"

Gurrah turned. "You? Oh. *Tel-e-phone!*" At his shout two little workers, a trifle less bedraggled than the rest, trotted up. One hopped up and perched on Gurrah's right shoulder; the other draped himself over the left, with his head forward. Gurrah grabbed the latter by the neck, brought the man's head close and shouted into his ear. "Give me Iridel!" There was a moment's wait, then the little man on his other shoulder spoke in Iridel's voice, into Gurrah's ear, "Well?"

"Hiyah, fancy pants!"

"Fancy— I beg your— Who is this?"

"It's Gurrah, you futuristic parasite. I got a couple things to tell you."

"Gurrah! How—*dare* you talk to me like that! I'll have you—"

"You'll have me in your job if I tell all I know. You're a wart on the nose of progress, Iridel."

"What is the meaning of this?"

"The meaning of this is that you had instructions sent to you by the producer an'. you muffed them. Had an actor there, didn't you? He saw the boss, didn't he? Told you he was to be sent back, didn't he? Sent him right over to me instead of to the play, didn't you? You're slippin', Iridel. Gettin' old. Well, get off the wire. I'm callin' the boss, right now."

"The boss? Oh—don't do that, old man. Look, let's talk this thing over. Ah—about that shipment of three-legged dogs I was wanting you to round up for me; I guess I can do without them. Any little favor I can do for you—"

—"you'll damn well do, after this. You better, Goldilocks." Gurrah knocked the two small heads together, breaking the connection and probably the heads, and turned grinning to Harry. "You see," he explained, "that Iridel feller is a damn good supervisor, but he's a stickler for detail. He sends people to Limbo for the silliest little mistakes. He never forgives anyone and he never forgets a slip. He's the cause of half the misery back here, with his hurry-up orders. Now things are gonna be different. The boss has wanted to give Iridel a dose of his own medicine for a long time now, but Irrie never gave him a chance."

Harry said patiently, "About me getting back now—"

"My fran'!" Gurrah bellowed. He delved into a pocket and pulled out a watch like Iridel's. "It's eleven forty on Tuesday," he said. "We'll shoot you back there now. You'll have to dope out your own reasons for disappearing. Don't spill too much, or a lot of people will suffer for it—you the most. Ready?"

Harry nodded; Gurrah swept out a hand and opened the curtain to nothingness. "You'll find yourself quite a ways from where you started," he said, "because you did a little moving around here. Go ahead."

"Thanks," said Harry.

Gurrah laughed. "Don't thank me, chum. You rate all the thanks! Hey—if, after you kick off, you don't make out so good up there, let them toss you over to me. You'll be treated good; you've my word on it. Beat it; luck!"

Holding his breath, Harry Wright stepped through the doorway.

He had to walk thirty blocks to the garage, and when he got there the boss was waiting for him.

"Where you been, Wright?"

"I—lost my way."

"Don't get wise. What do you think this is—vacation time? Get going on the spring job. Damn it, it won't be finished now till tomorra."

Harry looked him straight in the eye and said, "Listen. It'll be finished tonight. I happen to know." And, still grinning, he went back into the garage and took out his tools.

"I Say . . . Ernest . . ."

Fiction is fact the way it ought to be. "Ought" in that sentence is the malleable word, and it's slippery as an eel in a barrel of oil. How it "ought" to go depends entirely on the author's convictions (if any) and sometimes on his skill in obeying the dictates of someone else (an editor, for example, or the Ministry of Propaganda, if he has one in his neighborhood).

Fact, on the other hand, if reported with accuracy and completeness, has a way of making laughingstocks of people, especially when they do silly or dangerous things, and such reportage can hurt the people who have done those things.

Sometimes, however, a moral can be drawn from real events, and, like all fables, can acquire a meaning far greater than the events themselves. Who gives a damn if an improbably vegetarian fox does or does not reach some grapes which may or may not be sour? Yet the fable illuminates the human condition (predicament); a "moral" drawn from reality can do the same thing.

For a short-lived little Los Angeles newspaper, in 1973, I did this:

When I was a kid I ran a hotel in Jamaica. I had a wife and a baby by then but I was still a kid. I was still a kid for a lot of years after that, I guess, but that's another story. This story is about my grandfather.

The reason I was running the hotel was because of my uncle's asthma. He had asthma about as bad as asthma can get, but not all the time. He was supposed to go to Canada to get treatment about the time I arrived to take over the hotel and run it until he came back, but it was months before he left, and anyway he felt pretty good most of the time, and we got along fine. Then my grandparents arrived from England and it was a different story.

When my grandmother got anywhere in the same hemisphere with my uncle, his asthma got worse. Everybody thought that was a coincidence. Sometimes it would get so bad that we'd prop him up at 45°—if he lay down he'd choke and/or drown and if he stood up he'd fall over—and a servant and I would take turns watching him all day and all night for half a week.

You had to know when he was sleeping and when he had fainted; there were different things to do for each of these and you had to be right. Then for a week or more he might be just fine. Well, not fine, but anyway functioning. Usually he knew when he had a bad one coming up and he could head it off with his needle. His needle had Adrenalin in it.

My grandmother's job was taking care of my grandfather. That's all she did and all she'd done for nearly 20 years, since he retired. He was pushing 80 at the time and she rode flank on every forkful he ate and every step he took and almost every word he said. (She kept on doing it until he was 94 and fell downstairs and broke his hip and died the next morning. Out of a job, she died the same afternoon and they were buried in the same grave.)

My grandfather was retired from the Church of England—he used to be rector of St. Mary's Upchurch, which is what that song "The Bells of St. Mary's" is about, and but for the fact that his brains were beginning to melt just a little, he was about the sweetest saintliest little old man you'd ever want to see, with his priest's dog-collar and his little black bib, and his silver head cocked a little to one side like some kind of bird, and his precise Oxford English singing out of him in a full high tenor voice.

We were all sitting on the veranda after dinner one evening when there was a full-fledged family fight. It was of course couched in genteel voices expressing British restraint, but it was a fight all right.

At base, the fight had to do with the weird effect my wife (she was also just a kid at the time) had on my grandmother, who always suggested that my wife sleep with her when the hotel was at capacity, and who was looking forward to my departure for Kingston, 94 miles away, in a couple of days. 94 miles in prewar Jamaica was no game of hopscotch, and I proposed to take my wife with me and leave the baby—we had nine girls working for us, every single one of them a born nursemaid.

My grandmother got very nettled—honest to God there's no other word for it—at the idea and began coming up with objections, none of which made any sense because none was the real one, and my uncle spit back, and I spoke my piece, and my wife sat there with our 11-month-old baby on her lap, feeling miserable, and my grandfather guarded the teacup on his knee with both hands and smiled gentle beatifications out into the middle distance. My grandmother's voice began to get an edge to it and I began to hear my uncle's breath as his bronchia began clutching up. "He will jolly well go to Kingston and she will jolly well go with him," he acquiesced, "and the baby will jolly well stay here."

My grandmother batted this macho pitch with a high foul. "And what if the baby dies while she's gone off to Kingston?"

My uncle leaped to his feet, croaked, "We'll bury it, dammit!" and went charging away up the veranda toward the office. I looked at my wife. She looked the way I felt. I looked at my grandmother. She set three heaping spoonfuls of sugar into her tea and said placidly, "He's just gone for his medicine. He'll be back directly," and she carefully placed a fourth spoonful and began to stir.

She was right on both counts. He'd hit the medicine very hard and the medicine had hit right back. He's swapped his wet pallor for a dry lividity, and he had clownlike patches of red on his cheeks and a .38 automatic in his hand. His pupils were drawn down so small that his green eyes seemed to be all iris, and he shouted, "I shall kill myself!" and took from his jacket pocket a full magazine of bullets. He slid it into the grip of the gun and banged it home with the heel of his hand, and added, "And burn down the hotel!"

In that order? I thought to ask him, but it's kind of nice that I didn't. I looked at that shiny gun seeking back and forth like a snake wondering which was the best side of the mouse, and I looked at my wife sitting there with the baby on her lap, and I hunkered right out to the edge of that wicker settee, saying to myself, I've got to jump . . . but which way?—when my grandfather came back from Out There, set his teacup down on the low table, got up and stood nose to nose with the wild man.

"I say, Ernest," he said in that soft oboe voice of his, "why cawn't we all be chums?"

My uncle shoved the gun into the old man's stomach and tipped him back into his chair. He started to laugh and he started to cough, which collapsed him into his chair; he folded up and the gun lay down gently on the big gleaming tiles of the floor and slid out of his hand, and it was away from there and into my jacket before he was done with his first spasm.

* * *

I've told this story a number of times and it always gets a laugh. People have written whole books about laughter—even Sigmund Freud wrote one—and sometimes it's pretty obscure, finding out what exactly makes people laugh. In this case it's pretty clear. The naivete, the simplistic detachment, the totally unexpected insertion of childlike idealism into a harsh reality—it comes out shock, it comes out laughter. A story like this appeals to every cynical bone in our heads, and cynicism is popular because it always carries with it the jolt of reality, a hard boot on hard ground, and reality is not all that easy to come by these days; it's a comfort to feel the jar of it and know it's there.

For many years this anecdote has been an "in" joke with those who know it, who can watch a couple of cats churning up each other's faces in a parking lot, or a flight of B52s, and murmur, "I say—Ernest . . ."

But I'm not a kid any more, and it comes to me that perhaps people like my grandfather, who without guile can say such things, are not less than the cynics, but more; and it could be that what he said that day is no different in substance from the sentiments of those other targets of the cynics' merriment: Spock, Pauling, Bertrand Russell and their kind.

Mr. Justice Douglas, in his beautiful, futile decision on Cambodia, wrote that he was merely granting a stay of execution, because unless the bombing were halted, people would die. I guess that's pretty funny too. In six hours his eight colleagues—realists all—shut him down, and in twenty, our 52s flattened a Cambodian village and killed a gross lot of innocents. By mistake.

So really—why can't we all be chums? Why can't we? Why?

FINE SCIENCE FICTION AND FANTASY TITLES AVAILABLE FROM CARROLL & GRAF